## TOR BOOKS BY LARRY NIVEN AND STEVEN BARNES

*ACHILLES' CHOICE*

*THE DESCENT OF ANANSI*

*BEOWULF'S CHILDREN* (WITH JERRY POURNELLE)

*SATURN'S RACE*

# SATURN'S RACE

## LARRY NIVEN AND STEVEN BARNES

A TOM DOHERTY ASSOCIATES BOOK
NEW YORK

This is a work of fiction. All the characters and events portrayed in this book are either products of the author's imagination or are used fictitiously.

SATURN'S RACE

Copyright © 2000 by Larry Niven and Steve Barnes

All rights reserved, including the right to reproduce this book, or portions thereof, in any form.

A Tor Book
Published by Tom Doherty Associates, LLC
175 Fifth Avenue
New York, NY 10010

www.tor.com

Tor® is a registered trademark of Tom Doherty Associates, LLC.

ISBN: 0-812-58010-9
Library of Congress Catalog Card Number: 00-028646

First edition: July 2000
First mass market edition: June 2001

Printed in the United States of America

0  9  8  7  6  5  4  3  2  1

To the architects: Samuel Morse, Alexander Graham Bell, and the men and women of the Advanced Research Projects Agency. By giving us the telegraph, telephone, and ARPAnet, you created Humanity's central and peripheral nervous system, and opened the way to the future.

# PART ONE

PART ONE

# 1

## June 2020

The sun had fled the sky hours ago, and with it, Xanadu's winged children. Before it dipped beneath Bombay's horizon, a thousand kilometers to the east, Lenore Myles had taken one last dive from the central tower. She trusted her reflexes and balance less than the central computer that kept her and a dozen others dancing on the thermals.

One long, perfect arc followed another, swooping out to the breakwaters, a kilometer distant from Xanadu's core. Sensors at the edge of her hang-glider's batwing read winds and temperatures, coordinated their data with weather satellites sensitive enough to detect a gust of warm breath. Slowly she began the return journey, high above the ring of orchards and gardens, the beaches and ponds, the flowered parks of the floating island called Xanadu.

The roofed, tiered hexagons extending from the central tower were each about two hundred meters in diameter. Eight concentric rings, rising toward the center, afforded four million square meters of potential landing room. She had sufficient lift to make it to a little park, four rings out from the central tower.

A pair of late picnickers applauded delightedly.

Even encumbered by artificial wings, Lenore managed to bow. The couple, an Asian woman and a man with a British sergeant-major's mustache, were all smiles. "UC Berkeley?" the woman asked.

"Los Angeles," Lenore replied. She shrugged out of the wings and gazed out over the rooftops, down toward the parklands below. Her fellow students were beginning to cluster down there. With the setting of the sun, festivities would begin. She glanced at her watch: just time to take a shower, change, and get down there for the party.

She triggered her rented hang-glider's pickup beacon and waved good-bye to the couple, who had returned to their cheese and wine. Probably waiting for moonrise, she mused. Tropical breezes, perfect weather . . .

A night for romance, and adventure. She felt loose and tingly all over. Adventure's promise had been kept, and the aftertaste was delicious.

Stars and a crescent moon silvered a restless ocean. At the rim of Xanadu's southwest lagoon, eight hundred of the UCLA science department's most recent graduates sipped champagne or sparkling fruit juice. Just beyond the breakwater, impossible human shapes walked upon black and silver waves and offered the Council's greeting.

"Welcome to Xanadu," a titanic blond woman roared. "Your minds and hearts are the hope of the world. Today your path of intellectual achievement has reached a crossroads." Her words echoed among Xanadu's towers. "Albert Einstein said, 'We should take care not to make the intellect our god; it has, of course, powerful muscles, but no personality.' Contrast this with the words of French philosopher Michel Foucault: 'The work of an intellectual is not to mold the political will of others . . .' "

Lenore debarked from one of the little robot carts and found a waiter with a tray of champagne glasses. The reception was jumping by now, covering one of the promenades between the outer breakwater and the containment ponds, vast arcs of water extending beyond the central ring of floating hexagons. Here parks and playgrounds swarmed with parents and children. A little farther out, fruit trees provided a lilt of citrus on the night breeze.

She searched the crowd as she sipped, looking for a particular friendly face. She barely noticed the special effects show, although many of the other graduates gawked. Through some optical trick, the titanic blonde seemed to make intimate eye contact with each individual. "Who shall lead us to the future, if not the pride of our universities? And what tool will blaze your way, if not intellect? We salute you: your hearts, which brim with courage and commitment, your bodies, so strong and filled with the promise of youth, and most especially your minds, which this day have fulfilled your academic potential. Welcome to Xanadu!"

"Welcome to Xanadu!" the other titans chorused, and the looped greeting began again.

Lenore's not-so-distant ancestors would have dropped to their knees at such a display. Her reactions were a grudging admiration for the technology and a mild resentment of the Council's sheer power and ego.

The twelve most powerful people on Earth. . . .

Her mood brightened as she spotted a short, rounded shape, her roommate and best friend, Tooley Wells. She nudged Tooley from behind and whispered, "What do you think? Do they really look like that?"

Tooley turned, hoisted her glass in greeting, and arched a dark eyebrow. "Some do, some don't. And I never trust a man prettier than me." Tooley was six and a half feet of energy compressed into a five-foot chocolate container. For three years she had been Lenore's roommate and closest confidante. "Joe Blaze is fiction, of course. The blond god-

dess . . . Shannon, is it? She was that age when she married
Halifax ten years ago."

"Then the image came right off the Playboy Channel."

"With clothes added. Halifax looks ugly enough, but that
Medusa coiffure is a program. But look at the tattooed lady
over at the end . . ."

The woman to the right looked Bengali or Sri Lankan,
with dark skin but Mediterranean features, a hefty shape
even discounting her five-story height. She would be Diva,
representing Asian labor interests. A traditional red *tilik*
mark upon her forehead watched them like an unblinking
third eye. Her hands and lips were laced with spiderwebs.

"One of the scandal nets." Tooley wrestled with a memory. "One of those one-name shows with an exclamation
point. *Vince!* Or something like that. Anyway, *Vince!* said
that Diva was the real thing, but the tattoos are only half
finished. The rest are overlaid with a paint program. He had
pictures."

"Those came out of a computer too."

These twelve Councilors controlled the most powerful
corporations and unions in the world, with greater power
than most geopolitical governments, save only three: China,
the United States, and Greater Germany. In a world too dangerous for any sane person to desire celebrity, anonymity
was a greater wealth than gold. There was good money in
crafting virtual images to carry one's presence on the Network or in virtual business meetings or public speeches.

Synthetic images were protected and regulated like brand
names or company logos. (Lenore remembered her Greek.
*Logos*: a principle that stands as an intermediate between
divinity and mortality.) Whoever the real rulers of the Council might be, these twelve were the only faces known to the
general public.

Lenore wondered which were here present.

"—The world is ever growing and changing," spake Joe
Blaze, Energy's international logo. Joe was a darkly tanned
blond with a six-pack belly and a blazing smile, impossibly

handsome in a late-twentieth-century Malibu fashion. Lenore agreed with Tooley: She wasn't entirely certain she would enjoy meeting such a man. Rather perversely, she fantasized that Joe's flesh-and-blood counterpart was a dissipated sixty-year-old with liver spots and a sagging gut.

"The primary interest of the Council is the prevention of future wars, a hideous waste of human and natural resources . . ."

Joe Blaze made her feel downright homely, not an easy thing to do. Lenore Myles was a bit over five and a half feet tall, with brown hair and eyes and perfect skin to match. Her cheekbones were high and lovely enough to earn her occasional income modeling. Artists liked her faintly challenging smile and the touch of Asia in her northern European features.

Lenore Myles watched as her fellow graduates dispersed, arms entwined with spouses or lovers. For them, the evening promised romance and easy camaraderie. At another time she might have felt regret, or loneliness, or isolation. Tonight she bubbled with self-confidence.

An hour's assisted gliding and a second glass of champagne were helping her to slough off four years of brutal discipline. Tonight was a celebration. The Master's thesis had been accepted, her grades had come down at an overall 3.89, and two dozen job offers were already in the chute. She had thumbed a two-year contract with an Augmentation Technology firm in Washington State but might return to school afterward to begin her Ph.D. work. Her future was unfolding like a flower, and there wasn't a thorn in sight.

"Tooley? You told me once that any man can be seduced."

"It's the way their brains are wired. Who you got in mind?"

"Nobody."

"You know Dwayne and Marley?"

Dwayne and Marley, the grads now moving toward them,

had lectured Lenore on the airbus. Enough of that. She squeezed Tooley's hand and retreated from the Promenade. The towering Councilor images and their voices faded, and she moved into a shadowed, oddly peaceful darkness.

Graduates had full access to Xanadu's public areas, and couples wandered off along the curving seacrete walkways, toward the breakwater orchards, back toward the towers rising from the central hexagons. Stars clustered above her like swarms of frozen fireflies.

From somewhere came a laugh, musical even at a distance.

At the western edge of the lagoon, a silver-gray streak rose and smacked flatly against the surface of a containment pond. A man crouched by the concrete lip, until this moment hidden in shadow. The dolphin danced and pranced for him. Was he *talking* to the animal? A trainer?

He stood, uncoiling like a human spring. It was the kind of balanced, practiced motion that her grandfather used to have, without, of course, the accompanying arthritis. Dancer? Yoga teacher?

His right hand fluttered. As the party lights behind her changed, the dolphin became a dark blue streak. It arced through the air again, slipping back into the water with barely a splash. She had the distinct impression that the man knew she stood behind him but wasn't turning yet, almost as if . . . Hmm? As if prolonging a moment.

Now he stood, now he turned. Her breathing quickened.

He was only an inch taller than she was, with very black hair and a boyish face that might have seen thirty summers. Closer, his eyes were older than that. They showed no wrinkles, but instinct told her that they had witnessed the world for more than his apparent years.

He wore denim pants and a black open-collar shirt, a loose brown coat with four black buttons on each sleeve. It hung comfortably on him, although she doubted he spent much time or effort selecting his clothes. He was Japanese, she guessed, or Chinese, with a golden tan, a muted severity, an Amerindian attitude.

Then he smiled, and the entire effect was softened. "Hi." He extended his hand somewhat shyly. "My name is Chaz Kato." His voice was like warm honey.

Her hand shook a little as their palms touched. His fingers were warm, strong and moist with the ocean mist.

"Do you live here?" she asked. The next thought hit her fast: Kato? Kato Foundation. The simple "KF" initial at the top of her monthly expense check . . . ? Her expression must have betrayed her sudden insight, because Chaz was instantly amused.

"Yes," he said. "That Kato was my grandfather."

She could only mouth the word *Wow*. She had to talk fast, for fear of tripping over her words. "I . . . I guess I need to—" She laughed at herself. "I mean that I want to thank you for all of the help. I never would have finished my education if K. F. hadn't supplied the grants."

Chaz held up his palms in supplication. "No false modesty, please. Never doubt that someone would have recognized your talents. Ah." He paused, pointing. "A celebrity in our midst."

Three men and one extremely attractive woman approached along the seacrete path. One lectured nonstop, holding his audience rapt.

"Gregory Phillipe Hernandez. Biology department," Lenore breathed.

Hernandez was the biology department's most popular instructor, a prodigy whose Master's thesis had been marked *classified* by the Council before it could hit the library shelves. Many had heard that story, and nobody seemed to know its subject matter.

Hernandez nodded to Chaz in polite acknowledgment, his eyes brushed Lenore, but he never broke stride or conversational thread. When they had passed, Lenore asked: "Do you know those people?"

Chaz wrinkled his brow. Damn, he was cute. "Hernandez,

of course. I recognize Summers—the blackest black man. He supervises one of the food production facilities. And, ah, I think I've seen the woman. She's something to do with upgrading the generators. I haven't lived here that long."

She laughed ruefully. "Then I'm surprised you recognize them, considering the size of this place."

"We're pretty insular."

"Still. I mean, this is my first floating island. It's hard to get used to the scale."

His smile was buoyant. "We do a lot here. Six million tons of fish meal, thirty gigawatts of electricity, and a billion dollars in minerals every year." He suddenly seemed even younger than his (at least!) thirty years.

"What do you do here?"

"Carry on Granddad's research."

"He worked here?" Wait—

"Oh, no, he never saw this place. And I've only been here fifteen years as a junior whatever. I took up Granddad's work when—"

"Metaphors and augmentation?"

"Pretty much." His face suddenly seemed to glow. "Would you like a tour?"

"I'd love to." She slipped her arm through his, amused by her own daring. Mmmm. It was going to be one of those evenings, was it? How delicious to watch it evolve.

## 2

**X**anadu was the second of the Floating Island chain of independent international corporate entities. Ultimately they would be strung along the world's equator: new islands bringing life to a watery desert. Six of the islands were in place, two as mere skeletons. From the air they looked a little like lilypads, a little like snowflakes five kilometers in diameter. Counting ponds and water recreation areas, the farms and breakwaters, each enclosed an area closer to forty square kilometers.

Chaz walked her about the edge of one of the concrete lakes. The graduation party took up one corner of a single outer lagoon. Built in a series of hexagons spiraling out from a central tower, the island was of a scale that was disorienting.

"How many people call Xanadu home?" she asked. At the moment she didn't really care, merely wanted to keep him talking. Voices had always fascinated her. She thought she could listen to his, low and musical in an utterly masculine way, for days.

"Almost sixty thousand. But we could support five times that many."

Most of the Floating Islands would be grown five degrees to either side of the equator; but Xanadu "floated" five degrees farther north. Rougher weather, but trade was easier with India and Sri Lanka. They'd need that.

Temperatures were notoriously hospitable in the Doldrums. The evening breezes were docile and warm. A cool, distant moon danced distantly on the waves, just visible beyond an artificial horizon.

Chaz was in a mood to walk. Two-seater cars hummed along a rail that rimmed the path. Once he spun her out of the way as a cluster of teenagers scooted past on motor skateboards.

Their strides matched comfortably. The silvered waves, the susurration of the surf, the bubble of the champagne inside her . . . the total was more than the sum of the parts.

She listened, pretending to study Xanadu's sights, while actually evaluating her companion.

Chadwick Kato III. His grandfather was a legend, one of the seminal minds in mid–twentieth-century consumer electronics. Chadwick Kato had survived California's infamous

Manzanar detention camp, emerging an orphan with remarkably little emotional scarring. He completed his education and earned six patents before his twenties. Enormously wealthy by his fifties, he established a series of foundations to distribute his wealth before dying of . . . was it cancer? in his early sixties. She knew that much, and knew that his grandson was reputed to be brilliant and somewhat reclusive. And hadn't there been something of a legal mess? Chadwick the Third, sired by an illegitimate prodigal son, emerging to take control of Grandpa's financial empire . . . ?

Music drifted east from a palm-dotted, canopied breakwater. A delicious tremor worked its way up her spine. Lenore felt slightly dreamlike, as if the evening's conclusion was something preordained and tantalizingly beyond her control.

"You like orchids, don't you?" Chaz asked.

She nodded. A smile tweaked the corners of her mouth. "Interesting timing with the dolphin," she said. "I mean, she looked pretty peaceful until I walked by, and then all of a sudden, gymnastics."

"And?" he asked innocently.

"And it makes a girl wonder, that's all."

He laughed shyly. They left the path and walked out toward the breakwater, into the park. Couples strolled its manicured grass, arm in arm.

She asked, "How many universities are having their celebrations here tonight?"

"I think about thirty. All the UC campuses, probably, and maybe some from Arizona and Oregon. This is a West Coast affair. So there are about twenty thousand students here right now. That strains . . . no, *tests* our guest facilities pretty thoroughly." He reeled off data easily. Computer access?

The park was dotted with fruit trees. So close to salt water? Some Xanadu boffin must have bred salt-resistant fruit trees. A row of plastic rectangles stood up ahead: greenhouses, their walls lit from within and lightly misted. Her arm pressed more firmly against his, and he answered the pressure.

*He knows who I am*, she thought. *And if he does, then this is no accident. And . . .*

As he opened the greenhouse door, she thought back over her life and the ways that the Kato Foundation had assisted her. Her first science fair experiment was a fledgling bio-cyberneticist's attempt to cue computer response to eye movement. Although she had climbed no higher than third place, one of the judges had personally congratulated her and told her conspiratorially that she had been noticed, and to keep up the fine work. Was that man somewhere here on the island?

The college scholarship and the grants providing books and housing (and weekend beer) . . . these had made a quality education possible. Without them, she could have aspired to no more than a local education: UU Salt Lake, perhaps. With them, her life had become a dream. One success followed another, rolling toward some culmination as yet unglimpsed. On previous occasions Lenore had felt that curious emotional weight which signaled a turning point.

She sensed that same fluid pressure now.

The door sighed closed behind them. The greenhouse temperature was a humid twenty-six degrees. Within was an incredible riot of colors and scents. Miniature orange and lemon and unrecognizable citrus trees, pear and apple and cherry and mango each nestled in its own nook. Some had tags attached, naming Xanadu citizens or co-ops as owners. The greenhouse was about ten meters wide and kilometers long. From the air she'd seen it ringing the entire island just within the breakwater's hump.

As far as the eye could see, plants and bonsai-size shrubs grew densely. Every fifty meters or so overlapping plastic curtains sealed sections off, so that each maintained its individual temperature and humidity.

He led her down the central corridor excitedly, bouncing along like a kid showing off a secret clubhouse.

"You were waiting for me, weren't you?"

He cocked his head to one side, and she knew he was debating the merits of a lie. He said nothing.

She thought of asking something else, but when he brushed another plastic curtain aside, her question froze in her throat.

She didn't need to ask how he knew that she loved orchids, that her mother had owned a flower shop and that she had spent much of her childhood working among the tender, fleshy blossoms and sinewy, delicate scents. As a child, she had relished her skill in choosing the precisely appropriate flower for the occasion. He would know. Lenore intuited that since that first science fair he had watched her, had, incredibly, cared for her although he had extended greetings only through a surrogate.

With practiced care, he snipped a blossom. It was violet, with a scarlet tongue so bright it appeared to glow. He came close. "Do you mind?" he asked, and fixed it above her ear. "Do you recognize this?"

She shook her head dumbly.

"A variant of *Nervilia aragoana*. Women in Indonesia use their leaves to ease childbirth."

"Functional beauty," she said.

"My watchword."

She inhaled, breathing not only the orchid's singular perfume but also the milder scent of his own perspiration. His hands were broad and smooth, the fingers long. His eyes met hers very directly for a moment and then broke off, finding an excuse to look away.

*He's shy.* Sudden suspicion confused her initial impression. Not shy. It was something else. It was something she had seen in the survivors of bad love affairs.

Her fingers brushed her hair back and found the orchid there. She traced it appreciatively. "Beautiful."

"Practical too." His eyes were locked on hers again.

For almost a minute, there was no sound but the distant,

muffled music. Then he took her arm again. "Would you like to see more of Xanadu?"

"Yes," she said, and then heard herself say "There's a sweet job offer in Washington State, but who hasn't heard about the island life? Are the apartments and condos like the guest suites?"

There. She had given him an opening and was somewhat terrified by her own daring in doing so.

"Nicer," he said. "Perhaps I could show you one."

"That,"—she smiled in return—"would be simply *charming*."

# 3

E very half kilometer along the breakwater a central transportation spoke thrust toward the hub. A five-minute walk brought them to the nearest. Chaz tapped a seal on his pocket. A silver two-seater robot cart hummed merrily down its track, then sighed to a halt before them.

Lenore slid in and leaned back. The wind riffled her hair as the cart glided into the complex. On the way, they passed a broad lake similar to the one where she had seen him with the dolphin.

"Are those just . . . I don't know. Swimming lagoons?"

"No, fisheries, actually."

"You let the dolphins into your fishery?"

He laughed. "No. Manny was in our lobster farm. Dolphins don't eat lobster; people eat lobster. Very big export for Xanadu. Do you like seafood? Swordfish steak? Mahi-mahi?"

"Yum."

"Then you'll like it here. Any saltwater fish imaginable,

and the world's best collection of fresh. And hey, if it's out of season, we can texture algae to taste like anything you want."

Xanadu's main cluster of concentric hexagons rose above them, low towers crested with parks and low buildings. Her designers had deliberately avoided the concrete-canyon feel of most modern cities, inverting the priorities: Buildings were crowded underwater, human beings got the open air. The few spires aboveground tended to have wide, airy windows. In their offices and apartments the Floating Islanders probably had more recreation space and breathing room than any other industrial society on the planet.

She thought that this seemed less Coleridge's dreamscape than the Emerald City of Oz. Lenore had never seriously considered inhabiting one of the Islands, but this was starting to look good.

"What percentage of you guys give up national citizenship?"

"Not many. Anyone who can't get tax waivers, like Americans. Considering the hefty tariffs we pay on our goods, most countries are eager to maintain good relationships."

They zipped briskly along a slender bridge. Below them, an algae lake sparkled blue-black in the moonlight. They entered a tunnel, descended, then rose out of shadow. The cart eased to a stop.

"All out," he said, and took her hand again.

Although she had enjoyed a brief tour of Xanadu's guest facilities upon arrival this morning, Lenore had been too occupied with unpacking, jet-lag napping, and then trying out Xanadu's legendary hang-gliders to really absorb everything. In effect, she had seen more of the outside than the inside. She'd been on Xanadu almost eight hours, but she'd had little chance to appreciate its inner workings.

This was the opportunity, and it very nearly took her breath away.

*Aquatic organic*, some newsbyte had called Xanadu's interior architecture. The natural free-flowing lines, gently curving floors, and towering pillars reminded her of a conch shell or a coral reef, underwater lava tubes or the valves of a giant heart: something grown or accreted, not constructed by human hands.

She felt at home and at peace. Something about these curved spaces, the constant gentle breezes, the distant, barely perceptible salt smell triggered a hunger new to her experience. How could she crave something she had never known? Certainly she had seen pictures, had even enjoyed a virtual tour of Xanadu's corridors. But there was a world of difference between simulation and body knowledge: the cool, filtered ocean air brushing her skin, or the whisper of her footsteps against smooth tile.

The walkways wound naturally through the curving halls. Some opened up into mall-like store enclosures. As overhead lights lazily changed filters, the wall colors shifted slowly and subtly between pink and blue and then to yellow, so gradually that she never quite caught the moment when one shade merged into another. The cumulative effect was one of efficiency and organic wholeness. A tiny knot of tension melted in her lower back.

"I feel . . ."

Chaz glanced at her quizzically, waiting for her to finish.

"I don't know. It feels like this is all somehow familiar."

He nodded. "I've heard that. Want to hear what our design psychologists say?"

"Sure."

"They say that lubber architecture—"

" 'Lubber'?"

He winced. "Jargon creeps in. Sorry."

"You would be referring to us normal, sane people who like dirt between our toes."

"We've got dirt. Like Los Angeles has snow. We keep it where it doesn't get in the way . . ." He waited for her smile. "Anyhow, most lubber architecture is based on straight lines and angles because the math is easier. It's rare to find straight lines in nature. In some geologic formations, I guess—"

"Horizon."

"Horizon. But living things come in curves and arcs—"

"Redwoods."

"—unless they're fighting gravity." Chaz gestured around him. *"We're floating!* Boats and ships don't need to be rectangles! So all of this is curves, arches, gently contracting or expanding spirals. The overall effect is very seductive, very much like reentering the womb." He seemed to drift off for a moment, then was back with her again. "Listen—I pulled you away from the banquet. May I . . . feed you?"

"I'd like that very much. Xanadu must have wonderful restaurants." She said it teasingly. Just as she felt that she had been here before, she also had the sense that she knew him. They were playing out an elegantly choreographed *pas de deux.*

Could it really have been eleven months since she last took a man into her bed? All her emotions, all of her energies had been focused down to a single, topologically clean, manageable point: completing her education. Now all of the desperately encapsulated needs were breaking open. The knowledge that the man beside her had enabled that education fairly boiled her blood.

Consider it adventurism or *quid pro quo* or even simple animal appetite. One way or another, that this was going to be a *very* good night.

"Excuse me," he said. "I'm being paged."

The walls were paneled in overlapping scales. They might have been strolling through a roll of fish skin. Chaz pressed his right forefinger against one of the nearest ovals, and it lit up.

A woman's face appeared. She reminded Lenore of Diva, the Bengali union leader, but without the titan's pleasant cushion of fat. This woman looked athletically trim, almost severe. Worse, she was royally pissed off.

"Dr. Kato," she said in precise but accented English.

"Guests are restricted to public areas and transportation, of course." Lenore sensed that the formality was artificial. These two *knew* each other. English was this woman's second language, probably learned in late childhood. Lenore thought she might be Indonesian.

Chaz said, "I showed her the gardens, and then we wanted to get into the main sector quickly. The shuttle was right there, Clarise."

The dark-skinned woman (Clarise?) smiled shallowly. She turned to Lenore and inclined her head. "Welcome to Xanadu, Miss Myles."

"Thank you. Is there a problem?" Lenore asked. Was this a security glitch, or . . . ?

"We rarely entertain so many at once. Our residents expect their privacy to be maintained." And she was the one to do it. Proud, intelligent. *"We rarely . . . ?"* Clarise took her job very personally. An Indonesian girl recruited at an early age and raised on Xanadu? She held Lenore's eyes a moment more, then glared at Chaz. "You know better."

"She's my guest," Chaz said. "This is my private time, and it's really not a security matter. We are going to dinner."

Clarise's lips drew into a thin line. "At your apartment?" Her eyes remained cool, but narrowed.

"Is *that* a problem?"

Beat. Then all personal emotion vanished behind the professional mask. "She will be cleared though all checkpoints. And to both of you, a pleasant good evening."

And her image winked out.

Lenore felt whiplashed. "Chaz, am I poaching?"

"That's Clarise Maibang. She's deputy chief of security, and we . . . had a contract once. I didn't renew." He turned and looked at her, and she locked into his gaze instantly. "I've admired you for years, Lenore. I'd like you to know me."

She shook her head, trying to feel her way into his words. He seemed simultaneously naive and extremely mature. The entire situation was strange . . . and wonderful. "I'd like that," she said. He took her hand. Fingers tingling and intertwined, she watched as scales slid aside, revealing a concealed elevator pod. They entered.

"Aerie," he said to the wall. He turned. His eyes were very warm.

## 4

*Damn. I've known him for all of half an hour, and I'm in love with his voice. I've got to know how it feels to kiss him.*

Chaz stood very carefully on his side of the elevator, his fingers knotted behind his back. His gaze slid appreciatively over her dress. She was glad it was her very best outfit: A tightly knit peach dress, it clung to her hips, and was slitted to expose a tanned length of thigh. Without conscious thought she shifted her stance, presenting her most delicious angles.

A dizziness enveloped her as if she had swum into the midst of a warm, friendly shoal of fish. Chaz laughed, enjoying the game.

As they slid swiftly along, the elevator walls turned transparent. Lenore felt as if she were moving through a beehive, among countless, faceless thousands of Islanders bustling even at this late hour. Time seemed to matter not at all. She sensed interlocking purpose, as if she were peering through a microscope at blood cells rushing through myriad veins and arteries.

She detected no whiff of L.A.'s ultra-competitive desperation. In the industrialized world, nobody starved unless they hid themselves in the system's shadowed crevices. But a roof and a full belly merely gave one time to crave love, community, contribution.

Lenore had watched her mother struggle to build a life of meaning, armed with a bachelor's degree that now meant less than a nineteenth-century grade-school diploma. Without an advanced degree or family connections, finding meaningful employment could be murderously difficult. Forced to create her own venue, Melissa Myles had done it honorably and with style. But Lenore's mother had dreamed of a better life for her child. Chadwick Kato III had helped make that dream come true.

The tube shushed to a halt. Her bones felt a massive subsonic *click,* and then the capsule moved upward again. After a brief moment of diminished weight, they came to a final halt. The door slid open.

Lenore caught her breath.

Chaz took her hand and led her out onto an open patio. She gazed out across the rooftop toward the ocean far below them, a vast, darkly purple expanse whose surface crawled with flickering silver crescents. It was hypnotic, but no more so than the place Chaz called home, his "Aerie."

Her first impression was of pale orange light, of curves intersecting straight lines; of a rectangular two-story apartment strongly influenced by Frank Lloyd Wright, with an entrance like an igloo's. Vast expanses of transparent plastic molding were interrupted by sheets of darker material attached to panels taller than a man. She intuited that the position of those panels shifted from day to day with Chaz's mood. Yesterday's lighting design would never resemble tomorrow's.

He led her through the main hall into a foyer floored with a copper-colored hardwood. Directly opposite the door, a tight spiral of staircase led up to the second level. Gaps in the stairwell revealed it to be office, library, and bedroom all in one.

Milky rectangular eyes looked down at her from a shelf that ran just above brow level. She recognized one, then another of these old machines. Quaint ancient computers, every one of them. She had been in the Gates Museum. She

recognized the progression: These were the micros that had
changed the world. The tiny flat panel of the Sinclair ZX
with its membrane pressure-plate keyboard, an Osborne and
the similar Kay-Pro, the first all-in-one "luggable" systems
(had anyone ever really used a screen that flat and tiny? Her
eyes ached just thinking about it!), the Apple II, and . . .
God, was that an early Macintosh?

From there the machines became more generic. A proto-
IBM and a clone from Radio Shack, both running ancient
MS-DOS. A box capable of running Windows.

"You recognize?" Chaz asked.

"Yeah. Some. Where did you get them all?"

"Collectors dig 'em up and fix them. They all work too.
This one—" He pointed out a machine labeled COMPAQ.
"It was one of the first coprocessors. It ran both major home
systems. Granddad wrote a lot of that code."

Her hand slipped out of his as she walked wonderingly
from one room to the next, mesmerized by the dwelling's
simplicity and good taste. Black leather chairs and a table
of steel and white marble graced the living room. A walkway lined with white pillars melded seamlessly into a gently
arching ceiling. A recessed book nook was capped with a
plush chair and sofa sets, material unknown. When she
pushed her hand against the chair, it vibrated beneath her
palm.

She wandered over to one of the bay windows and an
Olympian view of fields, greenhouses, and breakwaters. She
pressed her fingers against the glass, blocking out first one
group of flea-size humans and then another.

His breath was warm on her ear. His fingertips, light as
butterfly wings, brushed her shoulders. He slipped a flute of
champagne into her hand. She sipped. It sparkled like milled
diamond. The champagne was the best she had ever tasted.

His hands slid down her shoulders, fingertips tracing the
roundness of her shoulder blades and the deep V in her
backless gown, down to the notch that stopped a bare inch
from the cleft of her buttocks.

But his fingers stopped. "Dinner will be here in a few minutes. I believe you enjoy grilled tuna?"

"Very much." She leaned her head back against him, enjoying the warmth. "I didn't hear you order."

"In the tube," he said. "There are chorded touchpads all over Xanadu, keyed to our handprints. I just modified one of my standard menus."

His word was good. Not three minutes later a food dispenser in the kitchen bonged. Chaz said "Aha!" and bounced away. He donned insulated gloves and opened the oven, drew out two trays, and presented them with a grand flourish, as if he had labored over them for hours. "Dinner," he said, "is served."

He waved her toward a dinner table carved from some dark, polished driftwood. After setting out the food, he pulled her chair out. He sat opposite, never taking his eyes from her. The dinner tray was sealed with transparent film. As she peeled it back a tide of savory aromas overwhelmed her. She was suddenly ravenously hungry.

Maybe this was processed, or reheated, or cooked in some super convection oven, but as far as her taste buds were concerned, the tuna had been slow-grilled over mesquite, and every mouthful was perfect.

*I could get used to this*, she said to herself. *I could seriously get used to this*.

Still, the nattering voice of caution buzzed like a fly in her ear. It was all just so wonderful, so blessedly easy. He was exotically beautiful, possessed of an odd combination of naïveté and cultured elegance, simultaneously older and younger than his years.

"You know a lot about my dreams," she said. "What about yours? Your granddad made a fortune with Gates and Sony and Disney. I'm sure you work hard: We used some of your teaching systems at UCLA. But your life must have been . . . sybaritic? Would that make it a little hard to identify with us working stiffs?"

She expected indignation, or some comments about the

value of immersion in culture or science, perhaps a declaration that Xanadu was a community unto itself, with sufficient social stratification to familiarize him with every level . . .

He assembled a bite of grilled fish and chewed, stalling. A little smile tugged at the corners of his mouth.

"Money just creates another level of problems and opportunities. I lost friends to cocaine," he said, "and they never saw it coming. Lenore, I don't wake up in the morning thinking 'I'm rich'."

He poured wine from a crystal decanter. Although it bore no sign of refrigeration or insulation, and had been sitting on the table since they entered his apartment, it was deliciously chilled. He tasted. He said, "Maybe I should."

"What do you dream of?" she asked.

"You'll laugh," he said. His eyes, so serious just moments ago, so intense that she thought she was talking to an old man, were now filled with light and laughter. This was a boy, and a boy in love with life, at that.

Or with Lenore Myles?

Or it was the champagne, or the setting. The night sky melted into the ocean's blackness, forming an indistinct horizon. Where did the sky end and its reflection begin?

"Maybe," she said. "Maybe I'll laugh. Take a chance."

"I want adventure," he said instantly. When she didn't react, he said, "All my life I've played mind games, and they've been good to me." He gestured at the wealth surrounding him. "But most of my . . ." He hesitated. She could almost feel the gears turning between his ears. "Most of my grandfather's work was created under the assumption that the more we know, the happier we'll be. Easy to understand where he got that idea. After all, he spent years in Manzanar, the Nisei concentration camps in World War II. All the result of ignorance. Americans saw the Japanese as alien, and treated them like BEMs. Only familiarity and communication can change that."

He took another sip, his mind drifting. "Well, knowledge

became an obsession. He wasn't *wrong*. I mean, if children are dying from diphtheria, and you know how to make the vaccine, that *will* increase the level of pleasure in life. And if you can prevent your family from starving, that's nothing to sneeze at either. But there's a point beyond which information about the external world just isn't useful any more."

"What point is that?"

He hesitated. "Okay, so it's more a big broad fuzzy line. My grandmother died of Alzheimer's." Was that a snarl trying to form? "Granddad never really recovered. He was convinced that we should know how to *deal* with this. The disease stole Ako's mind long before it killed her body." Lost in his memories . . . hey, no, in his *grandfather's* memories . . . he had damn near forgotten she was there.

"But couldn't more knowledge have cured her?"

"Consciousness is a tricky thing. What if we could've linked a computer to Ako's brain? Write a program to replace what she's lost."

"Mmm."

"But would it be *her?* Or a program turning her into a marionette? I still don't know! But . . . but Kato One didn't have even that. He hated himself for not being able to help. He had to help her dress herself, clean herself, remember who he was. Who *she* was. He wanted to know *how do we know*? What makes us us? But he'd run out of time. His own brain was turning to mush."

"Then you inherited his estate. You're more or less continuing his work, are you?"

*Tick*, he was back. "More or less. He kept good records. I'm into metaphors?"

A technical term. She nodded: *I understand*. Reassured, he said, "If you look at a given set of data as a building full of books, everyone needs a customized entrance to take advantage of his own learning style. This way of using metaphors is *older* than *these*." He waved at the line of ancient monitor screens. "Bar graphs, pie charts, accounting systems."

"Poetry?"

"Poetry. Damn! I never thought of that at all. Poets are trying to do what I do. Simplify. Codify. Politicians talk about our economy being like a tree that needs to wait out a winter's frost. We talk about business as war, or the body as a machine. You can show or hide what you like by switching accounting systems. All of these are attempts to make the unfamiliar familiar, to make the complicated merely complex.

"Once upon a time, computers talked only to people who understood punchcards, who thought in long strings of zeros and ones. Then we got more complex languages and command lines. Metaphors. You don't have to think ones and zeros if you can make pictures. DOS shells let nonnerds who didn't know a command line from a punch line actually navigate in cyberspace. Then came Macintosh and Windows and the other stuff Granddad worked on. A desktop is a nice, useful metaphor. Some still use it.

"The point of a metaphor is to let you find your way around inside this maze of information. Three-dimensional metaphors of the nineties and the kino and multiplex metaphors we use now give us even more flex. You and me, we're both working on ways to do this more directly. At Xanadu a lot of our experimentation is done on animals."

She nodded. "It's hard to do that in the States. The animal activists have almost shut it down."

"Good reason to set up base in the Bay of Bengal. I'm into metaphors and augmentation technology."

"Is that your main function here?"

"Not sole. I'm on a dozen boards. I teach classes. No real power, but lots of responsibility."

"Are you on the Millennium Project?"

He smiled. "Everyone in Xanadu is working on the Millennium Project. We're learning about our world, our selves. We're building the social systems and tools that'll give us the planets. And it works. It all works. You know? I can see." He tilted his gaze up at the sky, and for that moment, she could see as well.

"I can see where it might lead us, but even if I go to the stars, I'm not sure we'll be any happier. We'll be smarter, but we may not be wiser. That's what Chaz One would have said."

"And you?"

"Oh, I'm going." Suddenly he was grinning again, almost as if flipping a switch. "To hell with ultimate knowledge."

"What, then?"

"The adventure of it all," he said, and there was that nine-year-old's voice again. "Test ourselves. Push our limits. Why else are adventure novels and movies and so forth always so popular? We want to know what we would be like under pressure. Could we cut the mustard, or would we crack?"

The seductive energy had temporarily vanished. And if he wasn't stalking her, suddenly she felt herself wanting to close the gap between them.

*Okay, boy. I'll stalk you.* She put her fork down, and leaned toward him. "What kind of adventure?"

"Um . . . there are the great heroes in books and movies. James Bond. Indiana Jones. Modesty Blaise. Luke Sky-walker. Tarzan. I want to feel what they felt."

"Fighting mighty enemies. Research isn't enough?" She had never had the time or inclination to actively seek out danger but could still empathize. Perhaps, in a strange way, his life of wealth and comfort had been as much of a trap as her poverty.

She was almost surprised to discover that her plate was clear. He put his own glass aside and took her hand, leading her back to the living room window. A little espresso device at a coffee table chugged and whistled and produced a matched pair of lattes. She sipped, and gazed.

She said, "There's more than enough work, more than enough adventure for a hundred lifetimes right in front of you. Have you really spent so much of your time behind walls?"

Something dark floated behind his eyes, something swiftly veiled. "Too much," he replied.

"Then barking your shins a bit would do you a world of good."

He grinned. "Want to help?"

"That's not what I want at all," she said, and now they were very close indeed. She was close enough to see the stars reflected in his eyes.

"Don't you believe in adventure?" he said softly. They were sharing the same breath now. His lips brushed hers. Electricity burned between them. "They say pirates still haunt the straits of Java."

"Fantasies," she said, and leaned her head back. He kissed her again, and this time his tongue brushed the underside of her upper lip. Her lips parted.

His voice was a whisper now, but only a whisper was needed. "They say miracles still occur in the jungles of India."

"Wishful thinking." Suddenly they were kissing furiously. She molded herself against him.

When they broke, his eyes were dark, his voice slightly slurred. Good. She wasn't the only one experiencing a core meltdown.

"And did you know," he began, something teasing in his voice, "that aliens are said to haunt these very waters?"

"Right."

"Really," he said. The little-boy face was there again. She was beginning to understand his moods and patterns. "Would you like to meet one?" There was something crazed and daring in his eyes, as if he had said something almost unspeakably naughty.

He started to say something more, and she silenced him with a kiss. Her hands strayed down his chest to his stomach, and then farther still until he groaned in delight. They lost themselves in that kiss for a full minute, then he broke away. Without speaking, he took her hand and led her to the spiral staircase. "My lady," he said quietly.

She preceded him up the stair, up into a Plexiglas dome sheltering a round bed. Below them, the ocean. Above them, the stars.

His hands played over a chord keyboard, made some quick adjustments, and the star display changed. "I can give you any sky in the world."

"Stars are fine," she said quietly.

He spun her to face him, making something like a dance step. "I've waited five years to meet you," he said.

"Why me?" The bed pressed against the backs of her knees, and they fell together upon it. It molded itself to their bodies. She breathed him, for a moment not certain where she stopped and he began. A quick pause, a fevered gaze as incandescent as solar plasma, and then a whirlwind disengagement from all clothing.

They lay in his perfect bed, beneath a perfect sky, and she suddenly realized that she hardly knew this man, and drew back from him an inch. It was a moment when the alcohol and excitement, the pressure of her studies and the disorienting intoxication of this wonderful place all came together in her mind.

She expected aggression. Instead, he seemed to retreat into a watchful state. There it was again: that strange, patient part of him, something distant and yearning, like an old man watching children playing in the snow, separated from them by glass, and distance, and impassable years.

What was it her old boyfriend had once said about the Council? That they watched the rest of humanity as if men and women were rats scurrying through mazes for cheese long gone? "Worse than rats, Lenore," Levar had said. "At least rats will eventually stop looking. . . ."

She wanted Chaz to seize her, to pull her toward him, force his body against hers. Instead, there was that watchful quiet. "Where did you go?" he asked.

"Old ghosts," she said. "I'm sorry. Now where were we?"
She kissed him thoroughly.

"Whatever you want," he said when they came up for air.
"I've loved you for five years. And now that you're here,
I'm afraid of doing the wrong thing."

"I won't let you," she said. "And if you make a mistake,
I'll just make you do it over..." She kissed him. "And
over." Another kiss. "And over again." She took his hand
and began to guide it. "Until you get it absolutely perfect."

Then, with fingertips like fire, she showed him absolutely,
perfectly, exquisitely what she wanted.

And, wonder of wonders, he got it right the first time.


# 5

As sleep's dark tide receded
Chaz lay quietly, studying
Lenore's elegant, golden length. He marveled, reveling in
visceral recollection of her slow soft energies. Remembered
how her controlled urgency had given way to something
primal, molten, and demanding. He wondered if he, or any
mortal, deserved the affections of so magnificent a creature.

The answer to that question, he knew, could change his
life. *You want to love. We all do. But can you take that kind
of risk again? Loving Ako almost killed you.*

But this time he could protect her. He had already protected Lenore for five years.

He hadn't played her false. Just little lies, for her protection and Xanadu's. There were proprietary secrets here...:
but any lie, no matter how small, opened the door to betrayal. He traced his finger along her thigh, gazing lazily up
at the ceiling.

Though daylight was flooding through from the living

room, the dome above his bed displayed a night sky, constellations ordinarily seen only in the southern hemisphere: Tucana, the parrot, Triangulum Australe, the small dim Microscopium, and Sextans. How different were these names from the zodiacal references of the northern constellations. But then, those had been observed by Europeans for uncounted centuries. The first European eyes to view stars in the southern latitudes were sailors and merchants, who gave them names more eccentric and modern.

He could change them with a whisper, creating an aurora borealis, or a summer lightning storm, or even the undersea images from Squark City.

Well, no, she shouldn't see *that*. Not just yet. He must make it possible. One day he would share Xanadu's secrets with her. Not yet.

Lies made everything difficult. A relationship, he believed, was a castle. Lies fissured and weakened the foundations. He prayed that his evasions had not made a life with Lenore impossible. But if they had, he would weather it. He had been alone before, and for more years than Lenore could dream.

He brushed his fingers against her lips, depositing a kiss there, then started at her ankle, gliding the fingers slowly up her calf to the bend of her knee and then up the superbly muscled upper thigh and the rounded globes of her buttocks.

She rolled luxuriantly, yawning, her lips curling in a sleeping smile. One of her hands reached out and slapped against his, then groped to find him again. She grabbed his finger in a gesture as guileless and possessive as a newborn baby's.

Her eyes opened, then closed again, and she flared her nostrils wide. Without opening them again, she said: "Breakfast. Sir, you have won my heart." She rolled over onto her side and stretched like a big golden cat. He allowed himself to gloat just a bit. Last night she had been his! She was his again, if he reached out.

She worked her way up to a seated position, and he slid

the breakfast tray over her lap. She raised a glass of orange juice to her lips, swigged, swished, and gargled with it, then pulled him down into a lingering citrus kiss.

Her hands stopped in his hair. "What's this?"

"Busted!"

"What?" Her fingers traced a small circle at the back of his head, then tugged hair.

"All right, let me show you." His fingers moved hers aside. He pushed the plate in and tugged false hair to tilt it. The plug came out.

"Interface plug," he said, watching her eyes. Was she squeamish? She wasn't drawing back. "Makes it easier to link with most computer systems, especially Xanadu systems. When I was—" He stopped for an instant, then spoke a half-truth. "When I was getting over being sick, the Xanadu medical systems used it to track me. It's turned off now."

"Something serious?"

"Oh, yeah. Pneumonia and complications." Perhaps some day he would add detail.

She kissed him again and then pushed him away to arm's length. "There," she said. "I just wanted to say a proper good morning."

"Now think improper."

"Down, boy, down. God, I'm famished." Wordless for the next five minutes, she worked her way through eggs and fruit and hashed brown potatoes and toast. Sometimes she nibbled, sometimes munched ravenously, but finally she lay back against her pillow and gazed at him from behind drooping lids.

"You should be very careful how you treat a lady on a first date," she said finally. "You might find it hard to live up to."

The unspoken question hung between them like a wisp of smoke.

"You're looking for work now, aren't you?"

"I'm considering offers," she said in a poker-player's

voice. This line of conversation was business, and she was smart enough to handle it that way. Good.

"Well, there are hundreds of different job positions open here, and dozens of them are shareholder slots."

"Suppose I said that I was interested?"

"Well . . . there's a cocktail party this evening. Semiprivate. Only a few of the graduates are being invited. I could get you in."

"You'd do that?"

"I could be bribed."

"Could you now?" She leaned forward. Even without brushing, her postbreakfast breath was tangy and light. His groin tautened, followed by an odd sensation, something like warm honey dripping up his spine. *Oh, Chaz—you're in trouble.* She gazed into his eyes at lash distance, as if trying to pierce him, see into parts of him that he couldn't allow her or anyone else to penetrate. Then her eyes closed, and she leaned forward, stilling all thought, igniting all sensations.

# 6

Awake again, two hours later. A pale blue window drifted in the air in front of his face, flashing once a second. It was in that moment that Chaz realized he was alone in the bed.

A moment of panic.

"Message," he said, and the screen cleared. The beautiful, exotically severe visage wasn't Lenore's. "Clarise," he said. The image flickered, and real-time Clarise Maibang came on line.

"So, I trust you had a restful evening?" Her voice was cold. Anger seemed to stimulate her Javanese roots: From the choppy, almost explosive accent underlying her English words, she was furious.

"Thank you, very refreshing. And what can I do for you?"

At times like this, it was easier to imagine her as the brilliant twelve-year-old child she had been when discovered in western Java, an orphan raised by the reclusive tribe known as the Bdui. Twelve years of twentieth-century education was little more than a veneer over that fiery native girl. For a time, he had reveled in that fire.

He had enjoyed letting her run his life, while he was recovering from seventy years of entropy. Later—well, Clarise was a control freak.

"I wish to be certain you understand with whom you consort," she said, picking her words carefully.

"Clarise, I've observed her for years." He was distressed to hear the defensiveness in his voice.

"I know that," she replied. Suddenly Chaz wondered *how long* she'd known of his obsession. A year and two months they'd been together. "Doubtless, you are currently aware of the"—an instant's pause—"lady's academic performance and personal preferences—"

"Please."

"But I doubt she discussed her political affiliations."

Chaz rolled out of bed and chorded the buttons on the nightstand. The bed slid back into the wall, revealing a polished patch of hardwood floor. When the bed clicked into the wall, a waist-high railing became available. He held it and began his daily exercises.

"Where does she lean?" he asked. "Nationalistic, I suppose."

"More antiquated and radical," she said. "Spinners."

Chaz's holographic triplets appeared at the bar. The randomly generated fitness program waited until he slipped into position between them before they started to move. He simply followed along, sighing with painful pleasure as his hypothalamic implant began to reward him.

"Students for the Preservation of Nations?" He huffed out

a laugh. "She was a typical college kid. What of it?"

"That is the surface, Chaz. Spinning is Nationalism on top and something called Internet Libertarianism beneath. I think she is—" She said a word that was all harsh consonants. She didn't translate.

The Chaz to the left performed a careful turnout, and he followed. He raised his leg and held it suspended there, savoring the agony. He knew he was only supposed to do this for fifteen minutes a day, but it felt so painfully good. Maybe he should reset the mechanism for another few minutes, just to save a millimeter's wear and tear on his joints. The fact that it felt . . . well, rather autoerotic was of entirely secondary interest. Honest.

He said, "She seems harmless to me."

"Harmless? Ask those at the Antarctic base. Do you remember them, Chaz? The ones who can never come home?"

He stopped and stared. "Are you suggesting Lenore was involved in the Sandefjord massacre?" Sandefjord was the worst act of bioterrorism in recent history: thirty dead and eighteen pitiful spooks who would never see Norway again. Wait now, *Levar* was a Spinner—

"Her college lover, a radical named Levar Rusch, was implicated. Chaz, she is poison."

Chaz hadn't liked Levar. He'd been pleased when they separated, but the pudgy, self-important boy hadn't looked *dangerous*.

His pulse rate was up to a hundred and forty now, ideal for maintenance of basic health. His entire system was engaged, pain and pleasure. Induced masochism it most certainly was, but it served its purpose.

*We can fix you,* Xanadu's doctors had said, *but you have to help us. Learning about your body, and slowing down the damage, is the best way you can do that.*

He had said, *Every survivor becomes his own doctor,* still thinking that this was only another exercise program. His mind was recovering, but he still didn't believe that they really intended to make him *younger*.

The hologram led him like the ideal personal trainer: tireless, pitiless, with perfect knowledge of his capacities and needs. It took him through his routine with infinite patience. When he failed to perform a movement properly, his triplets flashed rainbow colors in the corresponding muscles and joints until he made a correction. He bent forward at the bar, relaxing into it. Hip flashed orange: The system read muscular tension there, and he made a conscious effort to relax. In 2006 he had not even known there *were* nerves there.

Clarise waited for him to complete twelve intense minutes before he spoke again.

"Was *she* implicated?"

"No." The syllable seemed to cause her pain.

"What happened to Rusch?"

She paused, her dark lovely eyes half lidded. He thought that he heard something evasive in her voice. "Vanished for the past two years."

Chaz stopped and gazed up at her, sweat trickling down his forehead.

"Thank you, Clarise," he said. "That will be all for now. Please adjust my itinerary. Put Miss Myles on the Atlantis Room dinner list."

Clarise's voice was cold, precise. "Of course."

And the picture faded out. Chaz continued his workout for another thirty minutes. The intensity increased almost unendurably, then began to decrease. The heartbeat monitor said a hundred and twenty-eight. The system was happy with him and beginning to reduce the endorphin high, taking him into the "back-off" phase where he would want to stretch out and rest.

Chaz mopped his face, feeling more apprehensive than he would ever have allowed a certain deputy security chief, and ex-wife, to know.

* * *

Clarise Maibang gazed at the empty space above her desk, where a magic window to Chaz Kato had closed. There were moments when the incongruity of her life came near drowning her.

She turned away. She calmed herself by spending precious minutes etching charcoal designs on huge square sheets of pulp paper. They filled the walls of her apartment: Xanadu's towers and hallways, parks and gardens emerged from her fingertips with effortless ease.

On Java, the Bdui were considered magicians of great power. The civilized world took her tribe to be almost Stone Age. Their sophisticated philosophical and spiritual life . . . she had tried to share that knowledge with Chaz, but never with anyone else, not since school.

In Xanadu, the magic was of another kind completely, reliable and reproducible at a whisper or a finger's touch. The window of light floating in front of her now would have impressed even the most stoic mystics of her tribe.

She sketched a seagull spiraling above one of the lower towers, suggested a sunset with a single arc of the charcoal stick. Almost perfect; smudging the arc with the tip of her thumb made it even better.

Clarise had come so far, crossed a gulf of culture and language and technology in such a short time.

And yet she was the same girl who had played happily in the mud, who had gathered yams with her long-dead mother. The silly circuit teachers were amazed at her facility with art and languages. That had mystified Maibang. Art was the duty of a Walking Daughter. Language was just a gift, the ability to look beneath sounds and link meanings.

The gift was a double-edged sword.

Chaz had noticed her at an art contest three years ago. She had submitted drawings created on her own time, previously kept in the solitude of her small, comfortable room. Without condescension the judges had praised her "neo-primitivism," and she had taken second place.

Chaz had handed her the ribbon.

During her year of marriage to Chaz, she had been convinced that she could win him, could make him love her. One day they might even return to her people to have their union sanctified by a holy man of the "White" Bdui, the inner folk who never spoke with outsiders.

He had not lied. He had said that their contract would expire in a year. He was frail then, reveling in his returning abilities, though still weak as a kitten. She would heal him and guide him as only a woman of the Bdui could.

Such year-long arrangements were not unknown among the Islamic peoples of Indonesia. Among the Sufis it was called a *muta* contract and was honorable. On the Floating Islands they were legally binding but spiritually void. But when he gave himself to her, she knew that they could make a home, a world together.

She had virtually begged him to extend the contract another year.

Wrong, wrong. She had left him two months into the second term.

And if she had made a mistake to give him her heart, it was a mistake that was damnably difficult to undo. She remembered walking out to the farthest northern breakwater, sitting cross-legged and burning a handful of rice, symbol of their love, to send the smoke to her ancestors. Hoping for a healing.

The ancestors did not hear. Did not assist. She could not forget.

He did not love her, and it would kill her to pretend otherwise. But if her mind had been strong enough to go, her heart still called to him, still wished to share her nights.

Now this!

Now the Myles woman. What kind of game was he playing?

He had not been good at that. Brilliant, somehow a man between worlds, a kindred spirit . . . though he sometimes acted as if the entire world revolved around his needs. A man in his eighties! Older men should develop a sense of proportion.

Where was the Myles woman now?

Her hand stopped in midstroke, her eyes losing focus as her mind drifted. She set the stick down, wiped her hands on a towel, and walked back to her desk.

Hah, this much magic was hers. Xanadu's identification badges also functioned as three-dimensional Personal Tracking Devices. Maibang spoke Lenore's name into the system, and a tiny blue dot lit in one of the guest units.

Two blue dots: another visitor. The security unit pulled up the information. Tooley Wells, Lenore's roommate for the trip. College roommate as well. Safe to assume they were also friends.

Clarise drummed her fingers for a minute, then chose. She would eavesdrop. It was her duty.

# 7

"Girl," Tooley said, "wipe that smile off your face, would you? Everyone will know exactly what you've been up to, and your reputation will be trashed."

"Mmmmm." Lenore lay back on the bed, fingers stretching out and wiggling in the sheets, luxuriating in a bed she hadn't slept in. Tooley stood over her, an exaggerated expression of alarm scrunching her dark face.

"I mean, what kind of woman sleeps with every handsome, brilliant multimillionaire who happens along?"

"I'm a tramp," Lenore agreed.

"Round Heels."

"Madonna."

"Hopeless."

Lenore rolled up off the bed and took Tooley's slender hands in hers. "He's wonderful."

"I don't want to hear the gory details. . . ." Tooley agonized through five seconds of modesty, then surrendered. "I lied. Speak."

Giggling, Lenore gave her fifty seconds of steamy reminiscence, then squared her shoulders. "And as for the rest, you will just have to use your imagination."

Tooley pressed one hand to her chest. "Ahhh . . . I don't know how to tell you this, but you did more in an evening than Mel and I have in the last four months. I'm not jealous. I'm in awe."

"It might be love."

"At least it's sex. But he's a *cyborg?*"

"Augmented somehow, anyway. His head bulges out in the back. There's a plug. Probably a whiz at computer games. There's another scar on his belly, abdominal surgery, years old."

Tooley looked at her. "So, what next?"

"A job interview was mentioned."

"Here? What about Washington Synaptech?"

"It never hurts to window-shop. Anyway, I brought old all-purpose—"

She launched into the closet and extracted a black pantsuit that had served Lenore on occasions as varied as field trips, scholarship interviews, and first dates.

She hemmed and hawed, tinkering with the accouterments, and suddenly realized that Tooley was quiet behind her.

Lenore turned slowly. "Deep thoughts?"

"I'm just wondering," her roommate said, "what Levar would say about this. Remember his 'Councilor exploiters of the world, rape the Earth and then escape to stars' routine? And you're talking about love with a man you've just met, who is probably a member of the Council. Levar detested the Council."

Lenore wagged her head. "Levar isn't here. Chaz isn't on the Council."

"You *know* this?"

She *knew* it. Chaz had power, but she'd seen how he flinched from authority. His ex-wife intimidated him. He bent the local law with a conscious sense of getting away with something. Chaz hadn't made these laws.

She said, "Tooley, I'm telling you that I woke up in the middle of the night, with this incredible man next to me, and I was thinking a lot of the same things that you're saying right now. And you know what? I decided that maybe it was time to grow up."

Tooley sighed in exasperation. "I don't know. Either maturity has arrived late in life, or you've dropped your values like a hot rock. It must have been some tumble."

Lenore smiled wickedly. "Honey, he has the body of a teenage surfer and the imagination of a ninety-year-old letch. And that is quite enough for this girl. One other thing." She paused. "His voice drives me up the wall."

"God, the girl is mad."

Lenore swatted at her friend playfully. "Now do you want to criticize, or help me get ready for tonight?"


Graduates from around the world were gathered in Xanadu's central auditorium, a cavernous stadium decorated to resemble a vaulted sea cave. Xanadu had gathered these thousands of brilliant young minds into one place at one time. Lenore expected part lecture, part showboat, and part recruitment spiel. She saw no way to avoid it, and besides, Chaz was speaking.

Naturally most of these graduates already had offers. Some had already thumbed contracts. Their guides made it clear that Xanadu's extensive legal staff knew how to break such documents. Xanadu, despite its merry façade, could be adroitly piratical.

Recruiters roved the crowd. Selected grads were cut out

of the pack, then guided to smaller groups for an individu-
alized spiel.

She searched the room for Chaz. Before she spotted him
she saw a big, pale, solid, totally bald man gliding through
the room, moving like some kind of smooth machine. A
cool, meaningless smile curved his lips, and the crowd
parted before him. He never paused, never engaged in conversations, never stopped looking. Lenore guessed he was
Security.

She spotted Chaz against the far wall holding a small knot
of prospects entranced. He hadn't seen her yet, but as she
increased the intensity of her stare he looked up and their
eyes met. His lips curled into a smile, but he continued with
his conversation.

Good. She just wanted him to know that she was there.

The tall man at the front of the room—thin, freckled, with
too much forehead and a careless thatch of rapidly receding
red hair—was Arvad Minsky. A Council member! He might
as easily have been a Martian. He wore an elaborate customized set of V-goggles; it partly covered his ears and right
eye and the crown and back of his head. His left hand was
a spidery gauntlet—it must have been lighter than it
looked—and he used it more than his right, moving it too
fast for Lenore to count the fingers.

He didn't act like a Power. He gestured, he finger-tapped
empty air, he made shapes with his arms. Words tumbled
from his thin lips in a cascade, as if he feared he might be
shot before he got everything out. "We grow our own islands! We're colonizing the ocean! How can you not love
it?"

The voice in the audience was inaudible. Lenore caught
a phrase or two and recognized Spinner rhetoric.

Minsky answered. "Xanadu and the Floating Islands have
been integral in the sharing of biosphere resources. We provide food, building materials, and medical aid to the needy,
on a worldwide basis. *We* don't damage the biosphere.
There isn't a community on Earth that's better at recycling!"

Another question. Minsky waved his gauntlet hand. The floor before him blossomed into a map: a lilypad made of hexagons, an aerial perspective of Xanadu.

Minsky was a polymath of intimidating magnitude: biologist, chess grand master, and one of the core architects of Xanadu's design. His hands were more expressive than his voice. He was talking nonstop while his fingers danced. The floor map shrank; the viewpoint pulled back from Xanadu's artificial atoll to reveal Sri Lanka and the Coromandel coast of India, then another fractal hexagon southeastward, deep in the South China Sea. Colored outlines flashed and mutated: trade routes, air routes, fish populations, currents of ocean pollution, slender neon comet tails for the tracks of satellites. But Lenore watched Minsky.

As his head swiveled and shifted, Lenore became sure that his headgear was fixed to the bulging back of his head. Like Chaz, he must have a plug back there.

Other guests had donned V-goggles, enhancing their view of the superstructure. Lenore slipped hers on. At the moment the images matched, but she knew that would change shortly.

She heard a recorded voice, not Minsky's, accompanied by flashes of holographic text and some exploded-view sectioning as explicit as a fly-by. Her specs painted pastel outlines around medical facilities on Xanadu and Sri Lanka and links between. The voice whispered a customized invitation:

*"Lenore, here at Xanadu you would find your biological research meshing smoothly with that of our prize-winning cyberneticists, who have pioneered artificial, self-replicating synapses—"*

The spiel's synthesized sincerity was compelling. Curious, she slipped her goggles down and watched their faces, wondering who was entranced, who still skeptical, who already saw Xanadu as heaven.

The Xanadu snowflake rotated until one of the southern towers rose high in her sight. There were blank spots. Her soaring POV glided in close, pierced a wall, and suddenly she was in a gleaming hospital unit. Now her goggles gave her a more customized view. Where others had a general tour of the hospital, she was taken instantly to the medical research facilities, to gleaming halls filled with glittering computer displays and stainless-steel apparatus.

*"—if you choose to become part of Xanadu's family or, indeed, to participate in the world of the Floating Islands, you will find yourself part of the most advanced team in the world, Lenore."* The whisper was direct, sincere, seductive. *"You have dedicated your life to creation of synthetic neural tissue. We believe this to be one of the three most promising augmented biocybernetic approaches. Here in Xanadu we stand at the cutting edge of that research, much of which we cannot yet share with the outside world. We can give you a glimpse of our efforts, if you wish."*

She watched as a hydrocephalic child entered an operating theater. A brief clip showed a pale redheaded eight-year-old attempting to fit basic block shapes together to make a rectangle. He failed miserably. In fact, he didn't seem to grasp the nature of the test.

In the operating theater, a team of doctors first electronically anesthetized the boy, then performed a series of exquisite laser surgeries. Lenore suddenly recognized the music: background music from the recent remake of *Charly*.

*"If you remember, put some flowers on his grave . . ."*

"After a brief convalescence," the voice-over said, "look at what we were able to achieve."

The boy was sitting up now, alert, and playing chess with Arvad Minsky himself. Minsky was teaching the boy his own favorite move: rook sacrifice.

Chess. Lenore smiled, remembering Chaz's remarks about his grandmother. Could this same boy, say, compare the characters of Huckleberry Finn and Tom Sawyer? Or write an essay comparing the aesthetics of flowers and snakes? Or was he a computer's marionette?

Any computer could beat a human being at chess. Had

there ever been a debate? It now seemed as quaint as John Henry's race with a steam shovel. This pointless posturing on nonessentials always drove her crazy.

She wound her way through the crowd toward Chaz, who was locked in a discussion with Hernandez. She was peripherally aware of the conversational buzz around her and even more distantly aware of the change in tone as the auditorium's high walls suddenly flushed red. The central display had changed. As the subject rotated from one facet of Xanadu to another, differing portions of the crowd paid attention. Others broke into conversational units, picked through the canapés, drifted off with recruiters for private tours.

The crimson flicker indicated that the engineering display was about to begin. The immense grid of the Oceanic Thermal Energy Converters appeared above them. Distantly the announcer discussed the OTEC generators and how power for Xanadu—and for export in the form of methane and liquid hydrogen—was extracted by harvesting the ocean's heat differential. Engineering geeks bored by the plight of a retarded child now clustered in fascination. Several were badge-beeped and moved in groups toward a personal inspection of the generators.

She drifted, trying to get close enough to Chaz to play with eye contact and also close enough to hear Hernandez.

"—implantation is a dead end," he was saying. "I'll be happy when there is less emphasis on the cranial anatomy or surgical procedure and more on the philosophical implications."

An attractive redhead smiled and said: "There he goes." Her voice was teasing and admiring. She licked the edge of her glass. Lenore had never seen her before, but she *had* heard that voice.

"And which implications are those?" Chaz asked.

"This is Freshman Philosophy 101," Hernandez replied. "The question isn't merely one of giving a damaged mind access to, say, basic mathematical skills. Not wiring a calculator into his head." Lenore was surprised to hear his thoughts mirroring her own.

"We'd want to give him the ability to gather and sort information for himself. Tighten the 'weave' of the neural net. What do we *wish* him to catch? After all, the philosophical and perceptual filters we provide an Auggie will determine which slice of reality he perceives."

Chaz smiled tolerantly. "Are you a Universalist, then? You believe concepts exist independently of the minds that perceive them?"

"Realism and Conceptualism are just positions on the board." Hernandez seemed slightly contemptuous of Chaz's question. "I want to screw with the board! The inability to agree on its design doesn't preclude its existence. I would hope we could at least agree that the lens through which we view reality changes our interaction with that reality. For instance: Earlier today we had a lecture on a variety of Xanadu's ecological concerns. It's all nonsense."

Chaz remained outwardly calm, but other members of the circle stiffened at the calculated barb. A dark-haired young man called indignantly, "Professor? Are you suggesting that damage to the ecosphere is irrelevant? Or hopeless?"

"I've suggested none of that." Again Hernandez gave them that pitying expression. "We do our share and more. Xanadu and the Floating Islands have been integral in the sharing of biosphere resources. We provide food, building materials, and medical aid on a worldwide basis." Silver fingers gestured intricately ... and Arvad Minsky was standing knee deep in a curved map of the Bay of Bengal. Neon lines drew themselves out from Xanadu: medical supplies, hydrogen, fish ... but the dark-haired man was trying to yell over Arvad's amplified voice.

*Jesus, he's one smug son of a bitch! I can't believe I once had a crush on Phillipe.*

Chaz spoke in a conciliatory tone; his voice was amplified too. "Let's cool off, shall we? After all, this is a celebration. I happen to know that Phillipe, for all his cocktail-party cynicism, has made serious contributions to the AIDS and smallpox vaccine programs. I believe that he contributed his entire year of doctoral research."

Hernandez looked a little flustered. "I don't like to talk about that."

"Modest," Chaz said, and smiled. The tension eased a bit, and several members of the circle chose that moment to excuse themselves.

Behind them, the wall colors shifted to green and blue as the display began to sink into the oceanic depths. Gliding aquatic shadows drifted through the room.

Lenore drifted up behind Chaz and slipped her hand through his arm. He smiled warmly and kissed the cheek she offered.

Hernandez watched them with bemusement, but Lenore sensed that something nibbled at the edge of his calm. Then he managed a more genuine smile. "As Mr. Kato said—it's just cocktail-party conversation."

The redhead tugged at his arm. Again Lenore wondered where she had seen the woman. No, wait. . . . Heard! But the face didn't match. The voice belonged to someone else.

Chaz guided Lenore away from the group. "So, what do you think of Hernandez?" she asked.

"Smart, but pedantic," he said. "He's definitely of a type."

"What type is that?"

"Arrogant, brilliant. Invaluable, especially in his own mind. We have a lot of them here, and frankly, anyone like Hernandez has a lot to be arrogant about. But . . . we could use more like you."

"Me?"

He nodded.

" 'We' could use me? Or is that a personal preference?"

Chaz leaned forward to kiss her lightly on the mouth. His breath was spearmint. "As personal as it gets. I tell you what . . . are you in the mood for a swim?"

He was changing the subject, but she let him get away with it. "Love it."

"Grab your suit and we'll visit the dolphins."

# 8

Chaz dove deep, eyes open against both rushing currents and the lagoon's mild alkalinity. He surfaced again, gulping air and reveling in the sunshine. He was content to dog paddle and watch as Lenore, sublime in an opal bathing thong, glided through the water like a sprite.

Effortlessly pacing her was one of the most beautiful creatures in the world, a five-year-old *Tursiops truncatus*. Manny was six feet long, his skin a slick and glistening gray, a bottlenose dolphin who, from the moment that Lenore dove from the lagoon's concrete lip, seemed absurdly delighted to play with her.

Manny was choosy about his playmates. He had embarrassed Chaz before by refusing to make friends with visiting guests. But he had immediately taken to this particular human female, gliding around her in a lazy loop, clearly relishing the game.

Chaz observed her efforts to keep up. Manny's first circuit was slow and easy. Her long, graceful sweep of arm and leg served her well as she shadowed him. Then he began to get ambitious. She came even with Chaz and bobbed up gasping and laughing. "He's staying just ahead of me," she said. "I think he wants to play."

On the next circuit Manny threw in an occasional twirl, then an extravagant spiral. He glided back to Lenore and nudged her with his snout. She giggled and took the hint. When Manny did his spiral trick again, Lenore duplicated his efforts. The dolphin fairly raced around the tank, then returned, nudged her again, and indulged in even more erratic gyrations.

After a moment's hesitation, Lenore followed him. Chaz stroked the pool lazily as Lenore and Manny played around its edge. With every revolution, Manny's gyrations grew more elaborate. Finally Lenore broke the surface and paddled over to the pool's edge, propping her forearms up on the concrete.

She blew water, shaking her head in frustration. "God, he wore me out. You know," she said, "if I didn't know better, I'd think he was testing *me.*"

Chaz laughed at that, and continued to chuckle as she climbed up out of the tank. But as soon as her back was turned, he gave Manny a nasty look and chopped a handful of water at him. Manny skated away, making a derisive *eee-eee-eee* sound.

Dolphin laughter.

They shuttled back to his apartment and showered together in a stall large enough for a decent game of volleyball. She wiggled up against him in the hot water, and they made wet soapy love again. He completely lost himself in her feel, her taste, in the strong soft heft of her. When they once again became aware of the pounding water, they slipped out and toweled each other dry.

After his heart stopped pounding, he couldn't help but say: "Stay."

"Hmmm?"

"Stay with me, here in Xanadu. There's a place for you here. There's always a place for someone as bright as you."

She laughed and wagged her head at him. "You know," she said, "you're really good at this."

He stared at her, a bit dumbfounded. "What?"

"Well, you must have a book, something that helps you play it line-by-line perfect. Did you order up the moon last night too? Was that a real moon?"

He worked his mouth without finding the words to keep it propped open and let it shut.

"I have a life," she said. "We've had fun. But what I do for the rest of my life—or for the next few years—will be decided very soberly, and not in the midst of a romantic buzz. I've got another offer, and I'll just bet you know it—"

"Washington Synaptech. Good company, good prospects. Climate isn't as warm. They're as nutty about seafood as we are, and if you like cappuccino you're in heaven. I'm offering more. Preliminary approval is on file. If you accept there would be the usual deep background checks and interviews, but I've never had a candidate declined."

She leaned back against the wall and crossed her arms insolently. "I've thumbed their contract. I have to show up for the first month, at least. What's the contract length here?"

"Usual corporate contract is five years."

"And citizenship? Loyalty oaths?"

"*I* had to take those." It sounded lame even to him.

"Umm-hmmm." He felt that he wanted to turn away from her, his cheeks burning, and suddenly knew what she was thinking:

*The scandalnet term for this was* Honeypot. *You choose the brilliant, vulnerable ones. No family, just out of college. You romance them and lure them into breaking legal contracts and traveling halfway round the world with promises of romance and adventure. Then come loyalty oaths and long-term ironclads. After that agreements of ownership for the first ten years of patents, how long do the romances last, Chaz? And that woman Maibang. You say you had a contract with her? Was that part of the recruitment package too?*

He couldn't really blame her for being suspicious—but he could hate the Spinners and the geopolitical propaganda machines.

He raised his palms in the universal gesture of surrender. "No more pushing," he said. "I've put in a bid. Dwell on it. And if I've been a little too pushy, Lenore, you're very easy to love."

Some of the humor returned to her eyes, and his chest relaxed a bit. She slipped on her clothes, her expression carefully neutral. "Let me think for a while," she said.

"You're leaving tomorrow?"

"I'm sure you already know that."

"There's tonight's dinner."

She smiled at him again, and he knew that he had said the right thing. "We'll have dinner, and talk," she said. "And then we'll see."

She kissed him lightly and left the bathroom. Chaz's mind whirled, and as he watched her dress, he knew that he had to get her to trust him, *now*.

"Wait!" Naked, he stepped from the shower and picked up his shirt. His thumb skritched the curve of the little crest above his pocket, the little wave symbol worn by every citizen of Xanadu. Crests, cuff links, watches, earrings, somewhere on their bodies every one of them kept a tiny memory bubble holding all of their medical, financial, and security information. Visitors were issued cards that served much the same purpose, but limited them to approved areas of the Island.

What he was about to do was strictly *verboten*, but . . . what harm, really?

Lenore watched, mystified and still half dressed as he snatched the badge from her blouse and ran into his office. "Clarise would pass a starfish if she knew," he said, more to himself than Lenore. "Tell you what: I'll put an eighteen-hour limit on this."

"On what?"

"I'm going to write my security access onto your badge." As he said the words, he slipped the plastic rectangle into a slot in his desktop data system and chorded a few quick commands. "Now you can go anywhere I can go, and *I* can go almost everywhere. Go where you want, do what you want. We don't have anything to hide." He popped it back out and handed it to her. His hands shook.

She held the badge by its edges as if it might singe her. "I don't know . . ."

"What harm?" he said. "If you leave tomorrow, and I never see you again . . . if I haven't done everything possible to reassure you, I'll never forgive myself. If I have . . . then it's just out of my hands, you see?"

She smiled wryly and closed her fist around the badge. "All right," she said finally. "Maybe I do understand. But no promises, right?"

"No promises. Just . . . give us an honest chance."

"Promise," she said, and kissed him.


Chaz sat heavily on the bathroom bench, gazing between his hands. The steam smell was evaporating. It seemed to have washed her scent from the air. There remained no trace of her in his shower. He wandered into his bedroom. No trace of her. The rumpled sheets had been replaced; her scent was gone.

He wandered out to his office, his naked body drying in the filtered air. "Projects," he said. Crafted and weighed for his own personality, his current projects appeared, cloaked as an apple tree. Taproots represented potential avenues of research. His cursor touched those roots. The view zoomed on individual roots labeled for papers and books and files. He saw he had neglected some recent molecular biology papers: nanotech interaction with autosomes, the possibility of co-opting human DNA strands to store data, modifying redundant circuits in the human brain as a kind of biocomputer . . .

That last sounded interesting, and he highlighted it with a touch.

Moving up the tree to the trunk, he found basic issues dealing with Xanadu itself. As an owner-employee of the massive facility, he was expected to make decisions that would influence the island's future.

Proposition 12-V was up for another vote. Lower the cost of energy to Sri Lanka? He might want to attend a virtual meeting on this one: It was good for Admin and Public Relations, bad for the Business office. Worse, Energy (the corporate superunion representing petroleum, solar, geothermal, OTEC, nuclear, and radical energy production worldwide) would want a say in this. God, he loathed politics.

Following the model up into the branches, he could trace the workings of any of a dozen different divisions, but the green line continued up into Chaz Kato's own leafy domain: augmentation technology.

As the old familiar excitement returned, thoughts of Lenore faded from his mind. He split his study time between the old and the new. A paper on the interaction of Freud's phallic stage of infant development (three to five years, the point where sexual attraction produces an oedipal complex) and how unresolved echoes of that conflict create learning blocks in a Maslow-like model of human development.

Here was a new book cross-referencing twentieth-century concepts of intelligence with vector and coordinate physics. "Attention," he commanded. "Synopsis of content."

His personal processing system spoke in a cool feminine voice. "This book attempts to reconstitute a workable and measurable definition of mental function. This is no small task. The ongoing debate between liberals and conservatives resulted in a psychometric wasteland, rendering linear measurement of strictly digital-visual qualities, e.g., the Stanford-Benet, politically passé. Unfortunately, the late–twentieth-century castigation of such measurements as Eurocentric and culturally elitist was almost as useless."

"Does the author have a remedy, or is he just thrashing around?"

"Multiple models. Intelligence measured as a vector rather than a scalar quality, and as a hypercube, with a complex core model representing all of the data currently available on inter-

and intracultural communication, neurophysiology and culturally dominant representation systems."

That could be interesting. "I'll take that in fifteen minutes."

Still naked, Chaz wandered through his apartment, ultimately drawn back to the bedroom. He gathered the sheets in his hands and sniffed deeply. Nothing. What of the blankets? For a moment, nothing, then . . . there she was.

He savored her scent. He had taken extraordinary measures to compensate for the lies he had been forced to tell Lenore. He prayed that those lies wouldn't shatter the first fragile happiness he had known in almost twenty years.

# 9

Lenore sat alone in a little corner booth in the Caribbean section of the Level Six food court. The map promised a hundred such courts distributed throughout Xanadu, and many true restaurants as well.

A real restaurant would be too intimate for her purpose. What she needed was room and time to think.

Why couldn't she just accept Chaz's gift? Two weeks ago, before she thumbed the Washington Synaptech contract, this would have been her fondest wish. Now she was staring into a legal and ethical mire. Yuck.

She picked halfheartedly at barbecued ribs slathered in a tangerine-based sauce. Wonderful. But was she eating textured algae, ribs and meat and sauce? Not the sauce—tangerine trees were too easy—but the meat . . . and the bone. *She* would make the bones of plastic, and recycle. She gnawed at her rib, imagining herself to be reenacting a Pleistocene diorama.

The restaurant's steel and plastic chairs were filled with busy, buzzing people. It was impossible not to be at least partially swept up in Xanadu's air of activity. Everyone was part of a single giant machine, a machine anchored in the ocean and aimed at the stars.

Tooley Wells approached. The glowing hologram ghost of a half-grown boy in a bellman's uniform trotted two steps behind her above a little motorized luggage cart that otherwise would have been low enough to trip people.

Lenore patted the seat next to her and said, "Have one."

Tooley plucked a rib daintily between her fingers, nibbled, then dug in. Looked up. "You look twitchy."

"Well, I got a job offer," she said. She leaned her head conspiratorially close. The room's constant murmur pretty much guaranteed that no one around them would hear, but it still seemed prudent to lower her voice.

Tooley grinned. "Rejecting your straight line as too obvious. . . ."

"Right."

"Most of the class did, didn't we? That's why we're here. The Floating Islands are still expanding like mad. They need people. We're the right people, honey, and they damned well know it."

"Yes. But. Washington Synaptech expects me in three days. If I break that contract, it goes on my permanent record. Who'll trust me again? If things don't work out here, I could hurt big time. Arrggh."

Tooley suddenly looked at her friend compassionately. "No wonder some people stay perpetual students."

"I don't like being an adult." Lenore pouted, then laughed at herself. "Listen to me. There are people who would kill to have my problems."

"Thumbing a contract doesn't sell you to a company. Thirty days, pig out on salmon, then opt out. Honey, you've slaved for years to make yourself into what you are."

"And what exactly is that?"

"Someone deeply deserving of success. Someone who

worked while the rest of us partied. After you and Levar broke up, golden eggs got laid more often."

Lenore laughed, but it hurt a bit. The isolation was still a vivid memory. Lovers had been few and far between, and unsatisfying. Real sex takes time, requires some depth of communication. In those years her fear of failure, of not fulfilling her mother's dream, had driven her so deep into her studies that only the most determined seducer would follow.

"Hell," Tooley continued, "I had to pry you away from the books to take Christmas in the Bahamas."

Lenore remembered that time fondly. Sparkling beaches, waterfalls, moonlight dancing, and long lazy afternoons with Tooley's family. She remembered envying Tooley's easy camaraderie with her sisters, her stern but loving parents, and doting grandparents. Even more than the siren song of the warm and welcoming sands, she remembered the feel of being surrounded by love. Remembered wondering why she worked so damned hard. Was it to earn the love and respect of people already gone? Or in hope of one day creating a family like Tooley's?

She knew only that she longed for that sense of connection. She would earn it with her intellect. Her intellect had always proven more trustworthy than her emotions.

"Anyway," Tooley said, "this kind of ends the Dynamic Duo."

"Time flies like an arrow—"

"Fruit flies like a banana," Tooley said, completing their time-worn catechism. They slapped hands and hugged.

"This isn't the end of it," Lenore said.

"Good." Tooley seemed relieved. "Listen. I spoke with Mom this morning . . ."

"How is she?"

"She's on the wrong end of the curve, and she has to fight to get gas. She doesn't make enough to go solar. Anyway, she said specifically to ask if you'd get violently ill at the idea of spending another Christmas with us this year."

"Where's the reunion?"

"Maui."

"Owie!" Chills ran through her. This was just wonderful. Fear that Tooley would drift out of her life had been a persistent, nagging irritation. She extended her hand. "Deal."

Lenore watched Tooley disappear from the food court and felt a terrible pang. She wished fervently that she had booked the same flight home. But *Chaz!*

She nibbled at the last rib. Cold, it still tasted fine. Most synthetic foods had a specific temperature range. Too warm or too cold, the taste degraded. Xanadu's gnomes were better than merely good.

Regardless, her stomach had passed the "fill" point. "Quit while you've got a waist," she murmured, and rose to dump the bones. The nice thing about the food court was that real, live human beings still worked the counters. She approached the boy working the barbecue shop. He lounged, momentarily between customers.

"Excuse me." He immediately gave her wide eyes and toothy smile. "Are the artificial ribs manufactured here? They're really very good."

He grinned broadly. "They should be." He laughed. "They're flown in from Sri Lanka. They used to oink."

Oops. She excused herself, feeling the perfect fool. Sometimes, dammit, you were better off just taking things at face value.

# 10

The little green plastic rectangle on her blouse gave no warning, and no security officers materialized to escort her, politely or otherwise, out of the east wing's cybernetics lab.

She had planned to take a shortcut, slipping over to one of the express elevators shunting from an outer to an inner ring, and technically that forced her to walk through an off-limits area . . . and she *had* to try the badge. If he'd lied about *that*—

But Lenore's badge didn't beep, and that put a secret smile on her face. She began to wonder how far Chaz's special access might reach.

The first polite warning should have been followed in a few minutes (were she to penetrate more deeply into the complex) by a sustained tone. If she were so unwise as to remove her badge, sensors would pick up a warm, unidentified human-size object and begin to pay it close attention. Xanadu's security probably studied thermal patterns. They might even have retinal scans.

Were their cameras so sensitive? She guessed they were, but there was a difference between having the capacity to gather and analyze data and consistently examining every passing warm object. That was prohibitively expensive, regardless of the system in question.

But it didn't happen, and now she saw a delicious option.

A closer look at the medical center might be of interest. Lenore's own work lay mostly in synthetic neural tissue. Sometimes she worked with doctors engaged in animal testing. She didn't exactly *need* clearance into the surgical theaters, but Chaz's pass might give her a look at some really interesting stuff.

Lenore hopped one of the elevators and headed over.

Clarise Maibang set charcoal to paper, drawing a long, broad line, the muscles in her forearms playing like cables beneath her golden skin. The drawing was crude but precise: a woman standing guard before a floating tower. She brandished a spear at a second woman, who had the head of a crocodile.

It was a healthier outlet than simply tearing Lenore's head off and pitching her to the sharks.

Clarise longed for the *kampongs* of her youth. The Bdui were less agricultural than most Javanese—they were virtually hunter-gatherers. They didn't, couldn't carry wealth about with them. But whatever their relative material poverty, no one from her village had to deal with problems like this. All grew into their roles, and there were no strangers.

Clarise had reason to investigate her Lenore Myles. The Spinner who shared Myles's bed *must* have shared her view of the world. Clarise recalled the Antarctic bioterrorism. At what point might Energy decide that the cost/benefit ratio was unfavorable and simply allow those maintenance and technical workers to die?

To a woman who still clearly remembered her Malaysian childhood, there were natural means of determining worth: *Do you contribute to the* kampong? *Is that contribution measurable? If so, we will welcome and feed you and shelter you through the storm. If not, the leopards are always just beyond the campfire's light.*

Those innocent men and women who no longer had the ability to contribute might be cast to the leopards because of men like Levar Rusch.

Maibang's better world was a place where everyone was exploited equally, where sexism and racism were as outmoded as rusty old automobiles. It was only in such a world that a woman like Clarise Maibang might travel from Stone Age to twenty-first century in fifteen years, and rise to power and authority. Eventually she would bring wealth home to the village of her birth.

No threat to her new home's stability would be tolerated.

Most of the visiting students had already left Xanadu. Some stayed on. Security had been deliberately relaxed to avoid the impression of an armed camp. But that latitude created new headaches.

It was difficult to justify continued surveillance. Lenore was wandering harmlessly around the island, sightseeing. If she penetrated any secure areas, an alert would trigger, and Clarise would know.

Lenore was no threat. Let her go home. Let her go far enough away that Chaz might recognize the gem within his reach and forget the fool's gold from afar.

# 11

Lenore wandered the halls. The med section was in a northern tower, one ring out from the center, as beautiful, clean, and spotless as the rest of the island. She daydreamed of a Xanaduan future.

What if Xanadu's lawyer loopholed her, and she *did* come to live here? Hell, there was even a virtual university, affiliated with colleges ranging from Hamburg to Tokyo and Johannesburg. She could earn her Ph.D., maybe an M.D., and Xanadu would fund it. She didn't think she would ever want to actually walk a scalpel through anyone's medulla, but she should have the credentials!

The maternity section was down a floor, along with pediatric medicine and the fertility clinic. Lenore drifted down that way. She found herself standing outside the maternity ward gazing at babies. Rows and rows of them, dressed in pink and blue and lined up for display in their bassinets and incubators.

She looked at those little faces, little pink and brown cheeks, some of them crying while nurses scurried about, and something in her chest relaxed.

Would Chaz make a good father? Purely a hypothetical question, of course. She was years away from any excursion into motherhood. Chaz was an older man; it did show. Nonetheless . . .

Just the thought of him made her smile. He was so damned sweet it made her teeth ache. Still, he was with-holding something. She knew it. And truth be told, that challenge was appealing. Something deep within him was begging her to open him up.

Perversely, her very freedom of access reduced her urge to ask questions. Chaz was a clever bastard. She toyed with the idea of calling him, just surrendering and telling him she would have a chat with Xanadu's legal staff, when she noticed a bright yellow line on the floor and then a cheery LEVEL THREE CLEARANCE sign.

How interesting! She took a few more steps, giving the security system a better chance to kick in. Nothing happened.

These generic hospital hallways lacked Xanadu's Aquatic-Organic look. The pale blue walls hummed slightly, almost alive. Workers passed with polite smiles, too pre-occupied to notice an unfamiliar face. *That* couldn't last. Surely she couldn't penetrate more deeply into the complex without attracting attention.

She turned to leave.

Behind her a woman laughed, and Lenore flinched.

She had heard that voice in the briefings, with its curiously nasal qualities. Why did her spine crawl at the sound of it? Why the almost overwhelming sense that something was . . . wrong?

She'd watched how Chaz used the interlocking oval panels in the walls. She summoned up a menu, then MAP.

The nearest sections crawled with light and produced a flowing schematic of Xanadu, all of its public access areas and perhaps a few more restricted pockets. Her face was hidden, and oddly lighted too, as she looked into the glow of the wall map.

She turned her head just enough to search for the voice.

There. That laughing redhead running down the hall. A perfect body, carefully weight-trained into symmetrical perfection. She actually looked *too* good, suggesting the kind of medical sculpting that only serious money provides. Hell, she could be forty, or fifty.

Lenore followed the woman down the hall into the reproductive biology section. She was delighted that Chaz's credentials had gotten her so far. Even so, surely there was a limit to his clearance. He'd implied as much. *He* knew where the borders were; she didn't.

The redhead paused and adjusted her dress coyly. Lenore pretended to be fascinated by the computer display, but the woman never noticed. Instead, she took off at a trot, virtually burbling with joy. Then she accelerated and flew into the arms of . . .

Gregory Phillipe Hernandez, of course.

Lenore felt a swift and irrational pang of jealousy, followed by the kind of guilty pleasure experienced only by the successful voyeur. The Great Hernandez had a lover? Oooh. This was *priceless*. She'd have to tell Tooley! Via e-mail, of course, not a murmur in the dark. God, she was going to miss Tooley.

The redhead clung to Hernandez like a lamprey. He walked her out into a side corridor, their faces glued together. Feeling foolish, Lenore turned and started to walk away, when, with a jolt, she realized to whom that distinctive, husky cracked voice belonged.

Impossible.

It was Dr. Mary Kravitz, guest lecturer at her high school science club five years ago.

Mary Kravitz, who had not merely impressed them with her intelligence and depth of perception in the ethical minefield of bioengineering but had won their hearts with her enormous courage.

Kravitz had weighed little more than 100 pounds, hadn't been able to rise from her wheelchair. Looking at Kravitz conjured mental images of the tragic, brilliant Steven Hawking. Which illness was killing her? Lenore didn't remember. Some variety of myoneural junction defect.

Mary Kravitz had died eight weeks after the lecture. Lenore remembered seeing the obit in *Science Newsletter*.

Mary Kravitz looked better five years dead than she had while living.

There was no visual resemblance. Even the young Mary Kravitz couldn't have looked this good. Kravitz had been blond and rather chunky. Now that Lenore thought about it, the eyes, the turn of the head, the bone structure in her face, some small things about her smile . . . matched.

Lenore followed them out.

The door opened into a broad, deserted hallway. She stood quietly, listening: nothing. A winding staircase led up to unknown levels. Distantly feet scraped against metal steps. Too distantly. They couldn't have gone so far so rapidly. Where, then? Lenore, feeling very foolish and juvenile, crept down half a flight and watched silently.

They stood on the stairs below her, arms twined around each other, necking like teenagers. Hernandez's hand roamed beneath Kravitz's blouse, hers groped the front of his pants. Their mouths were fused together.

This was *intense*. Lenore wanted to pull herself away but couldn't. The two of them partially disrobed each other and went at it right there against the wall. Hot, steamy, sweaty, damned-near public sex. It was over in about six minutes. They collapsed against each other, kissing wetly again. A few murmured endearments drifted up to Lenore.

The words were indistinct; the walls muffled sound. "Thank God . . . could get away."

Lenore dared descending another two steps.

"We're almost finished, darling," she said. "Just a few more stats." Kravitz made a warm chuckling sound. "A billion doses in *twelve* years. Double that rate now, thanks to you, my beautiful brilliant prince." She threw her head back, laughing giddily. "God, I don't know what they did to my hormones—or is it just you?"

"It's just me," he said, and they dove into another frenzied kiss.

Starting up again? Lenore was about to leave them to it,

when Hernandez said something that caught her attention.

"With air and water dispersal," he said, "it's a whole new ball game."

"We've poisoned the Collie stats. There's just nothing. No one will believe Triguna until it's too"—kiss—"damned"—kiss—"late."

Hernandez laughed nastily. "What a pitiful *maricón*. It was his own idea. You'd think he'd be grateful."

"I know what I'm grateful for," she said, and pressed herself against him again.

"I think they *did* double your hormones. But who's complaining?" The rest was muffled.

Lenore slipped out. What was all of *that* about? Her head whirled. A dead nymphomaniac was humping her teacher in the hall. Not Xanadu, but maybe not Shangri-la either. Had she found Unknown Kadath?

"Triguna"? "Poisoning the Collie stats"?

She backed out of the area quickly. Every nervous step increased her overall sense of fear and alarm.

Triguna? And Hernandez. Triguna was Hernandez's mentor at UCLA, a brilliant but eccentric Bengali, politically *most* incorrect. And what was that about dogs? "Collies?" She couldn't quite remember, but she had the sense that she had heard something about Triguna and his dogs somewhere before. And she knew just where to find the answers.

## 12

Linking, the most common form of augmentation, could be like having a dozen geniuses evaluating your every act. At other times it could be as simple as accessing a recipe template when cooking eggs Florentine, or gliding through a tango with a ghostly hologram dancer.

At the moment, Lenore's needs were hardly so exotic or entertaining. She merely needed data.

The nearest library nook was easy walking distance, tucked between a walk-in clinic and a bank of elevators. She chose a vacant shell and eased in, and presented her badge to the scan-eye for access.

A flat vidscreen descended, placed itself at perfect focal range, and began to display. She noticed that the library was debiting Chaz Kato's account. With voice and chorded keyboards beneath each handrest, Lenore commenced her search.

Triguna. Collie. (Dogs? Had to be wrong, but try it.)

The shell warmed her, and subtle tones from hidden speakers lured her down into alpha. From long experience, she began to slip into a twilight trance-state in which information flashed and wove itself around her mind at accelerated speed. She no longer perceived the edges of the vidscreen.

A series of papers arrived, highlighted according to her possible interests. Some were linked to flat video (although they could be altered to resemble holography, she noticed. She declined. The result always felt tinny, synthetic).

The only hit was a paper delivered to the American Humane Association on overbreeding of show dogs, written by a "Deskachar Triguna" in 1999. What now? She decided to let the search get fuzzy.

The search engine tried different spellings of Triguna (yielding one odd commercial for a "Tribunal Pet Shop" in Peoria, with a special on collie pups) and then it burped and did something different: It searched phonetically.

Paydirt. It was a snip from the UCLA Bruin newsfax, January 2018. The headline read: "Kali Lecture lands Triguna in hot water—again."

Kali?

The article suggested that Triguna had been censured for

"racism" due to some controversial lectures the previous semester. He had used the phrase "lesser breeds" in a lecture on mass birth control. Triguna was known to display statues and paintings of Hindu deities in his home and office. Some pundit nicknamed his lecture "The Kali Option," a bad-taste reference to the Hindu goddess who brings life through death.

Lesser breeds, but not collies. Kali! She requested the full speech—sound, video, and notes.

A classroom at UCLA, front-row center. To either side of her, intense young students scribbled notes or watched the lecturer. Holding forth at the head of the class was Balaraj Triguna, a round dark little man with stringy goatee and pince-nez glasses. She adjusted the volume and sat back to listen to the infamous Kali lecture.

"The reality," he said, "is that none of the problems currently plaguing mankind—war, scarcity of food, pollution, et cetera—are hallmarks of failure as a species. They indicate success. 'The ape that got what it wanted,' in Jack Cohen's wonderful phrase. We have become too successful for our own good. War is a problem because we have become too accomplished at this terrible, vital art—our weapons are too powerful to be used without risking all that might once have been gained. Scarcity of food is a problem only because we live so long, so few of our children die, and we have grown too used to rich living. Pollution is a direct result of our mastery of the environment, and, again, our vast numbers have turned what once might have been a minor problem—one tribe urinating in a stream upriver from its neighbor—into devastating catastrophes.

"The difficulty is that there are points of no return, points where the environmental reactions are sudden and irreversible, where they assume a momentum of their own. The population has leveled off, or even dropped, in the First World countries: Europe, North America, and much of the Pacific Rim. But Africa, South America, and the Middle East are swarming. Education will decrease their numbers, given the chance, but by that time their ecosystems will have collapsed under the burden of too many mouths sucking food and minerals from the soil and too many biological and industrial anuses dumping waste products into streams and rivers."

He paused and drew in a strong, cautious breath. "It may be suicide to wait so long."

An uneasy silence filled the classroom. A woman stood: in her sixties, short and wide and massive with authority. "Professor," she said, "our education programs cover the world. The tools for population control are available everywhere. There's no language in which you can't hear the voice of reason—"

"And still the ghost of Isaac Asimov haunts our dreams. Deputy Warner, if you persuade people not to have too many children, what traits are you breeding for?" A heartbeat's pause, then, "Unpersuadability! You're selecting for parents who don't understand your arguments, or can't read them, or who understand the *voice of reason* but don't give a damn, or who are too stupid to find the right end of a condom, or would rather watch cartoons or football!"

A young man raised his hand. "Professor," he said. "What options are left?"

The vidscreen's border flashed red. This, then, was the section that had led to Triguna's trouble. "We can fight their grandchildren for air and water in thirty years," he said. "Or we can reduce their numbers now. Which is the higher moral ground? Killing grown men and women, or dumping contraceptives into the Ganges?"

She froze the screen. Triguna's scenario? Her mind rocketed. Triguna was Hernandez's mentor, a man with a controversial vision. He had thrown away his tenure for a dark dream. Hernandez had worshipped Triguna! There must have been a falling out: "Maricón" is hardly a term of endearment. Hernandez was a brilliant, egomaniacal molecular biologist, lecturer, and researcher. Mary Kravitz a bioengineer who "died" years ago.

Lenore found her thoughts fracturing like a kaleidoscope image, but there was a pattern, and somewhere below conscious thought she understood the implications precisely. Horror waited down there.

Kravitz was alive. She looked younger than she had a decade earlier. Why had her death been faked? Xanadu's medical techniques must be near godlike. . . . Did that relate to the odd sense she had about Chaz Kato? Old and young . . . how old *was* Chaz Kato?

And why would the Council be interested in Triguna, and why would Hernandez be involved in a worldwide immunization program?

*You can get young again if you're rich enough, or powerful enough, or have the right friends!* Time always makes such things cheaper. Triguna sees a population explosion out of nightmare, and now *people can stop dying?*

("We can fight their grandchildren in thirty years . . . or we can reduce their numbers now.")

Millions and millions of men and women were given free vaccines against AIDS and smallpox, vaccines developed by a collaboration of geniuses including Hernandez and a woman whose brilliance was such that the Council rescued her from the grave and hid her away from the world. And Chaz Kato was sometimes young, sometimes very old.

Millions of men and women. A year. For what . . . ?

(When had Hernandez performed his doctoral work? Had it been fifteen years now?)

She wanted to vomit. Instead, nibbling her lower lip, Lenore shifted databases and began to examine global birth records.

Nothing.

Nothing anywhere. There had been no change in birth statistics, and she was starting to relax. A flood of embarrassment followed; she fought it. Just a paranoid daydream, but wow!

She almost giggled, the storm clouds receding; she smiled back at a young man in a lab coat. Lenore Myles, in a

restricted hallway under a false name, turned back to the
wall display, hoping he'd keep going.

Wait, now, she didn't *have* to let this go.

Forty years back, Carl Sagan's name alone had the power
to back a *dynamite* movie. Her own name wasn't a match
for his, but she had credentials, and. . . . With virtual actors,
Chaz Kato could be played as and *by* Dirty Harry Callahan,
aged *and* youthful. Talk to Tooley about this—if she could
stand the embarrassment. . . .

Then with a chilling *clunk*, another small, final piece of
memory fell into place.

*"In utero inoculation."* Kravitz's lecture, five years ago.
Vaccines could be designed to cross the placental barrier,
creating genetic or somatic effects in the unborn fetus . . .
not in the mother.

"Oh, God," she whispered, and went back into the statistics. The nightmare she was toying with now was a plan to
lower birth rates in the Third World. The method? Give the
mother a shot. The *baby* grows up sterile. It won't show in
the statistics for . . .

Call it thirteen years minimum, in Third World countries.
(Just after Chaz Kato reached Xanadu.) For these past two
years, then, birth rates might have been dropping. Gradually
at first, of course. The sterility statistics might be rising . . .
maybe those could be altered. *The Kali stats.* Start another
pox—a resistant strain of syphilis or herpes, something nobody really likes talking about, and that will mask the effects
of an inoculation given a decade before. One could explain
the sterility wave as uterine scarring, or effects from childhood fever. . . .

And did that make sense? Her memory tugged at her:
Hadn't there been a series of biowar outbreaks a decade
ago? Banana Republic and Central African biological attacks on neighboring countries? Africa too, if she was right.
Not many fatalities, but a lot of sickness—and the United
Nations investigatory committee concluded that, indeed,
someone had sold toxins to dictators all over the Third

World. Not many fatalities. It was assumed that the suppliers were virtually con men.

She looked more deeply, knowing where she would have to go to get the information. She would need to make a direct correlation between the inoculation program begun fifteen years before and the birth rates of the first generation following those inoculations. Even in the Third World, fifteen years would barely be long enough. . . .

In a fever, she began to type.

# 13

Like a spider hunched in the middle of a world-spanning web, the being who called himself Saturn felt the first tentative shiver of a jeweled strand. His fibers spread out around the globe, connected to a hundred different projects, but this strand wound close to the core of his being, connected to the most important and secret of his efforts.

Thousands of requests for information, inquiries, investigations, downloads, and web hits impacted the Kali project every day, far too many for Saturn to monitor personally. But there were triggers, tripwires. Certain queries in specific clusters or sequences could indicate more than casual interest. Someone was too close to a secret.

The energies composing Saturn drifted from their slumber and turned ponderously, searching for the searcher, and found . . .

Dr. Chadwick Kato.

Chaz Kato was no threat. In a year or two Kato would play his own part in the Kali scenario. Then let him babble any secrets he liked. Nobody would ever believe him. Meanwhile he was barred from certain domains in Xanadu.

But these current inquiries were in forbidden domains. Chadwick Kato must have hacked his keycard, extended its limits. Not surprising. Kato was easily intimidated but far from stupid. Lead him down the right paths, he might change the human race itself. Saturn reached for Kato's interface plug.

Kato was in two localities at once.

A glitch? Security cameras found Kato teaching a seminar to a group of interns on the university concourse.

A swift crosscheck of facial characteristics and retinal patterns identified the second "Kato" as one Lenore Myles.

Backchecking revealed that Kato and Lenore had spent considerable time together. She had gained access through him. Stolen it? If she had, then she had also compromised the security codes, which implied that she was far more competent and dangerous than the twenty-three-year-old scholar profiled in her records.

Kato, besotted, could have given her such access. That would fit his profile . . . but she had access where Dr. Kato was not permitted. *She* had hacked his keycard. A spy.

Saturn watched her watching, listened to her listen. He demanded and received a full dump on her life, and quickly focused in on her activities for the past seventy-two hours.

Futures splayed out like the wandering runnels in a river delta. Some futures were more likely; others were more interesting. Any minor decision could change the flow pattern forever. Saturn computed possibilities. . . .

This woman had the intelligence, the training, the connections, and apparently the inclination to cause trouble. Timing was a problem. He did not know why she had begun her current line of inquiry, but "Kali's" key players were on Xanadu *now*. She might have seen or heard something. She might go beyond exposing "Kali," the project Saturn himself thought of as the Fertility War. With a bit more bad luck, she might glimpse Saturn himself.

There were special reasons for care with her, but those could be handled. Best if she just . . . died.

Saturn put a full-time trace on her. He had to know everything she said and did now. He hoped that she wouldn't
speak to anyone about her findings. Every killing was risky.
More than, say, five deaths would raise his risk to an unacceptable level. With any luck, the killing would stop with
her.

He hoped she wouldn't speak with Dr. Kato.

# 14

Chaz decided to take one more
question and then conclude.
"Mr. Wozniac," he said, pointing to a short, turnip-shaped
little man in a crew-necked sweater.

"Dr. Kato," the intern said. "Your grandfather's pioneer-
ing augmentation work was cut short by his wife's death.
Almost a decade later you picked up the threads and carried
on, backed by the Council. Chadwick Kato the First was
something of an iconoclast, rather apolitical. Do you think
he would approve of your current situation?"

Chaz closed his eyes, wishing he had chosen questions
more carefully. "The past is past," he finally said. "This
research needed deep pockets, and none is deeper than the
Council's. I think Grandfather would understand my motivations, yes." He gathered his papers. "That ends our talk
for the day. I want your work uploaded by Tuesday, thank
you."

He left the room swiftly. He didn't like the way his heart
pounded.

Chaz took the elevator down to one of the seven main
dining halls in the north wing. Should he have selected a
more secluded and romantic spot to meet Lenore? He allowed himself a few steamy fantasies about the evening's

games, and the discomfort accompanying the intern's un-expected question began to fade.

But where was she?

He sat, confident that she would arrive within a few minutes, and wondered what he might say to her.

Given time to think, she would come to the only reason-able conclusion: Her best and brightest future lay with Xanadu and Chaz Kato.

He was quite certain that in a few months he could com-plete his wooing, and then . . . what? After Clarise he had forsworn future entanglements. But Lenore was so very dif-ferent . . . something like a pool of warm butter melted in his stomach when he thought about her. That awareness, that sense of fullness oddly made him more rather than less hun-gry.

Distraction: He ran menus through his mind. On Xanadu, a self-indulgent man could still eat a perfect diet. The link-age system would automatically calculate every micro- and macronutrient, contrast it with the monthly (painless!) blood panels, hair and skin analyses, and automatic stool and urine samples, and make recommendations based on health needs. Any protein or starch could be disguised to taste like any other. Synthetic, indigestible fats could be added to pro-cessed algae to create diet foods disguised as staggeringly rich desserts.

He settled on a plate of pasta and clam sauce, and waited for Lenore.

A smiling young man brought the food quickly. His smile seemed rather plastic, as if he were too aware that his job existed only because of Xanadu's commitment to total em-ployment. His parents were probably technicians somewhere on the island, and due to lack of education or ability, this boy had yet to find a berth. Never mind. Autobots might be more efficient, but the human touch was soothing.

The pasta was delicious . . . tomatoes fresh-plucked from the gardens, clams from the lagoons. They were a few cred-its more expensive than the synthetic, but that hardly mattered. He could burst his belly ten times a day and not exceed his food allotment. Chaz ate slowly at first, waiting for Lenore; then realized that he was famished, and began to bolt it down.

He wasn't exactly certain when he became aware of the little voice in the back of his head, the voice that was saying: *Where is she? Why isn't she here?*

He could know her whereabouts in an instant, but lubbers were touchy about privacy. Of course she need never know. . . .

Clarise Maibang appeared in the doorway to his left. With her was Whittlesea, Xanadu's chief of Security. Chaz didn't know the man's first name. Whittlesea was a hair under six feet tall, totally bald, pale, and as solid as an oak door. He had been in British MI before recruitment. No genius, and unimaginative, with little sense of style and almost no political savvy, but totally loyal to Xanadu and obsessively competent at his job.

Chaz experienced a quick and puzzling spectrum of responses: happy at the sight of a familiar face, then *Go away, Clarise. Whatever this is, I don't need it right now.* Then: *Why is she with Whittlesea?*

But when she locked eyes across the room, he saw a remote pity, and his spine crawled. They could have paged him. Taking time to find him personally implied a surprising level of concern.

He stood to meet them.

Maibang folded her fingers carefully. "Dr. Kato," Whittlesea said.

Chaz shook the offered hand. "What can I do for you?"

"Officer Maibang said that your lady friend left this afternoon."

"Left where?" A sudden sour hollow spot in his gut informed him that he knew damned well where and what she had left.

Clarise said, "She left Xanadu."

"Flight plan for Boston via Sri Lanka." Whittlesea watched his reaction.

Clarise's face was a mask. "So. You did not know?"

"We had a dinner date." To himself he sounded pathetic.

"She packed and shuttled out an hour ago." She leaned in closer. "Before she left she accessed files, Chaz. She has violated island security."

Crap. "I can explain that," he said quickly. "I—I wanted her to see what we have to offer. I gave her my access codes."

Clarise said something under her breath, and Whittlesea shook his massive head slowly. "That was stupid, Dr. Kato," Whittlesea said bluntly, "but it is worse than that. She entered files to which you had no access."

His mouth suddenly felt leathery. "What files?"

"That's classified. But she fled soon afterward. I think she is a spy."

Was that triumph on Clarise's face? No. It was pity. She didn't like where this was going any more than he did. He tried to be angry that she had brought her boss in on this, but couldn't. It was her job. And she had talked him into speaking to Chaz calmly, publicly. Politely.

He needed to match that energy. Stay calm. "No. I'm sorry. I'm the spy."

Silently and motionless, they waited for him to continue.

"Mr. Whittlesea, I'm very embarrassed. I don't know what to say."

His embarrassment was nothing to Whittlesea. "Go on, Dr. Kato."

"Sometimes I need access to information, and there's no time to go through channels . . . or else I just don't feel like it." He gritted his teeth. "Sometimes I play little games and see how they come out. Modify the visual and auditory moodscapes, add new ergogenics to some of the community foodstuffs—"

"Dr. Kato!"

Chaz felt his face burning. This was humiliating, but once

they combed the computer records, they would find everything anyway. Best to hear it from him. "I know, I know. But blame me, not her. I overrode some of the security, and when I passed my clearances to her, she got it all. My fault. Stupid."

Whittlesea was outwardly calm, but Chaz wasn't deceived: Xanadu's security chief was boiling. But there was something worse in there, something more than the accessing of classified files. "Very well, perhaps that explains *how* she did it, Dr. Kato. But not *why* she did."

"Curious?" God, that sounded lame. "I'll make a complete list of all my intrusions—nothing against the Covenants, I assure you. But I did look for loopholes. . . ."

"Really, Dr. Kato?" Whittlesea asked coolly. "And precisely which loophole allowed you to pry into the security codes for Xanadu's air traffic control system?"

Chaz' mouth fell open. "What?"

"And please tell me: How many times did you attempt to crack the algorithm on the main communication line?"

A gap, wide as the Marianas Trench, opened in Chaz's mind. He felt stabbed. Twisting the knife, Clarise continued. "Chaz, if she succeeded, she could raid our trading houses, spy on secure negotiations, even crash incoming shuttles. I am afraid someone planted her on you."

His tongue felt thick and numb. "That's not possible. I chose her, when she was sixteen."

Whittlesea bore in. "Then someone recruited her, Dr. Kato. Taught her what to do and say, and played you like a fish."

Chaz groped for some kind of emotional balance, and foundered. He needed time. Hours. Minutes, at least, to get himself back together. "Listen," he said. "I need to riddle my way through this. There's an answer. Please. Will you give me some time?"

For a moment, Clarise shared Whittlesea's obsidian gaze. Then the strong line of her mouth softened. "Idiot," she said, so softly that only he could hear. She turned to her boss. "Sir, I can handle it from here."

The security man nodded slowly. "We have no evidence of damaging intrusion. The investigation is just beginning, but out of respect for your contributions, you'll have a chance to clean this up. Dr. Kato, you owe Clarise a thank-you."

He stood and left the restaurant.

Chaz blinked hard, fighting to calm his breathing. Clarise said nothing, waited for him to sort it out. Finally, miserably, he said, "Thank you, Clarise."

"I have been aware of your interest in Lenore Myles," she said. She chop-gestured at a waiter, and he flinched and disappeared. "I was foolish not to take it more seriously. Chaz, tell me how you brought her here."

"Clarise, it didn't seem—"

"How. Process. Procedure."

He told her what he'd fiddled with, what he'd arranged, the programs. She listened, nodded, nodded. "It wasn't her idea, then. It was nothing she or any ally of hers could have meddled with?"

"No."

"All right. Perhaps we have misinterpreted the data. Twenty-four hours, Sherlock." She reached across the table and took his hands in hers. Her brown hands were large for a woman, and strong.

"Chaz," she said, "I know Whittlesea. He will expect something in return."

He was too numb to look at her. "What? Money?"

"I doubt it. He may demand your help in tracking down Lenore Myles."

Perhaps he nodded agreement. Perhaps not. He left the cafeteria.

No one noticed him as he walked the halls, the slowly shifting colors washing through the tiles as he hurried to the nearest elevator. As soon as the doors shut, he leaned back against the wall, struggling to catch his breath. He looked up at the wall, until the camera caught his eye. In that position, it could verify his retinal patterns as well as his face and voiceprint. He requested a secure channel.

It obliged him, and he said: "Messages?"

"None," a female voice answered.

"Nothing?" He felt like he had been kicked in the chest. He leaned back and let his eyes slide shut, feeling the acceleration, the shift, lost in the sigh and whisper of hidden mechanisms. When the elevator arrived at his penthouse, he stepped out onto his patio and asked, almost absently, "Have I had any visitors?"

"Yes," the voice said. "A woman, Lenore Myles, approximately three hours ago."

He straightened. "Did she enter my apartment?"

"No, sir."

"What did she do?" he asked.

"She left a piece of paper," the voice said.

He opened the front door and found the note. When he unfolded it, her handwriting, which (he suddenly realized) he had never seen, was neat and cautious and said, very simply:

*Personal emergency. Will be in touch. L.*

He crumpled the paper into a ball and dropped it. What was going on here?

What had he done wrong? And where had she gone?

He stormed into his office, plopped down in his chair, and said, "Privacy." That single word denied Xanadu's security forces the right to casually spy on him. Whittlesea could break in, no doubt, given motive. If he needed a higher level of privacy, he could encrypt his communications, but that would merely signal Clarise that something was up.

He didn't intend anything so ambitious.

He plugged in and summoned an environment to fit his current mood. A movie theater seemed an appropriate metaphor for his voyeuristic intent, '80s Cineplex style, without the smells. He watched as the screen retraced Lenore's path.

Security cameras had recorded her wandering the halls, researching in the library, meeting her roommate. The camera work wasn't seamless: Not every inch of Xanadu was monitored, but most public walkways were scanned twenty-four/seven. He picked her up, lost her, picked her up again in the bioresearch section, lost her when she entered a stairwell.

Damn. Many of the stairwells were monitored, but not all. Had she gone to another level? No, here she was again, and the timing strip claimed that only a couple of minutes had passed. Had she known that hallway wasn't monitored?

She walked briskly to a research nook. He saw her log on at SW21 as Chaz Kato. That was convenient. A touch of his own keys summoned up the record.

He'd watched her skill with metaphors evolve over years. For a year she'd used unicorns; one day they'd become horses (Levar!) and then a whole menagerie. Now he watched Lenore's cartoon-animal sigils dance through Xanadu's airspace patterns, touching security walls and flicking away, dancing on . . .

Jesus, Whittlesea was right. Lenore was trying to penetrate their air traffic control system, a high-security area. Of course Whittlesea had never suspected *Chaz* of using dancing animals. What the hell was she doing? Trying to put a dirigible under the incoming Shibano suborbital!

He couldn't stand to see more. He skipped and watched her board a flight to Sri Lanka.

She'd had no time to do real damage.

But Chaz Kato's life was tied to the medical facilities of Xanadu, and Lenore Myles could never be allowed on Xanadu again.

# 15

Lenore rode the gondola of a Beetle—a hard-shelled dirigible: silent, roomy, all picture window, and no faster than a galloping horse. Lenore could see more of the tossing sea than she really liked. She didn't like flying, never had and probably never would. Today she felt like a brightly painted target.

In the last twenty years, automation had removed much of the risk, but knowing that a human pilot sat in the cockpit didn't entirely calm her. Emergencies were better handled by the computer. The human presence was pure public relations.

The flight was only half full. It was too quiet.

She would have preferred a gondola jammed with notables, political leaders, entertainment celebrities, and maybe the Pope. In such company the forces of Xanadu could not make her vanish so easily.

Paranoia? She had seen horror, but in intuitive leaps as much as evidence. There must be an alternate explanation of the whole "Kali" mess. She might be acting a complete fool. She closed her eyes and tried to think, tried to rearrange what she knew.

But she'd seen a pattern; she knew its shape.

She remained drowsy but jumpy, unable to rest, unable to rouse herself to full waking. She thought of Chaz. Of touching him, of his smile. Of the way her heart had begun to awaken as if from a winter's slumber.

\* \* \*

Where there had been nothing but ocean for millions of years, a strip of lights and seacrete now ran out from the beach. Like Xanadu, Sri Lanka Airport had been precipitated from seawater and grown up from the ocean floor. The strip of seacrete was still growing at the edges. The altered currents grew more beaches.

The Beetle touched down like a feather. Landing tethers reached down to the mast and then drew it snugly into the dock. Lenore stayed with the meager crowd. Fear had drained her, and her eyelids felt as heavy as sandbags. The shuttle to Boston was two hours away. She decided to try to walk her fatigue off. Eat something.

Lenore roamed the terminal, with its bright, sweeping ceilings and its milling crowd. The spiced scent of a dozen cuisines, from marinara to curry to hamburgers, mingled in the sterilized air, but she took no joy in any of them. Fatigue bent her like decades, and she was overjoyed to see the blinking yellow sign of a Napcap rental facility.

A few meager credits remained on her debit card. She would invest them in a decent snooze.

She punched her card into the Napcap's slot. The lid lifted and she crawled inside. It *shoosh*ed down. The inside received her as a womb. The prospect of rest triggered an avalanche of yawns, and she was asleep before the lid sealed fully back into its place.

The induction cap was not needed, but it snuggled neatly onto her head anyway. Servos wound their way to their appointed places with automated ease. Premoistened contact points hugged temples and brow. A trickle of entraining current eased her into a deeper slumber.

Within a few minutes, her heart slowed to about fifty beats a minute, her respiration down to about six. She eased deeper into the delta, spiraling down toward perfect rest.

Ordinary human sleep varies greatly in depth and quality,

a vestigial remembrance of the time when *Homo habilis* needed to cycle between deep sleep and near waking, lest in comalike slumber he fall prey to carnivores. In the Nap-cap a client became an instant yoga master, able to stay in the deepest states for hours, increasing the value of each minute's rest manyfold.

Lenore never knew when she began to die.


Cocooned in darkness, Saturn watched.

He knew an opportunity when he saw it. All over the world there were men and women who served an unknown master for financial or political gain. Saturn knew who they were, who they served, what words or codes would command them.

He needed two such agents now. Their hands could reach where his virtual limbs could not.


Jorge Chandra was a small, grubby man who had worked at small, grubby jobs much of his life. His foggy view of Paradise was to slip through life with a minimum of pain and discomfort, to be drunk as often as possible, to win occasionally at gambling, and to indulge in whores discreetly enough to avoid his small, grubby wife's notice.

His wife had driven him out of their ramshackle house in one of Jaffna's outlying slums to apply for this job at the Sri Lanka Airport. He had been mildly surprised to actually win it.

For sixty hours a week he performed minor repair and maintenance duties at the airport. Irregularly, perhaps one hour a month, he performed special services for an unknown someone who provided untaxed income unsuspected by Jorge's shrew of a wife. When his beeper gave a special, once-in-a-month tone, he read its instructions and immediately complied.

Jorge used his key card to enter the central processing station. He punched a series of commands into the console, changing the time signal sent to Napcap #C-38, Concourse "D." He might have wondered why, but a thousand credits answered many questions.

It was a harmless adjustment. The occupant would sleep longer than she had planned. Might miss her connection. Might file a complaint. All such matters were handled at a level far above Chandra's head.

If someone wanted the inhabitant of C-38 to stay in Sri Lanka five hours longer than she had planned, then so be it.

# 16

Chaz? We were expecting you in the habitat." Arvad Minsky squinted at him from the viewscreen. Chaz understood the confusion: He had thought to descend to the ocean floor this afternoon with Lenore at his side. It would have been another flaunting of protocol, but . . .

But work would take his mind from his troubles.

Minsky looked back at him from the screen, thin freckled face concerned. "Something wrong?"

"No." Chaz slipped his hands into the glove box. "Let's get the modifications under way, and I'll try to get down tomorrow. I just can't spare the time to depressurize."

"All-righty." The screen expanded. Behind Minsky was the wetroom, Xanadu's combination operating theater and recovery room for their aquatic charges.

On a table hydraulically raised above the surface of a kidney-shaped pool, Trish, their youngest mature bottlenose, lay quiet and anesthetized. Behind her in the water was Manny, her mate. Manny swam a lap and then watched as

Minsky and one of the other techs cooed comfortingly to Trish.

Chaz got comfortable with the gear. There was no time lag this close to the patient. He had once watched a telemetric operation conducted in Clavius Crater. It was disconcerting to watch a three-second hesitation in the surgeon's actions. He wouldn't have wanted to try that. It required surer hands and a more confident spirit than his.

But this would be a standard implantation adjustment, and he could almost perform it on automatic.

Behind the plastic wall, Manny had ceased his swimming. He watched as Trish settled onto the operation platform. Several exquisitely modulated bleats emerged from his throat. After a pause, the synthesizer spoke: "Chaz? You there? Always worries when you not here. Please careful."

"I'll be careful, Manny," he said soothingly. Manny could understand human speech far better than Chaz understood dolphin. The scalpel touched the outer layer of skin, and he paused, studying the holographic chart floating before him.

Trish's head and body were already laced with plastic and nylon, superconductor wire and computer chips. Because of the bulges, the alterations to her shape, she'd had to learn to swim again.

"Tomorrow. She can hear speech?"

Trish's hearing was fine. She hadn't evolved as humans had, to untangle the sounds into a code. Dolphins could learn a little of that, as apes could, as Trish already had, but the computer add-on would hugely expand her vocabulary— if Minsky's interface worked. . . .

Too complicated. Chaz said, "Yes."

Today he'd go through the implanted nylon cap, through the corpus callosum and into the septum pelucidum. Then Trish's second upgrade could begin.

Enhancing intelligence could be shocking even for a dolphin, a process best performed in stages. After this operation, perhaps Trish would finally make the leap from tic-tac-toe to basic chess. Perhaps one day she would even challenge Minsky. Chaz himself had long since abandoned all hope of *that*.

# 17

His name was Hiroshi Osato, and he took his duties and heritage most seriously, as befitted a man who could trace his ancestry back to A.D. 650 and the Hakuho era of Japan.

The world had changed in many ways. Emperors and shoguns were less important to the survival of Japan than the mysterious forces of the Council. He was not always certain whom he truly served. That didn't matter. He obeyed his father, who *did* know such things. He could not betray or accidentally reveal what he did not know.

Osato was as content as a man could be in these degenerate times.

In the sixteenth century, Japan had been at its cultural peak, an exquisite balance of royalty, military, merchants, and farmers. Everyone knew his place, roles had been prescribed and adhered to for many generations.

The bane of the Samurai system was the rifle. A master swordsman trained for thirty years in his secret family arts could be killed by a peasant with an afternoon's rifle craft!

It was disgraceful. It was dishonorable. It was inevitable.

Some Samurai families remained in military service or sank into obscurity. Others made the transition to industry, where families who had once slain each other's sons on the battlefields now supported one another ferociously against the *gaijin*, the outsiders.

Some of the Samurai's greatest assets would never be printed on a balance sheet or a tax report. These secret assets were the loyalties of families who had never been Samurai but nonetheless performed as soldiers in countless wars.

Ninja. Masters of deception, disguise and assassination. They had their own family secrets: poisons, traps, explosives, evasion and escape. The Samurai fought with a rigid code of honor. The Ninja fought only to win. Hated by many, feared by all, they were "untouchables," social inferiors doomed to live and walk in a shadow world between polite society and the criminal classes.

Five of the ancient Ninja families had survived the wars and purges. The Osatos were among them. They banded together for mutual support, passing their skills, knowledge, and connections down the generations. And one day they discovered that in the modern world, as in the ancient, their skills were marketable.

Hiroshi left the island north of Hokkaido shortly after Lenore Myles went to sleep. His route had been prepared for him. A jet helicopter took him to the Hokkaido police airport, where a UN Riot Control suborbital carrier lofted him like a bullet to Jakarta and another helicopter. Four hours after the urgent transmission reached him, he nonchalantly approached the Napcap facility.

The capsule to the immediate left of the target was empty. He purchased its service. While waiting for it to open, he casually laid his hand over the dials of the target capsule. Hidden in his palm was a plastic rectangle. Initially flat, it molded itself to the Napcap's contours. At first beige, it shimmered and shifted colors until it was indistinguishable from the instrument panel.

He slapped his forehead, then checked his pockets as if he had forgotten something. He left briskly, never looking up directly at the ceiling. The security camera would have a devil of a time identifying him: mask, wig, and false fingerprints would prove an adequate, casual distraction. Within moments he had mingled with the jump port crowd and disappeared.

# 18

Chaz was exhausted after the operations. His hands trembled. Surgery was a skill recently acquired in his new life here at Xanadu. He had yet to practice it on human subjects, and probably never would. Making basic adjustments on cetaceans was frightening enough. Probing a human brain would paralyze him, he thought.

Making aliens, undersea. After years of careful practice, he could make it through an intense day without getting the shakes. And for three grueling hours he had not thought of Lenore at all.

He performed two operations. Trish the dolphin was straightforward. He did one of the specials too, a squark, a sea lion given computer enhancement and mechanical fingers.

His repressed concern about Lenore was beginning to hammer him again. What in hell would Lenore want with the air traffic control codes?

Her closest friend had just left for home. She had no family. "Personal emergency"? It was a kiss-off . . . but Lenore was no spy. He had watched her. He would *know*.

She would have arrived in Boston an hour ago and would be almost to California by now. He could page her on the plane, catch her there, a captive audience. And they could talk, before she had the chance to disappear back into her life!

Chaz slid into his private console chair. The fiber optic cable was a mere thread, but the interface plug was as big as his hand. He lifted the patch of artifical hair in the back of his head and plugged in.

Lenore's credit files were encrypted. That was fun! A few seconds of conjuring brought them up. His conscious mind interpreted the data as a series of blurred visual splotches. As his hands chorded the keys, the splotches focused into a congruent picture. He just needed to make out the image. Focus a bit *here* and shift the colors a bit *there* . . . Why wasn't it working?

Clever girl. It was Lenore upside down, in a handstand, and he was in.    Her recent credit history revealed a flight from Xanadu to Sri Lanka, a second leg from Sri Lanka to Boston aboard Benares Air. He checked times. Had she made her connection in Boston?

She had not arrived in Boston.

Then where was she?

There. A Napcap purchase made six hours ago. Napcaps were a service of the Health conglomerate, and Xanadu's extensive medical facilities required deep access to those data banks. Chaz penetrated the accounting unit for the air-port's vending machine system, to determine when she had left the Napcap.

Her fee was still accumulating.

Alarm crackled up his back like electricity. Jesus! She had never left!

The medical monitoring system opened to him. His com-puter system created a cartoonlike image of a funhouse. He strolled in along a midway crowded with Disneyesque car-nival barkers, into a tent big enough to house Dumbo's mother. Under other circumstances, he might have laughed: This entire metaphor must have been devised for school-children learning geography or history. It was amusing and interesting, and not his own work . . . but Xanadu's contract with Sri Lanka had opened a door he could squeak through, giving him access to the Napcap timer.

The timer and the medical monitoring equipment were out of sync. If he was to believe the timer, she had only been asleep for fifty minutes. Medical monitors said that she had been under for five hours and fifty minutes. Someone had dominated the circuit, forcing it to recycle, keeping her in trance. But why? All of the data existed here, along with a floating picture of a smiling Lenore, extracted from her credit banks. If she was still there, and not due to awaken for another hour, then maybe, just maybe, he could jetcopter to the airport, talk with her, get her story straight from her own lips.

Just for reassurance, Chaz took a look at her life stats.

The shock almost crashed him out of the illusion.

Her pulse was 48 and dropping, and she was someplace down through the delta floor. The bioencephalograms were flatlining. And no alarm had sounded! This was impossible. The entire airport should have been in an uproar.

He spun back out of his chair and clapped his hands. "Get me emergency. I need a message through to Sri Lanka security," he said.

"All lines," his computer said with numbing placidity, "are temporarily busy."

Chaz made a quick check. Satellite communication with Sri Lanka was unavailable, but Xanadu maintained secure fiber-optic transmission systems with dozens of countries. He could put through a priority call to any of them, reroute, and be through to Sri Lanka in seconds.

In seconds he'd tried them all. Nothing he tried gave him a response.

"All lines are temporarily busy," the computer said again, maddeningly.

He began a search, and found himself stymied. Without pausing, Chaz flipped to another metaphor.

"Metaphors," structured views of a given data set, could take many forms: virtual filing cabinet, classroom, library, mentor, or formal brainstorming sessions with a dozen favorite teachers or historical figures. Each had its advantages and disadvantages. Each worked better for some people or some purposes. Each had its own specialized security strengths and weaknesses. Now Chaz sought weaknesses.

*He floated in an immense pool, a perfect visual and auditory illusion of a dolphin training pool.* A computer-generated dolphin swam up next to him and challenged him to duplicate a complex series of gyrations. Using eye motion and hand chords, he stayed in pace . . . and was bounced back out.

Try the microwave relay stations. Blocked again, but not yet bounced out of the circuit.

Emergency main-cable transmission, exclusive to the Floating Island chain?

Unavailable.

This was absurd. If all transmission was out, Xanadu would have been screaming with alarms. A dozen different telemetric systems would be malfunctioning. He didn't need to test another route to be certain that someone didn't want him talking to Sri Lanka.

Someone with the powers of a Council member had sentenced Lenore to death.

He could hardly breathe. Suddenly the womb of safety he had woven around himself for fourteen years had become a trap.

He was certainly being observed . . . but Lenore was dying and he couldn't communicate. What could he do?

Ordinary security and communications channels were blocked. If the medical stats were accurate, in a few minutes she would slip into an irreversible coma.

The dolphin metaphor still held. He wasn't consciously aware of his attempt to penetrate the Napcap system, but found himself incapable of executing the metaphor-dolphin's final dervishlike permutation. Damn. Stymied.

Chaz shook himself out of it and read the digital input. There was no way to control Napcaps from Xanadu.

Turn off the power, then.

*A deeper ocean, no longer a confined tank.* His metaphor-dolphin dashed ahead of him, navigating a virtual Sargasso.

Swiftly, unexpectedly, a shark swept in. Dolphin Chaz moved more swiftly now and ran into—

A reef.

He popped back out of the metaphor. There was no way to turn off the power to that single unit. But Xanadu supplied power to Sri Lanka. As a shareholder Chaz had access to the system controlling the power grid, the gigantic OTEC system that was Xanadu's primary income source. He could spend precious minutes trying to convince a human being to help him—

No time. He tried the dolphin metaphor again and ran into another reef. Damn. He needed something different to crack grid security.

*Chaz trotted through the woods.* The Linkage system was more fully engaged now, and the illusion was tactile as well as visual and auditory. He looked down at his compass, seeking true north. He was linked to a gaming module used to teach nature study as a student resolved problems related to wilderness survival.

Voices to his rear. A virtual troop of Floating Island Sea Scouts floated through the woods behind him. He recognized their leader: That was Anson Teil, a gourmet chef and chemist who commuted between the islands, and was a scoutmaster in his spare time. His metaphor was lean and fit. They waved at each other.

Chaz needed to adjust the illusion. He made one swift mistake, ended up in the Arctic for a freezing moment, and then found himself in Sri Lanka walking through the Clarke Memorial Space Museum. Good. From there to a working display of the airport, and he was in the power grid and—

Bounced back out.

Chaz sat in his study chair, tired, wired, and tapped, in a stench of fear-sweat. This was very bad. Lenore was running out of time, and not only the usual but the unusual lines of approach were blocked. He couldn't call security. He couldn't turn off the power to the individual capsule or the entire section.

Wait. There was another way.

Lenore had done her work under Chaz Kato's name. A few quick commands booted it up. Cartoon animals, unicorns and rhinos, antelopes and lions and gazelles, danced through Xanadu's air traffic control system.

Yes! The codes were here, represented by a series of nonsense symbols. As Clarise had said, Lenore had slipped past some of the external security systems. But that wasn't Lenore!

Horses and unicorns, elephants and gazelles and tigers moved through metaphor space, but not like themselves. Their legs weren't moving right. The spy was misusing Lenore's borrowed metaphors. Even Whittlesea should have seen it. They floated like ghosts . . . no, they wiggled. Wiggling moved them. Not like landgoing mammals, nor like birds, nor insects. Microbes?

Chaz's relief flared and was ash. Lenore was still dying. How could he save her? She—*someone* had penetrated far enough to trip a silent alarm. Far enough for him to complete the job?

There was another truth about the relationship between information and machine. There is finite time and money to spend protecting systems. Go through the front door, and it was Fort Knox. But the right back door, or unexpected metaphor, might expose a vulnerability in the system design.

What would be the most unlikely, little-used way of looking at *this* information? What would be the most improbable doorway? He needed an access that had been approved, for whatever purpose, as a means of interacting with Xanadu's main system. He could pervert it to his own purpose, if only Security had never taken it too seriously.

Minutes remained. He wasn't thinking fast enough and knew it. Chaz went into emergency mode.

A reservoir tap in the skullcap made contact with his implant shield and administered a few milligrams of neurotransmitter-enhancing chemicals. Simultaneously patterns of thought implanted through electronically augmented hypnosis triggered. The world around him slowed, stilled, froze.

Chaz fell through the center of the universe, into a world without time.

Now then: Lenore-the-spy had gone into forbidden territory through the medical facility. That would be his entrance as well.

Saturn knew he had made two mistakes.

He watched Dr. Kato's frustration with growing satisfaction. Within a few minutes the Myles woman would be beyond hope. Saturn could block any system to frustrate a rescue attempt until it was too late.

But Saturn should never have allowed Napcap medical readouts to reach Dr. Kato. Idiocy! It would have been so simple to create the illusion that she was traveling comfortably to America and sustain it until she was safely dead.

He had drawn a picture of Myles partially penetrating the air traffic control system. He had drawn it too well: his second mistake. Now Dr. Kato was inspired, now he had the first steps. Saturn could not have anticipated Kato's choice of metaphor.

Even so, how could the prey wriggle free? What could Kato *do*? Saturn's curiosity was too strong: He waited.

Now Dr. Kato was running the education programs. Each had challenges and rewards, each was a different "window" or "door" to the same data sets. He went for Pathology, then Autopsies. Baffled there, he switched from human to animal, specifically to Marine Biology. His skills, combined with the unlikeliness of his choice, moved him further. The data he needed were flashing around him like koi in a pond, but he couldn't quite grasp them.

Dr. Kato was chewing up milliseconds, running out of

time. He couldn't reach the Napcap system. Perhaps Saturn was safe after all. . . .

Then with all sane avenues closed against him, Chadwick Kato III did something crazy.

# 19

Although almost no one realized it, a war was being waged in the skies above Sri Lanka.

Because of political stresses, air traffic between East Africa and the Far East tended to stop in Sri Lanka rather than Bangladore or Chennai. This wasn't ordinarily a problem, but when Gunnar Osterhaus, the pilot of South African Airlines flight 345 to Da Nang, was told to join a holding pattern above Sri Lanka, he declined. Flight 345 was only passing through Sri Lankhan air space. On this trip there was no scheduled stop.

A moment later his autopilot took the controls away from him.

Osterhaus was shocked. Emergency engagement! His efforts to contact the control tower were fruitless. Something was terribly wrong, but he had a reasonable safety margin of fuel, and there was no reason to panic . . . yet.

One at a time, six planes and two dirigibles diverged from their flight plans, moving into an emergency holding pattern. None was able to communicate directly with the control tower, but there was still no panic. The condition had existed for less than ninety seconds.

The chief air traffic controller working the main screen at the Jaffna airport had just begun to notice something wrong.

Three planes had begun to diverge from their logged flight plans.

The pattern was strange. They were all (four now) converging to intersect a microwave pathway, flying between one of the immense dish targets south of Jaffna and the orbiting solar power satellite that fed Sri Lanka's thirsty grids. (Five; six.) Not an immediate problem for modern, well-shielded aircraft, but several other craft were turning toward the same zone. That was just too bizarre. It verged on frightening.

Only seven seconds had passed since he first noticed it, and in the next few seconds, he debated initiating an emergency alert. It had happened once before, when Spinners seized control of a dirigible carrying a load of precious hardwoods from Indonesia to Xanadu. But between that thought and the next, the situation began to resolve itself.

Chaz existed in a split reality. He had found his door, a specialized education program he had used only once before, to remove a viable brain from a diseased and dying shark. If the entire operation hadn't taken place between one heartbeat and the next, his pulse would have raced. If his body hadn't been deep in trance, he would have been sweating.

The *Galeocerdo cuvieri* had been augmented and released to the seas: an early auggietech experiment. The tiger shark's change in behavior had triggered attack frenzy from its cousins. Near death, mangled and diseased and starving, it had traveled over a thousand miles to return to Xanadu. With no way to save the body, Arvad Minsky himself had performed the operation on the stinking near carcass, seventeen excruciating hours that ended in moderate success, the living brain networked in an artificial support system, the memory of the dreadful attack still encoded within.

It was one of the most lauded and fabled successes in the augmentation effort, and thousands of perverse grad students had made a game of it, called Frenzy. There were two stages:

The Gamer began with surgery, removing the brain. Any mistake sent him back to Start empty-handed. But with all blood vessels perfectly sutured, all nerve stems flawlessly joined to the synthetic neural bundles, the Gamer could play the Guest of Honor in a three-dimensional, real-time, full-sensory mass shark attack.

Chaz had played it a dozen times but never more seriously than now. He had been bitten and scraped raw, his nervous system jolted with pain for every mistake. He was exhausted and disoriented. The virtual water about him foamed red, and it was all he could do to retain higher brain functions. One of the most viciously entertaining things about the simulation was its tendency to cut logic when blood hit the water.

But every evasion, every subjective second that he survived, twisting and turning through the crimson murk, gave him greater access. The system's defenses had maneater teeth. They tore at him, probing for his innards. But he turned them against each other, biting and slashing to confuse their delicate and powerful olfactory inputs, and swam along the bottom to raise silt and sand in a vast cloud, then slunk swiftly away, leaving his tormentors to tear at each other.

And suddenly he was in. He had control, and if it was only for a few vital seconds, that was enough. In this world, seconds were like hours.

He took control of the main tower. He sent false messages to the planes, shuttles, and dirigibles within its reach.

They were turning. He projected lines of intersection, foresaw crashes minutes before they could possibly occur, and began a juggling act. He didn't need actually to block the microwaves. He didn't need actually to bring the armada together. He need only stay in charge long enough for the emergency program to kick in, and then Lenore's death trap would reset itself.

But he was no longer alone.

* * *

The voice was not a voice. At this level of temporal abstraction, a hundred thoughts would pass before human vocal chords could vibrate. But the same mechanisms that made it possible for discrete thought at such compression sought to reinterpret data into its least confusing form. Sounds seemed tinny and somewhat artificial, as if massively compressed for transmission and then imperfectly reconstituted. Colors seemed too red. Shapes were not wholly convincing imitations of reality.

But even given those limitations, what Chaz heard next did not seem human.

The voice was utterly asexual, the tones of a bearded woman or a man halfway through a sex-change operation. "Release the aircraft, Dr. Kato."

Some part of Chaz relaxed. He had hoped for this. He knew that there would be someone watching, the same person or persons who had sentenced Lenore to death.

"No," Chaz said. In a few more seconds the airport would enter a condition of emergency. All nonessential power would be turned off. The Napcaps would reset.

Chaz felt his hold on the aircraft tremble. For an instant the illusion shifted, and he felt pain in his side. Damn! His unknown adversary had dumped him back with the sharks. Could time be more of an ally? He could increase the temporal distortion, but it wouldn't help. He needed another six or seven seconds before Sri Lanka's security apparatus would kick in. Greater distortion could work as well for his enemy.

In fact . . .

Now that he was engaged, now that he was in, he could take the security systems with him back up to normal time. He didn't have to win. All he had to do was convince Sri Lanka that they were under attack. Perhaps they would reset, and perhaps not . . . but could his adversary take that risk? Could his unknown foe, whatever force had pronounced a death sentence on Lenore, let Sri Lanka discover that Xanadu had attempted a murder on their territory?

*Let's find out.*

In order to function at such speed, Chaz's personality had been simulated and cached in the main system, moving at the speed of light rather than a human nervous system's agonizing ninety meters per second. The transition back to normal speed returned him to the visceral world of the shark attack. He felt every bite, could feel the blood pumping from his wounds, fouling the water: This was no longer a game of evasion and escape. This was death and delay.

The planes converged. The microwave beams jittered in their shadows.

The voice howled. A tiger's snarl would have been friendly, intimate, compared to that sound. Chaz spasmed, kicked hard against his chair back. He thought of a tiger's snarl only because this was so *alien*. A tiger would have run.

Then, "Cease your manipulations, and I will cease my attack upon the woman. We must speak."

Chaz had kept a tiny thread of consciousness linked to his original medical scan of Lenore. He dared not release it. His enemy could send him false diagnostics. He allowed himself a peek at that data: His adversary had spoke the truth. Lenore's death had been arrested.

"Show yourself," Chaz said.

A face appeared before him on the screen. It was male and female, African and Caucasian and Oriental, a composite of human genetics and genders . . . and it lacked detail, until he saw it smile. The teeth were triangular, jagged, rows behind rows. A shark's teeth. A shark's smile.

Whoever hid behind that mask was a killer in possession of Councilor-level codes. The face was fiction, but Chaz believed the smile.

"You don't have to kill her," Chaz said.

"This is not your decision to make. She possesses information dangerous to the Floating Islands."

"Who are you?" Chaz asked.

"Call us Saturn, if you must call us anything at all."

"Why are you hurting her? She's not a spy."

"Everything we do, we do for the protection of Xanadu. We appreciate what you have contributed and have no interest in giving you pain."

"We?" he said weakly. "Does the entire Council know?"

"We have full authority in this matter," Saturn said. "Release the planes!" Saturn wasn't waiting: although the aircraft involved could barely have moved a dozen meters in real time, Saturn had disrupted his controls. The lines of flight danced as they wrestled. Chaz felt his grasp disappearing.

He didn't have to win. A draw would save Lenore.

"Lenore's death is unacceptable," he said. The planes he still held dived. In five seconds of real time, alarms would sound throughout the airport. If the new courses were not corrected, flaming aircraft would rain down on commuters within five minutes. Chaz asked, "How much attention can you stand?"

When Saturn spoke again there was the unmistakable ring of truth about his words. "She penetrated our systems."

"I beg the Council's pardon. I gave her access. She wandered afield, but I am at fault, and I will stand for it. But she did not penetrate as far as it seems. That is a clumsy fiction written by someone else."

A pause of milliseconds, but it felt like eternity. "She knows our secret," Saturn said. "She knows who you really are."

He didn't answer. Couldn't.

Deal with the devil, Chaz. You made your bed. He had signed papers giving Xanadu his life and future. During his time on Xanadu he had allowed others to make too many decisions, had slid into an odd pseudoadolescence.

Saturn said, "She knows that you are Chadwick Kato the First. She knows that you are your own grandfather. That you are almost a hundred years old. That information must never leave Xanadu. The rules of Xanadu and other Floating Cities specifically mandate the use of lethal force for the protection of our interests. You agreed. It was the price of your new life, Dr. Kato."

His mind screamed that she was innocent, that she had certainly not come to rob Xanadu, that her questing mind had seen secrets and probed them at his invitation!

"You signed the covenants. Do you understand? As of this moment, she has not passed the information to her controllers. But every moment she remains alive increases the danger. *Dr. Kato, you must act!*"

The planes were still diving.

Lenore was in Sri Lanka, with whom Xanadu had an extradition treaty, but they would never give her up without legal formalities. During those formalities, she might . . . *would* come into contact with hundreds of people. She could convey information to any or all of them.

Chaz checked the stats: The progress of her death was in suspension while they argued. *Quid pro quo.* Chaz eased his control of the planes.

"Do you wish to see war?" Saturn said. "Then tell the poor of the world that they could live forever, if only they were citizens of the Floating Cities. Tell them that they die because they are poor, that there is a means to sustain their lives, and that we withhold it from them. What then comes of all your efforts to feed the poor? What then?"

If Chaz lost his airplanes. . . . Saturn would have a thousand ways to kill Lenore. He couldn't allow himself to be drawn into a debate.

"There's another way," he said.

"There is no other way."

"You lack imagination." He meant it as an insult, but he sensed it was true. "You've created some kind of link to her capsule. Let me in. Maintain her life signs at the current level and just trust me for . . . one minute of real time. In exchange, I will release the planes."

"She must not regain consciousness," Saturn said. A single line opened between Xanadu and Sri Lanka, leading him to the Napcap unit.

Saturn had already compromised the Napcap. Chaz had no need to waste time there. What he needed now was a metaphor to represent Lenore's memories.

He chose a standard university-style twentieth-century library. Sketchy images gathered detail: endless rows of books and tables, the high windows and low murmuring blend of footsteps, page-turning, and computer key clicks.

As he wandered through the virtual environment, he ran strategy and tactics through his mind. What did he know? That the sleep-induction system worked by trickling current through her brain. Being in a dreamless state when she would ordinarily be experiencing REM sleep, she experienced an accelerated state of physical rest. So the field was set up to manipulate core mental processes.

When had she learned what she learned? Certainly within the last thirty-six hours.

The human mind has three basic memory systems, working in series. Sensory memory only lasts for about two seconds but creates a copy of the information or experience. Short term is a limited capacity system, usually seven plus or minus two pieces of data, held for about thirty seconds before uploading to long term, which stores and retrieves information by category.

What he needed was to destroy her last day and a half. He would delete what she had learned. Just take it away.

"That isn't going to change things, Dr. Kato," Saturn said patiently.

"We made a bargain." Anger surged within him. "Either keep it, or I'll bathe that airport in flame!" He had lost every airplane; he was bluffing.

Saturn went silent again.

Chaz did what he had to do. The metaphor was deadly accurate, and he was disturbed at his own imagery: He walked to a section of shelves marked "March 17, 0100–1400 hours" and swept up an armload of books. Books slipped free. He carried the rest to a central incinerator chute, dumped them, and watched them burn.

God, what did that mean? Were axons being destroyed? Synapses blunted? He went back for the books he'd dropped and watched them burn too.

What was he doing to the woman he loved? As the books burned, volumes on the surrounding shelves were singeing. A little browning. A little crisping. But the fire was controlled and never spread. Then the flames died, leaving only smoke.

He watched a smoking hole in the middle of a shelf. He finally allowed himself to understand what he had done. He could only hope that along with the obscene invasion of privacy, he had managed to save her life.

"That isn't enough," Saturn said. "Very clever, but the fact remains that she is a spy."

"That isn't a fact without a trial. Now that she knows nothing dangerous, she can be returned for trial, can't she?"

Saturn paused. "That . . . could prove embarrassing."

"Then what's your problem? She can't hurt us. She won't remember. I guarantee it. You know my skills. But if you touch her, or hurt her in any way, I will never work for Xanadu again."

"You can't be serious. You would lose all privilege, including access to hospital facilities."

Chaz took a deep breath. "What good is any of that? I've been alone for years. I finally fall in love, and you tell me she's a spy. My privileged status disappeared so easily that it's pretty clear it was never there. I'm telling you that she is neutralized. For God's sake show a little mercy," he said, and instantly remembered the sound of Saturn's frustration. Whoever Saturn was, that person was not likely to know mercy.

"Agreed," said Saturn. Then Chaz was linked to nothing but sleeping Lenore.

He began the delicate process of bringing her back to life.

# 20

Lenore's hands shook, spilling cocoa on her pantsuit. The men standing over her wore expressions of polite interest. They were lean, brown-skinned men of intelligence and discipline. None spoke English as a native language, but all understood the tongue.

The shortest was a man whom others referred to as "Commander," and he was nattily dressed in a brown uniform with a security chevron on the shoulder patches. He had arrived shortly after her questioning began.

He reviewed the notes one of his men had taken during her deposition, glancing at her from time to time. Her head pounded. She held tight to her anger, because panic was eating it from underneath.

Finally he looked up at her. His eyes were light brown, his features combined Indian and perhaps English. "Miss Myles," he said. "I regret the imposition, but your situation unfortunately took place at the same time as a minor disturbance in our power grid. Our staff physician has examined you and found nothing, but we have sent for a specialist who will arrive within the hour. Before she does, I would like to hear your story again, please."

Her head throbbed intolerably. She said, "I would like to avoid telling it again."

He merely waited.

"I got on a plane at Boston. I must have boarded. The last thing I remember was the boarding line. Showed my passport. Then I woke up with my head coming apart in a Napcap in Sri Lanka!"

"And you were en route to . . . ?"

"Xanadu."

He frowned. "I see. Well, we have spoken to the guest registration facilities there, and you were indeed on the island. You checked in. You checked out. You boarded your transport and disembarked safely. The security camera shows that you entered the capsule and remained there for nearly six hours, four times the usual duration. There must have been a malfunction."

"And two days of my life are just *gone?*"

"This is what you say, Miss Myles. We have a doctor coming, and a psychologist. We suggest that you may wish to remain here for a more thorough series of tests."

Panic won. She stood. "No! I want to go home. Now."

The security men looked at each other. "Miss Myles. If you intend to file suit against the capsule manufacturer or the airport itself, it would be better to have you examined now, before any further time has passed."

They regarded her with what they doubtless considered helpful, even solicitous expressions. But to her they seemed alien. One minute she had been boarding a plane in Boston, and the next, she was in Sri Lanka, shaking off the effects of the worst hangover a human being had ever survived.

"Commander," she said finally, trying to find some bit of resolve. "Do you have any legal reason to keep me here?"

"No," he said, in a tone that suggested regret. "But for your own good—"

"I want to be home. With my friends. In my own country. If you will not allow me to leave I want to see the American Consulate now, do you understand?" She hardly recognized her own voice. Who was this strident woman? The real Lenore, at the moment, was a small, frightened girl. This was sheer lunacy.

Two days? Gone? The men, all strangers, leered at her. She was certain that she would go mad if she didn't see something familiar, and soon. It was all she could do to keep from screaming.

He sighed. "All right. An Air Asia transport departs in a

little under an hour. You have an unexecuted ticket, and the airline is happy to make the adjustment. We have no grounds to hold you." Something seemed to occur to him. "Excuse me for asking, and I mean no disrespect, but . . . are you accustomed to drinking, and perhaps . . . other entertainments?"

She actually felt her spine stiffen. "What are you trying to say?"

"Some pretty wild parties on Xanadu, hey?"

She found the implication in both words and tone insulting. She gathered her belongings. She recognized the suitcase. She had packed it herself. She didn't remember putting the pantsuit on, but it was hers.

The commander said a few words in a language she didn't understand and then stood aside as a blocky, dark-complected woman helped Lenore to her feet. "Then we have no reason to detain you. If you wish to file against Soma, I would suggest you do so within seventy-two hours."

She nodded without speaking. Her legs were unsteady, and she moved like an old woman, but she moved. One step at a time, away from these strangers, away from this place, back to a life that she understood. Then, in quiet, privacy and safety, she would find out what had happened to her. Determine who and what might have caused those missing days.

And then, by God, somebody was going to pay.

# PART TWO

# 21

## MAY 2021

*There are minds that think as well as you do, but differently.* In the science fiction of Chaz Kato's youth that had been the one unchallenged truth. Mankind had not found extraterrestrial intelligences, but Xanadu was making them.

Barrister the Squark came at Chaz like a runaway bus. He stopped inches away, suddenly motionless in the clear warm water, maybe watching for Chaz's flinch. Barrister was a modified Great White, twenty feet of muscle and glistening hide, and two fleshy arms. The arms slowed his swimming, but the big flat hands made him *incredibly* maneuverable. Earlier scaliens had to make do with tentacles grafted from octopi.

He focused on Chaz with mechanical goggles affixed over his flat black lifeless eyes, ignoring the five students clustered behind him. "Want eight rods," he said. "Fish in exchange."

Three other Squarks swam in lazy circles, squidlike tentacles trailing fleshily behind them. They were tool users, but Barrister's arms were more advanced. They were short flat fins, but each ended in four flat gristly fingers, one opposed to act as a thumb. They looked like hands on a Disney character. Barrister hovered, holding Chaz's stare with his own mechanical gaze. His fingers wriggled restlessly.

Chaz, Minsky, and the students floated on the outskirts of the Scalien Village a kilometer southeast of Xanadu. Beside him, Minsky floated contentedly. "Barrister is a Type Three," he said, on a closed circuit, lecturing the students. "We've done several basic modifications here.

"Type Ones are enhanced neurotransmitter models. Usually they just get slyer and more aggressive. We lost a grad student to a Type One who acted docile, then grabbed a chunk, so be careful. Type Twos are straight link jobs: basically biological robots. They look like fish or aquatic mammals but are controlled by the computer system. I started Barrister as a Type Two. I've been modifying him gradually. Now he's a Type Three, the new breed, synthetic cortex piggybacked like a third lobe on his brain, interacting and occasionally overriding the other two. Most of these subjects died or seemed to short-circuit. Three percent of them not only accept the new capacities but seem to embrace them."

All the humans wore standard deep-operations gear: rebreathers with modified gas mixture, fuel-cell oxygen extraction gear, the works. No bulkier than twentieth-century SCUBA, but it allowed unbroken hours of usage, assuming one possessed the physical endurance.

"Village" was the word they would use until someone dreamed up a better one. None of the major structures in the Scalien Village were domiciles in the human sense. They looked more like corrals and frameworks than human habitats. Construction areas. Maze tests. Fishy gymnasiums.

"Scalien" they might keep as a generic term for all of the varied experimental animal/computer interfaces that tested and displayed Xanadu's augmentation technology. Arvad

Minsky preferred "frankensteins." Arvad had no sense of public relations at all.

For ten years they had run the village with implants, forcing the sharks and dolphins to behave as humans might dictate. But with increasingly sophisticated technology, it was possible to slowly release them from control, leave them their computer links, their augmented senses and intelligence, and see what they would do.

The experiments were of varying success. Release a shark from implantation control and it might run away or devour the fish it should have been herding, or something crazier yet.

Dolphins tended to act like old men awakening from bad dreams: agitated, groggy, confused. They often became too erratic to return to the wild and were best returned to total control.

But from time to time, if control was eased by, say, 20 percent, a Scalien might emerge who seemed to enjoy its new perceptions and capacities. Played with them. *Intelligence? For me? Wow!*

The experimenters argued incessantly as to whether programming was at work here, or something innate. But what remained inarguable was that most scaliens were, to all appearances, far smarter than dogs and not human at all.

Barrister the Great White had arms. His precursors had clusters of squid arms. Barrister's also came from a squid, but Minsky and Kato had reshaped them and channeled new nerves before grafting them into place. His periscope goggles allowed him to see what his arms were doing. He could assist in construction as well as herding. A squark.

Now Barrister was negotiating for some of the reinforced building rods squarks used to pen their own young and the fish herds as well. Sharks had no natural enemies save bigger sharks, and in a few of them, the urge to protect their young combined with their new intelligence to promote an appreciation of building and trade.

The first alien civilization.

"Must build," Barrister said. His mouthful of jagged triangular teeth belied the implied confusion in his words. "Eight rods or lose . . . your fish." Even the confusion, the uncertainty, might have been programmed. How much of this entity was Barrister? That was what they were trying to learn.

Negotiating wouldn't improve the bargain. Barrister knew how to count rods, but fish came in too many sizes and varieties. He would deliver fish until he thought the bargain was satisfied. Chaz held back only because the students wanted to talk to Barrister. Give him his rods, he'd swim away.

The Squark swam in a lazy circle and looked down on the buildings and pens. They were all in perfect geodesic dome formations or in various linked configurations.

Behind Minsky's faceplate, Chaz glimpsed a proud, deeply freckled paternal grin, a bit asymmetric, like his skewed face with its mismatched eyes, one human, one glittering multitask camera. Frankenstein indeed. Minsky said, "Last week a couple of repatriated squarks made it back."

Chaz asked, "Really?" because that was rare. About half of the Type Threes wandered away from Down Under. Most were never seen again.

"Really. And what was incredible? They herded back a baby! Unreal! It didn't want to come, either. They had nip marks all over their tentacles."

Chaz stared at his friend. Was he kidding? They'd been herding an infant tiger shark! Grafted tentacles and increased intelligence were not traits to be passed along to their young.

"Don't tell me?"

"Yep. They brought him right to me. Said 'Make smart.' "

Sharks had no vocal chords, not even the blowhole vocalizations of dolphins. The voice of a squark was a microphone speaking its thoughts directly, however much those thoughts might have derived from a computer program. Type Threes could talk, but this was above and beyond.

" 'Make smart.' They thought of this themselves?"

Minsky shook his head. "Damned if I know. I've been quizzing some of the programming staff. No one will admit to inserting that command. It might be a practical joke, but if it isn't. . . ."

In college Minsky's experiments had been dangerous. Stories had worked their way into his record. At Xanadu he had become more daring, well beyond the point of playing God. Chaz had noticed his friend's godlike ambitions before . . . but in these matters, arrogance was a goddam job description!

Chaz said, "Let me go over the code for you."

They rounded one of the larger, skeletal domes. On the other side of the bars swam baby sharks.

What Xanadu hoped for might be impossible. No one seriously believed that any combination of augmentation technologies, circumstance, and time might create or reveal a true pseudospecies . . . nobody but, possibly, Minsky. Most of them only hoped that these biocomputer interfaces might help humanity anticipate a true alien encounter. The oldest Council member, the Nigerian dictator/CEO whose logo was *El Cid*, seemed sure that add-on intelligence was the answer to Alzheimer's. Chaz wasn't sure he was wrong.

For now, they held conversations in the special bite-proof suits and acted out prearranged scenarios, allowing computers and sometimes programmers to decide how much of the animal's "personality" would be allowed to come through.

An absurdity, detractors said. You could attach a sea snail to the linking apparatus and make its slime trails work out differential calculus, but you'd never get the "snail personality" into the equation. Inarguably true. But every now and then Chaz sensed a mind pattern that had never been on Earth before.

The student floating to his left offered Barrister the next gambit. "Which are more valuable to you: the males or the females?"

The squark tentacles waved quickly, and Chaz thought he saw pain in that expressionless face. The goggle eyes stared. "Like females. Mate with females. Work better."

"Sharks are sexist?" a girl behind Chaz asked, bemused.

"Some successful squarks develop a kind of pride behavior similar to lions," Chaz said.

"What's the ratio of successful males to females?"

"About four females to each male. Males compete for them until they reach a distribution of about five to one."

"Let me rephrase that," the student said. "All right. Let's say I'm not talking about your personal preference. Which do you think is more valuable to the group, Barrister? Males or females?"

"Females can build," Barrister said in his flat, synthesized voice. "Make babies. Fight. Hunt." He paused. "Taste better."

Barrister swam on, down to the level where stresses on the cage had created a warp in the existing bars. Chaz could easily see where more were needed.

The students followed him down. Nadine, no older than fifteen but a true water sprite, asked the next question. Her face was lined and serious in the artificial light. "What is the meaning of life?" she said.

Some of the others groaned. Barrister turned and looked at her, right at her. For just a moment, Chaz thought he was going to lunge. Shark-proof suits or not, there was something primal and terrifying about a creature this size, with pudgy hands strong enough to work a pry bar and an apparent vocabulary the size of the Merriam-Webster dictionary.

Barrister stopped dead in the water. Very slowly he began to drop. Then with a flick of his tail and a tight loop, he came back to them. "The meaning of life," Barrister said. "If you don't keep moving, you sink."

The class looked at each other and at Barrister for a disbelieving minute, and then Nadine said: "Dr. Kato, I think they deserve their rods."

Chaz nodded. *If you don't keep moving, you sink?* Who had programmed that? Or . . .

"Eight rods, Barrister. Class over," Chaz said.

His class took one of the dozen Bubbles back to the surface: slow-moving pressurized elevators that traveled up and down Xanadu's gigantic tether chains, ferrying work crews, researchers, and students. Each was large enough for ten people to lounge comfortably, with food processors, entertainment centers, Napcaps, and linking facilities. They had spent less than four hours down on the floor; the trip back would be a leisurely lunch.

Minsky lounged on one of the couches, eating a thick sandwich. "Well? What do you think?"

Nadine raised her hand. "Dr. Kato? Are we to assume that that last comment was not directly programmed?"

Chaz looked at Minsky questioningly.

Minsky nodded. "It gets a little sticky. The computer can parrot back phrases, of course, but that specific phrase wasn't placed in Barrister's bank. More likely to be a literal translation of a series of definitions of 'shark' and 'sharklike behavior' in the pseudobrain. An attempt to give Barrister some kind of self-awareness. He's as sophisticated as they come, but still a shark genetically. Genetic manipulation will be the next step, and we're toying with that, but this latest permutation . . . I don't know." Minsky scratched his head, smiling boyishly. "It is just possible that one of my grad students was playing a joke on me. Barrister is way smarter than a dog or a normal dolphin. But so are the grad students."

They laughed. He said, "Barrister's speech patterns have always been canned responses. If he wants food, instead of making a special loop in the water or pushing a lever, he says 'Want food.' Does he know what it means? Yes. Could he conjugate the phrase? No."

"He can make puns," Chaz said. "It's a level up from

what we programmed into the system. He nudged me once, after he had finished eating some tuna. He wasn't hungry. He wanted me to follow him."

"So what was the joke, Dr. Kato?"

"He put two set phrases together. 'Want food . . . to follow.'"

Taking the elevator back to his apartment, Chaz was caught three times by various Xanadu folk seeking audiences.

In the last year he had steadily and surely felt the hand of discipline closing around him. There seemed to be endless demands for his services, and it would have been impolite and impolitic for him to refuse.

There were standard linking questions: amplification and modifications to installed equipment bases. New equipment to be tested and installed in Xanadu and abroad. The operation of telemetrical systems around the planet and beyond. Interpretations of data from subjects like Barrister, questions about whether this or that action or reply could possibly indicate true intelligence or awareness.

Then there was the arena of finance. As little as it might mean to him, his money continued to amass, and there was a call from a broker. . . .

"Chaz?"

"Van Buren. How's the weather in Geneva?"

"Fine, thank you." Sober banker the fellow might well have been, but Chaz still remembered Van Buren's last visit to Xanadu, when Chaz had talked him into a descent to Squark City. It was hard to forget the image of Van Buren in full rebreather gear, goggle-eyed and incoherent at the sight of the first Squark dome ever shown to an outsider and fourteen armed and dangerous squarks juggling steel rods underwater.

Today: "I want to discuss the disbursement of funds for the month. You have a standing order for the purchase of Synaptech. We know that there will be a new offering soon and wished to be certain that you hadn't changed your mind."

"It's been awhile, hasn't it?"

"Yes, and frankly, we feel that there are some better opportunities available."

"I'm sure. Keep me there, Carter."

Pause. Van Buren didn't like it, but then there was no reason for him to. Chaz's motivations were not shaped by money here.

The image winked off.

The last call requested that he attend a board meeting in the afternoon. Decisions had to be made about copyright piracy in India. He made useful noises and signed off just as the elevator reached his apartment.

The door opened and closed behind him, and the new security systems went into operation.

Chaz entered his library.

He loved his collection of computers. It was hard to recall his enthusiasm over the Sinclair's membrane keyboard, or that he had once been involved in a lively debate defending the minuscule CRT screen on the Osborne as "Almost exactly the size of a paperback book held at arm's length," as if anyone read that way.

No outsider knew, or could know, that he had personally purchased every one of these at retail. But any citizen of Xanadu would understand.

And it was hard to believe that the Macintosh computer case had once looked so strange, or that its sealed system had once caused so much frustration to its devoted fans. If he used the special tool and took the case apart, there, engraved on the inside of the composition plastic, would be the names of the original design team. Flush against the right edge, halfway down the list, was the name Chadwick Kato.

Ten months ago he had waited until his standard meditation time and placed his apartment under full security seal. He'd established that habit long before the Lenore incident. It wouldn't attract unwanted attention. Chaz had disassembled the Mac case, and not merely to view the name of the young man he had been so many years before. He had rebuilt its innards.

He knew nothing of Saturn. How could he outguess an opponent of unknown intelligence, unknown experience, unknown background? But even the most basic understanding of human psychology would suffice to warn Saturn that Chaz would be disturbed by what had happened eleven months before. Chaz Kato could not be expected to leave this alone.

His apartment could be, *would* be, searched or bugged. Saturn was watching.

Chaz must be seen to react.

Publicly if quietly, Chaz had engaged the services of a detective agency to keep a steady, long-distance check on Lenore and her roommate, Tooley Wells. It was only after the terrible duel with "Saturn" that he realized that anyone who had been in close contact with Lenore might have been entrusted with dangerous knowledge.

He only guarded her. He had never approached Tooley Wells in any way.

Lenore had been targeted for death. Why? Lenore the thief and spy was a fiction, but what was the truth? Had she learned something? There were too many factors, and too much information, to sort through with his unaugmented mind. He could not even be seen asking the right questions. He did not believe that any level of security could protect him from Saturn.

He couldn't rely upon Clarise. He dare not even question her directly. But he needed to search.

This was his current solution.

Chaz lifted the ancient Macintosh down from the shelf and plugged it in. He touched the switch on the back, and the little "Mac" icon smiled at him from the middle of the screen.

Under routine security seal, sealed into a womb of privacy and silence, Chaz had, for the next half hour, a window of opportunity.

The screen blinked. "PLAY BLACK DOG?"

"N. PLAY PONG," he typed.

The screen lit up in black and white. A little white ball bounced from one side to another at moderate speed. It was difficult to believe that the game had ever been anything but a child's toy, but the simple blip-blip of it, called "Pong," had once been the most popular computer game in the world.

Simpler, happier days. He was well practiced in the game, his coordination perfectly synced so that the minutes passed fluidly, his wrist flipping and flipping, catching the little ball of light as it zipped to and fro, until the score read 83101021—Chaz's age, plus the date.

He let the ball dance past his paddle. "Now Quest Gold," he said.

Inside the innocuous case was the most advanced processor that Chaz had been able to obtain secretly. Knowing that all of his accounts could be monitored, and most of his movements as well, he had done the only thing he could. He had stolen the parts. He needed a processor and an independent power source, so that Archie (the hardware) and NERO (the program) could sit in their shielded box and work even when the plug was pulled.

He took the VR headset from the machine at the far end. It was a standard Dream Park rental; hundreds were stolen out of the park every year. He rotated a component inside Archie and plugged the headset in and put it on.

A street scene formed, foggy, then sharp. Tall buildings and long shadows and a three-story brownstone dark with age. Sudden sounds: blatting horns, a prolonged shriek of bad brakes. Three antique cars danced with each other and the parked cars and dirty brick walls along the street. Chaz escaped a swinging chrome fender by jumping his character onto a parked car. All three cars somehow escaped with no more than dents and roared off in a wave of faintly heard curses.

The brownstone's front door emitted a tall, brawny, actor-handsome white man. He looked up at Chaz perched on the Heron's hood.

He said, "Dr. Kato, a problem. I can't let you in. I don't work here any longer."

This was new. "Some argument?"

"Resolved. But if you want him, you'll have to ring." He walked off down the street.

Chaz pushed the doorbell button. Waited. Would a program adapted from a detective puzzle game waste his time this way?

He tried the door handle. It opened. He walked in.

The office was locked. The front room was empty of life, barring a few *Polystachya* and donkey orchids. A clock above the sofas matched Chaz's wristwatch at just past six in the evening. At this time of day he wouldn't be on the top floor with the orchids. Chaz wouldn't consider invading the bedrooms and such, but . . . what would the game show? It might just kick him out.

Chaz was still exploring. The dining room was set with dinner for two, half eaten. Small birds—squabs—tiny potatoes, a vividly orange tart. Squash? Carrot?

Chaz rapped on the kitchen door and went in.

Both men were massively overweight, though it didn't seem to bother either. Lupus Nero snapped, "Who the devil—! Oh, it's Dr. Kato. Doctor, I must apologize. Ritchie is in a snit, and of course we don't hear the doorbell in here. Have you eaten?"

The NERO game had featured a first attempt at full sensory input. In 2001 C.E. it had not worked well. Chaz Kato Senior had fiddled with it. This version would be upgraded one day when it was safe. For now there was only sight, sound, touch. Chaz couldn't smell the stench of cars outside,

nor Nero's orchids, and what was the point of eating at
Lupus Nero's table if he couldn't smell or taste anything?

Chaz said, "I've eaten, thank you."

Nero said, "Dinner is ruined in any event. Shall we continue in my office? Yes, Fritz, I'll tell him."


Chaz loved MAD MASTER. He'd grown ever fonder of it
over the years. A kind of playful AI program designed to
evolve varying answers and interpretations from a given set
of data, this type of metaphor provided scenarios based on
what it thought the programmed personality would have said
or done had he been present. Companies used it to get virtual
answers from absent bosses. Sons used it to figure out how a
deceased parent might have dealt with a family emergency.

But there was fun and mischief in it as well. One could
interact with a virtual Napoleon, or Attila the Hun or Jef-
ferson or Robert Frost or Heinlein, or any number of fictional characters. All of this was originally in the spirit of
determining how a computerized personality might react.
What was awareness or creativity, what was mere information sorting?

And who wouldn't burn a library of books in exchange
for the chance to be taught political science by Lincoln,
physics by Hawking, American literature by Twain, or gender relationships by Hugh Hefner and Dr. Ruth?

The Y2K panic in January 2000 C.E. had driven good
software companies out of business. Chaz had acquired a
batch of commercial computer games nearly ready for market.

NERO, from Low Road Games, showed signs of haste:
a bit too intellectual, and the sensory input needed more
work. Instead of buying rights to the Rex Stout characters,
Low Road had just made up new names. Chaz toyed with
the game, then lost interest when his wife died . . . and no
other living human being knew that NERO had ever been.

Chaz had written NERO into the character template in

MAD MASTER. Over the past year, he had fed NERO random communications from members of the Council.

NERO couldn't have complete data access. Chaz could provide his desktop detective with all of the usual news feeds. He could carry copies of files for Nero to chew through. But he daren't allow his spy to make direct inquiries, or even draw a suspicious level of power.

One thing they could do was search for Saturn's "fist."

"Fist" was a nineteenth-century term used to describe the eccentric patterns of rhythm that would identify a telegraph specialist by the way he used the key. Programmers had individual "fists." Saturn's communications had been an impeccable weave of fabrication and disguise, but what Saturn had done, how he had done it, would suggest things about the man behind the curtain. Comparing Lenore's true metaphor patterns with Saturn's counterfeit might yield additional clues.

There was no way for Chaz to sort through possible variations. He wasn't even certain what he was looking for. NERO worked at it full time.

Lupus Nero glared at what had been Ritchie's desk, cruised around it, and dropped into a chair big enough to hold him. He was Nero Wolfe exaggerated to four hundred pounds, and tall enough to loom. The green blackboard behind him nearly covered the wall.

He was holding his temper, but the effort showed. "Fritz would want me to tell you," he said, "that nobody enters my kitchen without Fritz's permission. Don't consider yourself unwelcome on that account, Dr. Kato. Without invitation I don't enter either."

"I'll be more careful in the future," Chaz apologized. "Have you had the opportunity to look over the other material?"

"Indeed, Doctor. Eight months is a much longer time for

me than for you. You have also increased the ... ah ... clarity of my thought through additions to the speed, depth, and number of the processors available to me."

"I hope they've been sufficient."

"No."

"Can you suggest—"

"Upgrades? The problem is not with my intelligence! Input may be the problem. My latest news feed came from Entertainment at six-twenty today, and I have a fax from Transportation concerning the proposed Ecuador Beanstalk." The blackboard was a window: It flashed displays to match Nero's words. "Both purported to be direct communications from their respective department heads, Yamato of Japan and the Nigerian who calls himself 'El Cid.' Plausible?"

"I'd say so."

"I know everything you've learned in this matter, everything that makes its way into the media, and proprietary information gained from various sources through security lapses and carelessness, though you've restricted me to passive observation. If that were sufficient, I would have answers! This is the core of what we know."

The blackboard was running two windows now. One was a voiceprint of Saturn as he traded threats and bargains with Chaz Kato over dying Lenore. In the other, Lenore's cartoon animals ate into Xanadu's airport programs. The beasts looked odd; they were too agile; their legs didn't move right and didn't move often enough.

Nero said, "Is it clear that Saturn's metaphors are sea life? The pictures are Myles's, but they are imposed on fish." Certain animals flashed green borders: gazelles, giraffes, zebras. "These two—" Borders blinked on zebra unicorns. "—match very well with swordfish. The elephant is too supple," yellow flash. "Giant squid, I think.

"There are many marine biologists on Xanadu, but few have Saturn's abilities. I eliminated them first. I consider them again because *every* approach has failed.

"Doctor, let us examine what we think we know.

"First, what did Lenore Myles know? She may know that three equals one, as Saturn said. Chaz Kato the Third is Chaz Senior. Saturn is not trustworthy, but this would explain why she left you so abruptly. She spent all night and the next afternoon in the bed of an eighty-three-year-old roué."

Chaz winced; but these were his own suggestions.

"But this is not a killing matter! There are other ancients in Xanadu. A good publicist—spin doctor?—might sell you as a mere freak. People have often lived longer than a century."

"They couldn't do handstands," Chaz said bitterly.

"Don't do handstands in public, Doctor. Or join a circus! Brag of your abilities. Let the story fly free, fodder for the tabloids. Radical experiments done in secret. Ten die for every survivor. *You* would be exposed, but Xanadu's secret would be safe. Killing a witness would only make the secret more interesting. Dr. Kato, if you hadn't been suffering from sixteen years of survivor guilt, you would never—"

Chaz barked, *"Survivor guilt?"*

Nero shrugged theatrically; his flesh rippled. "You abandoned them all. Friends, business allies, and partners and rivals, the factories you founded, the people you hired and trained. Ako Kato's grave. Saturn's transparent justifications triggered your password, Dr. Kato!"

"Triggered my password." Chaz swallowed his fury. Only fools get angry at a computer program . . . and the damn thing was right. Saturn had pushed the buttons that turned off Chaz Kato's defenses.

"Where was Myles during her hours at Xanadu? What did she learn? The attempt to kill her in Sri Lanka suggests time pressure. If she committed some criminal act, there would be no need to fabricate evidence . . . unless her crime exposed or revealed some secret of Saturn's."

"If Saturn's a Councilor," Chaz objected, "why a crime? They make the law."

"Crimes against other Councilors, or against world opinion. We seek evidence of a wrongdoing that would force a member of the Council to act as swiftly and ruthlessly as Saturn has. How can I investigate such a thing? I am restricted to news feeds." The blackboard was flashing a stream of headlines. "I must be a passive listener. I dare not make direct inquiries, or even draw a suspicious level of power, lest Saturn track me to my virtual lair. Over eight months I've turned up nothing.

"I have eight months of computer activity from the twelve major and five minor members of the Council, and from every major power here on the island. The exception was Medusa, the cosmetics and beauty care magnate. Born Helena Schwartz—"

"You got *that?*"

"That and little more. Her security is better than the tools available to me. That might suggest something to hide, or merely a love of privacy."

Chaz liked Medusa, her public persona, but he'd never met Helena Schwartz. "Can she be Saturn?"

Nero said, "No. Ten days ago . . . Do you recall the crash of Continental LEO-33? I have two minutes of Schwartz unloading stock before the news broke. She was conference-linked to four cities in real time, and Ritchie picked it up. She does not have Saturn's fist. I spent some effort trying to falsify the source. Do you understand this term *falsify?*"

"You tried to show that the input isn't to be trusted."

"Yes. I could not falsify. It was Helena Schwartz, not a computer persona or an agent, and she is not Saturn."

"One down. Anyone else?"

"Yes. Saturn knows you well, perhaps through research, perhaps not. A Council member resides here openly, and he knows you. I have been able to observe behavioral aspects that might have been impossible at a distance."

"Arvad," Chaz said.

"Quite. Arvad Minsky is not Saturn either. His fist clears him."

"Who else? Wayne and Shannon Halifax? Diva?"

"Diva the Brahman, racist from a nation of racists. Her fist clears her, but she might be Saturn's ally or minion or master. What then? I know no way to question her. Shannon Halifax the former Playmate of the Year is too public to hide secrets, and I think her husband is too."

"Right. Joe Blaze?"

"Energy? That is Yamoto. His fist clears him. Why, Doctor?"

"Country club white. Yamoto's joke, I suppose." Hating himself, Chaz asked, "Did you consider Clarise?"

"Pfui. Clarise Maibang, second in Security, briefly your wife? Am I a witling? She might want Lenore dead for reasons of jealousy, but she has no legitimate access to the kind of power Saturn displayed, and how could she act under Whittlesea's eye? But I have her fist," and the blackboard showed the graphs. "Maibang plods. The woman is wary of errors, and she learned to read and write late in life. Her style is superficial."

Chaz's cheeks burned. Clarise deserved better than that! "Of course you're only judging her by how she uses a computer."

"I considered Whittlesea. I considered Tooley Wells, who came as Lenore's companion." More graphs. "Wells types very fast, then backs up to fill in the mistakes. Whittlesea's education and programming style are classical British. Paul Bunyon's fist is artificially generated, with a delay of five seconds while a human input is rewritten. His real name is Valentine Antonelli, and he was in a frenzy of strike negotiations over a conference network while you and Saturn were dicing for Myles's life.

"But Saturn's fist is highly skilled, methodical in his approach, brilliant in basic programming, and I cannot identify the source of his education. I wondered if he might have been taught to program before he learned mathematics."

"That's not so strange. Children do that."

"Not to such an extreme as Saturn."

"Who's left?"

"Nobody, Doctor."

Chaz said, "Damn."

"Regarding your interface plug—"

"Yes, I tested it. You were right. After I wasn't sick enough to need supervision, they told me they turned off the finder feature. It was a lie. The thing is still sending my location. Saturn always knows where I am."

"Only that?"

"No, it's reading my pulse and temperature too. It's a decent lie detector."

"Whether Saturn arranged that or not, we must assume he has access. You left it still sending?"

"I did. *Who is he?*"

"Shall we reexamine our assumptions? First postulate: Only a Council member could intrude into your communication line at will. You may be better able to judge the truth of this than I. Can you think of a technique someone else might use?"

"No. I've tried. It wasn't some visitor, and we check the service people down to their DNA. I might still think of something." Chaz Kato, hacker. He'd never done that, never, and now it might cripple him. He'd known enough to protect his companies against hackers . . . sixteen years ago.

"Second postulate: Only a Council member, or one directly empowered to act in his service, could have blocked communications to Sri Lanka and implemented the lethal procedures used against Miss Myles. Dr. Kato, I know exactly how all of that was done. Only a Council member could pacify Security here and at Sri Lanka while monitoring the Napcap system too."

"One or more."

"Worth noting, but our only avenue is to Saturn. We find his allies by finding the individual who announced himself to you. Third postulate: Miss Myles attracted lethal attention because of something that happened on Xanadu. Fourth,

Miss Myles is essentially innocent. Her attempt to penetrate the air traffic control network is fiction. I have analyzed her fist; you were certainly right. She discovered something dangerous to Saturn. But was she innocent?"

"Have you—?"

"Lenore Myles did indeed share Levar Rusch's life and bed for nearly a year. She was faithful, and very busy at her studies. As for Rusch, he certainly organized the attack on Sandefjord. He procured the virus and arranged to move it to Antarctica."

"God! Could he have done it without Lenore's help?"

"Oh, yes, he certainly has that range of skills. Further, it was never Rusch's habit to confide in a lover."

"Where is he now?"

"That I could not learn. He vanished after the Antarctica incident. He may be dead. If not, he'll survive in some English-speaking region where his accent will not mark him. My estimate is that Lenore Myles did not share in his crimes and could not locate him now."

"Good!"

"Very well. Fifth," Lupus Nero said, and stopped to drink deeply from a quart-size glass of beer. "Ah. Miss Myles herself cannot help us unravel this mystery. Her memory of pertinent events was completely erased. Her mind has since deteriorated further—"

"Oh, God."

"Doctor, a cup of tea? Beer? A Calvados?"

"No, let's go on."

"Sixth, Saturn noticed Myles only after you gave her access to secured areas."

"Why?"

"She indulged in a dangerous sport, telemetrically operated thermal gliding, hours before you met. Saturn could have hurled her at a building, killed her or put her in a Xanadu hospital where he could work on her. Nobody's curiosity would have been roused, not even yours. And it was through you that she gained access to possible secrets. Elementary."

Chaz had to smile. "Good. So. What are your conclusions?"

"We know nothing of Saturn beyond what you learned during his attempt to kill Myles. The image 'Saturn' projected to you then matches no registered trademark, nor do its component parts suggest anything other than a carefully randomized ethnic and gender composite. I cannot match it to any member of the Council, nor to anyone directly connected to Council members, where such information is available. We have at this point examined the programming style of all persons who could possibly have access to such power."

Chaz said, " 'Saturn' was satisfied to let her live after wiping a portion of her memory. It couldn't have been a vengeance killing. It was preventive."

"It is suggestive that Saturn altered the record of her last research session."

Chaz nodded.

"She was not attacking an airport, but she was using a workstation. What *was* she doing? We can't read the record because Saturn wrote over it. What triggered her inquiry? Some conclusions might be reached if I had more access to the security tapes, all the comings and goings for Medical section for the hour before she began her research."

Chaz shook his head. "I can't do that."

Nero's simulacrum studied Chaz. "Do what you can. I have gone as far as I can with the present course of inquiry. Saturn's kinesthetic signature is no fiction, unlike Lenore's airport attack, but it doesn't match anyone with a legitimate, logical access to such power. I seem to be looking for the wrong 'Saturn.' "

"Suggestion?"

"The invisible postulate. We've assumed that the Saturn who confronted you is still waiting to be confronted."

"What?"

"You people alter yourselves in many ways," said the Nero persona. "You, Doctor, your knees have been replaced, you take chemicals to alter the behavior of the nerves in your brain, your exercise programs play you like a toy robot, and while you design and program computers, *they* shape *you*. Any Council member may have shaped himself into something beyond my grasp, by these means or by others known to you. Dr. Kato, this question wriggles in my mind like a double handful of fer-de-lances. Here am I, a mock-up of a fictional character from a line of puzzle stories. To know this is hard on my self-esteem. Here are you as you wish to be seen, and that too might be a matter of self-esteem. Here is Saturn, but is he human? Or a computer persona with an operator behind it, or a program running on its own? Or has he changed his intelligence and abilities until his programming technique is changed too? The Saturn we are investigating may be long gone. These are all possibilities, aren't they, Dr. Kato? I cannot explore them."

Chaz nodded. "But these suggestions lie squarely in my own line of research."

"A security officer could tell you much about the needs and fears and abilities of any Council member. Clarise Maibang is not Saturn. You have been intimate in the past. Try to pry something out of her."

Chaz logged off early. He should have time to exercise, to wear himself out. These sessions always left him twitchy, but this time he was in a rage. His mood might be noticed.

He stripped and chose a jump rope from his closet, a pulse-rate monitor built into the handles. "Sprint routine," he said loudly, and a hologram blossomed in front of him, an idealized version of his own body, dressed only in shorts, muscles rippling in shoulders and back. He'd never looked that good in his life.

The image took him though four minutes of sweaty warm-up followed by twenty wind-sprints: ten seconds of all-out action followed by a minute of lower-paced work. Ten cycles of this and his body was so filled with lactic acid, he was so oxygen starved, that all tensions were blotted out by pain and exertion. Five minutes of cool-down. Three minutes of stretches. A shower.

He felt human again. As he showered, he felt the muscles in his arms twitching a bit. He was still angry, but at least he was in control now.

All right. He remembered the computer's words:

*Try to pry something out of her.*

Such cynicism was very like Nero. Chaz had bottled his rage then. He already knew that he was going to have to involve Clarise.

He had been lonely. He'd spent a year letting go, mourning his fantasy Lenore. Now he needed the woman he had pushed aside. But—he flinched. Clarise would be easy to hurt, and he'd *seen* the depths of her anger.

# 22

"Ms. Myles, do you enjoy your work here?" The man asking the question looked like a thickset Viking, green eyes intense and earnest behind his full red beard. His fingers were folded tightly together, and he examined the woman sitting across from him with what he doubtless considered to be a paternal expression. His name was Cotter Thorson, and he was Executive Operations Officer of Washington Synaptech. A formidable power in the cybernetics field, Synaptech was located in a relatively rustic area of southern Washington, with a full-wall eastward view of Mount St. Helens.

The woman across the desk from him looked out through his office window at the spectacular view. Not fifty years before, the side of that mountain had exploded, leveling three hundred square miles and felling ten million trees. The eruption left a scar still visible after decades of slow growth, persistent weathering, and scrupulous cultivation.

While she studied the shattered cone she was watching her own reflection. A stranger. The face was somber and stern and devoid of makeup, the hair cut severely short. The eyes were a wounded animal's. If she had to make a snap judgment about the woman reflected in the mirror, she would say that she had done everything humanly possible to neuter herself.

Lenore Myles squared her shoulders and faced her employer. "Yes, sir," she said. *In fact, I'd probably say that I enjoy my work here more than any other aspect of my life.*

He regarded her carefully, like a horticulturist studying a prized botanical specimen suspected of harboring a parasite. "When we first invited you here we thought that your research would revolutionize the field. Your synthesized neural nets were bulkier but actually more sophisticated than materials developed in classified government laboratories. You were a find, Miss Myles. We still believe in you."

"But . . . ?" she said, encouraging him to continue. There was more, of course. She had been expecting this meeting. There was always more. *My dear, your work just isn't suitable. My dear, your work is excellent, but your coworkers have begun to complain . . .*

Or, most terribly, *My dear, your work is excellent, your coworkers adore you . . . and I was wondering if you were free for dinner this evening . . .*

It wasn't quite the horror she had anticipated, but still close enough for her to flinch.

"We think of Synaptech as a team, a family," Thorson said kindly. "Sixty hour work weeks are the norm. Such a workload is tolerable only if we function in unity, if we all understand and support each other, as might a family." He raised his hand to stifle any protest. "No, of course I'm not suggesting anything improper. But we've noticed that you haven't attended a single social function in your first eleven months."

She lowered her gaze. "I've been quite busy," she said miserably. She felt as if she were defending her sacred honor. "We're so close," she said. "The synthetic tissue has been accepted by forty-seven percent of the lab animals, but rejection varies with different kinds of damage. We're learning why."

Thorson nodded. "More successful with gross damage repair than toxic necrosis?"

She was desperately eager to shift the discussion from personal to professional problems. "Calcium ion buildup damages mitochondria in neuron cell membranes. That kind of microdamage is hard to detect. If we can't find it, we can't fix it. This is Alzheimer's and Parkinson's territory. We're making progress. . . ."

His smile widened without becoming either warmer or cooler. "I've been in this industry for forty years," Thorson said. "And one thing I've learned: There is always a breakthrough, always a project, always an emergency. I don't doubt the quality of your work or the depth of your commitment to this company. I *do* question your commitment to your own health. I don't know what is wrong, Lenore." His use of her given name created a one-way intimacy that made her squirm. "But I would like two things. First, I want you to visit the company psych unit."

Her protests died unborn in her throat. Synaptech's contracts placed them in intimate contact with corporate and government clients. Terrorism was up this past year. Sophisticated screening tests were used on anyone with access to the main computer grids, the prototype Linking system that was so rapidly transforming the world. Lenore could refuse to see a counselor, or she could keep her job. She couldn't have both.

"Yes, sir," she said.

"And second." His paternal mask was even more carefully in place. "I want to be careful about the way I say this. . . ." He sighed. "Because we are a small company, we occasionally have to double up on our duties. It was a research team member who originally toured you through the complex, and you have been asked to perform similar duties."

"In fact I have one this afternoon, sir."

"I know, I know." He waved at her. "Please, let me finish. Once upon a time, things like this were far easier to say, but we've all become so paranoid and litigious. One of the things noted on your earliest evaluations was that you conveyed . . . a certain *joy* in your life, in your work. It expressed itself in your carriage, and, frankly, in your dress."

He spoke on but she was already tuning him out.

*Oh, really, Mr. Thorson? Did you remember when I used to laugh? To wear makeup and dresses? Did you remember when I could sleep through an entire night without the need to claw, screaming, from my dreams?*

Lenore Myles thought but did not state those things. What she said was: "Do I meet your approval today, sir?"

Thorson nodded unhappily. "Your clothes are within company standard. Just . . ."

*Drab*. But her sense of style was *gone*. She allowed her butler system to assemble clothing directly from the company catalog. No better, no worse.

She felt itchy. Her need to end the meeting grew almost overwhelming. She stood, face wooden. "Yes, sir. I'll see the counselor. I need to get back to my work now."

She stood, and hurried from his office.


Thorson's mouth was slightly open, dumbfounded at her borderline rudeness. But there was something so hang-dog in her expression that he didn't have the heart to call her back. He watched the door as it closed, thrumming his fingers on his desk. Lenore's work was good, but she just didn't quite fit in. It might almost be better to have someone less brilliant, but more of a team player.

He chorded his desk plate. Her stats popped up in a vertical shimmer of light. Impressive. Most impressive. Over the last year, Lenore had contributed more to the project than any three coworkers. Nonetheless, she had a Negative Social Evaluation. She was slowing *them* down.

Before a first counseling two months before, her dress was often slovenly. A personal hygiene complaint red-tagged her file.

He drummed his fingers. Such complaints had been common for the Nerd Generation, the 1970s influx of graceless, unacculturated savants who first mastered the arcane syntax of computers. When Thorson first entered the tech field, every company seemed happy to have one of these troglodytes slaving away in the basement. This was a different time and place.

Even today, Thorson knew of companies where Lenore Myles's current incarnation would fit right in. They loved employees who lavished the kind of attention on their jobs that most preserved for newborn babies or teenage sweethearts. Drones who had no personal life, in office or out. Such middle-management zombies did valuable work before they burned out. Lenore would burn out soon.

There were financial moves afoot that might make a great deal of this moot, deals that would leave everyone, including the troubled and reclusive Miss Myles, quite wealthy when her division spun off and went public. He needed to keep her working and guided for another few months. Then, if she found herself at loose ends, so be it. Hell, he'd make certain she could afford the best therapists in the world.

Still, he sighed. This wan, drab, frightened creature was a far cry from the confident and vivacious woman he had interviewed two years ago.

Just two years.

So much can change in a few months, he mused. He turned to other business.

Horatio says 'tis but our fantasy,
And will not let belief take hold of him
Touching this dreaded sight, twice seen of us:
Therefore I have entreated him along
With us to watch the minutes of this night;
That, if again this apparition come,
He may approve our eyes and speak to it.

The monkey sat at the keyboard, its furry fingers a blur of motion. On the wall behind it, words appeared. The monkey stopped, looked around itself absently, picked at its butt for a moment, and then produced another line or two.

"At Washington Synaptech," Lenore said, reciting her practiced speech, "it doesn't take the proverbial ten billion monkeys on ten billion typewriters to duplicate the Bard's work." Her guests represented a panel of investors from around the world. They had little in common save the aura of wealth.

"The synthetic neural tissue is self-replicating within bounds. It can scavenge its own nutrients from the bloodstream. The implants are designed to interface with the surrounding human tissues."

"And caching? And speed of conductivity?" One of the investors, a little Japanese man with broad flat hands, was intensely interested. She had not learned his name. He was merely referred to as "a guest of the board," but acquisition rumors had been running through Synaptech for a month now.

"We could increase nerve speed tenfold or a hundredfold. Theoretically, we could achieve light speed." She shrugged. "It would serve no purpose."

"And why not?"

Lenore had the very definite feeling that he knew *exactly* why not. "Imagine a Swiss clock with its gears in perfect balance. Speeding up one gear doesn't make the clock more accurate. A human being is infinitely more complex and delicately balanced than any clock."

"So then, when does increased speed become useful?" he asked.

"At this early stage, largely in combination with cacheing." Caching broke tasks down into component aspects and handled them "locally," increasing speed by shortening nerve impulse travel time. The technique saved only thousandths of a second, but in some arenas, that was enough. "It makes for more effective jet pilots, shuttle jockeys, certain athletes, gymnasts, and dancers. In fact, the courts have already seen the first cases of illegal augmentation in professional sports."

"So? I thought that the process was still experimental?"

The monkey's fingers were a hairy blur. Words scrolled across the computer screens.

"Very true," she said. "But it leaks out. At the top levels of competition, thousandths of a second make the difference between gold and silver. . . ."

She stopped, staring at the small man's pleasant Japanese face. It was melting, like a glass doll subjected to a blowtorch.

Lenore frantically sank her fingernails into the flesh of her palm. The wave of pain shattered the illusion, and once again a pleasant, round-faced Asian regarded her politely.

Somehow she managed to complete the lecture without screaming.

Lenore wasn't entirely certain how she made it through the rest of her shift. The hallucinations were growing more severe, more bizarre: tastes melding into sounds, colors singing in metallic voices. She fought her way back to sanity a dozen times a day.

She was beyond exhaustion now, and no longer certain how or if she could continue to cope.

Traffic out to the Washington coast was light. She took the western strip, put her car on automatic, and let the 'pilot do the work.

In another, earlier life she would have taken joy in the surroundings, in the farmland and the mountains as she cut toward the ocean. Today she could do little more than lean back against the seat and close her eyes.

The sound of the monkey's *tap-tap-tap*ping filled her world.

Behind her closed lids floated something like a densely printed sheet of paper. A ragged hole was torn in the middle, as if someone had punched his fist through. Words flew from the typewriter, joining with the edges, but the words made no sense.

Wearily she raised her shirt and checked her left rib cage. There, a little higher than her elbow, was a rectangular flesh-tone bandage trickling medication into her system. It had browned slightly, warning of exhaustion. No wonder she had almost lost it on the job. Bless Tooley and her husband Mel for finding a chemical cocktail to hold her together. Far from comforting, the thought of her near addiction only deepened Lenore's sense of shame.

Numbly Lenore listened to the steady thrum of the car beneath her, and watched the mountains as they approached.

A terrible abyss gaped in her mind, in her past. Two days of time. Forty-eight hours on Xanadu. Gone. No therapist, no doctor had been able to coax them back.

And it was getting worse, by God. The hole was growing. If she didn't find a way to reverse the process, it was going to swallow her whole.

The ocean was a vast gray sheet, whitecaps rolling in toward the shore in impersonal, eternal rhythm. Northwestern beaches were harder, less fetching than their Southern California counterparts whether in Washington or a few miles south in Astoria, Oregon, her new home. Even in summer, there were more cold days than warm. But something about the gray desolation called to her. More than once she had thought of walking out to the waves, allowing them to embrace her, to gush in and fill the hole in her mind and heart.

Lenore had found a beachside condo in Astoria, a seaside tourist town in northern Oregon. A two-story wedge of wood and steel built in the '60s, it was weathered and comfortable, unencumbered by any sense of style. She had the upper floor. Her downstairs neighbor was an older man named Mark something, who taught virtual junior high classes from his living room.

Mark had attempted to engage her in conversations when she first moved in. She had tried to show polite interest in his studio, in his theories of child rearing and how a 40-percent reduction in teachers had benefited students ("you'll never get better schools until there's a penalty for being a bad teacher . . ."). The hole eventually began to eat its way into their conversations, until she began to feel like Alice's Cheshire cat, just a disembodied smile with no substance to sustain it. Perhaps he became wary of her increasingly glassy-eyed responses. His tea invitations had lapsed to almost nothing.

She accepted this, and in fact welcomed it.

She paused to gaze out at the ocean, eternal and beckoning. Her self-destructive thoughts, dark and terrible as they might have been, were also coldly comforting. *If it gets too hard, I have a way out. There is always a way out.*

The car parked itself. Lenore hurried out and up the stairs, ennui vanishing as she anticipated her regular call from Tooley.

Her room was a rat's nest of tumbled books and crumpled clothes. There were no decorations. A single window looked out onto the rolling Pacific. A convertible sofa heaped with books crouched in the middle of the living room.

A red triangle blinked on the wall screen. "Lenore," she said. It opened, revealing a new list of books to download. She highlighted two dealing with memory and one purporting to be a kiss-and-tell about the Floating Island chain.

But now that she was home from work, mental paralysis

began to set in. It was difficult to remember what she needed to do.

A sign on the wall, scrawled on poster board, said:

CHANGE CLOTHES
WASH FACE
EAT
CHECK MAIL

She nodded to her younger self, thanking herself for the foresight to create the note, and went through the steps, performing her afternoon ablutions. At the freezer, she popped out the first frozen meal tray she saw. There were over a hundred stuffed in the box, all purchased *en masse*, dumped in randomly to provide some semblance of variety. Guaranteed to provide all necessary nutrients.

She never noticed the taste.

Nearly a zombie, she stared through the door of the microwave as her food heated. She smelled the first savory whiffs and was aware of salivating, but still didn't move. Only the *ding* of a competed cycle roused her.

Lenore carried her meal to the couch and dumped enough books to the floor to clear a space. Another red bar appeared in the air. She spoke her name again, and Tooley's picture appeared.

As always, her friend's face was worried. "Lenore," she said. "You haven't returned my calls for two weeks, baby. I know you'd call me if there was an emergency, but you know how we pregnant women are: We worry about everybody."

Lenore shoveled a forkful of hot rice-and-something into her mouth. The pain of a scalded tongue brought tears to her eyes. That was fine. Pain told her that she was alive.

"But I understand, and I love you, and I just want to help. You wanted Mel to offer a second opinion on your tests. Still want it?"

"Please," Lenore said fervently. Tooley's husband Mel

was a stress expert, a clinical psychologist who ran a small empire from his home office. Career burnout was the least of her problems, but any trustworthy eyes and ears were priceless.

Tooley seemed relieved. "Good," she said, and the line blacked out, and Mel came on.

Mel was tall, pale, and bland. Ordinarily, his gold wire-rimmed glasses lent his features their only sense of proportion or balance, but when he smiled, eyes and cheeks and nose suddenly aligned, conveying an odd serenity. She hadn't seen that smile since the catastrophic Oahu vacation. She missed it terribly.

"Lenore," he said. "I got some of my associates to take a look at your tests. I know that you've been through the wringer on this. I've got good news and bad news." He harrumphed and seemed to consult mental notes before continuing. "You know there's nothing organic, but cross-referencing your tests, it looks as if someone or something deliberately created a schetoma. Psychological blank spot? Stole a chunk of your memory." He pushed his glasses up on his nose, as if he had suddenly smelled something distasteful. "Why, God only knows. If it was chemical, we certainly couldn't find it in your bloodstream. If psychological, say, trauma induced, then the trauma itself is hidden in that void. That's for your psychologists to look into."

"Yeah, right." Between the company and her own personal funds, she felt she had done little other than subject herself to a shrink's scrutiny for the last eight months.

"No lesions, no neurotransmitter dysfunction. I tell you, Lenore, my best guess is that someone or something has interfered with your brain's filing system."

"But there's no organic damage?"

"None."

She paused. "Then there's no reason to think that any memories were destroyed."

"Just made inaccessible, or misfiled. Look, there's a ton about the human mind we don't understand. But organizational systems are as critical as the information itself. Without it, well, imagine the Library of Congress with all of the volumes scattered randomly on the floor."

Hope flared in Lenore's heart, a lone flame in the darkness. The information wasn't gone?

Tooley returned to the screen. "What's the last thing you remember, hon?"

They had reviewed this over and over again. "I remember packing my luggage. I—" Wasn't there more?

Tooley glanced at her husband. "You used to remember the approach to Xanadu!"

"I used to! I remember telling you so!" Lenore felt a whimper building up inside her chest, but fought to keep it there. "The last thing I told you was that I had a wonderful time with this man Kato."

"And were considering his offer. But why hasn't he answered your queries? Doesn't that imply that something went wrong?" Tooley shook her head. "I'm only guessing. This is as far as I can go. But I have something else for you. Are you ready to encode?"

Lenore chorded a few buttons, and her system went crypto. Any attempt to intercept the discrete information packets would destroy the message itself. Either nothing came across, or the message was intact. There was nothing in-between.

She ran a series of filters on the packet, and an image appeared. One hundred percent Syntho—voice and image, Levar Rusche as he had appeared when she first met him five years ago.

He was unhandsome, unfashionably pudgy, and his mop of limp black hair simply begged for a slash-and-burn. But his eyes were feverishly intense, and his small straight nose was still somehow endearing. Rusche could be anywhere in the world, and might have changed his appearance in a dozen ways. By circuitous means Tooley had gotten a message to him: probably a list of questions, carefully drawn up, a statement of Lenore's basic situation as they understood it. Then copies were distributed to a select group of college friends each invited to make copies and distribute them to anyone whom they believed might know anything, and so on and so on, a fractal network branching and branching until it reached someone who truly knew.

Then the process had reversed, ending in a message left for Tooley to find on the seat of her car, or on her pillow, or in her web mail. And now it was with Lenore, and her hands trembled.

She had not seen him, not really thought about him in months. He was not a part of the hole chewing at the edges of her mind, that chasm yawning a little wider every day. He was on the far side of a canyon, a tiny, distant figure.

"Lenny," he said.

Tears ran from her eyes. She remembered the endearment. Remembered his touch, and the sweetness, even when both of them understood that they were heading in opposite directions in life. How could anyone have known just how opposite those directions would ultimately be?

She brushed her fingers into the air. It was merely a hologram of his face, but that was still as much human contact as she had allowed herself in a year. The sense of loss was devastating.

"Tooley says you're in trouble. I'll keep this brief. I'm giving you a web address where you can send queries. Use the encryption protocol attached to this message. If I don't acknowledge receipt within twenty-four hours, try again in three days. If you still get no word, I'm sorry, but the link has been compromised."

The face didn't change, but the voice was sadder. "I wish I could see you. What you're going through sounds terrible. But these are bad times for all of us. I warned you that it was coming, Lenny." The image sighed deeply. "Let me tell you what I think is going on, all right? I don't expect you to believe me, but I have to try to educate you.

"I think that this guy Kato raped you. Tooley told me he was trying to recruit you. I think you turned him down, and he just showed his true face, Len. That's the way these people are."

His eyes burned. She remembered Sandefjord. She had never known how deep his involvement ran. He said, "The Council is at war with the United Nations. Don't doubt it. As far as the Council is concerned, nationalism is an antiquated concept. Nations are dinosaurs lumbering toward the nearest tar pit. Be scared, darling. Assholes like this Kato respond to no law. He's protected on that floating island. There are no extradition treaties. They believe that they control enough of the banking, food, and power grids that they could collapse the world's economy. Problem is, they're probably right.

"They wanted you, and didn't get you, and now you have to ask yourself which side you're on. You used to be a fighter, darling. Who are you now? I've been hiding for three years, but sometimes you can see more from a basement than a tower."

*I'm beaten*, she thought. If she admitted that, he'd be gone. She was glad that he wasn't in the room with her. Levar. He'd been an important part of another life, back when she had believed in simple answers and happy endings.

Tears were running down Lenore's face. She wanted so much to see him. To Levar, the world was so simple, so Aristotelian. Good and evil, black and white. She could no longer pretend to understand her own heart, let alone the outside world.

When his message ran out, she considered for a few minutes, and then reread his directions. She was perfectly aware of her actions. Each time they communicated, the link between her and the Spinners would grow a little tighter. Every time she would edge a little closer to the most dangerous terrorists on the planet.

Were they? She was no longer certain. Only one thing was certain: Levar Rusche had cared about her. She needed him, needed some hope or reminder of normalcy.

"Levar," she began. "I'm so happy that you got my message. And so very, very happy that you answered it. I'm in trouble, and you may be the only person who can help. . . ."

# 23

Pepper Wiley found Chaz at the northern landing pad's observation window, just watching. Shuttles had winged in for hours, from Scandinavia and Burma, the Americas and Northern Africa. The pad was a seacrete declivity, thirty feet beneath Chaz and Pepper's protruding plastic bubble-perch.

In all, Xanadu expected to host eleven hundred dignitaries arriving for the yearly Councilor conclave. They alternated among the first four Floating Islands. Chaz would be happy when the fifth and sixth were completed, so that the responsibility could be more equitably distributed.

She tugged at his arm. "Boss, we have to get ready for the Circus." Pepper was in her early fifties, with starched blond hair and a model's body, and stood an inch under five feet tall.

"The Circus." he sighed. This was vacation time for many. Council members rarely appeared in person, but they all sent representatives and staff, and the staffers took the opportunity to fly in wives, husbands, and families. All of the guests carried priority cards, all of them would demand security attention and personnel resources better invested elsewhere.

A red-and-silver wing-shaped VTOL swooped in from the north, hovered, then landed in a flurry of heat distortion.

As Pepper pulled him away, a Filipino dirigible nudged toward a docking tower like a sleepy whale.

Too many people, too little time.

Navigating the hallway, Chaz allowed Pepper's chatter to return him to the matter at hand. "—Minsky has been working with the setup. We've got the programs strung together. I just have to keep them in order."

"That's the job, Pepper," he said, instantly regretting his irritable tone.

Before she could answer, a phalanx of large Japanese men approached him. As they grew closer he revised his initial estimate of their size: Three were somewhat shorter than average, four rather larger. But their presence, their *aura*, perhaps, was huge.

The man in the middle, the quiet one, was Yamato, Councilor-level master of a solar, geothermal, nuclear, and petro-energy empire. Yamato's alter ego was Joe Blaze, the Malibu beach boy. The large four would be bodyguards, no doubt, although no one wanted to believe that necessary on Xanadu.

They'd have been thoroughly scanned before Yamato ever approached him. Yamato looked to be in his forties, very strong and hale-looking. He was, according to public record, in his late sixties. Soon, Chaz knew, Yamato would "die," to be reborn as a distant cousin or grandson.

"Kato-san," Yamato said. "It has been too long." Chaz bowed slightly, then shook the proffered hand. Yamato glanced at his men and then drew Chaz to one side. "Kato-san. I would like the opportunity to speak with you." He paused. "Privately."

Chaz looked at this man, levels above his own station, and had the distinct feeling that the Council elder had contrived this meeting, that he had, in fact, come to Xanadu just for such face-to-face contacts. Chaz looked at Pepper, who shrugged. They might well be on a timetable, but he could not refuse to speak with a Council member.

"Pepper," Chaz said. "I'll catch up with you." She nodded uncertainly, then hurried on.

"Come to a Silence room," Yamato said. Without waiting

for a reply, Yamato turned and strode swiftly away.

Chaz noticed that the smallest of Yamato's coterie watched him as he followed. The man moved with a curiously flat-footed gait. His palms were flat, his fingers thin and strong-looking, with a slight tendency to crook. Almost like claws, those fingers.

Chaz felt a chill of recognition, although for the life of him he couldn't remember if or where or under what circumstances he had met this man, with his strong, flat, callused hands and a mouth as expressionless as a shark's.


One of the most vital and valuable commodities in the early twenty-first century was privacy. Existing outside of any national waters, the Floating Islands could offer absolute security for meetings of any kind: political or economic, National or Councilor. They maintained a strict policy of neutrality even when Council business was directly involved.

Yamato took him to one of the smaller rooms, just large enough for a desk and four men. His host sat and then smiled at him, gesturing toward the chair opposite.

For almost a minute Chaz waited patiently, and at last opened his mouth to begin the conversation. Yamato held up a cautioning finger and then looked at his wristwatch, which gave no sign of being anything other than an expensive timepiece.

He smiled again. "A minute has passed, and we have not been disturbed," he said. "If it had been possible for my subordinates to compromise this room in any manner, we would have been interrupted and warned."

"Mr. Yamato, Xanadu's security is legendary. In fact—"

"I need no reassurances." Yamato's voice flattened with irritation. "I have just received all of the reassurance that is required. Now, then, let me come to the point."

"Please do."

Yamato spent a moment gathering himself, then spoke. "I

would like you to design a new linkage network."

"Excuse me?"

"Kato-san," Yamato said expansively. "You are a great expert on the linking of biological and cybernetic organisms. The current technology is available to the wealthy and powerful. A bare handful, less than a hundred human beings, has access to the full spectrum of services available. I believe that the price and complexity of the overall process can be reduced considerably."

"I have thought so for many years," Chaz said. He didn't want to admit it, but this cool, aloof man had triggered several of his most personal buttons.

"I have seen some of your experimental results, and they are superlative."

"But untested on human beings."

"I have men and women willing to accept such risk."

Chaz felt the excitement grow. "And?"

"And as a result of this, you would accrue sufficient power to raise you to Councilor level."

There it was. The carrot he had awaited for sixteen years, his entire "second" life. His value had been acknowledged, and a sponsor had arrived. He could implement his lifework, reduce the cost of linkage to the level that it would be available to the average upper-middle-class world citizen, and within a generation after that, available to all.

"No, Kato-san" Yamato said softly. He might have been reading Chaz's mind. "Not available to all."

"To whom, then?"

"To all Japanese."

Chaz closed his eyes hard. He could pretend not to understand, to be dumbfounded, to be angry or disappointed. He was none of those things. This was just more of the same provincialism and simple pettiness that had divided the world for thousands of years.

*Please, God*, he said to himself. *Not thousands more.*

"Mr. Yamato. This is not what I have given my life to. I am sorry, and I hope that you will not take offense."

Yamato smiled at him as he might have regarded a child. "I knew it would not be easy for you to hear my words, Dr. Kato. But please bear with me. In the growing world economy, nations are falling. Half a dozen African and South American nations have already dissolved, 'Gone Corporate,' as they now say. We are losing our boundaries: Geography and language no longer define us. I merely wish to protect those joined to us by blood. In a homogenized world, the small nation of Japan will be mongrelized out of existence."

"Is this the worst that can happen?" Chaz asked. "Isn't this preferable to war, or starvation, or plague? We can control all of these things, if we can work together." His voice rose and thinned. "We have to look to our future."

Yamato's eyes blazed. "We can *control* the future. And we must, or die as a people. Kato-san, I have researched your family. You are of a warrior house. Your father died in Italy, fighting for a country that dishonored him. I know that you once kept an Indonesian peasant woman." Chaz stiffened, and anger tightened his eyes. "And for years were enamored of a Caucasian. Still, I ask you to remember our heritage, which cannot survive without minds and hearts like yours."

Yamato reached into his jacket pocket, extracting a sheaf of papers. He laid them upon the table and covered them with his own broad, flat hand. A warrior's hand. Chaz suspected that this man spent an hour every day practicing kendo or iaido, ancient sword arts that connected men like Yamoto to their ancestors, men of armor and steel, warlords and nobility, Samurai and shoguns.

Chaz picked up the papers and read.

And was astounded. These papers represented title to unbelievable wealth and power. Yamato could offer them to him, just that simply. Just like that.

He closed his eyes. What would his father have given to be offered such bounty?

And yet, ultimately, it was the memory of his father's face that hardened his resolve.

"Yamato-san," he said carefully. "I am a simple man. For many years I have thought only of perfecting these tools and sharing them. There may be much of merit in what you say. Would you give me some time to think?"

Yamato studied him, as if already aware of Chaz's ultimate decision. He nodded his massive head slowly. "As you wish. Take a week. And then give me the only sane answer."

He stood and extended his hand. Chaz shook it and locked eyes with the Councilor. Deep within the folds of Yamato's dark eyes, he saw a lineage of warriors who could never stop fighting, regardless of the cost.

He could not resist such a force. But he could not become one with it either. There was no easy resolution to this problem.

And a tiny, irritating voice whispered in Chaz's ear: *Does Yamato stand with Saturn?*

He had to talk to Nero.

Yamato rejoined his bodyguards. Together, in a phalanx, they moved toward one of the main conference rooms.

The man who worked his way in toward Yamato was shorter than the rest. His face was flat and expressionless, although it was capable of great animation when the occasion demanded. He could be a clown, or a priest, or an emotionless killer. A year ago, in Java, he had played the role of an anxious businessman. Weeks ago, in Washington, he had asked rehearsed questions of a troubled Lenore Myles.

"It is pleasant here," said Hiroshi Osato.

"I am not satisfied with the service," Yamato replied.

"I will have a word with the management," said Osato, completing the code sequence.

And without another word the little man broke away from the others. Using his guest pass, Osato unobtrusively rode elevators and sliding sidewalks to the base of the eastern tower.

The Xanadu Recreation Zone was a miniature amusement park, a gaudy marvel of neon and glowing, percolating fluids circulating through a fantasy forest of plastic tubes. A steady flow of vacationers lined up for entrance to the pools, the tennis courts and weight rooms, the myriad games and amusements . . . and the hang-gliders.

Osato rented a locker, safety harness, and a half-hour's computerized gliding.

The girl who rented them to him smiled, all perfect white teeth and golden European hair. Osato returned her sunny expression without revealing anything of his own emotions.

"Have you used a glider before?" she asked cheerily.

"Yes," he answered. "But not at this facility."

"Well, until you've charted twenty hours, you'll be on-line with the recreation system. The thermals are artificial. It's waste heat from the OTECs pumped into three of the ponds. We have one of the largest artificial gliding ranges in the world."

"Your reputation is excellent." Osato smiled charmingly. She rented him a large red set of wings with super-strong foamed steel struts and a cultured spider-silk fabric of almost preternatural resilience.

He suffered through a short holo presentation on the automated gliding system with a dozen other vacationers. From the corners of his eyes he looked at them, marveling at their weakness, their infantile softness. Comfort had made their men into women and their women into children.

Osato loved children. The very young should play, should cheer, should dance in the sun. But then the path to adulthood must be shown. Osato himself had begun that journey at the age of ten. By twelve he had taken his first glider off the cliffs of that island north of Hokkaido and south of the Kuril Islands, an island known only by the Ainu word for "home."

There the Five Families had made a home, and there Osato had spent his childhood and taken his first flight. He had been frightened, but would never have allowed his terrifying father to see that in him. He was Ninja, as was his father, and his father before him. He would master his fears, or he would die. His passage to adulthood had been the gate between life and death.

Today, only duty compelled him.

He joined the line leading to the elevators. Soon he would be on the roof, would dive into the thermals under control of the main computers. And then the game would truly begin.

Arvad Minsky twitched in his chair. His eyes and scalp were obscured by a silver induction helmet, but his thin lips whispered inaudible secrets.

Chaz closed the door behind him quietly. Minsky was hooked into one of the kino inputs and wouldn't want to be disturbed. Chaz didn't know which program currently obsessed Minsky but guessed that it would be one of the dolphins or squarks in action.

Chaz waited politely, standing. There were two chairs in Minsky's little control nook, but Arvad had his feet up on the second. The nook was on the ocean floor, six hundred meters beneath Xanadu and halfway between floating and undersea cities.

When five minutes had passed, Minsky sighed massively, then slipped off the helmet and blinked rapidly. His eyes were unfocused; his high, freckled forehead glistened with perspiration.

Chaz pretended not to notice. That momentary confusion was the inevitable by-product of jumping from virtual physiology to the real thing. A lengthier disorientation period was a sure symptom of the kino addict. And as much as Chaz liked Arvad Minsky, and admired him (he was the only Council member Chaz could even remotely consider a friend), the man was a full-blown wirehead.

The camera eye found Chaz; then the other. As if he had thrown a switch, Minsky bounded up to shake Chaz's hand.

"I'm telling you. You really should try kino just before you go into the water. Change your entire experience."

"I'm sure," Chaz said warily.

"You only think you understand. There's a time lag where it seems you have ghost flippers and fins. You experience both sets of limbs at the same time."

"Sounds yummy. Do you have an itinerary for the Circus today?"

Minsky couldn't disguise his disappointment. "You should expose yourself to more new experiences, Chaz. You'll stagnate."

"I tell myself that every day. Come on. The Scouts are waiting."

A sharp, moist breeze plucked at Hiroshi Osato. Atop the tallest of Xanadu's towers, two hundred meters above sea level, two dozen flyers waited for their green light, back behind a roped-off line, wings politely folded at their backs.

Six meters along the textured runway, two attendants read the results as weather satellites microanalyzed Xanadu's synthetic and natural thermals, awaiting the moment to motion him forward. Timing was critical. The gliding control system could monitor a dozen fliers at a time, but more might overload the system. Osato twisted his thin lips to match the silly grins favored by most of the others.

The "go" light flashed green and the attendants urged him to flight. He felt the motor servos in his backpack hum, tensing and releasing wires running through his wing's hollow "bones." Hyperthin fabric began to breathe and flex. He walked, trotted, sprinted toward the edge. A tuning-fork chime sounded in his ears, to warn him that he'd passed the point of no return. Osato felt his feet leave the edge and *he was falling!*

*He was flying.* So tightly focused had Hiroshi Osato been that he hadn't allowed himself to remember the sheer *joy* of the experience. It wasn't quite a sensation of weightlessness:

His body pressed against the wing's padded straps. But as wing and body moved in the same direction at the same speed, the sensation of freedom grew almost too rich for mere human senses.

The breeze was sharp against his face now, but with Xanadu's computers in control he could simply relax and float. The terraces and jeweled ocean glittered beneath him, brilliant blue out to a distant horizon.

Freedom! Osato had never experienced anything quite like it, and the voice he forever tried to silence said: *Life is brief, and what means duty when I can fly?*

Discipline reasserted itself. He remembered who and what he was.

Below him, thousands of vacationers strolled the terraced parks, wandered the groves leading to the breakwaters, swam in the lagoons. Some of them pointed up at the gliders, perhaps envying their freedom or their courage.

How did Osato feel about them? He knew things that would influence their lives forever. His hands were among those controlling the reins of destiny. Yet, at the moment, he allowed himself to feel very little. Yamato was an important client, perhaps his most important. It was time to fulfill a contract, that was all.

Osato plucked at his belt and engaged special apparatus smuggled onto Xanadu from his island home. Very quietly it disengaged the glider's computer guidance and placed the glider under the control of his own muscles.

This had to be accomplished without alerting the main system. No one could know that hidden in this group of beginners was a single expert who chose to fly with skill alone.

Immediately the air seemed *filled* with gliders, although the closest were still a hundred meters away. Xanadu's recreational air traffic system had maintained the distance effortlessly. With eleven other sets of wings gliding in and out, Osato needed eyes in all directions. Even a near collision would be enough to alert the safety system.

Fear squeezed his chest like iron fingers. Disaster loomed. He needed to feel the air, to stay flexible, like a surfer seeking oneness with a wave.

Osato glanced at the ground and for the first time in decades felt stark raving vertigo. The primal terror of falling filled and overwhelmed him. He envisioned himself careening off a tower, smashing into another glider and plunging lock-winged and screaming into the picnickers below.

He locked his mind on the task before him. His abnormally wide peripheral vision glimpsed a wing swooping in from the right. It was still perhaps sixty meters distant, but he had to hare off in the other direction, spiraling around the tower, into the restricted zone leading to a cluster of penthouses.

As he entered the space, the electronics on his belt intercepted the challenge signals and disarmed them, rendering him functionally invisible to the security system. A few more seconds, just a few more. Panic still hammered at him.

He crossed the edge of the roof and swooped in. He landed running, running, dropping, spinning to cut his forward momentum. He cut himself out of his harness and rolled to a halt ten feet from the far edge.

He ended in catlike balance, his body performing perfectly despite the fear that had overwhelmed his conscious mind. An observer would have seen a perfect landing executed with exquisite physical control and iron will. Discipline. Fear was replaced by pride in performance. Pride, and a sudden eagerness to complete his business so that he could don harness once again and glide to the parks far below.

He rose to his feet and approached the front portal of Chaz Kato's penthouse.

It would aid his mission if he could enter, but he needn't. First he sprayed windows outside the living room, kitchen, sauna. One *spritz* and a camera was splayed across glass in strands too thin to see, a fiber optic spiderweb spread to catch light. Without a power source it could only record, but a laser from outside would flash those pictures back to the source.

The Council might know these techniques. The same laser flashed from *inside* would record what was *outside:* the face of Hiroshi Osato. Though he was disguised, it was a risk. The cameras might be washed off or rained off; that was a risk too.

There was only the one door. Osato's instruments detected nothing in the way of electronic defenses. He bent to examine the lock and realized it was open.

Who was this fool who lived as if nothing could ever threaten him? Or were there defenses too subtle even for the Ninja? Osato slipped inside like a breath of wind.

No need to spray windows again. It often amused him to spray a mirror or a glass dining table, but he saw something better.

A line of monitor screens, high up, antiques that would never be used again.

With a glee that never reached his face, Osato sprayed his cameras on the glass. *Dr. Kato, your computers are looking at you!*

# 24

Underwater, Minsky was far more lithe and agile than he could ever have been on land. Chaz still remembered his friend at a Xanadu reception for Krup, the German Councilor with the largest industrial empire in all Europe. Arvad Minsky must have been slightly inebriated, because when a pair of pale sirens lured him onto the dance floor, he had exhibited all the grace of a beached narwhal.

Underwater, however, he moved more like a fish than a

man. With fluid, powerful strokes, his entire body coursed as if he were born for this, or had made himself over in the image of a great, aquatic predator.

Arvad led two dozen of them down toward three of the larger structures in Squark City. One was a skeletal dome, one a spire, and one an inverted arch. It would have looked strange by itself, but in the midst of the other construction it seemed very much at home.

Behind them, chef Anson Teil and the Sea Scouts formed a rough wedge. Behind wide faceplates, their faces glowed with excitement. This was only the second time that the Scouts had been allowed into the experimental area. It was a treat, a precursor to an even greater gift in the possible future: In a few months, several of the kids might come down and work in Squark City itself. Sea Scout merit badges were hard to earn, but squark duty would be a sure route.

Doors and hallways were wider in the sections populated primarily by sharks than those frequented by the dolphins: Size and temperament were important considerations. These hybrid hunters didn't appreciate crowding. In either case, the shark passageways were diamond-shaped, the dolphin doors circular. Those for general usage were squares. Again, a little additional respect for their guests' instincts. No one wanted an experimental bite taken out of a passing flank. Dolphin blood in the water would be bad for everyone.

A few sharks cruised through the hallways. Chaz looked back over his shoulder again: The Sea Scouts swam in a tighter bunch, and Clarise swam with them to one side, her shark prod at the ready. There was no genuine concern: When visitors invaded, all of the sharks in the area were tightly controlled by their computer routines. There was no more real danger than in riding a shark-shaped carousel. However, caution in all things . . .

Twin tentacles emerged from a shadowed hallway, followed by the clumsy bulk of a tiger-striped squark. It carried a bundle of reinforcement rods in two tentacles. The weight drew it toward the floor, and it was using the other grafts almost like legs.

Minsky continued to lecture the Scouts. "We've come a long way. If we program the basic maneuver of rod connection and then implant a basic geometric template, squarks will work virtually twenty-four hours a day, obsessively, to complete the shape of the arena—"

"Excuse me, but doesn't that hurt them?"

Minsky looked around at the scoutmaster. He said, "It kills them, Mr. Teil. We've learned to allow for a dozen short feeding breaks. Then they seem to be all right. We've actually leased worker squarks to one of the undersea farms off Borneo. We've been quiet about it, but the initial research indicates success."

Success, right, Chaz remembered, except that in Borneo and Brazil they kept cutting back on the feeding breaks . . . like nineteenth-century robber barons. Third Worlders just didn't understand capitalism.

They emerged from a hallway into an unfinished section. Much of this complex was designed to simulate a squark–human interface, a place where both species might interact with maximum comfort. Pressurized air chambers and corridors featured transparent walls. On the far side, flooded hallways allowed human and scalien to "walk" side by side. On the far side of this transparent wall was an immense underwater arena.

The group crowded into a lock. Water drained out. The Sea Scouts scrambled from their suits. Twenty of them, carrying genes from four different continents; they were energetic, hyperalert, and fascinated.

As soon as they passed safely into the observation chamber, Chaz and Minsky left them with Clarise and exited through a far lock, back into the water arena.

Months before, the engineers had blown holes in the ocean floor, carting away tons of stone. A skeletal kilometer of dome rose above that man-made pit. Nobody thought to pressurize it: The forces involved would have tested the most advanced materials in the world. Here advanced scalien training exercises and experiments were conducted. Few were witnessed by outsiders.

Bottle-nosed Manny and Trish appeared, nosing Chaz and Minsky affectionately. Trish led Minsky away while Manny took up his position next to Chaz.

Chaz swam to the middle of the big bubble, adjusted his buoyancy, and hovered. Back in Minsky's control room, Pepper switched on a bank of dancing colored lights and rolled the big gates back.

"Ladies and gentlemen," Chaz said grandly. Pepper would add reverb, echoing his words through the crowded viewing chamber. "Would you please direct your attention to the center ring . . . where, for your viewing pleasure, the wizards of Xanadu will present the one and only master of the finny denizens of the deep—"

Memory, shockingly strong, flooded him. He remembered dusty streets, long, low, greenish-brown buildings. *Japanese children, Japanese men and women. White American soldiers. A different arena.*

He shook himself out of it. "I now present Arvad the Magnificent and his aquatic entourage!"

The gates swung the rest of the way open, and Minsky rode in on the back of his favorite success story, Barrister.

An enormous Great White shark, Barrister had two different varieties of augmentation: computer linkage and a gel-brain "backpack," a synthetic neural network surgically attached to his skull. He could learn. Barrister was probably as intelligent as a mildly retarded adult, and as cunning as a wolf.

But now Barrister was as docile as a pony. He carried Minsky around and around in a circle as Chaz played ringmaster. His flattened boneless arms splayed out like airfoils: extra fins.

Pepper whispered in his ear. "All right, Chaz. Stand by for the next phase."

The opening notes of Chopin's "military" polonaise rang

through the arena, audible in Chaz's helmet as well as the
observation room.

Doors opened at the north and south end of the dome,
and a flotilla of sea creatures entered.

A dozen smaller sharks swished through the water in
rhythmic lockstep. A dozen dolphins followed, each sway-
ing back and forth in time. Chaz stole a glance at the Scouts,
and they were clapping along delightedly. God, he loved
this.

The tentacled squarks were slower than Barrister. The
oldest were clumsier too, though they looked like the rest.
Some had too little sensitivity in their "arms." Some were
too sensitive: They swam to protect their tentacle clusters
from pain, and it threw them off. Always the altered shapes
threw their aerodynamics off. Only Barrister had gristle-
backed fingers and flat hands, fins to guide his flight.

Minsky led Barrister through his paces, gliding through
the water with the facility of a rodeo star, and no cowpoke
had ever guided his pinto so well. Barrister and Minsky
moved as a single creature. Chaz sighed with contentment.

Dolphins and squarks began to weave in and out among
each other, a choreographed water ballet reminiscent of
something from M. C. Escher. They swirled, they played,
they dazzled.

The slow, sensuous winding of Ravel's *Bolero* filled the
water. Minsky and Barrister led the others on a spiral to the
top of the dome and then looped down, trailing the other
Scaliens like a majorette trailing a ribbon. Around and
around the dome they went, the music an embracing coun-
terpoint to their gyrations.

Minsky guided his mount over to Chaz. The two of them
changed positions for the next bit. The Sea Scouts cheered
as Chaz waved bravely to them from his mount upon the
goggle-eyed Great White. Chaz couldn't feel the rough surface of Barrister's body through his diving suit's legs, but
his hands were naked. Barrister's broad back felt like
thousands of tiny teeth. Chaz couldn't get his legs around

him as he could a horse's flank: Barrister was much too large. It was more like riding a go-cart, with his legs and upper body at a 120-degree angle.

As Minsky magnanimously lectured and led the children's cheers, the Circus continued. Fish and mammals dove and swarmed. Dolphins left the array in synchronized phalanxes to spend a few seconds breathing in special oxygen hutches conveniently placed around the arena, seamlessly rejoining the parade a minute later.

Chaz wasn't sure anyone could see his face, but he bravely kept a smile plastered there, waving his hands with a ride-'em-cowboy enthusiasm as Barrister took him for a spin. He had never liked roller coasters, but Pepper and Minsky had talked him into this—

Barrister took a loop *hard*, and Chaz almost lost his lunch, thinking that he was going to *kill* that woman when he got through entertaining the Scouts.

Then he realized that something actually was wrong. Barrister was in trouble. His Great White mount was losing synch with the music, tossing his head this way and that, writhing and plowing through the water, biting and snapping at invisible enemies.

Chaz hung on for dear life. The other animals, shark and dolphin, were only partially controlled by the computer system. Whatever remained of their natural instincts recognized Barrister's behavior for what it was:

*Frenzy.*

The organized choreography disintegrated. Sharks and dolphins fled in all directions.

"What the hell is going on?" Chaz shouted. Barrister slammed him against the dome wall. Chaz's teeth gashed his tongue.

Pepper was on his headset almost instantly. "*Chaz—oh, God—I've got the wrong program here!*" Barrister's big flat hands gripped at one of the smaller dolphins, pulled it close to the terrible mouth. Blood boiled the water.

"*Well, dammit, shut down, shut down! No, wait—*" If we shut down, the animals will return to their natural state.

They'd follow their instinctive patterns again. Barrister would remain in Frenzy mode, continue his attack.

*"Shut down!!"* Minsky's voice was distorted with horror. Chaz was nauseated by the red-black clouds filling the water. The hapless dolphin flailed in Barrister's grasp, life ebbing.

Every instinct told him to flee, but Chaz dared not leave his harness. Barrister would turn on him in an instant. There was a Chinese proverb about riding the tiger . . .

The problem, it seemed, was dismounting.

The Sea Scouts stared up at him with their mouths hanging open, as if unable to believe that this wasn't all just part of the show. Mr. Teil knew. He was herding the Scouts gently backward, away.

Another squark veered too close to Barrister. The augmented Great White surged, whiplashing Chaz, and chomped one of its grafted arms in half. Shark blood mingled with dolphin.

"Dammit, Pepper!" Minsky sobbed. "Full shutdown on all Squarks!"

The other squarks immediately went into neutral, lethargically floating, maintaining barely enough momentum to keep them breathing.

For an instant Chaz felt relief, then realized that Barrister was still attacking. Barrister's "third lobe" made his augmentation more independent. Simply shutting him down wasn't going to be quite so easy.

But Minsky saw it too, and was thinking fast. "Take the dolphins off all control."

Frantic Pepper might have been, but to her credit, she responded almost instantly. The dolphins responded with their natural instincts. A school of dolphins knew how to protect itself from a single shark.

They swooped into attack formation, diving, evading beautifully, ramming Barrister from varied angles, eeling away whenever he turned to snap.

Every strike enraged Barrister and shook Chaz. Barrister wheeled away, gathering himself for another attack. Chaz took that moment to calm his voice and bark a command to Pepper. "Get the Scouts out of here. Call retreat for the Squarks."

Barrister thrashed toward the top of the dome. Chaz lost sight of the kids. He saw the squarks line up for retreat. Another dolphin rammed Barrister, and Chaz screamed as his leg splintered. Barrister tried to reach the retreating squarks, and the dolphins rammed him over and over, thunderous impacts that *had* to cause internal damage and left Chaz screaming in agony.

The torn squark drifted by. It had to be dead; its head was nearly torn apart, but the soft plastic bulge of a computer add-on was still in place and its tentacles thrashed weakly. Barrister attacked it viciously. Chaz was whipped side to side. His faceplate filled with blood. The whipping motion broke a seal somewhere, and water began leaking, spraying his hair, trickling down into his eyes.

He couldn't breathe and was losing the power of coherent thought. All he could think, all he could bring into his mind was the repeated words:

*Oh, God, get me out of this. Oh, God, if you get me out of this, I swear that I'll find a way to thank you. Oh, God, don't let me die. . . .*

And a final thought: *Is someone killing me?*

And then blackness.

# 25

In mathematically precise array, sharks and squarks and dolphins paraded across the landscape of his mind. If he could guide what he was riding . . . but always he made some misstep, always the dance ended in thrashing bloody chaos.

Chaz was only vaguely aware of himself. He floated, an egoless, disembodied thing, just beneath the surface of consciousness. He heard voices: familiar, comforting voices. People he trusted and respected were caring for him, healing his body. He'd done this dance before. It was safe and perhaps even prudent to sink back down into the depths.

Chaz drifted back to a recent, curious thought.

*Manzanar.*

Strange. He rarely thought about the place where, seventy years ago, his young life had changed so drastically. Well-meaning people called Manzanar a concentration camp, where America's Japanese had been imprisoned much like Germany's Jews. The comparison was specious. Terrible the Japanese plight, humiliating their disenfranchisement, but there was little deliberate cruelty and no murderous intent behind Executive Order 9066, the document that turned thousands of peaceful Japanese fishermen and business folk into aliens in their own land.

His parents weren't considered Americans, and doubtless some of the soldiers who patrolled the fences considered them less than human. But they weren't demonized. True, Manzanar was a world apart, with barracks and mess halls and recreation centers. But the showers poured forth only tepid water, and the ovens baked only bread and meat.

Born April 30, 1938, Chaz entered Owens, California's Manzanar relocation camp, in April of 1942, too young to really understand what had happened to his family. Two years later, no family remained. His father died in Italy in the summer of '44 fighting Nazis. Shintaro Kato died to prove he was a good American. Shintaro's wife died of pneumonia the following winter, despite medicine and medical care provided by white American doctors. The doctors were solicitous, almost painfully polite, and . . . embarrassed. They seemed humiliated by their government's efforts in the name of national security.

But solicitous or not, embarrassed or not, ultimately their

skills and medications could not hold back the infection. His mother slipped away, only seven months after his father's death.

No deadly showers. No hideous, stinking ovens. But Manzanar did have a graveyard, and Chaz's six-year-old heart lay buried there.

In dream, Chaz followed himself through the postwar years. His former Manzanar neighbors, the Yamaguchis, gave him a back room to live in. Decent, hardworking folks, the Yamaguchis were old enough to be his grandparents.

He never suffered for want of food or clothing. The Yamaguchis never spoke ill of the dead, but in a thousand oblique ways they informed him that they resented his presence in their home. He was a financial burden, an invasion of their precious privacy, and a remembrance of humiliations past, but the Yamaguchis were too noble, too spiritual, dammit, too *Japanese* to turn him out into the American foster care system.

He studied, and slept, a boy who had left his childhood behind barbed wire in Northern California.

In school, and later in the job market, he found one solace, one salvation:

Work.

His family died because they were anonymous Japanese. To survive, to have any hope at all, Chaz had to prove his worth.

He had nothing that could be reasonably considered a social life. His excellent university work earned him his first job, at Motorola in 1959, at the age of twenty-one. Chaz numbed himself with killing hours. Murderous hours, hours long enough to crush the pain, to kill any chance of relationships, to test his sinew and spirit to the breaking point.

Money and fame followed, and also a hollow sense of incompletion. He drank too much and spent too many nights alone. Solitude was intolerable, companionship often worse.

And then Ako appeared in his life.

Her face rushed up to him as through a long, empty tunnel. A deep, carefully hidden lode of repressed emotions exploded into life. The detonation was massive and quiet, like Ako's presence. She was as strong and intelligent as his father, as gentle and irresistible as his mother. She labored in Motorola's marketing division, a graphic artist of scintillant talent. She had that rare and valuable ability to lose herself completely in her work and seemed as egoless as a snowflake.

They met playing softball at a company picnic. She was a bit plumper than the American ideal. Her dark hair was bound back, round face and eyes shining. Chaz burned, like Saul on the road to Damascus. For days he avoided her, understanding quite well that she would change his life forever.

But Ako made decisions for the both of them, arranging affairs so that their paths continually intersected. At first he naively considered it accidental when Motorola's in-house magazine ran a series of in-depth interviews with the engineering staff. "Coincidentally" Ako organized and coordinated the photo shoots and interviews.

Chaz never had a chance.

No matter where he turned, there was Ako. Even when she wasn't there, she was there. When he began waking from terrible dreams of barbed wire and armed soldiers, her name on his lips, her face in his eyes, he knew that she was his angel, his only hope of salvation.

Ignoring fear for the first time in his life, Chaz pushed aside all reserves and did the best and sanest thing he had done in his thirty-three years of existence:

He asked her to lunch.

Until now, Ako had been chatty and professional, but sitting at one of Golden Szechwan's back tables, she seemed overcome by shyness, and barely met his eyes. He breathed her scent, relishing the delicate way she seasoned her rice, the way her white, perfect teeth gleamed behind every smile. Every word and action reminded him of his mother. The smooth pale expanse of her arms recalled the blessed comfort of his childhood, triggering a rush of memory so intensely visceral he had to excuse himself for a moment. Splashing cold water on his face in the rest room, Chadwick Kato gazed at the man in the mirror, seeing someone on the threshold of rebirth or destruction. He gratefully chose life.

Their courtship lasted a year, the happiest of his life. They were married at a chapel in Marin, with two priests: Taoist and Presbyterian. His new life was one of hard work and sacrifice, triumph and setback, late nights and early mornings.

Ako believed in him completely. She sacrificed her full-time job to create a home office. He did not ask her to do this. Her friends seemed to think that she was slightly mad. But he remembered lying with her by the fireside, savoring a late snack of homemade sashimi and pickled cucumber at almost two in the morning.

Her eyes were ringed with fatigue, although he knew that she had napped in the afternoon. "Ako," he said. "Are you sure that you're happy?" When he had met her, she had been industrious, obsessively active. Now that fierce creativity had bent to the creation of a home.

Her eyes burned with reflected fireplace light and with inner warmth as well. "We all follow our own dream, Chaz. Mine was to be like my parents. My mother was an artist, and my father had her give it up when they married. I remember asking how she could do that. She smiled at me as if I was too young to understand anything of the real world. She said everyone makes sacrifices in a marriage, if it is a real marriage. She said she was happy. She meant it."

Her eyes were very wide. "I am happy. And the man I love encourages me to continue my art. I do as much of it as I wish, my husband. I am happy. What more can anyone want?"

And she kissed him gently.

*  *  *

Years passed, in which they mellowed together, aged together, suffered and celebrated together, and his love for her grew.

She withdrew just a bit, following the pattern she had learned from her mother before her. She became the world behind their doors and windows, while he attended life beyond their blue picket fence. The computer revolution was exploding, and Chaz Kato was at the center of it.

He was at IBM when the concept of the personal computer first became a reality. He was part of the Apple II's original design team, and later helped steer the Macintosh to market. He eventually formed his own company, Pandora Ltd., in Santa Cruz, California. There he explored the concept of the interface, the movement from the digital to the visual. Work hours lengthened once again, but Ako did not complain. Never complained. But their relationship became more of a formality. She cared for the home.

In a way that he could not acknowledge until later, she was his heart. His love for her beat there, within him, but he took it for granted and never ever considered how very easy it would be for his heart, or hers, to break.

The hottest fire burns eventually to comfortingly warm embers. Hand in hand, Chaz and Ako watched the years roll past. The love they shared was no less real, but Chaz, ever more deeply involved in Pandora, was often remote and emotionally unavailable for weeks at a time. Ako watched, and helped him, and was the perfect, devoted wife.

There were storms in their marriage, as in all relationships. But for the most part, what they had together suited them both, and it was good.

After all, Chaz thought, one day all of this would be behind them, and they would have the rest of their lives together. Then he would be able to travel with her. They would see the world together and share all of the things that they had previously cherished separately. And that would make all of the sacrifice worthwhile.


In September of 1994, when Chaz was fifty-six and a week past Ako's fifty-fourth birthday, something odd happened. For years Ako had chronically misplaced her car keys. It was a standing joke between them, and she sometimes claimed that she only did it to force him to drive her to the store. Hah-hah.

On this particular day, Chaz was about to walk out of the house when he noticed her standing in the middle of the floor, wearing the housecoat he had purchased for her birthday, staring down at something in her hand.

He had never seen her wear that particular expression before, and alarm bells clattered in his mind.

Unable to speak, barely able to breathe, Chaz watched until finally she turned and looked at him. She held the keys out, dangling them from her fingertips. Her fingers were pinched together. "Chaz," she said dully. "What are these?"

He took a halting step toward her. She seemed so small, as if saying those words had required some terrible, voiding effort.

"Your car keys?"

"My . . . car?" she said, and then suddenly she laughed, delightedly, almost like a child. "Oh, yes!" She shook her head. "I just don't know what's wrong with me." The temporary paralysis seemed to vanish, and suddenly she was fine.

At least, she was as fine as she would ever be again.


With horror, he watched her personality dissolve. The years were being stripped away from her, her memories degrading, and every day she was a little younger, a bit more pitiable. Her language skills and coordination began to deteriorate, and her once almost miraculously even moods began to swing wildly and disastrously.

He didn't want to see her that way. He didn't want to remember her in that state. Only then, perhaps, did he truly understand the degree to which she had been his strength, his center.

He couldn't work. Couldn't sleep, although he spent long lonely nights holding her, listening to the thickness of her breathing, staring at the wall over her shoulder, praying for it to end.

It seemed to take forever, but from diagnosis to death only four tragically short years passed. Before those final days, almost everything *Ako* died. She shambled out into the living room naked in front of guests. She dialed strangers on the phone and babbled until they hung up. She gathered the sheets around her neck when he entered their bedroom, the room where they had once rested and loved. And screamed at him to leave.

He calmed her, speaking as to a child. Feeling every day of his sixty-two years he smoothed the hair on her forehead, crooning to her, as she clutched at him and sobbed, uncertain who or where she was.

Much, much later that night, when she was finally quiet, when her breathing was the gentle burr that signaled sleep, he left her and returned to the living room.

Chaz sat in his overstuffed chair, staring around him at the trophies of a life that had contracted to five rooms and a bed, and he cried.


It was a fall morning, in 1998.

The leaves were turning, the Northern California days just beginning to shorten. He woke from a dream of golden leaves, his skin tingling with the cool autumn breeze. Ako walked at his side, not young, not old. Timeless. Somehow ageless. He walked with the essence of Ako, the spirit that had slipped away from the world. She smiled at him, holding his hand and then raising it to her lips with a gesture that she had used a thousand times before.

Only this time it meant farewell.

He awakened and held his breath. The bedroom was dark, but he didn't need to see. He could hear.

The gentle burr was gone. Ako was gone. His strength, his life, was gone.

Hand shaking, he took her time-furrowed fingers in his and raised them to his lips, and kissed her good-bye.

Work became torture. Where once Pandora Ltd. represented freedom, now it symbolized his neglect of the woman he loved, the bitch goddess who had wooed him from her bed, seduced the passion from their relationship. Once upon a time, there had been tomorrow, and tomorrow, and tomorrow.

And then there was not.

He could sit in darkness, listening to songs that they had once enjoyed together, or he could work in the laboratory that he had come to loathe, driving himself, flogging his mind, flensing his heart, excoriating himself on the altar of science.

His associates were horrified. They watched him work eighteen-hour days, a man in his sixties burning up what remained of his life creating video games and fluffy data-bases. He sat in the back of a meeting, silent until the presentation was complete. Sleeping, perhaps. Then he would say a word, or perhaps a sentence, and spin the entire project into a new, brilliant direction. If it hadn't been for that, for his constant, insightful contributions to their projects, his partners would have forced Chaz Kato into retirement for his own good.

He became an object of fear, and pity, and awe. A caricature of his former self. His tiny, dirty secret was that a self-loathing part found pleasure in this new identity.

* * *

In spring of the year 2000, a group of learning-disadvantaged children were brought from Oakland to Pandora to test a new desktop system. Chaz decided, very atypically, to watch the process. He sat behind a one-way mirror, in the cool and darkness, while the children sat at the various computer stations or played with monitors and keyboards for a few minutes, and then ignored these to play with blocks and toys.

Except for one station, a VR module equipped with virtual gloves and visor. Once introduced to the virtual world, children were addicted. They loved almost any game, from shoot-'em-ups demanding no more than simple hand-eye coordination to complex games designed to test and develop advanced arithmetic and spatial ability.

The project head told Chaz that several of the children had cranial lesions which limited their brain's ability to process information. And yet children confronted with kinesthetic challenges often responded more adroitly than those confined to verbal or digital responses.

Chaz was entranced.

He began to wonder about the human–machine interface and where it might lead in the next century. He knew that doctors and nutritionists had devised various treatments for Alzheimer's and related ailments, but he wondered what he might add to the struggle. And he wondered if he might have found some way to extend Ako's life, or at least lessened the slope of her decline.

For the first time in years, Chadwick Kato was a man on a mission. He worked the same hideous hours, drove himself to the same exhaustion, motivated now by love rather than guilt.

For six more years, Chaz Kato pioneered the basic technologies that led to the science of Linking.

Then, ironically and inevitably, his health broke. In the winter of 2006 the ailments he sought to alleviate in others descended upon him. So close to the most important break-through of his life and career, he became confused, disoriented, a shell of himself. At sixty-eight years old, he was a broken old man, confined to his bed, unable even to retain knowledge from technical journals he had once illuminated with his own insights and essays.

For hours each day he stared at the wall, struggling to remember who he was, what his life meant, recognizing fewer and fewer of the men and women who came to visit his sterile white room, until finally it was too painful for them to visit, and he spent his dwindling days alone.


He lay staring at the screen of an unplugged television set, its darkness and silence drawing him, calling to him as if it masked the gentle, undemanding sound of Ako's voice.

The door opened. A man walked in, a stranger, thin, dapper, dark, very polite. He introduced himself as S. P. Tata.

"Do I know you?" Chaz asked, embarrassed by the need to ask the question.

"No," Tata said. His voice was heavily accented, but cultured. "But I think you will want to." He pulled a chair up to the bedside and spoke in a clear, calm voice. "I can give you your mind back, Dr. Kato. I can give you new life."

"Who are you?" He attempted to struggle to an upright position. He desperately wished to confront Tata as an equal. "What do you want from me?"

Tata pulled a chair close to the bedside and set his briefcase on his lap. "Dr. Kato," Tata said, "I represent a group of men and women who seek unusual talent. They believe that you are such a one. We would like to offer you a new life."

"A new life . . . ?"

He leaned close. "Dr. Kato, would you like to be young again?" His eyes burned fiercely, and in the fire of those eyes, all Chaz's remaining doubts or reservations were consumed.

He remembered signing and thumbing documents and speaking into video cameras. He pledged the bulk of his work "for the next 100 years" to the mysterious forces Tata represented.

New doctors appeared among those visiting Chaz daily. The old attendants drifted away. There was a change in his medication, both pills and injections. Different bottles, different colors. After a few days, he was moved to another room in the hospital.

A week after that, a private helicopter moved him again. How long he was in the air he did not know. He was unconscious most of that time. He awakened dizzy, confused, and afraid. The flare of hope and clarity Tata had inspired seemed to have burned away, leaving only the realization that he was in the hands of strangers.

"My friends . . ." he tried to say. He wanted to contact . . . whom?

His new doctors regarded him with awe and respect seasoned with the sort of protective condescension generally reserved for infants. "That's all behind you now," they said. "As far as they know, you'll be dead in a few days."

"Dead?" A trickle of fear rose in him. What was it that they had asked him at one point in the extensive tapings and signings? *Do you, Chadwick Kato, agree that Councilor Partners, Limited, has the right to make any decisions regarding your security, including but not limited to rewriting your personal history?*

He suddenly had a revelation: that last bit of paranoid insight contained the longest string of complex words that he had remembered in . . . months? What had they done to him? His physical weakness and lack of coordination were still extreme, but hope flickered once again. Wherever they were taking him, whatever they had in store, clearly he had been snatched from his grave. Whatever his new future held, it had to be better than the past he was escaping.

*Good-bye, Ako*, he said silently. *And hello to the new me.*

* * *

He was transferred twice before landing on a small island off the coast of Java. There, in a private clinic maintained by his mysterious benefactors, they went to work on him.

He knew that some of the treatment involved regrowth of nervous tissue. When these sessions ended his mind was cloudy, as if some memories had actually vanished. Computerized testing sessions mapped his cerebral cortex. Speed, clarity, memory, mental and physical agility, rotation of multidimensional constructs . . . They replaced his knees; the muscles, tendons, flesh had to grow again. They made him walk with a stroller long before it stopped hurting.

He read omnivorously, devouring his own writings with particular interest. Often he could not remember having written them and needed to reread three or four times. Then came a cloudy understanding, followed by a delicious rush of insight.

Chaz's computer was linked directly to the medical and technical libraries of a dozen universities. He spent ten hours a day poring over journals from around the world.

Tata and the doctors watched his progress, and smiled.

Time passed. He regained his strength of limb and began to discuss his own medical condition with his doctors, researching feverishly, astonishing everyone, himself most of all, with his intellectual stamina and drive. Not since his early college days had he read like this!

And . . . and he *remembered* his college days! He dreamed as if actually on the campus at USC. His senses were sharp. He could smell the flowers and count the dewdrops on a petal. In dreamtime, colors and smells and tastes were almost unbearably intense.

Day by day his waxy, tired skin sloughed off, flaking away like dandruff. The nurses vacuumed it up and whisked it away for analysis.

The day came when he could walk without assistance again. A squat, alert female orderly named Gloria walking close behind him, Chaz stepped out into the daylight.

Never, ever, would he forget that feeling. The equatorial sun was high overhead, and its rays blasted him with health. A hundred and fifty feet from the patio, grass gave way to sand. On uncertain legs he wobbled out toward the surf, toes sinking into the sand. Knees blessedly pain-free, he knelt to cup a handful of water, the foam bubbling between his fingers and draining out again . . .

His back didn't hurt. The liver spots on his hands had faded. Soon they would be gone.

Standing, he thrust his arms into the air, balled hands into fists, and whooped with joy, whooped and strutted and leaped and danced, and didn't stop until a coughing fit slowed him and made him double up with the pain in his side.

Again, he knelt at the water's edge. Again, he cupped foam in his hands, watched it running between his newly smooth fingers. He knew that within the foam an entire microverse of tiny creatures lived out their brief spans with no more awareness of his existence than he had been aware of powers that could convey a gift such as he had been given.

But he had to become aware. He had to serve.

He turned to Gloria. "How many others?" he asked. "How many times?"

"That's not useful information, Dr. Kato," she said gently, and then steered him back inside.


"Your name," Gloria said, "is Chadwick Kato the Third. You are your own grandson. Illegitimate, of course. Your grandmother was a Chinese technician your grandfather met in Taiwan, in about 1965."

He flinched. "The year before . . . my *grandfather* met Ako."

"Yes," she said kindly. "There was some discussion that the event might have taken place after."

He shook his head adamantly. "I would not disgrace her memory. Not even for my new life."

She squinted at him as if regarding a lovable but rebellious child. "I told them that you would say that."

He had a desk in his room now, with a beautiful ocean view. He searched the Net for information about his own work . . . his "grandfather's" work. He read it all. In time he regained or replaced most of his memories. The beautiful thing was that he wouldn't be expected to know everything about his "grandfather's" life.

They watched as he body-surfed like an otter. They watched as he read, as he slept. Sensors surrounded and cocooned him, and he was content for that to be so. Gloria told him about the interface plug in his head: It didn't just link him into computers and virtual programs, it helped the doctors monitor his health.

He'd given up privacy. Perhaps they'd warned him of this; how would he know?

He drilled himself in core elements of his new personality. Chadwick Kato III. Born in 1985, in Hawaii. Attended the University of Hawaii, and then a technical apprenticeship in Taiwan, with additional training in Europe. Chaz III had maintained communication with his grandfather but not actually assumed his name until the elder Kato's death.

Then, with full blessings, he inherited a vast block of stock and began to emerge from the shadows.

"Not far," Gloria reminded him. "Media exposure is no part of your new life. Your cover story will hold up, but there is simply no need to dare fate, do you agree?"

He nodded.

Six months after his resurrection, in February of 2007 Chadwick Kato III entered his new home, Xanadu. It was only the core of a facility at that time, five seacrete towers an-

chored to a mothballed supertanker. Power from their
OTECs precipitated calcium onto metal mesh grids. In those
early days, the tidal tug was a constant, rolling force. As the
structure grew more massive, that residual motion shrank to
almost nothing.

His new life was one of wonder and contribution. He
discovered that his work consumed him as it had not for
decades. He was lonely, true. He couldn't talk to any of his
old friends, even in the guise of his own grandson. There
was simply too much risk that he might slip. He understood
the need for secrecy. The gift of youth could not be shared
with all.

He could talk to the other nerds, and he could talk to
Security. During the next three years his only refuges from
loneliness became Arvad Minsky and a beautiful security
operative named Clarise Maibang.

Chaz recognized Arvad's style of strangeness, or thought
he did. He'd known hundreds of brilliant, asocial nerds. Arvad was moving into strange realms of the mind; it was a
delight to follow him. Fifteen years ago Arvad had only
begun to amplify his body and mind. Later he became much
stranger.

Clarise was midlevel in Xanadu Security. As his mind
healed and he tried his wings, Chaz found places he
shouldn't go in the physical and virtual worlds. Such events
threw him into contact with Security, with Clarise and her
lilting accent and not-quite-certain English. He took to asking for her.

Clarise was exotic, born to some hidden tribe in Java. She
tried to tell him something of her girlhood. There were secrets she could not share; there were nuances he would
never understand.

But he didn't have to lie to Clarise! That was such a relief.
She would listen, too, whereas conversation with Arvad generally became a monologue. Circumstance threw them together: He loved the night hours she was frequently on the
night shift.

A long time passed before he *looked* at Clarise. She was lithe, powerful, economical in her motions. She never stumbled, never dropped anything. Her skin was amber, like Ako's, or his own. He thought her one of the most beautiful women he had ever seen.

He did not know when she decided. A night that began at the opera, before the huge monitor in Chaz's living room, ended in his bed.

He realized that she had claimed him.

He accepted that. He believed that women did that. For three years he'd been rebuilding his life, and it was time—

But with a precise perversity more often found in life than fiction, Chaz already loved a young and brilliant UCLA student named Lenore Myles.

He could not form relationships or attachments outside Xanadu. Of course not! But the Kato Foundation had its interests around the world, hundreds of young people whose work in synthetic neural material, or virtual teaching techniques, or biochemical ergogenics attracted his attention. Lenore Myles was following his own line of research. The paths he was pursuing when his health shut down, Lenore was following now.

He watched. He didn't guide. What if he'd been on one of a thousand wrong paths? He watched hundreds of students, worldwide. Maybe one of them could make it work.

*Real* cyborg interactions. Intelligence on demand. Mankind limps toward godhood just a little faster.

At first Lenore was no more than one of a thousand other faces. But over the years he was drawn more and more to the cool precision of her thoughts. He made the fatal mistake of wondering if the bland rotating head-shot image on her file really represented the woman herself. It took no more than a single, simply worded request to find video from Lenore's high school science fair, news clips from a swim-

ming competition, a holograph speech from her days in debate club.

No baby seal had ever been clubbed more adroitly. Chaz
was thunderstruck, in love and devastated before he knew
it, before he really realized that it had happened.

The impossibility of the relationship was obvious. *Right*.
He reached out for Clarise instead, and she came.


She must have wondered why he didn't offer marriage.

It was because she engulfed his life.

Most people did that. He was still growing into his new
life, just leaving his invalid state. Ako had kept order in his
home, and in his life when he was there. He and Clarise
shared a very different home; it extended throughout the
still-growing island. He was a lover and a patient and a
security risk. At first it seemed very natural that she would
surround him with patterns.

But he was growing stronger, looking for new challenges
. . . and Clarise was trying to follow him into the virtual
universe, too.

Chaz wondered if the Bdui understood privacy. Security
training wouldn't teach it to her! How deeply would she
rule him if she was his *wife?* He flinched, he dithered, he
compromised: He offered her what he had only read about,
a Muta contract.

A Muta contract could be broken.

But Chaz had given up his privacy for Xanadu's immor-
tality. She was in his life; she always would be. Clarise's
love was possessive, and she liked order.

Chaz had never quite admitted to his terror that Saturn
was another face of Clarise Maibang. Now it haunted his
dreams.

Images and sensations cascaded through Chaz's mind, ter-
minated only by the slow and steady ascent to consciousness, like a drowning swimmer thrashing up from the depths
toward a distant, healing light.

## 26

Clarise Maibang sat at the edge of his bed. Worry had hollowed her face, forcing her cheekbones into prominence.

A warm cocoon surrounded his left leg. Under the bandages a web of wiring would be running magnetic pulses through the leg. So, he had broken bones. His mouth tasted as if he had slept with pennies under his tongue, and his eyes weren't focusing quite right. He guessed that he was concussed as well. The wizards of Xanadu would have handled all of that before he ever emerged from his induced sleep.

Clarise held his hand in her two. "How are you, Chaz?"

Sudden panic gripped him. Someone had tried to kill him! He pulled her close. She mistook his intent and kissed him. He'd taught her that, a tasting of textures: not a Bdui custom.

He returned the kiss and presently asked, "Can your Security seal this room?"

"No . . ." Curiosity danced in her eyes. "What are you thinking?"

He gave back no signal. Not sudden lust, then. She said, "I can move you to a Councilor's suite, which *can* be sealed. Is it necessary?"

He nodded emphatically.

Almost an hour passed during which calls were made, beds rolled here and there, orderlies shuffled. He was rolled out into the hall and down an elevator to a lower floor. Then through security doors, where Clarise displayed her badge, and finally into a room with all of the personality of a fishbowl. Regardless of its unappealing Lucite decor, it was what he needed: a total security seal. Here he could speak.

Clarise sat next to him again, mystified smile crinkling the smooth brown skin. "Alone at last . . . ?"

"Someone tried to kill me," he said. He hesitated and then took her hand. "I know I can trust you."

"Really? I have better motive to murder you than most!"

He didn't smile. "Yes, but Saturn's fist isn't yours."

"What?" She was even more puzzled now, and Chaz found himself telling her the whole story, gushing it out, more relieved than he would have believed to tell the story to a real human being after a year of keeping it completely to himself.

He concluded by saying "Saturn must have decided he needs to remove me."

She considered. "Or if I might, perhaps Yamato wants to be sure you don't move against him."

He nodded briskly. That slight motion made the room whirl.

Clarise shook her head. "I'm not saying that I don't believe your story, Chaz. You don't tend to fantasies, and you're not a liar. But shouldn't I research this?"

He held hard to her hand. "No, you should not do that! Leave it to NERO. I don't want you trying to find him. You'd be noticed."

"There is one further problem, Chaz. Barrister's frenzy wasn't a murder attempt. It was a mistake." She watched his face. He waited. She said, "Arvad left one of his personal cartridges on a shelf in his office. Pepper put it with the Circus program. Do you understand? It was a stupid mistake, and *Pepper* made it. The session recorder caught the whole thing. You distracted Minsky while he was playing that, that game? *Frenzy.* It's the same format as the rodeo cartridges. Pepper couldn't have known what was on it unless she and Arvad Minsky were in collusion." She considered another moment, and so did he. She said, "No, not even then."

"Why not?"

"Pepper wasn't supposed to handle programming. I was. I decided not to. I wanted to be down with the Sea Scouts where I could enjoy the show." She was squeezing his hand, too hard.

He squeezed back. "Shit happens." Thinking. "Wait. Arvad . . . ?"

Clarise drove another nail into that coffin. "No. Arvad Minsky risked his life to get you off Barrister. Chaz, that *fish* bit a piece out of his leg—"

"Ai!"

"—before we could get everything shut down. The safety seal shut off his femoral artery. He would have bled to death in under a minute, and the blood in the water—Blood." Clarise shuddered. It took her a moment to find her English speech. "Accident, Chaz. Big, stupid, awkward, embarrassing accident. Lucky for us it wasn't worse."

"How's Arvad?"

"Walks twelve minutes a day. Electrical stimulation. Thigh muscle, a length of cultured artery. The knee isn't damaged—the shark broke some teeth on it—but he's redesigning it anyway. His mind is not damaged. He is working some huge, intricate medical program, working on himself. He wants to repair Barrister's programming too, but the doctors won't let him."

"Good." Minsky, the first friend of his second life. Arvad Minsky wasn't Saturn. Nobody was Saturn. Nero had compared the input patterns with anyone who could be.

*Except one.*

Clarise's expression had lost none of its affection. If anything, she was more concerned than ever.

"Ten days from now," she was saying, "We're taking a load of spirulina over to Benares. I think that you should come, Chaz. It's been a long time since you were off the island. There's a big world out there."

She waited anxiously.

"Big world. I can't even stand up yet," he said.

"You'll be walking. The doctors make you."

The kinks in his mind had put a wall between himself and Clarise Maibang, who only wanted to love him. Near-death experience could change a man's perspective.

Clarise didn't know how to flirt; innuendoes were foreign to her. She was making a pass at her once-husband. Where did she find the nerve? And his whole heart welcomed her, reached out to her, but—

*Who is Saturn, Chaz?*

"Can I tell you tomorrow?" Chaz said. "Can I make up my mind tonight?"

She didn't like that. Her eyes evaded; she brushed his brow with her lips and was gone.

When he was his own grandfather, Chaz Kato had barely dreamed this age. He had helped to shape a world in which any human being could find his/her ideal mate somewhere among the eight billion, if he were willing to learn the Net, if she were willing to search. Few did, and there were predators on the Net, but they *could*.

But Clarise had been pulled into Xanadu from a Stone Age tribe of . . . a few hundred? In a population that small, a woman would not find a million acceptable mates. With luck, one. The Bdui might never have invented coyness. When a woman claimed a man, he would have no choice either.

She'd *known* he was observing Lenore Myles. She'd told him so, when she and Whittlesea came to accuse Lenore. But when had she learned, and what had she thought? Did she know why he'd offered her a temporary contract, pulling back in terror from a greater commitment?

Twelve years ago Clarise had given her heart and body to a man whose soul belonged to a total stranger living three thousand kilometers away. She'd tried to change him. Ultimately she broke it off, continuing to love him all the time.

Chaz had a long reach. He helped Lenore from a distance. Her initial work study program was commuted to full scholarship. Chaz pulled more strings. Ultimately he caused her entire graduating class to celebrate on Xanadu. Clarise had known that too.

And still she loved him.

His heart broke beneath the weight of wasted days. But *who is Saturn?*


Chaz buzzed the orderly. When the wall opened and a concerned face appeared, he said, "I believe that my condition has stabilized?"

"Yes, sir."

"Then I would like you to transfer the files directly to my private lines and have my personal medical systems assume responsibility. Can you do that?"

The orderly said, "Just one minute." His image froze on the screen. He'd be calling the physician in charge, who would check Chaz's trainer program's capacity. In a pinch, his trainer could simply act under control of the central system.

The static image came to life once again. "No problem, Dr. Kato. We can transfer you back this afternoon."


Chaz's motorized wheelchair purred through the corridors to the smiles and quiet applause of staff and citizens. He nodded his head graciously. Apparently his fame had preceded him.

Ride 'em, cowboy.

Nadine the mermaid and several other Sea Scouts were gathered to greet him. Pepper took personal responsibility for escorting him to the elevator. Pepper looked as if she wanted to die.

"I can't say how sorry I am, Chaz. I don't know how I made that mistake."

Her misery yanked him out of his own thoughts for a moment. "Yes, well . . . how exactly did it happen?"

She took a deep breath. "Well, you'll remember that the entire rodeo was really more of a ballet. We call it a rodeo to catch the kids' interest, but we do it all to classical music. Your part was choreographed to Beethoven's *Für Elise*."

"I remember. Short, gentle, nothing too exciting—"

"Well, we kind of threw it together at the last minute, and some of the audio/kino carts were . . . a little confused. Mr. Minsky had just finished a personal game of *Frenzy*. His personal cartridge was labeled in his own handwriting, and there it sat, upside down on the shelf. I saw that upside-down 'F' and the rest of the squiggle, and oh, God."

"Got to speak to Arvad about his handwriting." This was getting cosmically funny. It was all he could do to keep from laughing hysterically, right in her face. He had to end this. "Meanwhile, I should get used to making my own way. Do you mind?"

He rolled forward, then spun the chair to watch the doors slide shut as his assistant looked after him, her eyes filmed with tears.

Jesus. He didn't think that he could have lasted another minute. His chuckle became a crazed giggle.

# 27

As Chaz rolled through the gardens toward his doorway arch, it struck him that he was tired of coming to this door by himself.

One word to Clarise . . .

But if a certain wild supposition was correct, then he was about to enter Hell. He would not drag Clarise Maibang along!

His front door opened at his bidding, slid shut behind

him. Chaz maneuvered himself into his living room and gazed up at the rows of classic computers. He was a bit off schedule, but no one would doubt his need to a little private meditation time.

That is, if anyone was watching at all.

He braced himself and stood. His cocooned leg would take the weight, but his balance was off. Little tickles of warmth buzzed through him as he changed position. Hobbling forward, he lifted the Macintosh from the shelf and lowered it to his desk. For a long moment he gazed at it. What he learned in the next minutes might change his life forever.

Chaz adjusted his virtual gear and engaged the apparatus. He summoned Pong . . . played like a zombie, winning, winning . . . panicked because he'd forgotten to check the date . . . guessed, let the ball slip past, and found himself in an alley in Brooklyn.

A burly man in archaic police uniform was sitting on the steps of the brownstone. The man grinned when he saw Chaz Kato. He stepped aside to allow Chaz to reach the doorbell.

Uh-huh. Chaz reached for the bell but didn't press it. Concealed by his torso, his other hand turned the doorknob. Unlocked. He slipped through and closed the door before the cop could quite get his mass moving to push inside.

"Slick," Ritchie said. "He's hiding in the orchid room. I have to stay at the door, but I'll call up."

Chaz took the elevator. Again there was a moment's temptation to stop off on the private floor. Ridiculous. If he needed to see Lupus Nero's dresser drawers, he could program them himself.

The elevator opened on the roof. It was a riot of color. He watched Lupus Nero sniff deeply at a blaze of lavender and yellow. He could imagine the smells well enough to make him giddy. This game needed a sense of smell!

Nero himself was ablaze in a yellow silk bathrobe. "Dr. Kato, it's good to see you again. Come and look at my new

*Habinaria*. Are you familiar with this breed?"

He was laboring over a delicately stalked, pale violet plant with fringed blooms.

"No, I'm afraid not."

"Ah. This is the rein orchid. Ordinarily grows in bogs. And here, what you sent me is thriving." Four great blossoms in a thousand soft colors and textures of *black*. "Most unusual." Nero sniffed deeply. When he turned his balance was off. "Intoxicating. From the *Fu Manchu* series?"

Chaz laughed. "Caught!"

"Appropriate. A virtual detective growing fictitious orchids."

Was Nero offended? Chaz saw no sign of it. He asked, "How's Lenore?"

Lupus Nero shook his head; jowls swung massively. "Dr. Kato, I once thought to observe Saturn observing Lenore Myles or Tooley Wells. But you've hired Wayne Intelligence to do that, and you *expected* to be caught at it. I have never directly monitored Lenore Myles at all. For ten months I have listened passively to communications at Wayne. I thought to observe Saturn observing the ladies through your detectives."

"And?"

Shrug. "I see no trace of Saturn. He is as passive as I. I know nothing of Lenore Myles that isn't in your Wayne Intelligence reports."

"Mr. Nero, I need you to perform another fist comparison for me."

"Doctor, we have examined everyone capable of penetrating your defenses on Xanadu, including all members of the Council and two hundred and twenty peripheral—"

"Not everyone," Chaz said. Nero's eyes glittered, and Chaz grew more specific in his request.

Nero grew quiet, and Chaz knew that the program was active. And then he scowled. "Dr. Kato, Saturn's fist does not resemble yours at all. I suppose that would be good news?"

Chaz felt something deep and cold melt in his belly—the lingering suspicion that his mind had cracked after all; that the regeneration process was imprecise enough to allow some virulent and subtle madness to emerge.

He had not willfully destroyed the mind of Lenore Myles.

"Very good news," he said.

"But we are left in the same frustration. I've tested the fists of several more of Xanadu's workmen or, in four cases, established that they are not computer literate. He can still track you, and we can't find him!"

"I can turn it off," Chaz said.

Nero blinked. "Yes?"

"I couldn't stand it. I built a switch into the interface plug. Give me a pen point and a mirror, I can turn off the sender. Of course Saturn—"

"Saturn would know at once. You would have to be already running."

"I've been offered a chance to get off Xanadu," Chaz said, "for a week or two."

"Take it."

"I'm not ready to go into hiding—"

"Become less predictable, Doctor. Give Saturn something to do, something to worry about. Make him react, and *I* will watch the result. Give him less reason to jump the next time you do something unusual. Take a trip, take up juggling, take up hang-gliding!"

Chaz nodded. "I will," he said, and broke the connection.

The air filters were performing: No dust showed the outline of a computer that sometimes moved from its row. He staggered as he lifted the ancient computer back to its shelf.

Who was Saturn? He would continue the hunt. But while he did . . . a certain wonderful woman had waited years for him to come to his senses.

He chorded his desk pad, dropped the security shield, and called Clarise. When she appeared, even before he spoke, she seemed to know what he was going to say, and her smile was magnificent.

* * *

For days now there had not been a Saturn. Now Saturn looked at the world.

The world didn't know it yet, but it was ready to riot. Deforestation in the Mato Grosso had driven Indians, miners, and laborers of all stripe east to Rio de Janeiro, overcrowding their already notorious *favelas*. There in the shadow of the statue of the Virgin, some of the worst police atrocities of the century had taken place, and some of the most savage reprisals.

In South Africa, the gap between the haves and have-nots had never been wider, with wealth still disproportionately distributed across racial lines. De Beers was rumored to be closing its mines and transferring billions out of the country. Millions of blacks were living at near-starvation levels, millions of whites in constant low-level terror.

Radical Islamic suicide attacks in Israel had transformed the streets of Jerusalem into a war zone. Repression against the kamikazes merely polarized the surrounding nations. Jewish retaliation, in the form of a fuel-air explosion on the outskirts of Mecca, had killed hundreds and brought the entire region to nuclear twilight.

Defenses were in place on the Floating Islands. They would put up a fight worth seeing.

In the main, members of the Council were playing their usual games, taking their accustomed risks, with no extraordinary defensive precautions. It would seem they thought themselves immortal, untouchable. Saturn smiled in anticipation.

Chaz Kato . . . Saturn had feared Chaz Kato lost, killed in a stupid and trivial accident. It seemed he would recover. He would travel to India aboard the dirigible *Gilgamesh*. The timing was elegant.

Lenore Myles was . . . gone.

Saturn hadn't expected that. He narrowed his focus.

Records: a jet train to Portland, Oregon, to see yet another doctor. Records: examination fee, prescription fee, both paid. Cab fare . . . accumulating. No cameras on the cab.

Saturn, busy with a thousand other things, watched Lenore in motion. Amtrak station. A ticket southbound to Studio City . . .

# 28

The doctor's office was in Portland, Oregon.

"Just relax," the woman behind the glass said. Lenore reclined on the table as the scanning arm hovered up her body.

"We'll just be a moment," the voice repeated, and Lenore closed her eyes. Darkness seethed behind her eyelids, and in that darkness lay a deeper, colder pit. She calmed herself. Although her eyes were closed, when light crossed them a webbing of veins grew bright and fractal as a road map. The brightness increased to a point near pain and then subsided.

"Thank you. You may dress now."

A male attendant brought her clothes back into the room. Lenore's whole body clenched like a fist. He smiled at her face without examining her nakedness, and left.

She dressed in haste . . . but these were not the clothes she had worn into the office. Something bland and loose-fitting, casual without being particularly comfortable. Simply scanning the old garments might have missed something. If she protested in any way, the clinic would simply apologize and bring her own clothes, and that would be the end of her contact.

This was her first step down the pipeline. She had to walk carefully: Though unknown and frightening, the path ahead was her only route to salvation.

There was a mind to reclaim. There was truth to learn.

The other patients in the waiting room were lower-middle-class folks, either uncomfortable with home medical robots or unable to afford one. The free clinic was one of the alternatives.

The doctor who finally saw her was in her sixties, slump shouldered with a face like sun-dried leather. "Well, Miss Myles, you're fine. Fit to travel, as they say. I did notice a bit of a scalp infection. I've written a prescription." She tore a sheet off a tablet. "You can get a good price at this pharmacy." She scribbled an address at the top. Lenore looked at it.

She had been told to take public transportation. The pharmacy was across town. "I didn't bring my car."

"There are autocabs right outside," said the doctor. "We'll call you one. Have a pleasant day."

The city of Portland was crisscrossed with rail lines and guide strips. Buses, trolleys, automobiles, and computer-routed vehicles all shared the same streets. Traffic jams were a rarity.

A little double-occupancy autocab broke from the flow of traffic and pulled to the curb. A lighted panel on the side displayed her name. She slipped into the back and spoke the pharmacy's address. The cab popped back out into traffic.

A speaker mounted on the backseat spoke. "Good afternoon, Lenore. Please just relax." The voice was synthesized, impossible to identify.

The cab whirred through the streets, drawing a maze to throw off visual pursuit. She had few doubts that it was scrambling its own ID numbers. The guidance network itself would take it for one of the thousands of other automated vehicles gliding through the streets.

If anyone was watching. If anyone cared.

She dozed.

She woke when they reached the Amtrak terminal. The synthesized voice said, "There is a ticket under your seat. Please make use of it."

And then the door opened. The ticket was printed with her name and the destination: the Universal terminal. Well. She hadn't anticipated that, had imagined a more exotic destination. But she had no idea how many legs awaited her. She could take her journey only one step at a time.


The train took her down the coast, but she never saw the ocean. It stopped in San Francisco, and she longed to get out, stretch her legs, see the sights. She hadn't been warned against it but couldn't muster the courage. It had taken everything she had to get this far. She was so terribly afraid of losing some basic and primal portion of her memory. Her identity, for instance. Being unable to answer a question like "Who are you?"

Not until the train slid south of Santa Barbara did she first catch sight of the outskirts of the greater Southern California entertainment complex. From Valencia south to Orange County it stretched, incorporating amusement parks ranging from Magic Mountain to Disneyland and even older Knotts, from the Universal Studios Tour to Raging Waters. The growth of the Pacific Rim and Indonesia as industrial giants had shipped most manufacturing concerns out of the United States. Southern California had simply accepted the inevitable, and entertainment became its dominant industry.

The amusement parks, restaurants, movie studios and television stations, radio networks and publishing empires all linked together beneath the sheltering aegis of Entertainment and Communication. Their souls belonged to the Council, to Wayne and Shannon Halifax.

All were linked by electronic and subterranean communication. Tourists from around the world could spend weeks just shuttling from one dream-maker to the next and never see what used to pass for the real world. Beaches from Malibu to Playa Del Ray were all part of Universal's Baywatch City, with staged rescues on the hour, every hour, and no one seemed to remember that citizens had once entered the water for free. Drowned that way too.

Her train slid into Universal Station. Almost instantly, the rumbling and shaking began. An instant of panic: *earthquake!* Chunks of concrete ceiling rained down, and station attendants reeled back and forth in terror . . . mock terror. Everyone else on the car was laughing and cheering.

It was all part of the show. When the shaking stopped, the great pieces of concrete were reeled back to their former positions, and passengers filed down onto the glittering street.

Before Hollywood Boulevard itself became a 1940s museum, Universal had begun the process of building a faux avenue, one more attractive to visiting tourists than the addict-dappled thoroughfare to the south. Now museums and private streets were a simple fact of existence. You paid toll to the company, and a portion of every dollar found its way to the Council. Twenty-four-hour shopping, dining, and entertainment were available, and a zero street crime rate.

Most tourists—and citizens—found it a welcome trade. Gated communities were a common phenomenon of the previous century. Halifax had built the first gated city since ancient times.

Lenore's instructions pointed her toward the Planet Hollywood Café a block away. It was easy to follow the star-studded sidewalk, replete with Grauman's Chinese–style footprints and plaques. Here were little hoofprints from Babe, a performing pig. There the handprints for O. J. Simpson for his role in *Othello*. And in front of her a plaque from the NAACP praising Woody Allen's *Birth of a Nation* remake. Street performers panhandled in whiteface, miming disappointment or ecstasy as passersby ignored them or contributed to their March of Dollars collection cups. Holographic junkies with goofy smiles wandered the streets while hallucinations blossomed in the air around them.

Planet Hollywood beckoned. Lenore gave her name at the front desk. The girl zipped her finger along a book and then smiled brilliantly. "Ah!" she said. "This way!"

She took Lenore by the arm and led her back through the chattering tables. Lenore was glad for the contact: She felt more disoriented every moment.

She sat in a corner booth. Disappointment was sharp within her; she had hoped that Levar would be here. Her instructions ended here. She didn't know what to do next.

The wall shimmered with a menu. Her appetite a distant memory, she paged through it, past Schwarzenegger Supreme steak and the Babe-bacon burger to a Star Wars salad with "Lite" Saber dressing. There was nothing to do now but relax.

She had come so far. Insecurity was eating her alive. What if it had all been a wild goose chase? She didn't know if she could even find her way home.

Conversations buzzed around her. Everyone in the restaurant was making a deal of some kind. The man at the table next to her, a California-tanned parody of an agent, chattered incessantly, although he sat alone at the table. He turned his head very slightly, and she saw a vid screen reflected on the inside surface of his sunglasses.

Suddenly he turned toward her. "Pardon me," he said. "But do you have any Gray Poupon?"

For a moment she fumbled, seeking the little basket of condiments. But he was grinning at her, and the sound of his voice finally penetrated.

Dear God. California tan, bodybuilder physique, fashionably recessed hairline, shades, facial planes taut as if with shoddy plastic surgery . . . It was Levar.

Brilliant. Here in the land of make-believe he could alter his appearance, and even if his surgeon was drunk at the operating table, it would simply look as if Levar were disguising the passage of time with an iron-pumped torso, a bad wig, and waxy skin.

*Love ya, babe.*

She shivered.

He leered at her, the quintessential Hollywood pickup in progress. "Are you waiting for anyone?"

"I wasn't . . ." she began. It took all the strength she had to maintain the pretense of lightness. Smooth as a snake, he slipped from his table to hers. They ordered, and as they did he kept up a steady line of chatter. His name (he said) was Teddy Mercury, an agent at MCA who was putting together some really big deals for some really small people she had never heard of. She chewed her way through what might have been quite a good salad, while Teddy ate slow spoonfuls of yogurt and finished with a vitamin-enhanced dry piña colada.

After the meal, he leaned back and asked: "Would you like to see my office?" Without waiting for her answer, he paid the bill and escorted her to the underground parking lot. A little red two-seater Soweto Stallion stood at its charging post. The doors sealed and the dashboard flashed green. The Stallion nosed out into traffic.

"Lenore," Levar said. Not all of the California Sweetie-Baby had left his voice. "You look like shit."

"That's better than I feel," she said. "I'm not sure *what* to call your appearance."

"What I am," he said, "is safe. And hey—in a way, I guess I'm still in labor relations. I represent the actors and writers, not the studios, so it's still the good fight, right?"

It only took seven minutes to cruise through the gates at the sprawling Universal complex. The actual movie studio was less than 10 percent of the overall amusement park complex. His offices were crammed into a little brown bungalow at the corner of the lot.

"Yeah," he said as he showed her around his cluttered waiting room. "Universal has enough talent under contract that they keep us on line at all times. It's a bitch."

"So . . . you're really an agent?"

"On my mother's grave. See that poster across the street?" He pointed out a billboard filled with dancing images. The title was a giant Valentine heart with the initials R. L. and M. L. linked romantically.

"Yes . . ." She searched her memory and couldn't find a reference.

"Political scandal musicals are *in* this season. This is based on the old Lewinsky-Limbaugh affair. My clients are thick as fleas on that dog."

He sat her in a vast couch across from the tiny desk and peered at her owlishly. "So . . . it's been a long time, Lenore. I've set something up—*found* something—but it's a tight window."

"What's going to happen to me?"

He grinned. "You're going to disappear for a while. It's pretty wild. Truth is, as persistent as you were, if I hadn't vouched for you you might be vapor by now. Ironic as hell, actually."

His gaze drifted up the walls, which were covered with movie posters. "I guess in some way it's just the birds coming home to roost. I couldn't hide away forever . . ."

She had to ask the next question. "Levar . . . what happened in Antarctica?"

For a long time she thought that he wasn't going to answer, or that if he did it would be with a denial. Instead he fractionally inclined his head: a positive. "This is war, sweetheart. It doesn't seem that way right now to most of them, but it is." For just an instant, that fire she remembered from college days burned in his eyes once again. Then the lid came down.

"The virus was from a Councilor biochemical lab. It was only supposed to create high-grade fevers and disorientation, with a ninety-nine percent communicable rate. Seventy-two hours of nausea after a forty-eight-hour incubation period. Designed to break down the opposition without undue lethality. Well, their design screwed up. *Their* design. Not mine. We—" His voice rose a defensive octave, then dropped to a whisper. "—stole it, and we introduced it to

Red Ice Base, but the rest of it wasn't our fault. It was *their design.*"

His jaw set harshly, daring her to dispute him.

A giggle lodged like a bubble in her throat. Levar was claiming his *warranty* on a stolen experimental war virus! But she'd laughed at Levar, hadn't she, once? She remembered no details, only shock and distress as if a cherry bomb had exploded under her tongue. And this man was her last hope.

Levar studied her. She wanted to challenge him, to ask the hard questions. She came right up to the edge. Who stole the weapon, Levar? And where did they get their information, and why were you so ready to trust it? And why do you believe that *nobody* knew what it was going to do, and why are you so ready to believe that incompetence exists only on one side of an issue?

She already knew the answer. Levar was a fanatic. To Levar the world was black and white, no shadings, no colors. She couldn't even argue. Her mind was damaged. He'd make her out as a fool.

Tasting her own cowardice, she sank more deeply into the couch, and asked, "What do we do next?" Sounding plaintive.

"Next, I take you home and put you to bed." She tensed as if awaiting a blow. He raised a hard muscular hand and waved it at her comfortingly. "Sleep, hon, no funny stuff. Especially not when you were probably raped a year ago. You look like you haven't had a good night's sleep in months. And then in a couple of days we move."

That sounded good. She felt as if she were dying inside. Yes, rest might be possible, if this man from her past actually could help her. Gratitude overwhelmed her pitiful reservations and objections. Tears spilled hotly down her cheeks. "Yes," she said. "Please help me." She looked at him as directly as she could. "Levar . . . I know that I'm probably not much in comparison with the women you're used to now . . ."

He winced. "Lenore, don't."

"No. Let me say this. I am so grateful to you. Even if this doesn't work, I am so terribly grateful. If there is anything you want. Anything that I can offer, anything at all, just tell me." The speech exhausted her tiny store of courage.

Levar shook his head. "I'm just trying to help a friend, someone fucked over by the same beast devouring the rest of this tired old world. You'd do the same for me, wouldn't you?" He brightened. "I tell you what. After this is all over, maybe we'll go on a vacation together. No obligations, all right?"

She nodded her head, dizzy with gratitude.

"Besides," he said softly. His capped, perfect teeth gleamed. "What kind of a monster do you think I am?"


Lenore Myles lay sleeping on Levar's double bed, curled on her side, thumb very near her mouth.

Levar watched her for a few seconds, noting the long, slow draw of her breathing. Once a magnificently healthy creature, she looked like she'd been touring Bergen-Belsen. Remembering the times of their intimacy, he felt a twinge of remorse at what he was about to do.

But such an opportunity might never come again. At times like this he could almost believe in astrology, on the confluence of stars and destiny. How many different threads had tangled to create this moment in time? Their innocent UCLA romance, her sponsorship by the mysterious Kato Foundation, her later involvement with Kato himself, and . . . this. Whatever had happened on Xanadu, it was deliberate, and terrifying. Corporations had their own drives, their own needs. Not alive and not intelligent, still they fought and struggled and competed for supremacy with humanity and each other.

He saw them as devouring maws sucking life from the

planet to create wealth for men and women who had sold their souls to the demon.

Lenore was just another sacrifice on the altar.

And the last thread in the pattern had reached him only a week ago.

Levar sat in his entertainment room, facing the wall-size screen, flanked by surround-speakers in floor and ceiling and couch. This was his screening room, and on ordinary nights he might watch a vid featuring one of his clients, or a classic film, or something in the current box office.

The phone beeped and he answered. "Ciao. What's up, Sid?"

"We need you to look at some new holos. This is on the *Oz* remake."

*The Wiz* made with twenty-first-century special effects and an all-white cast. "Pipe it over to me, but I might not get to it until tomorrow."

He clicked the phone off and instructed his line not to put another call through for the rest of the evening.

In the top corner of the screen a tiny image of Lenore, asleep in his bed, continued to play. The rest of the wall divided itself up.

A satellite's view of the Xanadu complex, all ten million square feet of it, spread like a water lily on the ocean. He could amplify the infrared until individual human figures could be seen moving about on their myriad missions. He'd done that. He did not today, and doubted he would in the future.

He shivered. There are commitments one swears, and means, but never thinks actually to fulfill. The terror to come weighed on him like his own tombstone.

He summoned up Chadwick Kato III. Tiny photos filled his screen: crowd scenes. He zoomed on a single face. A Japanese face, not particularly handsome, with no evil showing. Levar shrank the picture and began to pull up records.

Brilliant, mysterious heir to a fortune. His DNA was fully Japanese, just as he appeared. The man could have been a force for good. Instead he had taken his grandfather's money and squirreled himself away on this corporate paradise. There were mysteries about the man, mysteries Levar longed to solve. A picture of his mother was on file, and her name, but she had been born in a rural area, so there was little documentation. His father? A bastard son of Chadwick Kato I. No picture, but certainly the estate must have been completely convinced of his parentage.

School records matched, but there were tantalizing omissions. It was difficult to find schoolmates or teachers. One security guard at the Swiss boarding school said that he didn't remember the boy. Said, in fact, that he knew of at least one case where someone had purchased records in the school, falsified his degree. But to what end? To make some rural kid seem more cosmopolitan? To dupe stockholders into believing that steady hands held the reins of power?

Here it was: not a newsbite, but an e-mail blip with an obscure Spinner logo.

Chadwick Kato III would be in India for at least a week, supervising the distribution of powdered fish protein, or perhaps spirulina. This, following another Spinner net report that he'd been ripped apart by a shark. Kato was not a member of the Council but was almost certainly a single level removed. He moved with them, knew them. For a week he would be vulnerable.

Sleeping in the next room was a woman who knew Kato's secrets. If Levar could restore Lenore's memory and then bring the two face to face, something interesting might happen.

Levar scratched his left leg. It itched. He glanced again at the tiny image of the sleeping woman.

A series of coded inputs wiped Kato and took Levar to a very private section of the Web, one invisible to anyone without the correct ciphers.

The network that had spirited him to safety after the Antarctic debacle, which had provided his new identity, was not supported solely by individual idealists. As the war between the Council and the national governments grew fiercer, funding from threatened countries became more lucrative. Obligations to various security services grew more extreme. America, Germany, and Japan all funneled money into the radical coffers. And from a hundred smaller countries flowed money and requests as well, filtered through a dozen cut-outs.

Something was happening. Something was causing disturbances in Central America, in Africa, in Southeast Asia, in China. Levar hadn't the experience or knowledge to make sense of the squawking. There were no ongoing epidemics, no disasters, no rise in death rates or disease rates. Starvation-based diseases were *declining*.

National and corporate health services, security arms, news media were alarmed about *something* . . . but certain livelihoods depend on bad news, like global warming, holes in the ozone layer, dying rain forests. . . . There might be no more to it.

But a clear request had filtered to him, without explanation.

*Need access to Xanadu*, it said. *All means and routes to be explored. Order to be carried out by October 22.*

That was in two weeks.

What was happening? Whatever it was, Levar was in the middle of it. Fate had given him the opportunity to rise rapidly in his chosen strata. Fate had delivered into his hands the instrument of his deliverance from the smarmy, meaningless existence he had fallen into.

Lenore Myles was his ticket back to the big leagues.


Saturn considered:

Eleven o'clock and Lenore Myles was somewhere in Studio City without a hotel room or a restaurant meal or a ticket home. Mind-damaged as she was, she could hardly survive under such conditions. She might be wandering the streets among the hologram junkies, her mind now gone completely. But that was a dangerously complacent bet.

Better to assume she was in the hands of secret friends.

Soon it wouldn't matter. All the chickens were coming home to roost . . . but for the next few days it might be bad if Lenore and Chaz pooled what was in their minds. If Saturn couldn't find Lenore, he had better do something about Chaz.

# 29

Prancing horse-drawn chariots and gold-wreathed elephants spearheaded the bridegroom's procession, displaying his power and wealth to Karaka Tata, their host's lovely youngest daughter.

It was a hell of a show. Eight hundred guests crowded S. P. Tata's palatial home: a Victorian masterpiece built at the height of British rule, refurbished in the 1980s. Indian and European design didn't quite work together. There were thousands of steps and no ramps. Chaz was out of his wheelchair recently enough to notice. He climbed them holding Clarise's hand. Her wiry strength was holding half his weight.

The bride and groom were seated opposite each other in straight-backed chairs separated by a curtain. The carpet beneath them was a frozen river of iridescent threads woven so masterfully that it fluxed and glowed even in shadow. They settled Chaz in a third chair.

The ceremony had already run on for more than an hour.

Chaz felt their eyes: *Why is this man seated? He doesn't seem elderly or ill. . . .* The only other chair held Tata's mother. Guests stopped to speak to her; she rarely responded.

The wedding party lined the canopied patio, all elegantly robed and wreathed in flowers, to witness the betrothed couple's vows. Clarise stood close beside Chaz, her own subtle perfume somehow amplified by the scent of rosewater on flowers.

This was a most propitious ceremony. They had been betrothed from birth, their astrological charts and palmreadings evaluated by the most erudite and accomplished seers. Although S. P. Tata was a cultured and well-traveled man, he still adhered to tradition.

The Parsee men and women glittered, immaculate in white suits or varicolored, richly embroidered dresses. They watched proudly as the only daughter of their community's most powerful man was given in holy matrimony to the son of a textile millionaire.

*"Be as pure as the moon.*

*"Be as illustrious as Zoroaster.*

*"As soul is united with the body, be you united with your friends, brothers, wife, and children . . ."*

Clarise's dark, sharp face was relaxed as he had rarely seen it. She looked almost angelic. It was impossible not to respond to her sense of centered relaxation. Certainly nothing in her simple Javanese village could have resembled this opulence. . . .

Chaz felt a sudden flash of insight and shame. Their Xanadu one-year marriage ceremony had been pure convenience, as synthetic as nylon. They called it a "muta" contract after the Sufi ceremony it imitated, but there was no genuine commitment, no spiritual foundation.

*This* ceremony represented permanence. The bride and groom were screened from each other, separated by a piece of golden cloth. Beneath the curtain the couple held right hands, as another piece of cloth encircled and knotted around them.

*"Praise Zoroaster as your spiritual leader . . .*
*"Treat Ahreman, the evil one, with contempt . . ."*

Their host came to them as they gazed out of a window
overlooking the gleaming white sands of Chowpatty Beach,
one of Bombay's favorite recreation spots. During the day,
when the heat beat down savagely, the beach was all but
deserted. But when the shadows grew long, it swelled with
life.

"Celebrate, my friends," Tata said. His beard was graying
now and he was round at the waist, no longer the young
lawyer who had once visited Chaz's hospital room to speak
of fabulous things.

The Arabian Sea sparkled beyond the white sands of the
beach. Thousands of Indians stood shoulder to shoulder
down there, enjoying the day. Chaz had a sudden, childlike
urge simply to strip his party clothes off and totter down to
immerse himself in the warm waters.

Clarise shuddered. "Such crowding would smother me."

*That* idea died. Without her he wouldn't get halfway.

Tata smiled. "You think that this is crowding? Wait until
the day after tomorrow, when the *Ganesh Chathurti* ceremony begins. For ten days you cannot see the sand. Hindus
from all India will come to celebrate." He shook his head
ruefully. "Then our notorious 'Crush Hour' traffic multiplies
manifold. It will be impossible to travel, best to just stay
home."

"Do you participate?" Chaz asked carefully.

"Dunk Hindu gods in the sea? No. My people and I are
Parsis, from Persia many centuries ago. India has room for
many beliefs, Bombay more than most. Did you know that
this city was built on religious tolerance?"

Chaz admitted he didn't.

"When Charles II bought Bombay from the Portuguese,
and the British later decided to build this city up from the
seven islands, everyone said that laborers would not come.

That the noble experiment would fail. One promise made all the difference: the guarantee of religious freedom. That single commitment has spared us the terrible violence which has torn the rest of our country."

Chaz knew that Bombay had been reclaimed from the ocean inches at a time, an unparalleled feat of British engineering. New Bombay, the expansion city across the Thana Gulf, had had the advantage of twentieth- and twenty-first-century technology, and construction had *still* been a challenge.

Chaz and Clarise had arrived three days ago, after a leisurely journey aboard the dirigible *Gilgamesh*. Cities and villages, jungles and rivers, forests and oceans had flowed beneath them during dreamlike days. Along the way, they had dispersed tons of fish and algae protein. The precious powder was Xanadu's way of saying "thanks" for the use of the oceans. The Floating Islands gave back to the world that nurtured and supported them. It was dynamite publicity.

Normally, *Gilgamesh* turned back after traveling a few hundred miles inland. But his old friend Tata had invited him to a wedding, and Clarise wanted to go. It had been so long since he'd set foot off Xanadu . . . it was sometimes difficult to remember that an outside world existed, that not all human beings lived in artificial, tethered environments.

The party, begun in absolute tradition, grew more modern with the addition of a band. The younger people gyrated to western-style music. Tata sighed with resignation. "Some things change, and others remain the same, my friend."

One of the groomsmen shyly asked Clarise if she would care to dance. She gave Chaz a single sidelong glance. It embarrassed him to realize that this beautiful, proud creature was actually requesting permission. He nodded, and off she went.

Tata laughed. "You two share a single destiny, my friend. Trust me. I know these things. For years you have danced around each other. It is the oldest game, but I think the game has entered a new phase."

Tata was immensely wealthy, heir to an empire of hotels, steel mills, trucking, and cabs. But on their first meeting Tata had been a lawyer entering middle age, eldest of six sons, sent into the western world by his philanthropist father. The young prince must learn modern traditions before assuming the throne.

By the end of the twentieth century, India's starving millions starved less horribly in any of her major cities: There was work for willing hands in the brave new world. But housing was more critical than ever. Five hundred new faces appeared in Bombay every single day. Modular building techniques, reclaimed land built on seacrete piers, and modern food cultivation techniques, all spawned by Floating Island technology, offered hope. The elder Tata saw this and, although not of the Council, knew that his sons, and their sons, would be Linked. He did the Council's bidding, and his son after him.

Chaz gazed at his friend. Tata had one foot in the twenty-first century and one in the sixteenth. There was a question Chaz had waited two decades to ask . . .

He spoke carefully. "I see that your arthritis is still bothering you, Sajid."

Laughter and the sound of music filled the room. The wall tapestries, images of sun and forest and ancient heroes, had been in Sajid Tata's family for generations. The sun, low on the horizon now, shone through hanging curtains of vari-colored silk, lending myriad tints to the vast reception room, tinting the marble floors.

Tata's mild smile creased a salt-and-pepper beard. "I know what you will say," he said. "You want to ask why I, who have served the Council for so long, do not request their greatest boon."

Chaz nodded gratefully. For a moment Chaz felt that Tata was struggling with his explanation. Then there was a glad cry of "Grandpa! Grandpa!" from across the room. Twin cocoa-creme tykes dashed into his arms. They looked to be a Parsee-English mixture, and a moment later their mother and father entered the room. The mother wore traditional Parsee dress and was a dusky gem. The father was a hale, red-cheeked, hearty man whom Chaz took for Australian.

Tata's welcoming hug was so intense he seemed to be pulling them into his heart. He secretly slipped his hand into his coat, then performed a feat of prestidigitation, producing gold foil-wrapped treats from each of their ears. The twins squealed delightedly, covering him in kisses.

He introduced his daughter and son-in-law (Chaz was wrong: the son-in-law was South African), and they talked construction and communications for a few polite minutes. Then both went in search of the bride.

"He is an important man," Tata said proudly. "He postponed the dedication of a dam to honor our family." The white of his hair, the crick in his posture seemed not such a tragedy anymore. "You see, don't you?" he asked quietly.

And Chaz did see. Tata might request and receive the boon of extended life, a reward for long and honest service. But he would have to leave his family behind. No more hugs from his grandchildren. No more glorious nights with his wife. All his friends left behind. . . .

Chaz's mood was spiraling downward when Clarise approached, a light dew of perspiration beading her brow. Her brown skin seemed golden in the muted light. She gazed up at him. "Dance with me, Dr. Kato?"

"This isn't my kind of music," he said. "And I'm not sure these legs will support me, yet."

Almost on cue, the band struck up a waltz. "We can just sway," she said. "Trust me. I won't let you fall." The younger dancers left the floor, and some of the older guests moved out to try their luck.

Clarise stood back, and Chaz pushed himself up from his chair. He was wobbly but all right. He took her in his arms. He had learned these steps when her mother was an infant, but she knew them. Her wiry strength held him stable during the spins. They maintained a very proper frame, but her smile was cat lazy.

"Some people say that taking a woman to a wedding is a way of asking a question without asking a question," she said.

"I follow," he said warily. The floor wheeled with guests in white and gold, western and traditional Parsee garb. The waltz had an exotic undertone that Strauss had never anticipated, but might well have applauded.

Chaz said, "We made a mistake. I don't want to make another one."

He could feel the webbing of good, useful muscle beneath the exquisite padding. She was not just a beautiful woman, she was one of the best security officers on the island, and part of the organism to which Chaz had pledged fealty.

He had left a world behind him. Why had they chosen him for the gift of life extension?

He had a trick of perception. He could see implications. ("Then Kato does his jumpshift trick and we all get whiplash of the mind." Bill Gates had said that.)

Chaz felt a sudden and very real ache. Tata might grow old and die, but at least he had lived. Was that the price? Had Chaz lived so long, seen so much, and just now understood?

Clarise stopped him, and they stood immobile in the middle of the dance floor. She studied his face with something like alarm. "Chaz? Is your leg all right? You're crying."

In that moment, Chaz saw his life clearly, and finally knew what he wanted. He pulled Clarise to him and kissed her, not deeply, but warmly. He held her, reveling in her sheer aliveness.

"Chaz?" she asked, shocked and delighted.

"Shh," he said, so softly that she had to put her ear next to his lips. "Weddings always make me cry."

# 30

Lenore Myles arrived in Bombay at 12:05 A.M. local time, three-quarters dead from jet lag. Every nerve in her body jangled. She was dressed in calculatedly tacky gold lamé that simply *screamed* "starlet."

She let Lavar deal with their luggage and rather numbly answered questions at customs. The airport was shoulder to shoulder. "You are here for the festival?" a round, mustachioed official asked.

Levar smiled with perfectly capped teeth, deep in his Hollywood persona. "Here to visit a client. Movies."

The official straightened proudly. "Ah! India has the largest film industry in the world! But if you can, see the Festival of Ganesh. It is world famous."

He stamped their passports and waved them on.

Bleary-eyed, she let Levar hustle her through an airport filled with lovely, dark women and exotic men in western-style suits. The humidity and squalor didn't hit them until they stepped out of the terminal, and suddenly all her fatigue dropped away.

The street outside the airport was lined with beggars in rags and robes. Police officers attempted to hustle them along, but there often seemed little difference between cab drivers, concierges, street corner flower sellers, and those who simply tugged at her coat, asking in stilted English if she wouldn't like a "tour of city"?

She was so overwhelmed by the sounds and the sights, even so late at night, that she might have stumbled and been swallowed by the crowd if Levar hadn't hailed a cab and hustled her into it.

She fought to catch her breath. "I know," he said, calmer than she would have believed. "The first time, it's a little overwhelming."

A human driver pointed the cab like a missile. As they wound among streets, pedestrians, and other missiles, she pressed her face against the side window. Bombay was a city of lights and darkness, odd remnants of British architecture and stone-carved Hindu deities.

And everywhere, everywhere, the streets were clotted with people. They slept on the sidewalks, families clustered together. Little cook fires crackled on streetcorners and in alleys, and every cranny seemed crowded with makeshift lodgings.

"Are they really so poor?" Lenore knew how naive the question sounded but couldn't resist asking.

"In comparison with the rest of India? These people are rich," Levar said. "There is plenty of work here. In fact, that's part of the problem. The poor flow into Bombay from all across the continent. Where can they live? But they aren't starving."

She was happy when the cab pulled into the underground parking garage of the Bombay Hilton. Apparently the Spinners were well-heeled.

At three o'clock in the morning, the Hilton was sleepy but awake. She had never seen half so many bellhops in one place, and everywhere smiling brown attendants hovered, eager to take luggage or escort them to elevators. Halls, lobby, and offices were narrow but luxurious. Seductive, nearly inaudible Indian music hummed through the intercoms. She stood back against the wall, her mind swimming with fatigue and disorientation as Levar checked them in. The officials were kind to her, the bellhops attentive but polite.

Did they know they were tending a corpse?

She couldn't quell the darkness within her, the sense of implosion, the slow deterioration of the most sacred and vital parts of herself.

Levar took her up to their narrow room via a narrow elevator. Their room was small and spotless. The plumbing and furnishings seemed antique . . . not genuine antiques, certainly, but the work of artisans who worked in the day and slept in the streets at night. Bombay lacked in roofs, not hands.

She was in the heart of New Bombay, constructed across the Thana Gulf from the original city. She knew much of the city was of recent construction, using refinements of the British land-reclamation technology that built its elder sister a century and a half earlier. Tomorrow they would cross to the other side. Tomorrow they would enter a hellhole, and perhaps there she would find the answers she sought.

*Xanadu*, she thought. Bitterness and wonder. Floating Island technology had built New Bombay. She should rejoice in that. But if something had happened on Xanadu . . . if Chaz Kato had raped her body and mind . . .

Her stomach churned with warring emotions. If Xanadu and the Floating Islands had protected him, then she and Levar would destroy Chaz Kato and Xanadu and the Floating Islands.

Her belly felt heavy and hard with rage and grief and pain. She was stunned with the severity of it, dizzied, and suddenly Levar's arms were around her. She sagged, knees turned to water.

Too weak to stand, she gazed out on the city, this new world wrought by Xanadu and her sisters, looked out on a canyon of lights. Invisibly far below them, families cooked meals on the open streets, and were happy to do so.

"Stop it," he whispered in her ear.

"Stop . . . ?" she asked, not understanding, and then saw that her fist was pounding against the thick glass, that the skin over her knuckles oozed red. Little smears of blood and skin marred the window.

Gently Levar led her to the bed. He didn't try to make love to her, and for that she was grateful, even as she wondered at his motives. Was she so unappealing now?

He held her as he might a child. She curled against him and cried, and thought about what she had lost and what she might find tomorrow, across the bay, in a city a world apart.

# 31

Chaz Kato slipped out of bed, lifting Clarise's arm as he rolled away. The room smelled of the love that they had made, of her sweat and other body scents. For a moment he stood over her. Weakness in his legs was beginning to subside. Days ago he'd needed a wheelchair. Judging by the last half hour, other weaknesses had healed. Xanadu's magic was strong.

Her face, angular due to her extreme fitness, in repose seemed almost cherubic. Like a dark angel, he thought.

Strange, how every couple, every *coupling* had its own perfume. Afterward you can simply breathe it in, and you know.

On his honeymoon with Ako, he had *known*. No, not on their wedding night. They had both been exhausted, and though they'd tried heroically to stir up a romantic mood, ultimately they'd fallen asleep in each other's arms. He remembered waking during the night, her plump cheek pillowed against his arm, the faint baby sourness of her breath somehow endearing. He had watched the sunlight creep across the room, until she began to stir. He kissed her awake. Slowly, gingerly, then with increasing joy they had joined for the first time.

Afterward, he had known. They had both *known*.

A hindbrain thing, he thought. The olfactory nerves are coterminous with brain tissue, bypassing the frontal lobes.

The older, more primal brain understands. He knew that this woman was his and he, hers. And it was as simple as that.

Clarise? There had been no room for anyone in his life when he and Clarise first met. Although he hadn't admitted it, would never have admitted it, there had been something distantly irritating about her scent, about the feel of her as she lay against him, her body seeking his warmth and comfort in the night.

Lenore! He shied from her memory. He had been so terribly, achingly, completely ready to wind his life around a woman. Lenore seemed to have bathed in rose petals, her every secret a sweetness beyond his experience. Was she a fantasy? Or had this devil Saturn ripped away their destiny?

The circle had come around again. Clarise was in his bed again, and he knew simply by his reaction to her scent that he was ready.

He looked out on the ocean. From his window he saw the beach where, tomorrow, Bombay's Hindu population would celebrate the Festival of Ganesh. Floating Islands would distribute tons of free food.

Weddings and celebrations, old gods and new. This was a heady mixture. That and the scent of sex almost overwhelmed him. He turned back, steeling himself against the lure of the moonlight.

Clarise slowly stirred and then came awake. She sat and held out her hands to him, the sheet falling away from her breasts. And when he came to her, and they loved again, he heard her.

*You are lost and have wandered*, she said. *And I am home to you. As you are to me.*

*Yes*, he cried out later, much later, in the fullness of the moment. *Yes.*

*I have needed you so badly.*

*And will not leave you again.*

Later, when they lay quietly in each other's arms, he asked her: "How could you wait for me so long?"

She simply smiled as if he was a silly child and said: "Where was I to go?"

There was no answer to that, to her, so they fell asleep in each other's arms, and remained that way until morning.


Lenore Myles and Levar Rusche took the ferry to Old Bombay. The ferryman was withered and nut-brown, his muscles like ropes wound around a skeleton. His eyes were very alive. When he peeled back his shrunken lips in a smile, his teeth were very white.

The waters were clotted with small craft, most with foul little gasoline engines, some few with small, powerful jet-stream designs, and many powered by no more than muscle and will. The boatmen all seemed to be cousins and brothers and friends. These people might have steered such craft for a thousand years. Their boatman chanted softly to himself, as if he had traversed these waters for so long that he sailed without conscious thought.

Levar paid him when they reached the far side, and two grinning street urchins helped her up out of the boat. They were paid off with a few small coins.

Finding a cab was simplicity itself: It would have been more difficult to continue their journey on foot. A three-wheeled putt-putt jostled its way through the streets, lurching this way and that, and squeezed in next to the dock. A young man with blindingly bright teeth and coal-black hair screamed at the other cab drivers, shaking his fist and glaring. He latched onto Levar's arm and pulled the two of them to his cab, keeping up a nonstop stream of English conversation as he did.

"You come for Ganesha-Caturthi?" he asked. "Very big, very good. Weather so fine this year. Rain no more than four-five days this week."

"Imagine that," Levar said. He passed a scrap of paper to the driver. "Can you take us to this address?"

A toothy grin. "Yes, sir!" With unlikely and disorienting

speed, the cab scooted through the crowded streets.

Street dealers hawked blue statues of a man with an elephant's head, or an elephant with a man's body. T-shirts, caps, jewelry; every time they stopped at a light or a street corner, urchins pressed up against the windows, hammering with flat, damp palms, offering bric-a-brac of all varieties. The smell of hot grease and fresh garbage filled the air, but curiously, there was little stench of decomposition and no trace of human waste. It was true. Overcrowding was rampant, but Bombay's sanitation services were up to it. There was a huge profit stream running through this city and an endless supply of willing, industrious hands.

This wasn't her idea of a Black Hole, Calcuttan or otherwise. It was more like the "Slumland" section of Disney World.

And a flow of dental floss and toothbrushes too! All those white teeth. Had the American Dental Association acquired a SWAT team? Lenore giggled.

Levar smiled back at her. "What?"

She clutched her head. It was gone. She couldn't remember.

The cab dove through a series of twisting alleys and finally stopped in front of a wide glass wall with twisting neon spelling out words in several languages. The sign in English said: WEB MALL.

The windows were wide and garishly lit, with muscular men and women posing in them, moving through slow-motion Tai Chi and yoga poses, displaying their bodies in ways that gave her the creeps—until she looked more closely and saw things that made her doubt her eyes: tattoos that crawled across the skin, beauty marks that fluttered away from the body like cilia or fleshy feathers, tongues that stretched and curled and coiled in serpentine fashion. A woman with her eyeballs removed and twin vidscreens anchored into her skull.

"What is this place?" she whispered.

Levar drew closer to her, as much for his benefit as hers.

"Councilor and National legal systems overlap in New Bombay. They're still working out the details. Because of the confusion, it's one of the few places in the world where untested Augmentation technology is available for human beings."

"Dear God." A beggar boy tugged at her arm. She looked down and saw that he had tentacles grafted onto his shoulders instead of arms. Clumsily, weakly grafted. They didn't look as if he could juggle a handful of coins.

Levar shuddered. "Beggars here have always mutilated their own children to make better beggars. Now they've gone to the next level."

They ducked through a curtain into a foul-smelling warren of tiny rooms. Noxious hallways branched off in all directions. The front door was guarded by an enormous man with a machine-pistol grafted to the stump of his left wrist. He challenged Levar, who produced a little plastic card. The door guard barked a command to a small boy who ran up, took Lenore's hand, and led them at trotting speed through the neon Beggar's Alley.

Up and then down stairs, past nooks where women moaned under the knife and prostitutes serviced customers by hooking genitals to genitals with glowing microfilaments.

Birth control, indeed.

She lost track of the twists and turns, and then they were through a door and into a small, surprisingly clean waiting room. A tiny Caucasian woman peered at her engagingly. She was about the size of a cricket, with gloriously white hair and eyes that twinkled.

"Miss Myles?" she asked, clearly delighted. She called to the back of the office. "Dr. Chandra? Miss Myles is here!"

A huge Indian man emerged, so large that his hands were like catcher's mitts. The confined space might have increased his intimidation factor almost intolerably, but his evident delight was almost childlike.

"Miss Myles!" His hands swallowed hers, and he shook them warmly. "I've wanted to meet you for three years."

Lenore was taken aback. "*Three* years?"

He spoke heavily accented but excellent English. "Yes. This is ironic, yes? You develop a technology and then cannot use it for your own affliction and must come halfway around the world. And here you find the Chandras, who adapted your techniques so that we might one day save you."

Adapted. Pirated?

The cricket chirped in pleasure. "Yes yes yes. Well, please sit." They produced tea and little biscuits for her, and sat closely as they explained tapes furnished by Levar and evaluated her preliminary tests. They needed now to examine her personally.

They shaved little plugs on her scalp and attached wires to the base of her skull, to her forehead and temples. They set up an apparatus to peer into her eyes, and for the next two hours asked questions, played tones, shone lights, triggered sensations, fed her samples of bitter or sweet paste on little spoons, and had her smell the contents of varied jars. The entire time the little Caucasian woman and the bearlike Indian man puttered and purred and sorted and evaluated and consulted with each other, made holophone calls and consulted books and computer screens, talked happily and concealed dark faces—

Then told her to wait a minute and retreated to the back room.

After about ten minutes Mrs. Dr. Chandra emerged with another cup of tea for Lenore, every inch the very proper hostess. Then she disappeared behind the curtain again.

Levar held her hand. She looked into the mirror at herself—tired, scared, and now half bald. But for some odd reason, this strange pair had instilled her with more hope than she had felt in almost a year.

"It's all right," Levar said confidently. "They're *good*. There was a little problem in Australia for the lady . . ."

"Problem?"

"Something to do with her method of obtaining fetal

nerve cells to treat Parkinson's disease. She ran from the law and ended here. She met Dr. Chandra, fell in love—isn't he *big* for an Indian? They've worked together ever since."

The two of them reappeared. The cricket spoke. "Miss Myles," she said. "You have been given a virtual stroke. Very precise and accurate."

Mrs. Dr. Chandra pulled her chair closer to Lenore, and held her hand tightly. "The procedure was done in a hurry by someone of great skill, intelligence, and, I think, compassion. Someone wanted to remove a memory without hurting you. Unfortunately, the edges have begun to unravel. I've never seen anything quite like it. It is almost like a posthypnotic suggestion given at the axion level. Part of your brain was instructed to turn itself off."

"Can it be reversed?"

She sighed. "No no no. Wrong approach, with the technology we have available. What we *can* do is *treat* it as a stroke. We can inject a combination of synthetic and immature neurons—"

"Culled from?"

Dr. Chandra cleared his throat. "Two sources. Laboratory-grown neurons extracted from testicular tumors."

*"What?"*

"Don't worry. There is an insignificant chance that they will develop into cancer cells. These cells, unlike most human cells, retain the capacity to develop into different cell types. We keep a culture."

In what was probably a completely unconscious reaction, Levar's hand had strayed to the fork of his jeans and cupped protectively.

Lenore resigned herself. "And the others are fetal cells, aren't they?"

"Yes." Dr. Chandra seemed uncomfortable with the topic. "But there has been more trouble than usual obtaining them. The abortion rate has dropped greatly in this city. Our usual source is abortions from the street people here in Bombay.

Often circumscribed by religious beliefs, but I'm afraid that has rarely stopped anyone, especially once there is an established market. But birth rates are down."

"The government's population reduction program is finally bearing fruit," Mrs. Dr. Chandra said proudly.

Lenore said, "No . . . wait . . ." A trapped memory hammered at the wall in her mind, fists dripping blood and bone chips. . . . She shook herself out of it. "Go on."

"We'll inject the cells using an MRI map to guide and tag them. The transplanted neurons will send out extensions, connecting with healthy neurons and establishing normal communication."

Lenore finally caught on. "So what you're hoping is that the new neurons will bridge the shut-down areas and act as conduits for information."

"That's the simplified version of it, yes. We've never tried to undo damage like this. I mean, it's not really damage, if you understand me."

Lenore stared at the ground. "And if you do this, how long before we know the outcome?"

"A week to ten days," Dr. Chandra said. "We must be sure that the cells are not rejected, that there is no bleeding or inflammation of the brain. We should know that in seventy-two hours. Then we will see. Dear, I wish your earlier self could supervise!"

There it was. She had come halfway around the world to try a technology stolen from her own work, bolstered by illegal fetal brain cells. Something inside her told her that there was more to this. That she needed to think, to ask why something that they had said struck a distant chord.

She couldn't think of a question.

"All right," she said. "Let's do it."

# 32

I t is just a rumor," Dr. Jois said. Their host kept a small house above Chowpatty Beach, where they watched thousands of Hindus participating in the elephant god's yearly ceremony. They filled the ocean and crowded the sands around multiple titanic statues of the Ganesh. Its colors were gaudy enough to hurt the eye.

"Clearly," Chaz had said at first glance, "this is not the god of good taste."

Clarise was horrified. Dr. Jois and Tata were more tolerant. Jois was a small, limber, dark man, a friend and schoolmate of Tata's who lived south in the town of Mysore. He had come up for the holiday.

Behind them the spires of Old Bombay rose as proud as they had been when originally erected by the British. The juxtaposing of old and new should have been jarring to Chaz, but it wasn't. Perhaps the presence of the historical, or the ancient, in the midst of a modern explosion was somehow comforting.

This was a time of celebration, when the old ways and superstitions came very close to the surface. It was not only laborers and artisans, the lost and hopeless who splashed out in that Arabian Sea in homage to the god of wisdom. Doctors, lawyers, legislators . . . the holiday brought Bombay to a joyous standstill, crowding the streets with revelers and engendering an almost irresistible urge to believe in things unseen.

Which had led to the current discussion.

"I am telling you, my friends," Jois said. "Two things

have come out of Mysore in the last year. One is rumblings from the health office . . ."

"To what end?"

"The government has made it quite difficult to obtain that information. If I were to speculate, it would be that the un-wed motherhood is virtually nonexistent. And the birth rate as a whole is dropping." He seemed troubled.

"Is that a bad thing?" Tata asked.

"A thousand new faces pour into Bombay and New Bombay every two days," Clarise said. "You said that. If something is working—"

"Why do they hesitate to take credit?" Jois took a long pull from his iced tea. "That is peculiar! But my friends have little to tell me, and it is difficult to read whispers."

"Well, what about this rumor of Ganesh?"

"Yes," he said. He turned to Tata. "I spoke of this over a year ago."

"Oh, yes. In jungles north of Mysore, the god Ganesh has taken fleshly form and is rousing the natives."

"Yes . . . but something has developed that might interest you." Jois turned to Chaz. "Xanadu's distribution of fish protein has made you many friends throughout India, Mr. Kato."

Jois had piercing eyes and skin so clear it looked like burnished brass. He was very thin but radiated vitality. "I have heard many things. But these stories I have heard from several sources." His accented English was excellent. "A celebration has been conducted on full moons, and many of the village's laborers attend. Ganesh comes. Some say such ceremonies are conducted all over our country." Again he shrugged. "Who knows? These are strange times. We have seen so many miracles."

Chaz remembered words that he had spoken to Lenore Myles: *"And they say that, in the jungles of India, miracles still happen . . ."* before he ripped them from her memory.

Chaz glanced at Clarise. She was alert, all her attention focused on Jois.

He just couldn't resist. This trip was bringing him back to life! "Might your people consider it . . . improper for outsiders to attend?"

"Improper but not blasphemous. You have brought much good to the villages. The food, the inoculation programs have reduced starvation and disease greatly."

"How long will the trip take?" he asked.

"As long or as short as you wish. We could be there in an hour or a month."

His various responsibilities back on Xanadu became a mental juggling act . . . and then Clarise leaned over him. Her lips nearly brushed his ear. "Chaz, once in your life you broke your health because you thought it was duty. Today your duty is to heal. Take the time."

He said, "Let's take a jeep. A little camera safari? I'd like to interview some of the villagers we've fed. I'll take the footage back with me." Good publicity. Or he might find a glitch—food that was in violation of religious proscriptions, or just bad—and how else could Xanadu learn? "And let's try to see this fakir's act with the elephant god."

"I tell you, my friend, it is more than that."

"Sorry. God of Wisdom? Dunsany's character Jorkens had a chance to meet her—the Sphinx—but he would have missed his sailing date."

"Fool," said Jois.

"Then we can jeep back up along the coast and take *Gilgamesh* home. Can you arrange that, Tata?"

"That, or whatever else you desire," his friend said expansively.

Clarise yawned. "I'm glad that's settled, Chaz. I'm feeling a little sleepy. Or maybe a bit restless. Would you like to come back to the cabana and help me decide which?"

# 33

Lenore woke in a cocoon, unable to move her head. She was fastened into some kind of white webbing. It looked as if a spider had woven her tightly into a large bed in a small room.

She moved her eyes to the side. It hurt, but the ache was a good one. She remembered a burst of air against her arm, then a swift drop into darkness. Of course, she recalled nothing of the procedure itself.

She blinked and resolved a blurry image of herself on the ceiling, hanging upside-down. What . . .

Mirror. The entire room was mirrored, rather tastelessly. Where the hell was she?

Levar was asleep on a chair to her right. Mrs. Dr. Chandra stood at the bedside, watching her react.

"Where am I?" Lenore managed to croak.

"Oh." The little doctor took in the room with a bemused glance. "We share the facilities with some of the cybermall's other tenants."

Lenore sighed. "Dr. Chandra's brain surgery emporium and cathouse?"

She *yeeped* in surprised laughter. "A little joke! And how long has is been since you indulged in humor?"

There was a dizzy pressure behind Lenore's eyes as she tried to answer the question, and found she could not. But . . . The corners of her mouth lifted in a smile. However small, however pitifully, she had attempted a joke!

"How long have I slept?"

"Almost a day since the operation. Part of that is the jet lag, of course. No postoperative complications. We're quite happy. You are something very close to an ideal patient. Do you feel up to a few simple exercises?"

She whispered "Yes" without nodding her head.

Levar woke up when she was halfway through a series of computer-assisted games: measures of reflex speed and cognitive choice, memory speed and simple logic. Then batteries of aural tones and light patterns while sensors built into the webbing took various measurements.

Throughout, Mrs. Dr. Chandra nodded and hummed. "Splendid," she said finally. "You're doing just fine." She almost twinkled as she pirouetted and left the room.

Levar took her hand. "How do you feel?"

"Like a baby butterfly," Lenore said. And laughed, found herself caught in a laughing jag that was out of all proportion to the merit of the humor. "Levar, I feel hope!"

Only twenty-four hours since the introduction of strange new cells, undifferentiated neurons, fetal cells, artificial dendrites, whatever. At the coaxing of the Drs. Chandra, the cells were building bridges and communication lines. It was impossibly premature, of course, but she could actually feel the difference, feel the aliveness within her, like a bubbling light way back behind her eyes.

Levar squeezed her hand. "Do you remember anything?"

He looked so earnest, so passionate that for a minute she could clearly see through the weight-pumped body to the chubby boy he had been in college so long ago. Before Antarctica, before so much in the world had changed for the worse. She could only laugh at his impatience.

"No, Levar," she said. "Nothing yet." But was that true? She remembered something odd. A taste. Meat and barbeque sauce, distinct and delicious, and bone between her teeth. Short ribs? And a voice: Tooley's voice? Now where had she eaten barbecue with Tooley? *Xanadu?*

Phone her! But that would be a terrible violation of security.

"I don't really remember much yet," she said. "But I will. I know I will." She squeezed his hand. Suddenly her vision shimmered with tears. She was almost overwhelmed with gratitude. She owed this man, her friend, her former lover, so much. And he had asked for so little in return.

"But it will," she repeated. "And then I'm really going to owe you." He turned away from her slightly, as if reluctant to meet her gaze. "No, really," she said. "You're going to help me think of a way to pay you back." She found her voice trying to put a saucy turn on that, but it softened into sincerity.

He squeezed her hand again and stood. Again, without quite looking at her, and she remembered the pudgy boy he had been. She'd *liked* the old Levar Rusche.

"Don't worry." His smile was forced. She thought she saw a kind of hunger behind it. Was it lust?

She owed him . . . but that wasn't it. She felt a sudden stab of fear, alarm trickling in from the periphery, dulling the joy and relief.

"Everything will work out fine," he said. "Now I'm going to make arrangements to move you back into the hotel. You'll be all right?"

"Fine," she said, and watched him until the door closed behind his broad, California-muscled back.

That was strange, she thought. Her mental clarity was returning, and with it a healthy dose of paranoia. Strange. One would think that as her mental acuity increased, it would be clearer to her that she was safe among friends. This must be some kind of transference, like a patient hating the therapist who uncovers a dark, abusive family secret.

# 34

For six days now Chaz and Clarise had followed a rude trail south. The jeeps were at least forty years old, gas-guzzling curios with stiff springs and worn seats. His backside was sore, but his spirit soared. He was hiking every day now, stretching and performing pliés and deep knee bends, and his legs were almost back to normal.

They had enjoyed six days of glorious scenery, of water buffalo and trained elephants, of smiling, brown-skinned laborers carrying loads on their backs or heads as their fathers and mothers had for a thousand years before them. Of thin, healthy children running beside them, begging for handfuls of vitamin candy that he distributed with delight.

He took hundreds of pictures a day and at night in their tent sorted though them, deleting 90 percent, uplinking the rest back to his scrapbook on Xanadu.

And later there was roast mutton cooked by Dr. Jois and his guides and a sky filled with stars every bit as glorious as those on Xanadu. Later still there was Clarise, luminous in the moonlight, the starlight in her hair sparking highlights he had never seen before. They stayed up after the others wandered off to bed and spoke of things hitherto unvoiced: her childhood and his, their dreams and hopes.

Once she said, "When you got well, you wanted your privacy back."

"My brain wasn't healed," he said. "You like to run things, right? But for a man like me, it makes sense to let . . ." How to phrase this?

"To let Ako," said Clarise.

"—to let Ako run my home. Keep my feet anchored so I can reach further. So I can . . . play." (Ako had asked him once, *Do you get paid for playing?* He'd said, *So do all scientists.*) "Well, my home is Xanadu and you."

The trip down to Mysore was delightful. He saw temples and rivers filled with crocodiles, passed villages where healthy, protein-fed children serenaded them and received blessings from thankful parents once Dr. Jois made introductions.

He saw many children but very few infants. It stirred around in the back of his mind. The villagers welcomed them, knowing that Xanadu's gifts had brought life and health to the village. But sometimes he saw something angry and dark behind the smiles. He had seen this in hospitals, in patients trying to forget that they were in pain. Nothing directed at Chaz. No, it was inchoate, unformed, like a black anvil of cloud drifting, awaiting guidance. *Shall I storm?*

*Is it time for the lightning?*

The morning they were to reach Mysore, Jois awoke them before dawn with hot herb tea. He told them to dress and come to the jeeps. The sun had not yet climbed above the trees when they approached the first outlying buildings. Jois held up his hand, and the minicaravan stopped.

Although the day had yet to warm, there in a broad flat area clasped by a U of dormitory-style buildings at least two hundred men and women, old and young, exercised in the morning air. In concert, their breath a teakettle's hiss of effort and exultation, they arced and twisted their bodies until they glistened with sweat, then forced themselves into even more formidably corkscrewed configurations.

At first Chaz thought the jeeps would bypass the complex, but Jois pulled his wheel hard, and they rolled into a hard-packed driveway. "Weather is good today," he said. "Or students would have to practice indoors."

They rolled down a driveway sheltered on either side with palm trees. Through the branches, he saw the students' glistening, sweaty bodies torqueing and twisting through their morning exercise.

They jumped back and forth with impressive athleticism, and Chaz finally couldn't contain himself. "What exactly *is* that?"

Jois smiled. "It is called *Ashtanga*. A form of hatha yoga. You know yoga?"

Chaz nodded. "By reputation. Looks strenuous. I thought yoga was sitting like a pretzel, contemplating your navel . . . that sort of stuff."

His host chuckled. "My grandfather taught it around the world. We continue his work. Perhaps you would like to try a class?"

Chaz held up his hands in protest. "That's a little much for me. I was injured recently."

But Clarise watched the students intently. Chaz realized that in all the time he'd known her, he had never seen her work out. She was Security; she'd be skilled in various techniques of restraint and defense. She moved like a panther, yet he had never actually seen her undergoing her rigors.

She squeezed his hand and said, "I'd like to try."


Jois told them that they would have to wait until nightfall and therefore had a day to rest and ready themselves. They were taken to a clean, spare dormitory. Running water was a welcome sight after days on the road.

He showered and napped, and awoke in a muggy afternoon. Clarise was nowhere to be seen. Chaz dressed quickly and went in search.

Lanky, lean yoga students strolled the halls. They looked to be from many countries, including Europe and America, and they smiled at him, assuming that he was one of them. Oh, he was lean enough, he supposed, but he wasn't . . . hmmm . . . what was the word? Supple. That was it. They had a quality of supple strength that was rather androgynously appealing. A few questions took him to a dining hall, where he piled a bowl with bananas and a kiwi-like fruit he didn't recognize. The hall was almost empty. A jovial, rounded chef informed him that afternoon classes were in session.

The building looked new but already well used. Three stories on about five acres of ground, with spacious patios and gardens. Many, many windows and open doorways looked out onto small patios where pairs or triplets of students worked at various arcane poses, meditated, or just lounged and enjoyed the day. He found the atmosphere re-

laxing, and music played almost continuously from hidden
speakers.

A few more inquiries took him to a larger room, where
at least forty students faced each other in two rows, exer-
cising. Jois conducted the class personally, and his meek
country doctor persona had evaporated, revealing a merciless taskmaster far more lion than lamb.

Jois barked commands, he cajoled, he joked, he insulted.
With hands and feet he prodded them into more precise
postures. He urged them to breath more deeply and slowly.

Pools of sweat dripped from them. The windows were
fogged up. Chaz sat quietly in one corner of the room and
watched. Together, as if they had done these things a thousand times, they rolled through the movements.

Suddenly he realized that one person was out of sync. It
was Clarise Maibang! Oh, she was lean and strong and flexible, but it was clear that she had never attempted these
specific motions. Her savage look of concentration was
somehow endearing. When Jois barked at her, called her
lazy and told her to "tighten her fundament," Chaz could
barely restrain his mirth.

He kept his cool. The last thing in the world he wanted
was for Jois to notice him and invite him onto the floor.
There was something about this art that was both beautiful
and intimidating as hell . . .

An hour later the torture was over. Students lay steaming
on their backs. An assistant drew blankets over them, and
soft, restful music hummed from the walls.

After ten minutes, some of them started to rise, fold their
blankets, and tiptoe from the room. Clarise was one of these.
She saw Chaz, and smiled as she had not during the workout
itself. She folded her yellow blanket and joined him. Her
white leotard was dappled with sweat, and she looked both
radiant and curiously relaxed.

She took him out into a garden, where they sat on stone

seats. She breathed deeply several times, centering herself.

"Strange," she said. "This does not look like home . . . but it *feels* like home."

He looked at her in surprise. "Similar how?" he asked.

"I have just limped my way through a form of yoga, not the Serak of my people, but it feels the same."

"Serak?"

She grinned ruefully. "Serak is never taught to women, but after my parents died, my uncle taught me a few things."

Again this was more than she had ever volunteered. Chaz asked, "Was he the one who let you go with the missionaries?"

She nodded. "I think that there was always something a little different about me, and he wanted me to see the world."

"You're different, all right." She didn't turn toward him, but her small, warm smile told him all he needed to know. He kissed her on the corner of her mouth. She took his arms and wrapped them around her, and he felt her aliveness, the softness and strength. Suddenly a flash of revelation that was almost disorienting: *She wants to have my baby.*

God. How do I know that?

She turned and looked at him, still not speaking. Her brown eyes were so clear, so calm and wise. He started to speak, but she just shook her head. "Shh," she said. "Let's just be here for a while." And then laid her head on his shoulder.

Sometimes, he thought, knowing is enough.


The sun had set hours before, and the trek into the forest to the east of Mysore was a slow thing. They followed trails hacked through the brush by traffickers in hardwood and bamboo. Some were old elephant trails adapted to footpaths and the needs of gasoline jeeps.

During the day they might have passed lines of native workers singing and laughing and making jokes about weird strangers as they walked to their various employments, carrying box lunches of rice and curry and spiced meats.

But now, at night, the silence and the absence of humanity set Chaz's nerves on edge.

Dr. Jois drove them, Clarise in the front seat, Chaz in the back. Jois too seemed a bit nervous, on edge. Chaz had left his Xanadu clothing behind. They were all dressed in simple, coarse pants and shirts, even Clarise, who had chosen to disguise her gender.

The closer they came to their destination, the heavier the foot traffic became. Finally they turned their jeep onto a side path and took to their feet.

The flow of devotees seemed endless now. Most of their companions were men, disproportionately between the ages of fifteen and thirty. They were almost silent. Jois walked between them, head down, quiet. Something in the air was . . . disturbing. This place seethed with a repressed current of anger or violence.

Because the walk was a hardship? No, he thought not. Too many seemed to be in their late teens, young fathers perhaps. Angry young men on hair triggers.

The path narrowed and then widened, and they came to an amphitheater cut in the earth, lined with split logs and round stones, concentric rings leading down to a wide, flat open circle at the very bottom. Opposite them, a broad path led from the forest down to the center, and he noticed that the attendees were careful not to block the path.

Other than this one throughway, the amphitheater was jammed full. A thin warm rain misted the air, and he hunched his shoulders. Clarise pushed against him, her strong shoulders comforting him even through the coarse cloth.

For almost half an hour they stayed like this, waiting. Chaz shifted impatiently in their position at the back of the amphitheater. Jois only shook his head and said, "I do not know. Perhaps . . ."

And then there was a disturbance at the far side and a

growing rumble in the crowd. Some tremendous mass thundered into the earth, and again, and again. Chaz realized that their impact had been growing for minutes now. As something approached them. His skin crawled.

Brush splintered, followed by a cry of fear and awe.

Entering the walkway was a wall of neon colors.

The elephant had been dyed in bright, iridescent pink and blue. It wore a garland of gigantic blossoms around its neck, and a *hat!*

Chaz's laughter died unborn. This creature could tear him to pieces . . . the *men* would tear him to pieces . . . and it wasn't funny. Look past the colors and it became the largest elephant he had ever seen. It stood fully fourteen feet at the shoulder, with vast ears and terrifying tusks. Its broad face was tattooed with Sanskrit, and its tiny black eyes gazed out at them. Chaz felt himself being judged.

Clarise whispered something under her breath. He'd only caught the end of her exhalation, but he knew what she was saying. She had said: "Ganesh?"

No, it didn't have the body of a human. That legend spoke of a young god or prince beheaded in battle, his body fitted with an elephant's head.

It moved like nothing on Earth could stop it, and the way it looked at the crowd, its vast gray trunk curling and uncurling. . . . The truth smashed into his mind like a two-by-four. Ganesh was *aware*. The animal was sentient.

With his sanity in question, Chaz looked for any abnormality about its head.

The hat was a dome of overlapping gold plates encrusted with gemstones. Chaz had seen so many of these on local statues that it had slipped past his mind; but it would hide Xanadu technology. There was something funny about the mouth too.

The elephant walked to the center of the amphitheater, accompanied by several human attendants, and spoke.

Chaz couldn't understand the words. He wondered . . . hoped that the voice was recorded, or broadcast from another location. But the words were perfectly synchronized with the bellowslike swell and deflation of the beast's sides.

*Not a microphone. Augmentation!* Ganesh was speaking with an altered mouth and a computer under the hat. This was no ordinary elephant, trained and conditioned and then painted to resemble an ancient god. This was as sophisticated an illusion as anyone could possibly create.

Without moving his lips, he spoke to Dr. Jois. "What is it saying?"

For a long moment, Jois didn't answer. Chaz saw that his host had grown pale. In the torchlight the men around him looked strained, eager, sulfurously angry.

Jois placed his lips close to Chaz's ear. He spoke in a whisper hardly audible beneath the elephant's modulated roar.

"This is very, very bad. Ganesh says that their young wives will bear no children."

As if on cue, the men roared their anger.

"He says that their government has betrayed them, sold their future children to the powers of the West. Ganesh says that their leaders are traitors and blasphemers, and that their time is near."

Perhaps it was just his imagination, but Jois's whisper had grown cold. His eyes were colder still.

Clarise grabbed his arm. "Chaz," she said. "We should get the hell out of here."

Men yelled out to "Ganesh," and the others fell silent to hear. "What are they saying?"

Jois still seemed numbed, but he spoke. "They are saying that the young wives are not bearing children. That they know this, and that the government has done nothing."

"Is it true?" Chaz said, already knowing the answer.

"Only the very young ones are infertile. The birth rate has been dropping for years in girls not yet . . . sixteen now. Only in the outlying villages do women bear children so young. It is natural that it would be seen here."

The men yelled and screamed. Ganesh reared up on his

hind legs and balanced there, forelegs stretching to the sky, trunk unfurling, trumpeting its challenge to the dark, rainy clouds.

Chaz was thunderstruck. The crowd fell absolutely silent. Except for Jois, who babbled now. "Ganesh . . ."

"It's a trick!" Chaz said. In English. His words fell into the sudden silence.

"Oh, God," Clarise murmured, and Chaz suddenly, horrifically grasped the depths of his error. The men closest to them turned and looked at them, and then those farther away. A slow, steady, angry murmur rolled through the crowd.

The great elephant cocked its head and looked at the back of the amphitheater. Directly at them. Slowly it rose to its feet. It shook itself as if awakening from a dream, absurd in its pink and green paint, terrifying in its unnatural intelligence. As it walked up through the crowd, men scrambled from its path.

Chaz stared into its eyes, looking for whoever or whatever controlled the beast. "Saturn," he said, for Clarise's ears.

The elephant screamed something in Bengali and charged.

Hands reached for Chaz, grasping his robe. He shucked out of it, from the corner of his eye seeing Clarise smashing a man in the face with her elbow, watching her move with incredible, disorienting speed to seize a torch. Screaming, she thrust it into the face of the augmented elephant.

The elephant reared back, trumpeting. The men who had grasped at Chaz and Clarise were frozen, horrified by the tableau, suddenly overwhelmed by the awe and mystery of the moment. But Chaz and Clarise ran.

Jois, fleet as a rabbit, led the way. Ganesh thundered down and came for them.

They had bare seconds before the crowd overcame their fear and did as their deity bade them. But in those few moments, Chaz and his companions fled the amphitheater. The elephant screamed its rage, a terrible, driven beast with the eyes of Saturn. It trampled its followers, it tore up trees, it flung great divots of earth into the air in its attempt to reach them. Torches and stone and battered men flew.

Someone threw himself at Clarise. She pivoted without breaking stride, made some kind of movement Chaz couldn't follow, and the man tumbled away, unconscious. A knife flashed from the shadows. Chaz screamed in horror, certain his life was over. Then Clarise was there, grasping the knife hand, torquing with her hips. There was a grinding snap, and the elbow behind the knife shattered, the acolyte's face distorted with terrible, stunning pain.

Then Jois had their jeep, and Clarise was pushing Chaz into it. Ganesh was close, tearing up bushes and trees in an orgy of pink rage, struggling to reach them through the protecting forest. A native threw himself on the back of the jeep. The sweep of a makeshift club brought sudden pain to Chaz's left shoulder. He balled his fist and smashed it directly into the man's face. His fingers felt as if he'd broken them all, but his attacker fell back and away. Then the jeep was off, racing down the road. The screams of the pursuing men and the trumpeting of the frustrated elephant faded behind them.

Chaz sank onto the floor of the jeep and sobbed for breath.

# 35

Within the shadow-tangled webbing of her sickroom, Lenore spoke her first intelligible word of the day. "Levar?" Her lips were chapped and coated with a soothing ointment that had yet to stop the splitting.

"Yes, Lenore?" He sat at the edge of her bed, his fingers smoothing her brow.

He had stood by her for almost a week now, administering antibiotics, antidepressants, and other medications he neither recognized nor understood. Twice the Drs. Chandra had visited them to check her readings and bandages. They nodded sagely, smiled, patted Levar's shoulder, spoke comforting words, and went about their rounds.

The disinfectant's ammoniated lemon reek still curdled his stomach. Sometimes Lenore reminded him of a terminally ill octogenarian, sometimes a feeble infant. He was uncertain which discomforted him more. The nausea and incontinence seemed almost a cleansing process, as if she were being emptied, or perhaps razed to rebuild anew from a firmer foundation. Eyes blazing with fever, Lenore had taken a brief turn for the worse. Now she seemed to be approaching normalcy.

For longer and longer periods, she was the Lenore Myles he remembered.

Fatigue consumed her, fed by late-night reading and fledgling attempts at exercise.

Gazing up at him, she whispered: "What's happening outside? I hear something. Not the festival, is it?"

Even here, on the thirtieth floor, screams streamed up from the streets below. A thousand thousand outraged voices melded into a hateful, chaotic chorus.

What if he, *they* were to fall into those angry hands? It nibbled at his mind. Something hideous had happened, something that the stone-faced newscasters had yet to address directly.

Fear leeched his resolve, but he refused to surrender. Somewhere here in Bombay was the key to the Council's deadly conspiracies. And he, Levar Rusch, would find it.

He scratched idly at his right leg. For the past few days, it had itched inordinately.

Lenore's grip weakened, then strengthened as she collected her thoughts. The tip of her tongue moistened her scaled lips. "Why are you here?" An almost childlike curiosity flickered in her eyes. "Why are you helping me?" She managed a weak smile. "Don't tell me it's love. Even at the beginning, I don't remember love."

"You underestimate your powers." He hitched his eyebrows suggestively, and they shared a brief, flat chuckle. When it died, he shrugged. "We have the same enemies. . . ."

But she seemed to be looking right through him. He hadn't the nerve to lie. "There isn't anyone else," he said.

She blinked hard several times. "I'm not sure that Chaz is my enemy," she said.

"How much do you remember?"

"I'm getting bits. Bytes. I remember thinking that he loved me. I wondered how in the world he could feel something like that. He didn't even know me."

"This is a man of wealth. Power. A man used to getting everything he wants. If you didn't return his love, mightn't he have become frustrated? Dangerously so?"

She blushed. "I don't remember everything," she said, "but I can tell you that there was no need for rape. That much I'm sure of."

Levar was jarred. Hell, what if Kato *hadn't* raped her?

But there were other sins, worse sins. The Council was raping the entire planet. He patted her hand and fed her a few capsules. He held her hand until she slipped back into a drowse. Lenore closed her eyes and began to snore.

Outside the window, Bombay was burning.

While Lenore slept, Levar Rusche retired to the living room. He opened the black rectangle of his briefcase and withdrew something that resembled a hypodermic needle with a glass thread attached to it. He plugged the thread into a port at the briefcase's hinge, linking to the powerful computer built into the frame. He pulled off his pants. He felt around his right kneecap until he could slide the patella up. That still made him queasy. He pushed the needle in and winced at that too. It hurt. The skin covering his thigh was his own.

Beneath it the femur had been surgically removed. Anchored between the hip and knee sockets was a structure that any X ray or standard scan would show as healthy human bone.

He slipped on his sunglasses. The lenses rainbowed, kaleidoscoped, cleared. The air in front of him blossomed into a shadowed human shape. He was hooked into the secret core of the Spinner network.

When Levar spoke, the words gobbled out of him in a cascade. "God's sake, will you tell me what's happening? I'm in the middle of a war zone!"

The male/female voice answered him. "There are disturbances from Bangladesh to Beijing. We don't know *what* is happening, only that it seems tied in with falling birth rates. Are you secure?"

Secure? His contact's words had opened a pit of panic just beneath his feet. "Let's hope. Do we have the new codes?"

"They've just come through. Please stand by to receive transmission."

Almost immediately, Levar felt an unpleasant buzzing in his bones.

The Chinese surgeons had promised that he would feel nothing, but he could never completely dispel the notion that the thing inside his right thigh was talking to him, had a personality and an agenda of its own, and meant him no good.

Just a minor malfunction. Just the shakes! The mission would be over before he could get these electronics repaired. He arched reflexively as the electrical tingle intensified. His mouth tasted as if he had bitten down on tin foil.

Then, suddenly, it was over. Levar choked back a curse. Manners! "Do we have any word on Kato and the woman?"

"Stand by. We're still searching. The current political confusion makes everything more difficult."

"For me, too, and my ass is on the line."

The creature on the other end was unimpressed. "You aren't the only one taking risks, my brother. Until the Council falls, we are all at risk." The image winked out.

Levar withdrew the hypodermic and slipped his pants back on.

He walked to the window and stared down on the town. Yesterday a thousand cook fires had twinkled like stars. Now a dozen buildings in his view jetted smoke or flame. Levar leaned his forehead against the window. He imagined that he could hear the voices, detect the crackle of the flames themselves, hear the vast and faceless masses as they discovered the depths of their betrayal. His doubts and anger fled, the pain vanished. He drank in those voices, intoxicated by their demands for justice, justice that only Levar Rusche could give them.

The Festival of Ganesh had transformed into something dark and hungry, a celebration of mindless rage rather than scholarship. It had happened in a twinkling, so quickly that Tata wouldn't have believed had he not witnessed it for himself. In the past forty-eight hours, retainers whose families had served his for a dozen generations had grown surly and uncommunicative.

Fearing for their safety, Tata had sent his family away to his beachfront villa in Ceylon. But the emptiness of the great house, so recently the site of a joyous wedding, now engulfed him like a tide.

Like thieves in the night, one at a time his servants had slipped away. Finally he had cornered Sohela and demanded an explanation.

"You must leave, Mr. Tata," the old Bengali woman had said. "You are not safe."

He was utterly baffled. "But why? Sohela, I don't understand."

"Because of the people you serve. The Council."

"The Council? But they've fed us and sheltered us. Just two weeks ago you were praising them for the work they've done. Should I flee now because I serve them?"

Sohela would barely meet his eyes. "It is true. I cannot change that which is true."

"But why?"

Her thin shoulders bunched and then relaxed. She sighed, as if a great, terrible weight had been lifted from her. Something between anger and pity shone in her eyes. "You think perhaps that I am a simple woman, that I am foolish to worship as I do."

"I never—"

"You didn't have to. I could see it in your eyes. But you need to know that this is real. No, not wild tales of Ganesh trumpeting human speech. Those are certainly fables for the ignorant. What is true is that the women are not having babies."

Tata was stunned. "Sohela, your niece gave birth last month."

"She is almost thirty. My great-niece, who is fifteen and properly married, should have borne by now. She has not. And neither has any girl under sixteen."

What was this? And if it was true, who had known of it? And how carefully must it have been kept under wraps? Sixteen years old? No woman under the age of sixteen giving birth . . . ?

He had missed the old woman's next words. "—must leave, sir, now. It is vital. You serve the ones who did this."

She turned and hobbled away.

Like a sleepwalker, Tata went to his office.

His computer was always on-line; it was the work of moments to begin the proper searches. This couldn't be true. It just couldn't. . . .

And yet, within moments, the truth was revealed on the screen before him. His nation's birth control program had encouraged young women to postpone their first children, urged men to use condoms and couples to use other devices. Even the sacred celibacy rituals of *Bramichariya* had been encouraged, with apparent success. But hidden deep within the statistics was the naked truth that birth rates for mothers born after 2010 to 2012 C.E. had nearly stopped.

The dropoff was precipitous and obvious. How could anyone have missed it? But if the cause wasn't birth control programs directed in an unfocused and uncoordinated manner by a faltering government, then ... then ... ? Something clandestine and awesomely effective.

But why was blame being laid at the Council's door?

A cold sweat broke across his brow, and he suddenly remembered something of terrible importance. A few quiet phrases into the computer and the information appeared.

He almost stopped breathing. His hand flicked out to touch the phone pad. The connection had barely been made when he heard a sound behind him.

"Mr. Tata?"

He spun in his chair.

This was no rioter. The man was thin, and pale skinned, and Chinese. The gun in the man's hand suggested that he was already quite certain of Tata's identity. "Yes." Tata straightened in his chair.

"Mr. S. P. Tata?"

Tata had no wish to enter the next world with a lie upon his lips. "Yes," he repeated.

He felt the beginning of something as soft as his granddaughter's kiss, touching him in the middle of his forehead. Then there was nothing, nothing at all.


Lenore Myles wasn't certain why they had left the hotel, unless it was because the world was coming apart.

Traffic in Bombay, always grueling, today was hideous. Panic filled the air like a sour perfume. Government bulletins begged people to remain in their homes, encouraged foreigners to seek shelter at their consulates. Skilled news commentators garbled their reports, faces flushed and eyes brimming with tears.

Even so ... the hole in her mind was beginning to heal. One hour at a time, it was raveling. Odd how blessedly wonderful that felt. The joy was twofold: Not only did it signify recovery, but also it implied that her research had been valid! She would return to the United States, walking proof of her own synthetic neural research.

Levar had rented a Land Rover with tinted windows and engaged a tall, leathery young driver he called Raul. These two knew each other. He'd be a Spinner.

Levar had emptied his wallet to move their luggage downstairs. The bellhops, so polite and cooperative just a week ago, now viewed them with suspicion or hatred. When tips were doubled and redoubled until they became extravagant bribes, he finally found men willing to assist them.

The streets were clogged with traffic and the rubble of burning buildings. She saw a European hauled from his taxicab and beaten on the side of the road. When Raul turned the corner, the man was still twitching. A twisted length of pipe descended on his head, and the twitching stopped.

She felt as if she were watching everything through a haze. Levar navigated, studying a folded paper map. Guided by luck and nerve and animal instinct, Raul drove them eastward, away from the lethal crush engulfing the downtown area.

The frenzied mob receded behind them.

"Where are we going?" she asked.

"To the dirigible docks," Levar said. "The airport, trains, and docks will be impossible, but we don't need them. We're getting the hell out of Dodge, babe."

His sudden enthusiasm confused and frightened her. "What are you talking about?"

"I've got new information. An old friend of yours is coming to town."

# 36

Route 60, the coast road leading from Bombay down to Mysore, had become almost impassable. In one town after another, rioting had erupted, violence grown rampant. Fires blazed out of control, government outposts and train stations stormed and destroyed by mobs hell-bent on vengeance. It was clear that every political, religious, and ethnic faction blamed all others for the hole in the universe where babies had been.

Chaz and Maibang kept driving. Stopping would have been suicide. Chaz had been on the phone to *Gilgamesh*: *Get us out of here!* and discovered that its hydrogen fuel tanks had been drained to apply new seals. For the next ten hours, they were on their own.

Twice they had been able to refuel the car. The first time a debit scan had been sufficient, but the second time the gruff, bearded attendant would accept only cash. He glared at them, and as they pulled out of the station and back onto the highway, he was already talking on the phone.

Eight minutes later someone took a shot at them from an overpass. Clarise cursed and spun them off the main road.

There began a jouncing, nightmarish journey along back roads roughly paralleling Route 60. Chaz scanned the radio constantly. The news was not good. Central health offices had contacted doctors across the continent. It was their terrible duty to inform patients that rumors of low birth rates were true. A massive series of diagnostic tests was being organized. . . .

Hindu blamed Muslim, and Muslim blamed Christian. Each said that the other lied about its own terrible statistics to cover its own genocidal intent. Towns along the Pakistani border were burning. India's prime minister had refused to rule out the use of nuclear weapons.

Chaz could understand little of what was being said. Almost none of it was in English. To his useless rage, their car had no shortwave radio. They were at the mercy of the local AM broadcasts.

Clarise dropped the engine to low idle so that she could hear. "A minute, Chaz." She stepped out, staring up the road ahead of them. Chaz wouldn't have been surprised had she dropped to her knees and put her ear to the ground. Her face was grave. When she returned to the jeep she said only "We're getting off the road," turned the wheel sharply to the left, and took them down to the banks of a stream.

They plowed the muddy banks in low gear as long as they could, sometimes going tire-deep in water.

The natives they passed stared at them, pointing, occasionally waving happily.

*Dear God*, Chaz thought. *They don't know yet. In two days the news will have reached every town across the continent. And what happens to us all then?*

In one of those villages they traded their spare tire and Chaz's watch for a few greasy gallons that strained their engine to the sputtering point. They might have chugged to safety, but within an hour their right rear tire exploded, stranding them on a tiny road between two heavily forested meadows.

Clarise got out. Chaz followed. The calm that settled over her was contagious: He felt his rage ebbing. Then she said, "We are going to die."

Chaz said, "Nah. Bombay's that way—".

"We could never walk to Bombay."

They were still two hundred kilometers south of Bombay, mere hours by car, an eternity on foot. They dared not seek assistance from any of the larger villages. No telling what news had filtered down. They needed to find a landing spot for *Gilgamesh*, hunker down, and wait. But where?

When Chaz suggested a two-kilometer trek to a town just east of them, Clarise's face tautened with fear and stress. "You have no gift for languages."

That last news bulletin? "Tell me."

She tuned the radio, listened to it for another few seconds. "It's been going for hours." She translated, " 'Unconfirmed rumors of the Home Secretary's office suggest the sterility epidemic is connected with the AIDS inoculation program of 2003.' "

Chaz stared at her. If people believed *this*, then he and Clarise would never leave India alive. But *he* believed instantly.

"Lenore," he whispered.

"What?"

"She found out. Saturn needed her dead. *Saturn.*"

"Ah." Clarise accepted.

A million considerations ran through his mind. Almost as quickly as one possibility gelled, he discarded it. Then the shadows of a cohesive plan came together.

He said, "They'll make the next connection, between the inoculation programs and the Floating Islands and the Council. We need to get *Gilgamesh* off the ground, and we need to do it now."

"Send her home?" she said, her voice glum and resigned.

"Screw that," he said. "Tell them to finish their repairs in the air, if they can. Then come and get us the hell out of here."


The field was east of Bombay, a huge flat razed area with gigantic hangers protecting lighter-than-air craft during monsoon season. Three dirigibles were parked there at the moment, a private airship belonging to a logging concern and two craft for the Floating Island chains. The logging blimp was a throwback to designs a hundred years old, a swollen cigar shape with a carriage underneath. The Councilor craft, *Gilgamesh*, used a spherical lift design, a cluster of modular gas sacks suspending a ship like a Viking galley beneath. *Gilgamesh* was a startling, vivid crimson.

Levar, Lenore, and the impassive Raul waited at the edge of the dirigible field, their Land Rover camouflaged beneath mud-and-leaf-colored netting. The two Americans alternated thin, queasy naps to the arrhythmic crackle of the multiband radio mounted beneath their dash. The band continually shifted, and Raul monitored it without apparent need for rest.

Levar had put down the backseat, extending the cargo space so that Lenore could stretch out. Her sleep was thin, crowded with dark, confused dreams. Several times she swam up toward the surface of consciousness to see Levar and Raul hunched over the radio, conferring in low voices. Most of the broadcasts were in a language she didn't understand, and these Raul translated. But some of the transmissions were in English: Spinner communications.

Spinners. Through Levar's connections, she had begun the road to recovery, and she should be grateful. As mental clarity increased, she became more certain that Chaz was no enemy. But her memories were slippery things, sliding across each other like eels in a night-dark sea. From time to time they coiled and linked, affording her a new level of clarity, a window into a misty past. So far, she remembered no taint of violence or betrayal.

Searchlights slid across their camouflaged vehicle, thinning her sleep even further. Hired guards patrolled the fence near the great balloons. Twice the night was split with bursts of machine-gun fire.

Levar turned to her, his eyes so bright they almost glowed in the dim morning light. "Wake up, angel," he said.

"What is it?" Shedding sleep was like struggling up out of a pool of oil.

"We have a rescue mission," he said excitedly. "Caught a communiqué between the blimp and Xanadu. Your friend Chaz Kato is in trouble, and we're the only ones who can help!"

She clambered up out of the luggage compartment into the seats. Raul turned the key, and the Land Rover's muscular engine roared to life. That power and off-road potential was a necessity: East of Bombay, smaller arteries were uneven and overgrown, foot or elephant trails invisible on even the best maps.

Raul backed out of the camouflage netting, across twenty yards of ruts and roots, then onto a road. He swung the Rover about and headed south.

Under the dashboard, the radio transmitter beeped at them. "Distress signal," Levar said. "Councilor frequency."

"Where did you get . . ." she began, and then closed her mouth. This was Levar. "Who? What kind of trouble are they in?"

"Car breakdown," he said. "*Gilgamesh* can't reach them where they are. They'll need to make a visual contact and then get *Gilgamesh* to pick them up in a clearing. But you know something?" She knew that he wouldn't wait for her answer, and he didn't. "This is what we've been waiting for. There's no way your boyfriend can turn us down now."

They roared south.

Ten minutes later, *Gilgamesh* lifted from its moorings and climbed into the sky. On hydrogen it rose, and hydrogen burned in its engines. Its only audible trace was a whiff of hot water vapor and a low, throaty growl as it prowled southward on a mission of mercy, black against the midnight clouds.


The temperature had dropped. The depth of the chill startled Chaz. Southbound, their trip had seemed an adventure. Gas heaters had produced a steady stream of warm air, bringing the tents to toasty perfection. Now Clarise idled the engine just to circulate warm air. Slow and inexorable as a shadow creeping around a sundial, the fuel indicator sank toward the red.

Maibang stared out into the woods.

"What are you looking for?" he asked.

She checked her little belt-pod tracking unit. "Our communications are coded, but the beacons aren't. Just because no one can understand us, that doesn't mean that the wrong people can't find us."

Despite the car's warmth Chaz was shivering, and he hated it. "How likely do you think that is?"

Her expression was baleful. "Don't you understand, Chaz? Even now? There's no way to tell how bad this is. *Gilgamesh* might not have been allowed to take off."

"They said they were in the air—"

"The signal might have been faked. Our crew might no longer be on board. Or someone else might find us before they do. You understand?"

He tried to think it through. Dammit, stress was slowing his mental processes to a syrup.

Her fingers bored into his shoulder. "The world over, most people consider children the greatest blessing a benevolent god can bestow. Someone stole that blessing from them. As far as they are concerned, the Council *murdered* their heirs. You are the closest thing most of them will ever see to a Council member."

"Saturn," Chaz said. His fists closed on an imaginary throat. Then, "We need someplace flat. Wide enough for *Gilgamesh*."

They began to walk north along the road, ducking out of sight on the rare occasions when another vehicle appeared. The road was rutted and mean. The moon hung low and swollen in the sky, balancing on a canopy of trees. To the west, the stream gurgled quietly. If the circumstances hadn't been so hazardous, their journey might have seemed almost idyllic.

In the distance, someone screamed in despair. Chaz tensed and then relaxed, and had almost convinced himself it was just a monkey when the quiet was split again, this time by a gunshot.

Clarise looked back along the moonlight-silvered road.

She wasn't his woman at this moment; she was far more. Her mind and body were weapons. She was sworn and ready to protect him even at the cost of her own life. It was only reasonable, only rational, but still somehow wrong, a reversal of primal roles. Should he have been surprised?

He'd never seen her like this, but he knew her instantly.

"Into the woods, Chaz. Get off the road."

To the south, the clatter of an ancient engine grew nearer. Someone was coming. Could they have been followed?

"Chaz!" Her voice was sharper this time.

"I'm not leaving you," he said. She turned to look at him, her eyes huge and dark. He saw the wild child she had been in Java, when the missionaries had found her among the Bdui and brought her into a new life.

"They'll follow the distress signal," she said. "Get away from me."

"Leave your belt," he said. "We can run together." She wore her finder on her belt; his was on his wrist. He stripped it off and threw it into the stream, and that left only the interface plug in his skull.

He didn't want to die there on a country road in India, but even worse than that thought was the obscene notion of this magnificent young woman dying to save a man three times her age.

She unbuckled her belt. She searched out a chunk of wood and knotted the belt around it. With a powerful whipping motion, she flung it out into the stream. He heard the splash.

"That might fool them for a while," she said thoughtfully. "But we can't count on it. Come on."

"My interface plug—"

"Yes, I remember. *Hide* yourself." She grabbed his elbow and led him out into the woods, away from and then parallel to the road and the stream. Then, by fading light, she pulled the hair patch out and probed the back of his head. They hadn't been able to test that; it would have alerted Saturn.

"Done. Come!"

* * *

He was savagely happy for the hours of exercise he had put in at Xanadu, the endless sessions intended to tone and trim his body. Here was the first true test. His legs ached, but he was almost keeping up with her. She wove through the shadowy spaces between the trees like a beautiful, wild animal. Every few minutes she stopped, turning her head as if aiming her ear back along the way they had come. He heard men whooping behind them and knew that their com links had been discovered.

"Shit," she said. It emerged as *stheet*. She'd never quite learned to pronounce that word.

Flashlight beams splashed the woods behind them, fluttered among the branches like glowing butterflies. He ran now, but his crashing, plodding footwork seemed certain to attract lethal attention.

A sudden shape loomed in the woods ahead of them, and a huge man threw himself at Clarise.

A gnarled, four-foot branch, thick as his wrist, appeared in her hand. The darkness had concealed it from Chaz's view until this moment. He had no idea where she had found it, and it looked too heavy to be used swiftly by a woman her size. Clarise was a blur. She spun the piece of lumber like a baton. She feinted, thrust the end at his face. When he lurched back she hit him in the crotch with the other end. When he doubled over, she reversed her grip with magical speed and shattered the branch against his skull. He gave a single muffled cry, collapsed onto his knees and then his face.

She cursed, throwing the pieces aside. "Go on," she said. "Keep running. A clearing can't be far."

But he couldn't leave. There were two more men coming, and one held a long, curved knife. Clarise slid sideways, posing a slender tree trunk between herself and the first attacker. The second carried a club the size of a polo mallet. The knife man came at her, swinging wild, trying to drive her from behind the tree. She lunged toward the club man. When he swung, she moved inside, under the swing, hit him with her knee and simultaneously had her hands on the club. She jerked and hopped. Somehow he was falling, and she was above him, both of her knees coming down on his elbow joint.

The crack was horrendous. He screamed as she rolled from him in a sinuous, snakelike motion. Her eyes looked like black mirrors.

The man with the long knife saw what she had done to the first two and wasn't about to be lured in. More men were coming behind her, and time was on his side.

Half paralyzed with fear and fascination, Chaz forced himself to stoop down, to grope in the darkness until he found a fist-size chunk of rock. Swiftly he calculated the distance and trajectory, grateful that the big man was standing still, not responding to Clarise's gambit. Chaz cocked his arm, exhaled, and threw.

The rock flew true, clocking the giant directly between the eyes. He yowled and staggered back. Clarise didn't hesitate. She rolled across the ground and thrust her borrowed club up into the man's gut. He slammed back against a tree and then sagged down.

She turned to Chaz, her face a mixture of gratitude and exasperation. "I told you to go!"

"They would have killed you."

She grinned and grabbed his hand. Together they stumbled through the woods, and then out of the woods onto another small road.

With shocking suddenness, a car bounced off the road toward them, its headlights blinding.

Clarise drew her club back and prepared to throw it through the windshield. Then they heard a woman's voice in American-accented English. "Chaz Kato!"

"Oh my God," Chaz said. He knew that voice. It was impossible, but he did.

Lenore stepped out into the light. "Chaz?" As if she didn't know him.

"Lenore? What in the hell are you doing here?" The Land Rover represented salvation, life where only death had loomed, but there was a great mystery here, and he couldn't move forward, even toward salvation, without answers.

"Chaz, I was in Bombay, having . . . a medical procedure. We heard you were here."

"That was classified." Chaz heard the undertone in Clarise Maibang's voice, as the security expert considered all the ways information might have leaked.

"Clarise," Chaz said, "a thousand people saw me at the wedding. Millions saw us distributing food."

She glared at him.

"Teddy Mercury, the Mercury Agency." Mercury held out his hand for a fleshy shake. He had capped teeth, massive forearms, and too much hair. Chaz disliked him instantly. He knew the type. Pure Hollywood. He'd have news agency sources and the money to bribe his way past the crowd. If he knew that three equals one, he'd be in heaven! Chaz might have been offended that his precious Lenore had taken up with this troll, except that the troll seemed to have saved his bacon.

"Hey, babe," Mercury said. "We've got a radio here and some transport. What we don't have is time. We came a hundred fifty miles to offer you a ride, and it's getting hairy out here. What say we have the rest of this chat in the air?"

Chaz and Clarise shrugged at each other and climbed in. Strange bedfellows, indeed.

## 37

One chair was a recliner, and the wall next to it was a medical laboratory. Chaz Kato was not the first of Xanadu's darlings to use it.

He lay in a torpor. A glass thread ran under his hair, and tubes and sensor sleeves led from his arms and his chest. His damaged body had been without sleep or Xanadu's medical supplements for nearly twenty-four hours under extreme stress.

Clarise had fallen in love with Chaz Kato while watching him blossom from a dying old man into a powerful . . . *wizard* was the word she came to use. Strong, outworldishly handsome, with amazing mental gifts; but with vulnerabilities too.

His mind would be skewed now. She could not trust his judgment. Any decisions regarding Security must be in her lap . . . but he was getting what he needed, though this gear was primitive compared to what he had on Xanadu.

Clarise watched Lenore Myles and the man she had introduced as Theodore Mercury. It couldn't be helped, but it was not good that they see Chaz like this.

For so long Clarise had had no chance to think. But Lenore's arrival with the dirigible went beyond serendipity.

They'd dropped Raul. Mercury had said, "In these parts me and Lenore stand out like albinos at a tanning salon. Raul can just disappear into the brush . . ." and she'd bought it. Too tired to wonder. *Why not* carry Mercury's servant?

The steady, humming pulse of *Gilgamesh*'s engines vibrated through the floors.

* * *

Maibang had observed Lenore Myles after she returned to
her contract in the States. She'd seen the woman mysteri-
ously diseased and incapacitated. If this was Myles, she'd
made a miraculous recovery indeed.

Clarise hunched near Lenore and spoke in a quiet, even
voice. "So, Miss Myles . . . if I might ask, what is the medical condition that brought you to India?"

"Something happened to me on Xanadu," Lenore said. "It
damaged my memory." It was impossible not to acknowledge the genuine confusion and fear in her eyes, but there
was something else there as well. Suspicion? "Damaged my
mind. I came to India to find a black market technology that
could heal me."

"And you just *happened* to want to look up an old friend,
just in time to rescue us?"

Lenore flinched at the sarcasm. "Of course not. Teddy
knew about my troubles on Xanadu. He got me a pair of
doctors in India. He wants my story after I recover."

"Lenore, the good Mr. Mercury will want your story for
a Hollywood scandal zine." Clarise hated the zines; they
were her natural enemies, always trying to get something,
anything, on the Floating Island chain. To watch one of their
shows, the entire purpose of the Floating Islands was to
provide orgy space for corporate perverts.

But Lenore, still studying her like . . . well, like an exotic
enemy . . . said, "And *I* wanted my mind back."

"It was Lenore's own techniques and software!" Mercury
grinned at her across the aisle, and Clarise wanted to put
her elbow through his perfectly capped teeth. "Pirated in
India so it could be used to cure her! Poetic justice *sells*,
babe. Not to mention the mystery. What happened on Xanadu? And you would be . . . ?"

*Babe?* The image of Mercury choking on his blood grew
more appealing by the moment. This was just the sort of
shallow parasite Clarise imagined Lenore bedding.

"I'm deputy Security Chief for Xanadu." She watched for the flinch, and thought she saw it. "So," she said, "I suppose that some of your spies discovered Chadwick Kato was a passenger on *Gilgamesh?*"

"I have stringers all over Asia. Never know where a good story might come down. Chief, doesn't the mystery appeal to you? What was ripped from Lenore Myles's head? What did she *see?*"

Her anger built and darkened . . . but then a bubble of skewed humor percolated through the bile. Privacy had ended in the last century, a passing fad. If these people hadn't been so eager to violate her beloved's privacy, she and Chaz might be dead now. She might actually owe this little troll her life.

Lenore said, "Security Chief? Were you there? Do you remember me?"

"You came as a group. I watched over you all." Clarise knew she shouldn't add to that, but she had trouble meeting Lenore's eyes. "You went hang-gliding."

"Did I? I couldn't get any Xanadu records. What else did I do?"

"Wait a few hours," Clarise said. "We will look." She did not say that she would show Xanadu records to Lenore Myles . . . but she hadn't quite decided not to.


*Gilgamesh* abandoned its remaining cargo before commencing the eastward trip. Unburdened, the dirigible could travel nearly a hundred kph on the homeward trip across the continent. With every passing kilometer Clarise grew more aware of their vulnerability. The dirigible's squat drifting shape made a fine target for an anti-aircraft missile. A hundred terror groups held such weapons.

*Gilgamesh*'s every previous voyage had been a mission of mercy.

Chaz was up and about, monitoring the diplomatic channels through Xanadu. When she went forward to speak with him, he nodded to acknowledge her presence. "Yes," he was saying. "I am aware of that. But, Ambassador, surely you can't think that our food distribution . . ." He sighed. "Yes. Those are the charges. Unsubstantiated charges. But the World Court will certainly want to see the evidence. All I am trying to do now is get my people home. Certainly . . . no, there is no intention to violate Indian air space . . ."

Chaz's voice went flat and hard. "We have treaties with you, Mr. Ambassador. They give us certain rights. We provide power and compute cycles for much of your country. Any attempt to force this vehicle down will be considered an act of war." He listened for another minute and then turned the communications link off.

"Well?" she asked.

"Relationships we've spent twenty years nurturing are unraveling in twenty hours. You were right." He took her hand. "I had no idea how deep the feelings went."

"How deep do your feelings go, Chaz?"

*Huh?* But he glanced sideways at Lenore, now asleep. A tired smile and "I'm with you. Of course I still care about her. I tore her brain apart! And I want to know what the living hell is going on. But I'm not jumping ship."

She squeezed his fingers.

The captain turned to them. "We've reached our cruising altitude."

Chaz pushed himself up out of his chair and looked down on the countryside. Tiny pinpricks of light glimmered through the haze. Fire, riot, murder, the children of rage. To the east, the first blush of dawn painted the horizon. A new day beckoned, devoid of promises, starved of hope.

Lenore was asleep. Chaz took her pulse without knowing quite why he did it. The touch triggered an intimate memory, a swift visceral flash:

*A memory of rolling against her, sliding atop her, into*

*her. Bliss, immeasurably heightened by long years of anticipation . . .*

He shook it off.

Teddy Mercury was fighting to stay awake, and Chaz could empathize. Adrenaline dump was incredibly soporific. Chaz said, "I think you saved our lives."

"All in a day's work. I tell you what. You can pay me with permission to tape on Xanadu. I'd like exclusive interviews—"

Chaz held his hands up in protest. "I can't promise any of that. In fact, we're in emergency mode right now."

"Natives throwing rocks, is that an emergency? I'll admit that the scene was right out of Edgar Rice. Give us the rights to *that* story."

"You could pull your footage out of old files. The copyrights have all lapsed."

Mercury laughed hugely.

The man was incorrigible. Chaz was too exhausted to fight. If he wasn't careful, Mercury would have the Floating Islands snarled in litigation for the next twenty years. There were far, far more serious fish to fry.

*Lenore.* So his efforts to save her had nearly driven her mad. So her only hope had been black market software, and this weasel had made the connection for her, maybe to get a nasty story for the scandal zines . . . or for pity, or love. Some men won't admit to heroic impulses.

Still, if Lenore's memory was coming back, she might recall information dangerous to a monster named Saturn. The decreased fertility, the augmented elephant with Saturn's eyes made a pattern with Lenore in the middle of it.

Perhaps Clarise could help him think. . . .

But when he turned back to his love she was already curled in a big plush chair, snoring softly.

*Gilgamesh* drifted on, its passengers all sprawled in the lounge, eyes closed, softly burring their fatigue, sound asleep, all but one.

* * *

Levar Rusche dared not open his eyes. Clarise and Chaz both smelled a rat, though they might mistake the breed. Better to give them an obvious rodent than have them dig too deeply into their memories or memory banks, to find an ex-boyfriend with Spinner connections.

They'd have found Raul's prison record on the first pass.

Levar's false identity would hold for another few hours. And by then . . . His heavy lips curled into a smile, and his next snore was genuine.

# 38

The final approach to Xanadu was tense. In its final hours over Indian soil, *Gilgamesh* had twice been buzzed by fighter craft and once urged to touch down for inspection. Chaz made additional unsubtle threats against India's power grid, and *Gilgamesh* was ordered to Xanadu with all due speed.

By the time of their docking, the mood aboard *Gilgamesh* was close to panic. If anything, the avalanche of new and verified information made the situation more urgent: Doctors inoculating Aborigines in Australia had been clubbed to death in the Outback. Medics giving AIDS vaccines in Central Africa had been given the "necklace": bound with a truck tire, doused with gasoline, and then set aflame.

Millions of children had been carted to overburdened clinics, and tissue samples had been extracted from mothers and daughters. Those whose mothers had been inoculated under an AIDS prevention program begun sixteen years earlier bore sterile girl-children. The program was connected with the World Health Organization and funded by forces now believed linked to that group known as the "Council."

From the docking area they went straight to Chaz's penthouse, too exhausted and haggard to interact with other Xanadu denizens. Once behind closed doors they stared at each other.

"You don't have anything to do with this," Chaz told Teddy Mercury. "I think you'd be safer somewhere else."

Levar Rusche answered, "Just help me get off this island, and I'm gone."

"What can we do for him?" Chaz said to Clarise.

She made a few quick calls. "The evacuation procedures are in order," she said to Mercury when she was done. "We're moving our people to safety, off the islands and away from any of the main areas of political instability. Parts of the United States are still stable, but all shuttles to the Americas are full. Here's what I want you to do." She wrote a pair of names on a slip of paper. "This will introduce you to Xanadu associates who can assist you when you arrive. That is, if they still live." She pulled a temporary badge out of her pouch and ran it through a slot on Chaz's desk. She spoke a few soft, coded phrases into the desk microphone and then extracted the card. "This will give you the clearance you need," she said. "We shouldn't be more than an hour. Meet us back here, and then we'll get you on that transport."

"Sure, sure," Mercury-Rusche said. "Would it be all right if I got myself a bite of food first?"

"We'll order in."

He took Lenore's hands. "You going to be all right, babe?"

"Sure," she said, but had difficulty meeting his eyes.

*Are they lovers?* Chaz wondered.

*Lenore isn't sure she wants to be alone with me*, Clarise thought.

Levar's mind was already abuzz with what he must do next. He looked back from the doorway, thinking, *I hope she can remember her cover story*, and was gone.

An uncomfortable silence descended. Chaz cleared his throat. "Wait a minute before we start. I'm going to call Arvad Minsky. He needs to be in on this."

"Why?"

"He's the only Council member I know personally. That could be very useful. And something else. I want you all to meet a friend of mine."

"A friend?"

"His name is Nero."

Levar Rusche hurried out of the penthouse. An actor's agent must sometimes swallow panic and smile at the taste. Levar knew what Xanadu's citizens saw: a fascinated tourist with a hasty need for a rest room.

He took the elevator down twelve stories, then exited and found the first men's room to his right. Anyone watching him would have been surprised at the ease with which he moved through the halls. It was as if he had memorized maps.

In the bathroom he found a toilet cubical flush against the eastern wall. He locked the door, pulled his pants down, and examined his right leg.

He had probably been scanned a dozen times since reaching Xanadu. The more he thought about it, the more likely that seemed.

The strain of maintaining his pretense suddenly hit him hard, and he collapsed onto the seat, trembling violently. Rusche wiped an unsteady hand across his forehead. Two minutes passed before he steadied his thoughts sufficiently to proceed.

He had been told that the bathroom on the twenty-third level of Xanadu's west residential tower shared a wall with a major communications conduit.

He didn't understand technical things. They'd told him that the system used wireless communication between certain nodes, and that a person with the correct codes, in close proximity to the conduit, could insert false commands into the system.

His task was simple, even if the route to its execution had been torturously complex and uncertain. The Spinner hierarchy needed someone to slip false authorizations into the security system. God knew how many Spinners were carrying artificial bones . . . but a series of catastrophes had put Levar Rusche deep inside Xanadu's security shield. He could hardly believe that he was here, right in the middle of the mess when the freaking Council finally tipped its hand, and the whole world could finally scope the extent of their greed and venom.

He pushed his leg against the wall. The coolness of the paint against his pale skin was a comfort. The dull ache in his bones, ordinarily mere background to his thoughts and actions, increased slightly in intensity, as if something were *happening* in there.


Arvad Minsky arrived breathless. He found Clarise Maibang and a haggard but still lovely stranger watching Chaz Kato play some simple and ancient computer game.

"Chaz, I'm busy. Everybody's busy. When you called, I—"

Clarise waved him to silence. Arvad moved up beside her. Maibang didn't shy away; she was used to his appearance; but the stranger flinched, then subtly moved to put Maibang between herself and Arvad.

The little white dot got past Kato's paddle. Kato said, "Now Quest Gold."


Minsky said, "Oh," a split second before the screen bloomed into color, into a hologram view of a street lined with baroque lamps and antique cars.

Chaz's finger *jabbed* and the viewpoint dropped under a

bullet as it ricocheted off concrete and *whirr/wheee* passed overhead. Still crouching, he ran their point of view behind a flight of concrete stairs. Bullets chipped the concrete, *wheeee*. In a pause Kato pulled them to the top stair and eeled through the open door.

A large lean man lifted the gun he'd been aiming at Kato. "We've had some excitement here, Doctor." His eyes and gun looked past Chaz, out through the screen. "Company?"

"Ritchie, I'll see your excitement and raise," Chaz said. "We've got to talk to Mr. Nero *now*. Sorry."

"I have to tell him who."

"Clarise Maibang, Security officer on Xanadu. Arvad Minsky, resident Council member, and Lenore Myles. Both are in Augmentation tech."

Ritchie disappeared through a door.

Arvad said, "Chaz, this is really neat. *Really* clever. What kind of processor—skip it. What's it for?"

"I've been hiding from whoever caused all this. He calls himself Saturn and he kills without a second thought—"

Ritchie reappeared and motioned. They went in.

Lupus Nero was as still and silent as a bronze Buddha behind his desk. A large antique handgun rested in front of him in what must have been a big copper ashtray. "Dr. Kato, you've never brought guests before. I assumed secrecy was paramount."

"Priorities change. Anything new regarding Saturn?"

"Dr. Minsky, Miss Maibang, I'm very pleased to meet you both. Miss Myles, I see that you've partially recovered from what was done to you. We never expected that. Has Dr. Kato had a chance to brief you all?"

Minsky said, "No. Chaz, can I interface with this setup?"

Nero picked up the gun. "I prefer to keep my mind intact, Dr. Minsky."

Chaz said, "The linking attachments aren't there, Arvad. Mr. Nero, you're quite safe." Being threatened with a picture of a gun: It might have been funny. "What have you got?"

"My news feeds indicate that a conspiracy of awesome scope has come to fruition. A billion girl-children born infertile are just coming to maturity. Half the Council is dead or imprisoned and awaiting trial. Scapegoats, I assume. I expect Saturn will claim their property. Wealth enough to rule the world. I still don't know who he is, but my list of living suspects shrinks hourly. Xanadu is under attack. Dr. Kato, have you anything to add?"

"I was out of touch when it all came down. We saw an augmented elephant dressed up as Ganesh being used to incite riots. It tried to kill us."

"The god of *wisdom?* Saturn has no sense of style nor fitness. We've noticed that before."

Arvad asked, "Why would this Saturn want riots?"

"Dr. Minsky, we needn't assume that Saturn wants riots. He needs to know *when* there will be riots. Otherwise he could get caught in the gears."

Chaz directed, "Mr. Nero, brief these people on Saturn. You've got the graphs."

"Security?"

"We'll assume Saturn is otherwise occupied. We don't have a choice, and it's a good bet."

"Very well." Nero stood. He pulled down a rolled-up screen that covered an entire wall. "Ladies, gentlemen, this was the heart of my investigations." Chaz knew it instantly: the graph that was Saturn's fist.


At first, Arvad's mask was one of amusement, but as the rotund detective spoke on, his amusement flickered and died like a candle in the wind. He turned to Chaz, and his face was drawn and pale. "How long have you been working on this?"

"Almost a year. Ever since . . ." He hesitated. "Ever since Saturn tried to kill Lenore."

Minsky shook his head. "The birth rate, it's just a statistical construct. The rest is paranoid fiction. Someone has falsified evidence on a massive scale."

In Chaz's living room, sealed off from the outside, the four of them sat sipping cappuccino. On the screen Nero was sipping beer. He said, "One or more Council members are certainly involved. These techniques were and are available to nobody else."

"Information can always be stolen."

"Arvad," Clarise said, "it doesn't matter if it isn't true. If enough people *believe* it, they'll attack us."

Minsky scoffed. "Who? These are international waters. We're protected by United Nations treaty. Any hostile action against us risks massive retaliation."

Chaz sensed that there was something wrong with his friend. Minsky seemed unwilling, or unable, to grasp the reality of the situation.

Fear, Chaz thought, affects each man differently. To some it was a stimulant, to some a soporific, and to some a hallucinogen. Arvad Minsky was in deep denial. He must be brought back.

Nero said, "I have a feed from Bolivia. Martial law has been declared by the government and army, separately. Rioting in the streets. Five officials of International Mining and Construction were hauled out of their houses and burned alive."

"But that doesn't mean . . ." Minsky began.

"The stock market has dropped two hundred and forty-one points in the past two days. It's going through the floor, Dr. Minsky. Anyone who could have anticipated or caused all this will shortly be the wealthiest person who ever lived."

Minsky stared at the screen, silent, perhaps temporarily unable to speak.

"Mr. Minsky," Clarise said gently. "We need to talk to you."

"What do you want?" he said weakly.

Chaz said, "Arvad, I want you to take the opposite position. Take all of this at face value: a year of Nero's research plus what we're getting on the news feeds. What does it imply?"

"Runaway sterility. Wherever they're breeding fastest and can afford children least. Okay." Minsky closed his human eye, though his prosthetic continued its rapid flicker. For a few moments there was quiet.

Arvad said, "We have at least five possibilities, and none of them is good. First is your conspiracy, Chaz . . . Nero. The age group selected itself—babies, vaccinations—and that let them keep it up for sixteen years. The drones with the hypodermics don't know. Nobody knows that doesn't have to. I could probably describe what they needed in software and tools—"

Nero asked, "Would it look like this?" Lists, designs, brand names crawled across his blackboard.

"Y-yes. Nice job, Nero. You've even got upgrade options marked in. Maibang, this *would* mean we're going to be attacked by the whole planet. I think you're right. The average paranoid-in-the-street will buy it all." He waved a dismissive hand. "Second, a natural viral epidemic might masquerade as another disease—or have no symptoms at all but have this effect. Or an engineered organism might have escaped from American or Soviet biological war facilities when the Sovs were shutting down. Third World hygiene spreads plagues fast. Or you could write it as a secret project between Third World countries, possibly funded by one of the superpowers to curtail population without the consent of their people. Or the Spinners. Save the planet?

"*I'd* have locked it into a massive propaganda program. That part didn't happen—misfired somehow." As if suddenly entertained by the possibilities, he looked up at the ceiling and almost smiled. "Fifth . . . consider an epidemic of spontaneous sterility, triggered by a biofeedback mechanism in the biosphere itself, when the human population reached a certain genetically preset density."

Nero said, "That last is only word games, Dr. Minsky,"

as Chaz was saying "You can't believe that."

"No, no, of course not." A thin sheen of spittle had coated his upper lip, and the flicker in the mechanical eye had speeded up. "But you must know that there are papers, papers written by good men as early as the mid-1980s hypothesizing—"

Chaz touched his friend's shoulders. Minsky flinched almost as if he had been struck. "Arvad," Chaz said. "It isn't any of those. This was deliberate, and focused. I don't believe it was done by a government."

Through the entire discussion, Lenore had perched quietly on her chair, watching and listening and thinking. Despite the fact that she might well hold the key to the entire hideous situation, she had hardly spoken. But now she moved up behind Minsky, and so did Clarise.

"Right," Chaz said, "Lenore. Tell your story."

Lenore grimaced. "I can tell what I remember. I don't remember any Saturn, Chaz." When Minsky turned his attention to her, Chaz noted the way she shied away, half concealing her revulsion.

Chaz remembered her touch on the plug at the back of his head, one magic night a year ago. Lenore had had courage then. *Strange* didn't frighten her. What had he done to her? Could she heal? This paranoid's paradise she'd been plunged into wasn't helping one damn bit.

Clarise said, "We're looking at this all wrong." She took the lost girl's hands in hers. "Lenore," she said urgently. "Do you remember the food court? You ate barbecued ribs—"

"Ribs! They were *real*. Tangerine sauce." Lenore looked like a child struggling to remember her ABCs. "I remember Chaz now," she said, and smiled sadly. There it was, a momentary awareness of something forever lost.

"Chaz . . ." she said softly.

"Yes?"

"I don't remember all of it, but I could retrace my research steps, maybe."

They were all ears. "What do you remember?"

Her lips pressed together, turning down at the corners as she strained for an answer. "In a hurry. Afraid I'd be noticed, and I guess I was, but it didn't take long. There was something about a dog."

"What kind of dog?" Chaz asked, mystified.

"A collie, I think." Suddenly, and unmistakably, her face brightened. "Goddam! That was a mistake. I thought it was dogs. It was the goddess *Kali*. The Kali Option."

# 39

Levar Rusche was on that cusp of sleep and wakefulness, a place where the facts of his life began to run back and forth, interweaving into the stuff of dreams. The device in his thighbone communicated with the computer on the far side of the wall of the rest room cubical. Drowsily he remembered the Bomb.

His parents had known many terrors and passed them on to him. The population explosion. Destruction of the rain forests, the ozone layer. Thermonuclear winter. The Bomb: atomic, hydrogen, cobalt. Global Thermonuclear War. Neutron bomb: wipe out all life, but leave tools and structures untouched.

Grade school teachers had taught his grandparents to hide under their desks if they saw a flash. That notion had been discarded when Levar was growing up. The United States government had decided that teaching people how to survive a war might "destabilize the balance of power."

But Levar the child daydreamed of a "neutron antibomb" that would smash the works of man and leave life intact.

By the time he reached college he knew that biological

weapons could fit the bill. Poetic justice: Life could use man to avenge itself upon man.

Once he had been just another radical UCLA dreamer. That youth had believed that the best possible political system was a representative democracy responsive to constituents within its geographic borders. Protesting and marching and striking seemed a natural outgrowth of those beliefs.

But when one of his oldest buddies had been hired from the USC biochemistry department to an Antarctic research facility, Levar saw an opportunity to do more than protest. He subverted Wayne. Together they joined the fledgling Spinner network. The results of these efforts had been disastrous, leading to fatalities and an infamy that had driven Levar Rusche deep underground. And Wayne could never leave Antarctica . . .

But Spinner funding didn't dry up. Opportunities for advancement actually increased. The powers behind the Spinners protected him, offering a new life.


Over the years he had asked himself disturbing questions. Whose pockets could be so deep? He had never sought to investigate more deeply, to seek honest answers to hard questions. It might well be better not to know.

Years had passed. He had seen and done terrible things, helped others escape, passed information, and twice been involved in assassinations of the Council's midlevel officials. Always for the Cause.

It wasn't enough. As the Council gained greater power, he understood that the world was, indeed, at war. Men of his ilk were the foot soldiers, both expendable and deniable. From time to time a Spinner was caught at sabotage. Trials led to imprisonment or, in two cases, executions. When this happened the Spinners bitterly complained that Germany or America had failed to comprehend that Spinners were their best and most secret allies.

Now, dozing, his mental censors down, Levar Rusche

wondered if they *did* know. If the nations understood quite well that in this Brave New World they must smile and make the deals and adjustments offered by the increasingly powerful Council. Make the deals, but fight covertly, using expendable soldiers.

He dreamed that the Spinners were, in cold fact, funded by the nations that denied and imprisoned and executed them.

Another, darker thought drifted up. Levar had heard rumor of a Chinese boy who worked his way into a position of responsibility in a Formosan factory, only two years after the little country had gone corporate.

The explosion had taken out half the building. The only question was; *How* had he smuggled a bomb into the plant? Their scanners were state of the art.

Levar had figured it out. As soon as the scientists who implanted the communication device in his leg had explained how it was possible to fool the scanning devices, to create a "false shadow," he had known. He had wondered, then, at the courage required to carry a bomb inside one's own body.

How brave, to live moment after moment with the *kamikaze* machine dormant in your bones. The stress must have been almost crippling. He didn't think he could take it. The Chinese boy had been a better man than he.

The buzzing sensation in his leg had grown slightly, and it felt a little warmer now.

The device in his leg would be sending out false identification signals for incoming craft. The signals would filter down into the main banks, and spy ships would enter the landing pattern. In the current state of emergency, security was likely to be fierce. He wondered if the Spinner technicians knew that the system would adjust. That too few minutes might elapse between the time that an anomaly opened the system to intruders and the moment the operators understood the nature of the threat. Intruders would have only minutes to disappear into Xanadu's crowds. And so would he.

He had been unconscious during the surgery. He had never seen what was implanted in his thigh, not before, certainly not after. But he *did* remember drifting up near the edge of anesthesia, no pain, but the distant awareness of voices. And he remembered hearing words that he couldn't understand.

Words in Chinese.

The buzz in his leg grew intolerable, and then it stopped.

A moment later, Levar Rusch was aerosol on a wave front.

The table was quiet. They had listened to Lenore for ten minutes now. She had spoken nonstop, as torrents of memory were released.

Minsky closed his eyes. "Let's try to put this together. Someone with the power of a Council member . . ."

"One or more," Nero said. "We have one voice, one fist, but how could one perpetrator do everything that our hypothesis requires?"

"Augmented." Minsky wasn't really talking to the NERO program. "Modern communications, enough computer storage, hell, it might be possible. Maybe he's got allies, maybe just staff. This person, this *Saturn* is behind a plan to reduce the population of the Third World by millions of people . . ."

"The claim is for a billion. That may be hysterics," Nero said.

Minsky nodded. "And we can suppose that he is responsible for the operation, or he's protecting those who are. Saturn could be somebody's servant. Maibang, you buy this? No one could keep something like that quiet."

Clarise didn't answer. Chaz said, "No. But if the plan began sixteen years ago, there was time to set up half the Council as fall guys. *Import* some fall guys. Survivors take all. A lot of us newcomers moved into Xanadu during the expansion period . . . around a hundred? You'd been here for three years, Arvad."

"Too many," said Arvad.

"No. You pick a hundred. Bring them here. Look them over. Maybe ten join the inner circle, the rest are cannon fodder. Did that bastard give me back my life just for this?"

Lenore seemed puzzled. "What do you mean, 'Give you back your life'?"

Chaz winced. It was far too late for lies. "Lenore, I'm pushing eighty-four. Chadwick Kato wasn't my grandfather. *I'm* Chadwick Kato. The Council has extraordinary means of life extension. It's the ultimate bribe."

"Wow. *You* built . . . ?" He saw an instant of hero worship; then other implications reached her. "This *Saturn* made you young again?"

Minsky said, "No no no! Chaz, if a Councilman has gone rogue, that doesn't mean he, or *she*, saved your life with some ulterior motive. *All* of us vote on candidates. We *all* voted for Chaz Kato. You were simply too valuable to die."

"Chaz Kato died. I remember. Wait. Yes! The redhead!" Lenore's eyes were wild, excited. "She was supposed to be dead. I heard her voice, and it drove me crazy. She was. . . ." Her face screwed up with the effort. "She lectured us at UCLA. Then she *died*. God . . . what was her name?" She struggled, but it wouldn't come.

"Mary Kravitz," said Chaz. "Diva's assistant. What *do* you remember?"

Lenore laughed suddenly, joyously. "She was screwing someone in the hall! I couldn't wait to tell Tooley—"

"In public?" Clarise asked, disgusted.

"In a hallway!"

Minsky seemed flustered, embarrassed. "In some cases the regeneration process unbalances libido, leading to unfortunate behavior. It's temporary." He smiled nervously. "Go on, Lenore."

"I overheard them. That was when the 'Kali Option' thing came up. I summoned up the Xanadu library and started looking, and that, I guess, is what almost got me killed."

Clarise was looking out the window, her dark, lovely eyes deeply troubled. "I remember something too, Chaz."

"What?"

"The people who came to my village and found me so many years ago. They were inoculating the men and women and children. I suppose it was this AIDS program. They were kind people. I believe that they were good and gentle folk."

"Why are you so sure?"

"Not everyone in the village was inoculated."

"Why not?"

"Among my people, there are the inner Bdui and the outer Bdui. The outer Bdui have contact with the outside world, but the inner ... they interact only with the outer circle. I was of the inner tribe, but when my parents died, a family on the outer ring adopted me. I was seven or eight when the doctors came. I remember the tribal council, and how we tried to convince the inner ring to let us submit to the needles. They refused. The doctors were saddened, but they understood and went away."

"And ... ?"

"There was no pressure. If this is the way the contagion was spread, then these people who adopted me and cared for me ... who educated me in the ways of the outside world and eventually gave me my life on Xanadu, these people would be angels of death. Chaz, they didn't know."

"Of course not." Minsky voice had grown thin and brittle, as if the implications, the enormous scale of the plot was beginning to hit him. He stuttered and seemed close to panic. "F-far too many people would be n-necessary to spread the n-nanocytes, the disease ... whatever the hell. And so only the people at the very top would ..." He stopped, his eye so wide and frightened that he seemed more fish than human. "What was that?"

The others stared at him.

Nero said, "Dr. Kato, my news feeds have stopped."

The blast came then, followed by a rumble that shook the building, as if the structure had become a semisolid just long enough for a powerful wave to run through the walls and floors. A sound so low it was heard more in the bones than the ears.

Then it was still.

"I felt a score of electronic minds go crazy all at once. Now there's nothing but static. Dr. Kato, I've lost all my connections," Nero said.

A moment later alarms began to sound.

# 40

Clarise excused herself and pressed her palm against a wall that was out of Nero's sight. A window opened, and her supervisor Mr. Whittlesea appeared. He looked flushed. "Clarise, we need you down on twenty-four," he began.

"What's happened?"

"An explosion. Someone has compromised security, and we don't know how bad it's going to get. Right now it looks as if someone entered a virus into our system, and perhaps some false commands, and followed it with an explosion that pulsed our whole network. We're up and running again, but on emergency mode now, and that means that some of our diagnostics will be off-line for hours. I don't know what's happening but . . ."

His eyes were distracted by something to his left, and he excused himself, went to mute, and answered the call. When he returned, he was ashen.

"Clarise, where are you?" he asked. She was even more alarmed. He should have known *exactly* where she was, and with whom.

"I'm in Chaz Kato's apartment. Mr. Minsky and another guest are here as well."

"Thank God. You are relieved of all other duty, do you understand? Code *'Anemone,'* Clar—"

His words were interrupted, and the screen blackened as the floor and walls trembled again. She sprinted to a side wall. Her palm-press transformed it into a huge window.

Thousands of pounds of steel and glass and torn bodies erupted from the side of the east tower, plummeting floors down to explode on a pedestrian walkway. This time she could see the tiny fighter craft zipping away. A second small black plane appeared. Smoke and light flared at its wing as it launched a missile at the tower.

Another roar.

She grabbed Minsky's hand. "Sir, you must come with me now."

"Anemone," Minsky repeated numbly. He stood on rubbery legs.

Clarise locked eyes with Chaz. "Come with me now."

"Can I take Nero?" Chaz asked, already knowing the answer.

"Go! Leave me!" Nero bellowed. "While you survive I can be rewritten!"

Clarise was already halfway out the door.

All the work! All of the hundreds of hours of secret labor, lost! Chaz spoke a few swift words, reencrypting the program. Then he ran for the door, dragging Lenore.

"They're taking out the command centers," Clarise said grimly as they ran through the rooftop garden toward the elevators. "Someone wants Xanadu."

The elevator doors opened as they reached it and sealed behind them soundlessly. It was frozen in emergency mode, but it required only a few intense seconds to override the control. Chaz felt his chest turn to ice. "If they're this mad, why don't they just nuke us?"

"Xanadu is too valuable. The Nationals are going to use this whole thing as an excuse to seize everything we've got.

Also . . ." She looked him right in the eyes. "They want Council members alive, to answer questions."


Clarise's override enabled an express run, straight down. Through the transparent walls of the elevator they watched Islanders screaming and bolting for transportation that was already overcrowded, for boats already gone, for ground transport that would scurry them in circles and deposit them where they began.

Desperate men and women hammered at the elevator doors as they slid down, slid past.

At least four explosions had rocked the towers. Wounded Xanadu folk staggered through the halls, dazed and bloody, ghastly in the flashing red emergency lights. Sirens, muffled by closed elevator doors, raised hair on the back of his neck. Chaz felt sick. Lenore and Minsky were very still, almost transfixed.

"What about Levar?" Lenore caught herself. "I mean—"

Clarise's head whipped around incredulously. "Tell me you are lying. That was Levar Rusche?"

Lenore swallowed and looked from one of them to the other. "He helped me," she said in a tiny voice. She shivered like a trapped animal.

Clarise's eyes were as cold as the heart of a dead star. "Can you really be that stupid? Could *I?* I knew he was trouble, but I never."

She moved in a blur, and Lenore slammed against the wall, the security woman's elbow at her throat. "Your boyfriend smuggled in a bomb. Hundreds of people will die because of *you.*"

Lenore struggled a hopeless second. As the effort died, something within her broke, and the first spark of something new, some strength Chaz hadn't seen in over a year, percolated to the surface. "Big news, Clarise—your 'Saturn' fried my brain. I was *made* stupid. Levar was my only hope.

You're the Security muck here, and you let him aboard *Gilgamesh*. How were *you* made stupid?"

Chaz said, "Clarise, *stand down,*" wondering if she would hear, or if she would simply lean in and crush Lenore's windpipe.

Eyes blazing, Clarise let the American go. Lenore rubbed her throat. "Why don't we find Levar?" she said. "Ask him. I'm sure he'll explain . . ."

"We scanned him coming in," Clarise said. "Any bomb he brought was inside him. There won't be anything left to ask."

Lenore closed her eyes, as if sensing the truth of that last gibe.

Minsky was walking like a sleepwalker, his good eye half closed, his camera eye flickering. Testing every electronic sense, Chaz guessed, finding only blanks, then testing again. Now he shook himself awake and said, "So. What now?"

"All ordinary routes are compromised," Clarise said. "If I read this right, the island must be crawling with Spinners. Levar gave them access to secured areas. If they want hostages, they have hundreds now. My instructions don't include fighting them. I am to take us to safety. There is a way."

"And that is?"

She looked at Chaz, and he knew the answer. "Squark City," he said, and she nodded.

# 41

The service level was already below water level. They could feel the pressure in their ears. The tunnels here, far beneath the living quarters and offices, entertainment facilities and malls, also served as maintenance tunnels for the OTEC units and food processors.

Some dozens of personnel were trapped down there, unable or unwilling to return to the surface. A tall rawboned brunette with an Oklahoma accent pulled at Clarise's arm. "What's happening? I heard say transports are thick as flies. Soldiers. Chinese and Indian soldiers?"

Clarise stopped for just a moment, something about the taller woman's fearful demeanor penetrating her single-minded focus. "They've crippled the communications and defense links," she said. "They don't want you. They want the executives. Surrender and you won't be hurt."

"But where are you going?" she asked. "You folks know something, don't you! You know something!"

The brunette tried to run behind them, but Clarise got a door between her and them and sealed it shut. They heard desperate pounding, but thank God they couldn't see the brunette's face.

"Come on!" Clarise herded them along at running pace. They raced through another hall, almost skidding into a pair of locked access doors. Chaz's heart stopped when the Security agent's first two efforts to open them failed. On the third attempt, the computerized lock yielded, and she ran them along. On the far side was a single service elevator, and she crowded her charges in, sealing the door behind them. The floor sank beneath them.

"What are we going to do?" Chaz asked. "We can't hide out in Squark City forever."

"No," Clarise said soberly. "And we don't have to. I have a plan. The cargo sleds are designed to haul tons. Take the cargo compartments off and they'll make good speed and distance."

"Where are we going?" Lenore asked.

Clarise finally managed a very slight smile. "Home," she said.

*  *  *

The elevator doors opened on the changing room, where Xanadu-model rebreathing gear awaited, racked neatly in rows.

Lenore was aghast. "Chaz? Chaz! I've never used a rebreather!"

Minsky said, "This equipment is so sophisticated that you won't even notice it. It does all of the work for you. Everything's taken care of. There are throat mikes built in."

Chaz said, "You swim like a fish, anyway." He was stripping as he spoke.

For a moment Lenore froze. Her frustratingly partial memories included the image of Chaz naked. But she didn't remember him in a swimming suit. Had they been in the water together? And if not, how did he know she could swim?

Her bare feet tingled against the changing room's plate metal floor. Minsky and Chaz had already stripped down to their underwear and were slipping into the suits, then sealing their clothing in waterproof bags. Minsky was a step ahead, with none of his earlier clumsiness or hesitancy. He was dressed and half stowed while Chaz was getting his pants off.

Lenore was frozen, questions racing through her mind, eating seconds that she knew were vital to their survival.

The air tasted of salt.

Clarise approached her and, with surprising gentleness, said, "Here, let me help you." She turned to Chaz. "Chaz, you get yourself ready. We'll handle this. It's a girl thing. Right?"

Lenore nodded gratefully.

"Fine," Chaz said. "I'm thinking distance, time, and fuel. It might work, Arvad!"

"Glaaad to hear it." His headpiece already muffled his voice. "How long for a stripped Wetcat to cross the . . . floor of the bay? There's a word."

"Embayment," Lenore said. "Embayment! I remember."

Minsky clutched his head. "I don't. Trying to think, it's

like my memory's been ripped out of my head. Bay of Bengal . . . a thousand miles across? It's not like we have a lot of choices. I have some suggestions. . . ."

They cycled through the locks. Minsky led the way out into the ocean. They swam toward the distant misty lights of Squark City, collecting an honor guard along the way.

The dolphins were there, Manny and his mate, Trish. In past months she had responded to their teaching (some would have said programming) like a champion. Although neither as intelligent nor loquacious as her mate, Trish was still a talkative beast.

"Hello, Chaz," she said. "Why you come?"

Manny nosed her out of the way. "Trouble up above, yes?"

"Yes. Trouble," Chaz replied.

Manny brushed along the length of Lenore. She floundered, then yeeped, "Manny!" and tried to hug him. He was too slippery.

Additional figures loomed ahead of them now, misshapen, grotesque, except that in their current situation they were beautiful. The arms of squarks gently pulsed and wove in the undersea currents, and Chaz felt his plan falling into place.

A few other sharks nosed around curiously, and Chaz waved at some of the human workers who were down in the dome. Several workers swam out to meet them as if wondering about their identity.

Chaz recognized one of them: Anson Teil, the scoutmaster, long and lean in SCUBA gear, his red-going-white hair tied so it wouldn't float around him. What in the world was *he* doing here?

"Mr. Kato! What's happening up top? Mr. Minsky?"

"We're being attacked," Chaz said. "It should be all right for civilians. Just wait for things to settle down, and then go back up, turn yourselves in."

"To *whom?*"

With a flash of guilt, Chaz suddenly realized just how hollow his reassurances sounded.

Teil led them down through the airlock. There, huddled in the reception area, were six of the Sea Scouts. Chaz recognized the Curry twins, a little redheaded girl named Crystal, and a swarthy boy, Mohammed.

*Now* he could see the mess they were in. The Scouts were related to some of Xanadu's most powerful folk. Crystal was a Councilwoman's niece. Up top, they would make effective hostages, if the invaders didn't kill them outright.

Clarise was way ahead of him. "We take them, Chaz," she said. " '*Anemone*' certainly extends to the protection of the innocent."

"Right," Chaz said. This changed their plans, made everything more complicated, but that was just too bad. Calculations spun.

He pulled Minsky roughly to the side. "Give me some help, Arvad. Sanity check. What does this change? We'll need one of the Wetcats and extra batteries for the rebreathers. If the kids don't panic, we've got a chance."

Arvad was twitching. He met Chaz's eyes nervously. "I," he croaked, and swallowed, and said, "haven't the vaguest."

Sanity check: failed. Chaz said, "Hang on, Arvad. We'll get you out of here."


In a castle on an island in northern Japan, video monitors were tuned to a hundred channels. Fully fifty of them carried the same horrendous carnage: Xanadu in ruins.

"Enemies are feasting," Osato said bitterly, "but fortune has tossed us a bone. I was to place cameras where we might spy on Dr. Chaz Kato, one of Xanadu's midlevel personages."

The voice behind him had a gravelly quaver in it, but it was in no way feeble. "This was ordered by Yamato?"

"Yes."

"Yamato is dead," said Osato's father. "His limousine was firebombed by the wild rabble. We have positive identification from his gene pattern and the amplifications in his skull."

Osato shivered, but he did not turn around. "Vengeance?"

"Nothing for you or me. He was a client, my son, not one of our own. Only his cause is our own."

"A pity, then, that he will never see the entertainment he bought from us."

"Show me."

Osato ran the film.

It wasn't just jerky; it was stop-motion animation. Osato said, "I must apologize. These organic-mode cameras record for an instant, then turn off while the cultured nerves recover."

"The view is awkward too. Did you retrieve anything else?"

"Sadly, no. I stowed my retrieval system against discovery. When the attack came—" Osato remembered gliding through the mob where he would have preferred to run; delaying to search his room for cameras; then anchoring his laser recovery system against vibration, aiming into Dr. Kato's domicile. It was fine-tuned and ready, just as every one of Chaz Kato's windows disintegrated in a shower of slivers.

But his father had no interest in excuses. Osato said, "When the attack came I moved too slowly. A missile destroyed all of Dr. Kato's windows with all of their spray cameras. I had a moment in which to aim my recovery system through the empty frames, into the line of antique computers above Dr. Kato's entrance hallway. I never expected such results."

"Play it again."

Osato did as ordered. The result was a blurred stop-motion view of a gently smiling rounded face, a bit distorted, looking up. Two hands grew huge, then edged out of view. The face wobbled and expanded. The view settled, the face at eye level now, hands half in view at the bottom of the screen. The hands jittered.

"Fast forward," Osato's father ordered. Osato skimmed past several minutes of Chaz Kato playing Pong, and stopped when Kato did.

Kato's hands typed. He talked, listened, talked, to a friend whom he held in complete trust. Osato's hands itched to turn the view around, but he could see nothing but Chaz Kato. Formality here; now a shared joke—

Osato said, "Even if we had sound—"

"Even if you still remember how to read lips, this stop-motion one-sided conversation would not help us. Was the computer destroyed?"

"A second bomb reduced the entire set of antiques to char and glass and metal splinters a moment after I recovered the data. I risked searching the ashes afterward for a misplaced floppy or a heat-proof safe. There was nothing."

Mas Osato sighed. "Still, we know that Dr. Chaz Kato was hiding a secret from his colleagues at Xanadu. A secret of vital importance."

Osato did not comment. It was not his place.

"For this one eyeblink of time, the most important question in the world is this," his father said. "Who was it that caused three hundred million children to give birth to infertile daughters? And the count still rises. Who orchestrated the Fertility War? Who chose the victims? Not Yamoto. The mob's victims would seem to be unsuspecting straw men, and Yamato was one of those, caught unprepared. None of us has found any trace of a prime mover, nothing until this moment, barring a name that must be a code."

Osato waited.

"*Saturn.* Yamato would not have chosen the name of a Roman god. An American might, even one of Japanese blood. An elder restored to vigor might choose the Roman god of time and age as his *logos.*

"We had no suspects. Now we have one. We must try to falsify the hypothesis that Dr. Chaz Kato is Saturn. Learn what you can."

Osato bowed.

# 42

Deep beneath the sea four tonnes of Mitsubishi Wetcat shuddered, lost traction, and ground to a halt. Chaz worked the gears with carefully leashed dread—he had piloted a 'cat only three times, helping Squarks move equipment from one locale to another, ferrying rock or logs. It had been a distraction, a dawdle, never the deadly necessity he now faced.

The Wetcat, designed in Japan and constructed in Detroit, looked something like an old-fashioned locomotive with a caterpillar tread, the underwater equivalent of a bulldozer or heavy cargo transport. It ordinarily sat four, with a storage space between seats and rear wall for basic gear, and a hookup rig outside for hauling serious freight.

They had stripped the cab of everything but batteries, some food paste tubes, and water supplies. The cab was not pressurized, so all passengers had to stay suited for the entire ride.

Twelve hundred kilometers. Fifty hours, minimum, from Xanadu to the Nicobar Islands in the Andaman chain, in the eastern portion of the Bengal Bay.

The Bay of Bengal, home to Xanadu, occupied better than a million square kilometers of relatively shallow embayment stretching from Sri Lanka and India to the West, Bangladesh to the north and the Malay Peninsula to the east. About sixteen hundred kilometers wide, the floor of the bay was now their only route to safety.

If, hope to God, or maybe Mitsubishi, they could make it.

They had fuel and the batteries for the air supplies ... if nothing went wrong. *Hah.* Something always went wrong. Disaster crouched out there in the darkness beyond the yellowish cones cast by the Wetcat's oversized headlights.

Much of the floor was relatively shallow, no more than two thousand meters deep. That was a thousand meters deeper than the floor beneath Xanadu, and more than Squarks or dolphins wanted to hazard. The Wetcat broadcast a weak beacon, enough to tingle the electronics within their finny friends. Manny and the others would follow as best they could. Chaz felt like an undersea Moses on a strange and desperate Exodus.

They had traveled for more than thirty hours now. The Wetcat's radio heard not a whisper from Xanadu: They would have been completely cut off from the outside world if not for the antenna wire bobbing up toward the surface. They dared not broadcast but could catch snippets of news.

Chaz finally noticed what thirty hours of grim news was doing to the six children behind him, aged eight (Jeffty) to fifteen (mermaid Nadine).

There had been a bit of sniffling at first and then an admirably sharp response to Mr. Teil's announcement of emergency. No tears, no more complaints: The kids had grabbed their packs and what food they could, and piled into the Wetcat as soon as the staff had prepped it.

The other Squark City staff had listened soberly to Chaz's escape plans. He would never forget their efficiency as they checked the Wetcat's every fluid and bearing, replaced worn sections of tread, and did everything in their power to enable their escape. After one initial, polite question, no one even mentioned that they were being left behind. No one needed to.

Xanadu had been seized by a joint Chinese and Indian incursion on charges of piracy and murder. In a flat, emotionless voice the announcer stated that there had been "little" loss of life—

(He remembered the image of the shattered wall, bodies exploding through walls of glass and seacrete, plunging to the parks below.)

—and that trials for all accused would be held expediently. Those conspirators who had evaded capture were requested to present themselves for judgment. It was promised that the trials would be fair.

(He remembered the sight of the rocket striking the side of the building and in his mind once again saw a pale round face staring out at the moment the attack helicopter unleashed its load. The face had disappeared in the thunderous blast.)

A fair and speedy trial. You bet. Chaz turned the radio off.

"How will I find Barrister?" Minsky asked.

Chaz was weary of hearing it. He said, "The squarks communicate with each other. He'll find us."

"My air is stale," Mohammed said with no trace of alarm.

"Clarise . . . ?" Chaz began.

"I'm on it," she said groggily.

Teil was asleep, curled up like an ungainly spider, his mouth a bit open. In sleep he smiled; all his wrinkles were smile lines. Chaz didn't want to wake the man for this.

Clarise twisted a valve at Mohammed's back. A few bubbles floated free as she cleared a connection. "It's done," she said. Mohammed nodded, took on a blissful expression as he began to relieve himself, and then went back to sleep.

Clarise clambered back to her seat next to Chaz. "That . . . could have been nasty."

"So far so good."

"What do we know, my captain?"

The 'cat jolted as its treads hit another pothole. Chaz wrestled with the controls. Nothing that they couldn't handle, thus far, but . . . a jam or a broken tread here didn't mean calling for a repair crew. It meant surrendering to a bloodthirsty pocket army, or slow suffocation two thousand meters down.

After a few nervous moments he was able to back the 'cat up and find traction. He took bearings by computerized compass and struck out into the murk.

The seabed was relatively flat, but given to abrupt declinations that lurched them all forward. The headlights gave them about ten meters of saffron illumination. Beyond that, gloom stretched off as infinite as the depths of space.

Lenore Myles stretched and came back out of her daze. "Where are we?" she said, and peered out into the darkness. A flat blue eel wriggled past their window, perhaps attracted by their lights, then scooted away with a sinuous and rather disturbing ripple. The absence of vegetable life was more unnerving than the lack of light itself. This was a dead world.

Fleeing across an undersea hell, searching for life.

"We're about two hundred miles . . . sixty klicks west of Nicobar. We had to swing south, change our plans to try the Andamen islands."

She rubbed her eyes sleepily. "Why?"

"The Java Trench is seismically active, and we'd never find a way across. Best to go farther south, even if it empties the batteries."

He looked at the gauges. They were three-quarters down, but the red zone represented a healthy inch of safety. They would make it. They had to.

The Scouts were in a stress-induced daze, in and out of slumber like hibernating bear cubs. Clarise too had dropped back off to sleep, leaving only Lenore and Chaz awake in the cab.

In her rebreather helmet, Lenore's face was distorted slightly by the plastic, but he thought that she was still lovely. In another time, another place . . .

For one brief moment, they might have had a chance. Then *Saturn*.

And if Clarise was his real best choice, when did that

become Saturn's business? He had the right to make a fool of himself in his own way, in his own time.

She caught him looking. Lenore said, "I'm sorry about everything, Chaz."

He shook his head. "We were mugged. No apologies between us. Let's just hang tight." His helmet's speakers made his voice a muffled echo.

Hers sounded like a whisper from the bottom of a well. "All right, Chaz," she said, and watched the headlights slide along the ocean floor.


Klick by slow klick, they continued their desperate crawl to safety. Chaz, Clarise, and Minsky took turns at the Wetcat's controls; and when Minsky had them, they watched him. Past the fortieth hour the engine needed nursing. Sand or rock or grit had climbed the treads and settled in the gears, which now made a nasty grinding sound.

Minsky gave the engine a rest but kept the headlights on for a few minutes. From time to time a bizarre, luminous fish twisted through the beams and then disappeared into the darkness again. At last he turned the headlights out, and only the dim overhead bulb dispelled the gloom. Darkness, stale air, and increasing static on their headsets increased Chaz's sense of claustrophobia until the urge to scream was almost overpowering.

Arvad gripped the wheel, body slumping, eyes closed. "We're going to die down here. I hope you know that."

"Jesus, Arvad."

One of the twins, a blond terrier of a ten-year-old named Barbie, began to sniffle. "Don't you say that!"

Her brother Clark chimed in. "You never ever *ever* give up."

Arvad turned and regarded them wearily. "I'm just . . . tired. I'm sorry. Didn't really mean that."

"Yes, you did." Barbie sniffed. "But you're wrong. We're going to be fine."

Arvad had such a chagrined, helpless expression on his masked and lopsided face that Chaz almost laughed. "Well," he said finally. "Who can argue with that?"

Teil nodded approvingly. "More survival points for Barbie," he said. He uncurled a little. "When we get out of this, some of you are in for merit badges. The rest of you had better monitor your attitudes, or the twins will eat you alive!"

Mohammed and Crystal were asleep. Nadine and Jeffty straightened shoulders, their moods improving 100 percent on the spot. Jeffty broke into a gap-toothed chorus of "Ninety-nine bottles of beer on the wall," which kept them going for another ten klicks.

It was amazing what a little competition could do.

At the forty-fifth hour they paused again. Chaz and Clarise swam out and swapped fuel cells again, for the last time. According to the Mitsubishi manual, they had a two-hour margin of safety. If the Wetcat failed to live up to that promise, they could whistle for their refund. But as the ocean floor began its slow rise from the depths, Chaz began to hope.

At a hundred meters they were joined by the dolphins, who gave them a quizzical "What kept you?" expression, and then the squarks and the entire misshapen cyborg menagerie.

Sudden relief gave him permission to experience his fatigue. Waves of visual ink crashed against his mind and then receded. Even the air seemed sweeter.

Until this moment, he hadn't realized how much he had dreaded dying at the bottom of the ocean. Perhaps they wouldn't make it. Perhaps they would all be captured or killed. But he wanted a last breath of clean, unfiltered air. He wanted his last vision to be of an open sky.

\* \* \*

Xanadu maintained a financial interest in a small tuna fishery off Kamorta, where Minsky had contacts. The manager was suspicious, but his tight little eyes grew wide when Minsky opened a leather pouch and spilled a dozen pearls into his brown palm.

"How did you happen to—"

Arvad Minsky said, "Trade goods. It looked like the end of the world, Chaz. Heinlein once said, 'You don't truly own anything you can't carry in both arms at a dead run.' " His voice dropped. "The way I look, I'd *better* be carrying a plausible bribe."

Chaz nodded. "You look like a Borg."

Arvad's shaky smile faded. "They don't remember *Star Trek* here. I look like a *Council member.*"

Clarise did their negotiating. When she took the pouch of pearls, Minsky made no objection. Title to the Wetcat got them the *Shompen*, a twenty-meter fishing boat, and the skills of an experienced crew.

All hands transferred to the new boat. The kids ate and drank ravenously and fought over the toilets. The captain was a round dark man who couldn't seem to stop gumming pearls in his toothless mouth. Finally and reluctantly, he went into conference with Clarise. She spread a map down on a table and traced lines with her finger, drew, discussed, drew again. They argued, and compromised, and more of Minsky's pearls changed hands.

The *Shompen* slid south, taking three days to cross the Andaman Basin, then slid past Indonesia and Sumatra to Java. Clarise guided them by guesswork or intuition, around a wild and heavily wooded coast to coves she had not seen since childhood.

She seemed to change before Chaz's eyes, shedding the Xanadu years like a snake skin. Her eyes were even more alert, her posture very erect, her every motion light and quick as any animal's. She was like a wild butterfly slough-ing a civilized cocoon.

At midnight on the third day after they beached the Wet-cat, the *Shompen* slid into a rocky harbor. Maibang piled everyone out, splashing them through the surf to a pebbled shore. When the captain asked what they were going to do, she only smiled and said: "Our bargain is done and well done, Captain. Remember—" And her fingertip touched her lips. He grinned toothlessly as she gave him three more pearls.

Then the *Shompen* backed out of the harbor and chugged away.

"And now?" Lenore asked her.

"We walk."

Chaz and Arvad Minsky walked to the water's edge. Only they had seen the scaliens that followed the *Shompen*. Now their finny friends came closer to the surface, and Chaz knelt on one of the rocks.

Manny and Trish rolled quietly in the surf, waiting for Chaz to tell them what to do next. Behind them, the squarks floated patiently, arms floating like jellyfish tendrils, content to follow Manny's lead. In this new situation, their differing species meant less than the common fact of their unique alterations.

These were his friends and, in another sense, his children.

Chaz stole a glance at Arvad. The man seemed remote and imploded. The word "friendship" didn't begin to de-scribe the connection Minsky felt to Barrister. The Great White had vanished into the wide ocean, and Minsky was lost.

Chaz pushed himself up. "Clarise, how far do we go?"

"I'm not certain. My people are nomadic. They're within a day's walk, I am sure."

To Manny and his aquatic companions, he said, "Three days from now, be back here at midnight. Then we will know more."

They chattered an acknowledgment and scattered.

They walked for hours in darkness before the eastern horizon began to blush. By moon and starlight, the shadowed brush seemed filled with hostile silhouettes and hooded eyes. In time, breath came more harshly, and legs ached. Clarise pushed them on. She picked through the brush finding trails that might have baffled a lizard. In the morning's sharp cool light the territory seemed primeval, as if nothing human had passed this way since the end of the Stone Age. It began to rain, a hot sticky downpour that felt and tasted like watery sweat.

Chaz was blowing air. Rain slicked his hair into his eyes. His left ankle had just begun a long, sour scream of protest when, without a whisper of warning, they were suddenly surrounded.

The men around them were thin and dark. Most were shorter than Clarise. They held bows and arrows at the ready, most of them pointed at Minsky.

Chaz froze perfectly still. One of them chattered something in a language Chaz had never heard.

Clarise answered in the same tongue. There was a long silence, and the men began to speak excitedly. In the midst of the happy noise, Clarise turned to Chaz. "This is home," she said.

# 43

Their escorts led them to the *kampong* after dark and in the rain, their shoes and clothing stained with thick red trail mud. The Lurah, an ancient village chieftain who seemed all knobby bone and sinew, welcomed them to his earth-floored house. His thin, sunburned wife clucked over the Sea Scouts, especially the twins, and regarded Clarise with something approaching awe. The pair lent them sarongs to replace their soaked shirts and trousers, then fed them rice and salt fish and stewed, leafy greens. Only then did the Lurah ask them their business.

Clarise spoke for them, talking alternatively in English and in the tongue of the hill people.

"I am a child come home," she said. "You knew I would return. I have songs and pictures of the world outside I would share with you. The journey has been long and dangerous. My companions and I seek asylum."

The Lurah rattled at them, and Clarise translated. "He says my people are still in the hollow mountain. 'At times we hear their songs, which sing of a child come home. They asked us to watch for her.' "

"Clarise, I thought *these* were your people."

"These are the outer folk. Only they know where to find the inner. He will take us deeper into their territory."

Lenore grew bold. "Did these songs say you were bringing guests?"

Clarise understood the implied challenge and was amused. "Yes," she said. "They did."


Chaz had barely closed his eyes in the previous seventy-two hours. As soon as he was taken to a hut he fell onto a bed and slept as soundlessly as a corpse. He remembered no dreams, and never approached the surface of consciousness for almost twenty hours.

He awoke in darkness, rain still beating against the roof. He felt Clarise's warmth next to him. He could barely make out her outline, which rose and fell with the burr of her sleeping breath. He pushed himself up on his elbows and gazed down on her.

On Xanadu, Clarise's exoticism had appealed to him. Here on Java *he* was the exotic . . . he and Minsky, and Lenore, and the children. Clarise was in rhythm with the brush and jagged hills, with every step up dusty winding trails.

She walked like a queen come to claim her kingdom. In his fancy, her beauty seemed to recede from him, as if she were returning to Fairyland.

But in the night she was with him again.

The rain died, and darkness finally thinned. As dawn feathered the sky, the camp began to stir. Clarise awoke to see him staring at her.

"What is it, Chaz?" she asked.

"I don't know," he said. "I should be terrified and miserable. People are dead and dying. We're hunted. We probably won't get out of here alive. But that's all yesterday, or tomorrow. Right now damned if I'm not happy, and it makes no sense at all."

She reached for him. "It doesn't have to make sense," she said. "Just accept what is, and what will be will come soon enough. Too soon. For now, just be."

Her body was soft and warm, as deep as the sheltering oceans. Together, they rejoiced and welcomed the new day.

The old man took them along a muddy path so narrow two men could not walk it abreast. Below them and to the left a twisting river sparkled in the morning sunlight like an emerald snake. Ancient, gnarled trees clustered along the tangled slopes. Chaz's calves and ankles screamed complaint before two hours had passed. The scouts trudged along, suffering in silence, but Anson Teil had to assist Lenore, who suffered from mild but disorienting dizzy spells.

Before they saw another human habitation, the sun was high overhead.

The huts were wood and bamboo lashed together as if designed to be taken apart and refitted on a whim. The Bdui *kampong* was small and neat, no more than five or six acres. A few ragged chickens pecked in the dust outside. Orange fruit dried in strips on small rows of wooden frames. To the left, pungent smoke curled into the air from the roof of a little shack. Ancient women sat in circles, threading chunks of meat and fish onto cords to be cured.

A few well-nourished, naked children played on the flat, packed dirt. They were darker than Clarise, with European eyes and Japanese peasant cheekbones. They were small, few above five feet, but projected terrific vitality. One glance at the newcomers and the children scuttled off to the huts in search of parents.

Their guide spoke, and Clarise answered him, bowing gracefully. The man gave them a smile filled with broken teeth and disappeared into the brush.

"Was this your home?" Chaz asked Clarise.

"No, but I remember the mountains. The outer Bdui travel the mountains following the game and the seasons. Sometimes they stay in one place for years, and sometimes they move every few months. This *kampong* is new."

A young woman appeared. She was a taller, more confident and mature version of the shy young girls who had vanished indoors. Chaz was startled by her resemblance to Clarise. Not as tall, not as lovely, and her teeth were not as straight or white, but the same clear intelligence shone in her eyes, and she carried herself with the same fluid grace.

At sight of Minsky she lost her poise, but only for a moment. Then, to Chaz's surprise, the new girl *sniffed* Clarise, then broke out into a delighted smile. She waved them all to the porch of the largest hut, while she disappeared back along a beaten footpath.

"Well," Clarise said optimistically. "I think I passed the first test."

Chaz decided not to ask.


While they waited, village teenagers, graceful and brown, appeared and offered them sliced coconuts, water, and a pulpy sweet-sour fruit juice Chaz could not identify. Several of them carried broad-bladed knives with stained, serrated edges. They chopped, juggled, and spun the blades as if they had been armed in the crib.

Then something odd happened. Several of the young girls began shouting, making teasing hand gestures to a well-muscled young man. He was unusually tall for a Bdui: almost five and a half feet, Clarise's height. Chaz had noticed him earlier: While the other village youths entertained them, this bravo leaned insolently against a tree, watching her speculatively.

Finally, one of the girls literally dragged him over to them. He laughed, flashing a mouthful of improbably white teeth, and selected a coconut from a pyramid stacked in the shade. He hefted it and laid it on the ground in front of them. He squatted, raised his flat right hand, and then slammed it down. The coconut splintered into a mass of juice and shell shrapnel.

He grinned at Chaz, looked significantly at Clarise, and swaggered away.

Chaz cleared his throat. "By any chance was he asking you for a date?"

"You might say that. His name is Morot, and he was showing off his *Serak,*" she said. "The fighting art of my people. He was saying that he is more of a man than my man."

"Than me?" Chaz said.

She nodded happily, never taking her eyes off the lad.

"I hope I won't have to fight him for you?" He hated the way his frayed nerves turned that sentence into an interrogative.

"Let's hope not," she said merrily.

"Could I learn this 'Serak' stuff?"

"Sure," she said. "Can you give me your full attention for twenty years?"

"Yes," he said. She smiled happily, so he didn't add, *I'd love to think we have twenty years, but I'm having some trouble concentrating lately. . . .*

The sun was an hour closer to the horizon before a tiny,

gravely courteous man appeared. He spoke to the teenagers, who by now had completely encircled them, politely smiling without displaying the slightest inclination to break ranks.

Tea and a battered copper tray of grain cakes were served as the small man exchanged a few Bdui words with Clarise. His eyes widened. He looked at her more closely and barked laughter. He grasped her about the shoulders. Despite his apparent frailty he hugged her tightly enough to wring a gasp from her.

He sat with them as if in parlay, flat on the porch. The teenagers surrounded them in a quiet, very polite outer ring, all the insolence and surliness evaporated. Beyond them a few younger children congregated.

The younger Bdui made way for the older villagers who wished to enter the inner circle as the conversation flowed. Clarise translated when appropriate.

Clarise, it seemed, was a "Walking Daughter," one of those children sent into the external world once a generation. These children were adopted into friendly tribes, sent to learn what there was to learn and then return with new songs and stories for the village. Clarise had been adopted by missionaries and found her way eventually to Xanadu.

"The Old Queen gave us our ways," he said. "And they pass from daughter to daughter, and we obey and protect them, never question."

After almost a minute's silence, Clarise spoke clearly and with formality. The village chief answered her.

Another silence. Chaz asked: "What did he say?"

"I asked for asylum among my people. We need to be in the inner ring, among the 'inner' Bdui. They never come into contact with the outside world. We would be safe there."

"And?"

Clarise sighed, but her expression was, if possible, even more determined. "A Walking Daughter must prove herself."

Smoke seemed to shift and coil behind her eyes, and Chaz

felt a chill. "Well, aren't we isolated enough already?"

Her smile was sad and gentle. "Chaz, our enemies have power. They will find the Squark City technicians. They will trace the Wetcat. I gave the captain pearls, but he will talk anyway. The trail might die at the coast if no one sees us again. No missionaries, no traders. We must be ghosts. Perhaps they will seek us in Jakarta. Only the inner ring is safe."

*A Walking Daughter must prove herself.* What exactly did that mean? There had to be another way. "Do we have anything to trade? Can we buy room?"

She shook her head. "It won't work like that. I have to prove myself a part of the village."

"Weaving? Songs?"

"I'll be tested," she said flatly. "It begins tomorrow. If I pass, then we will have shelter. If not, we must move on. And, Chaz, we *will* be found. And killed."

"Is there anything I can do to help?"

She leaned against him and shuddered. He felt helpless and furious with himself for the dark, cowardly sliver of his id that was relieved the burden rested on her shoulders and not his. "Just love me, Chaz. I'm afraid."


They slept in a private hut that night. There in the shadows, they held each other. Chaz hoped that they might make love, but she was far too exhausted and clung to him like a child.

Chaz lay awake long after Clarise sank into slumber. He thought of the hut nearby. There, Lenore slept alone. If he felt helpless and afraid, Lenore's anguish had to be almost beyond endurance.

And yet, and yet . . . the mysterious Saturn had drawn the line. He had started this. Hundreds, perhaps thousands had died already due to his machinations. Hundreds of millions of children would never be born.

The skein of the conspiracy would unravel if Chaz knew where to grasp the thread. As terrible as the consequences had been, if Lenore hadn't heard a single clandestine conversation in a shadowed hallway and pursued it, no entity called Saturn would ever have surfaced.

If Lenore was a sacrifice on the altar of truth, so be it. If his life and the lives on Xanadu were all forfeit, then so be it. In these waters, he swam as a babe. But Saturn would make a mistake, and Chaz would find his invisible opponent.

He slept, dreaming of empty wombs.

The women of the outer village arrived at daybreak, short dark thin women wearing filmy garments reminiscent of saris.

They stood in a crescent outside Chaz's hut and chanted until Clarise emerged to join them. They encircled her and walked her to a sheltered clearing. There in the shadows they held a conversation in song. They warbled for perhaps ten minutes and then paused. Haltingly, then with increasing confidence, Clarise repeated the songs back to them.

To her delight and theirs, as the afternoon wore on she improved. Occasionally she led them in a verse. When the afternoon shadows grew long, the village women rose smiling and led her to two tiny old women who shuffled her into a hut for physical examination.

As he waited, he watched the Sea Scouts, who were playing a makeshift game of kickball with the village children. No words were exchanged, just whoops and hollers and grunts of exertion as the afternoon wore on. Xanadu's offspring were a bit larger, but as the hours passed all were covered in dust and formed a single tribe.

Chaz and the other adults were too nervous to do more than smile politely as the elders argued with each other: Should Clarise be allowed to stay? Should she be sent to the Christian church, two days' march away? Or to a fishing village up the coast . . . ? A skinny twelve-year-old named Jaffie had studied with missionaries; he translated haltingly. An old woman who had known Clarise's parents spoke to all of them, followed by a wizened great-uncle.

After an hour Clarise emerged from the hut, adjusting her clothes. The old women followed her out, rapidly spoke some words that Jaffie blushed to translate, and then sat, facing her expectantly. Clarise took a deep breath and began to dance for them. The old women winced, grimacing at her errors.

After a half hour Clarise returned to him sweaty and dejected.

"They say that I have forgotten the old ways and that I might live in the outer circle, but that is all." Her eyes were vast and dark. "It's not enough."

"We could—"

"No, Chaz." She gripped his hand tightly. "Chaz, no matter what happens next, I want you to be silent, do you understand?"

He nodded, afraid to fully acknowledge the implications of her request.


The Bdui camp was spiked with paths leading into the woods, the mountains, down to the sea only three hours' march away. Traveling westerly was a path lined with trees bearing small, dark datelike fruit with the taste and texture of figs. The Sea Scouts had already explored them. At the end of that path, an hour from the camp, Chaz found Anson Teil, Lenore, and Minsky clustered on a cliff overlooking the ocean.

Minsky gazed out to the northwest in the direction of Xanadu. If Chaz strained, he could imagine that he saw smoke rising from the island's skeleton.

Minsky looked morose. Chaz put his hand on his friend's shoulder. "Arvad?"

His friend didn't answer.

"What is it?" Chaz asked.

The water sparkled in the setting sun. "He's out there," Minsky said. "He's not one of them, you know. He needs me."

The way he said it, the way his voice quavered, Chaz thought that he was talking about a lover. But Arvad Minsky had never been known to take a lover, male or female. It was Minsky and his sharks: four since he and Chaz had met, and the last was Barrister. And so it had always been.

Words eluded him. If Arvad had lost a pet, or a wife, or a parent, the words would come. But this . . . "He's got better weapons than sharks do. He's smarter, even without you linked in," Chaz said. He was guessing.

Lenore's hand rested on Minsky's shoulder. He didn't respond, but neither did he reject her.

Very quietly Anson Teil said, "It's hard, Chaz—being isolated on Xanadu for as long as he was, and suddenly cut off from everything he knows or loves. I'm not sure how you're managing so well."

"Clarise," Chaz said honestly.

"Don't you need diet supplements?"

"Oh, yeah. So does Arvad." His eyes met Lenore's. Had she told Teil? She had. "I'm getting arthritis. Nothing worse, so far."

Laughter twisted in Minsky's throat. "It's my mind. Maybe it's Alzheimer's! And maybe it's only the computer link. How would I know? I'm older than you, Chaz!"

"By a year."

Teil and Lenore were fascinated. They waited . . . but Arvad had no more to say.


# 44


"One child per generation," the elder said. Jaffie translated. "We choose one, and send the one out into the world to learn of the outside. A Walking Son or Daughter. Even in the beginning, the Great Queen bade us do this."

Sitting cross-legged in a semicircle, the Sea Scouts watched, silent with fascination.

"And now this woman wants to shelter within us, to return to the fold. We say that she has forgotten our ways, that she has lost what makes us separate and apart, what gives us our magic. She cannot join the women of the tribe. She will seek to join the men. It has rarely been done, but a Walking Daughter can make special demands of our council. We must allow her this chance."

Clarise was dressed as were men of the Bdui, with blue vest and pants. A band of blue cloth bound her breasts tightly. Vest and cloth band were blotted and streaked with sweat.

She squatted in a circle drawn in the dirt. Over and over again, grueling hundreds of times, she repeated the same eighteen basic movement patterns, sets of strikes with fist and elbow, grabs and blocks and throws performed in the air against imaginary opponents. Bent forward, 90 percent of her weight balanced on the front leg, hands held high, she strained her body through the peculiar patterns, *djurus*, of the Bdui martial art, *Pentjak Silat Serak*.

"Marrying the Djuru," this form of torture was called, the performance of a set of martial movements over the entire night, the only rest provided by shifts in tempo. She continued after the Scouts had wandered to bed, after Minsky fell asleep, and only Chaz, Lenore, and Teil remained awake to witness her efforts.

Chaz's lungs burned in sympathetic exhaustion. Surely this "marriage" was a greater exertion than any marathon. It was a performance worthy of an Olympic hopeful, almost beyond the capacities of human flesh. Until the violence in the Indian forest, he had never suspected that such reserves lay hidden in that slender, silken body.

Ironic that this fabulous performance was in the service of a dead man. Chaz could no longer deceive himself. He had left all his medical monitors, potions, and spells behind on Xanadu. The years would hit him like an avalanche.

At last will and sinew failed, and Clarise collapsed. She lay on her side, heaving, clutching at the spasming muscles in her right thigh. Chaz started up and toward her. Her eyes flamed warning. "Stay back! I have to do it myself." Trembling, she forced herself back up, balancing on exhausted limbs. Finding strength from God knows where, she began anew.

"Clarise?" he whispered, aghast. She turned to him, showing him a stranger's face, a lovely face that he had so often kissed now revealed as a mask over an animal urgency, an almost supernatural endurance and appetite for pain. She looked at him, *through* him, and never stopped moving.

At long last the village elders nodded their approval. Clarise staggered to the edge of the circle and collapsed. Lenore was asleep now, but Minsky was still awake. The three men kneaded her muscles in preparation for the next challenge. Jaffie brought Chaz a gourd filled with coconut milk. With a few halting English words and a good deal of pantomiming, the intent was conveyed: Clarise had a few minutes to prepare herself for a more realistic test of her skills.

Chaz cursed. Clarise lay motionless, exhausted, her eyes half lidded, almost comatose. How in the world could they expect her to . . . ?

Then he noticed something that had escaped him before: Her breathing was not ragged but tightly controlled—inhalations long, exhalations longer still, thin and hot like a steam whistle. Her diaphragm was taut, fluttering with each breath, hands tensing rhythmically. But through that, he saw her eyes focus on his for just a moment, and she was back with him and gone again.

He understood. *Don't interfere.*

Chaz swallowed his bile and continued to massage her knotted calves. A quarter hour later Clarise emerged from her odd semistupor and rose to her feet. She was remarkably recovered, as if she had slept for hours instead of minutes. Another small miracle.

The drum and cymbal music began anew.

Morot appeared. Chaz groaned: It was the coconut killer. The teenage Silat expert was stripped to the waist. Every visible inch of his sunburned body rippled with flat muscle. He moved like some kind of impossibly lifelike marionette, as if he had no weight at all.

Before the council of elders he danced and bobbed and wove, displaying his martial skills. Where Clarise had seemed like a leopard, this boy was a shadow glimmering in water: here, there, up, down. Each segment of his body seemed to explode in perfect form and independent motion, a remarkable exhibition of muscular control.

After Morot finished, Clarise stomped the ground with her right foot, spat in the dust, and commenced her own dance. The elders watched her closely. Miraculously, all apparent fatigue had vanished.

Clarise and Morot danced toward each other in a ragged spiral. They feigned kicks and punches, still out of reach. The drums and *gamelan* cymbals created a hypnotic, seductive rhythm. The villagers' chanted encouragement spurred them on. Closer they came, and yet closer. Then, as if someone had flicked an invisible switch, the mock fight turned real. With a blur of motion, they collided, scrabbled, rising into the air like fighting cocks.

Chaz's eyes couldn't follow the action, but when Clarise retreated to a safe distance, her face was smeared with blood.

Chaz forced himself to clarity. He knew that witnessing this ritual was a once-in-a-lifetime experience. Honor or not, he was aghast.

They clashed again. As before, Clarise seemed to get the worst of it. Morot's leg flexed, knee raised hip-high, foot drawn in. From this odd position the ball of his foot flickered out, hammering her just under the breastbone. As she stumbled and almost fell, her body corkscrewed awkwardly. Her opponent grew more confident. His leg swung surprisingly high, catching her on the hinge of the jaw. She crumpled, breaking her fall with her folded arms, all of the breath driven out of her. Fast as a striking snake, Morot was after her. Then, in that moment of ultimate despair, something unexpected happened.

Clarise's knee folded into her chest. Her bare foot shot out, unshod, as it had been in her childhood, when she had run the mountains of her native country. Her heel, hardened by rock and sand, caught him squarely in the gut. His feet left the ground, his eyes wide with shock as he flew backward.

As if connected to him by elastic bands, she was after him, she was on him. She caught his left leg with her ankle, sweeping it as he tried to regain balance. She spun him by an arm and his head, flipping his entire body horizontally, along the axis of his spine.

*"Puter Capala,"* the old chieftain murmured excitedly.

Before he could hit the ground her elbow crashed down—

Clarise's warning forgotten, Chaz was on his feet. This was just a boy, just a child!

—and stopped, an inch from Morot's head. Perfect control. Hours of grueling exercise, virtually no rest or food, and a brilliant adversary, and she had defeated the boy *without hurting him.*

The village elders nodded their approval.

Behind them, the sun was rising once again.

The Bdui chieftain conferred rapidly with the others, laughing and nodding. A great knot in Chaz's chest began to relax. Although he could see her tremors, Clarise faced them with her weight balanced on her left leg, the right crooked and balanced on the ball of her foot. Her hands were clasped, and she bent forward deeply from the waist, doubtless a gesture of respect.

She remained in that position as the village awoke and gathered in the new light. The six Sea Scouts clustered around them, rubbing their eyes groggily, and staring at Clarise, who hadn't moved, despite the perspiration that dripped from her face and speckled the dust at her feet.

When the entire village was gathered, the music began again, and the chief spoke rapidly in his native tongue.

"This ceremony welcomes back our Walking Daughter and her adopted children," Clarise translated. "And her brothers, and her man, and—" She stopped; her eyes fell on Arvad; her face twisted with effort as she said, "her demon servant . . ."

Now she looked directly at Lenore. The chief continued to speak. Lenore seemed to hold her breath. "And her sister," he said. In the early morning light, tears streaked Lenore's face.

They were safe.

More than that. For a time, at least, they were home.


They were given their white robes before they were allowed to pass beyond the outer ring. *Blue for the outer Bdui, White for the inner*, Clarise had said. The people of the outer ring sang them into the center in a procession, but there was a point, some invisible line scratched in the dirt, that the Blue folk seemed reluctant to pass. Jaffie continued on with them.

A small boy dressed in white ran out to greet them, followed by a second child, and then another, and another. They stared at the newcomers until an older girl shouted at them. Then they converged on Jaffie, welcomed him as a brother, and gave him white pants that he donned with evident relish. The children streamed out until the newcomers were surrounded by a flock of gigglers, who held their hands, hugged their legs, and finally, sang them into the inner village.

# 45

The path to the White village wound through a shadowed valley, then along the edge of a coastal cliff overlooking the Indian Ocean. The paths were deeply trod but overgrown enough to convince Chaz that these seminomadic folk remained within a familiar region comprised of some few thousand square kilometers. He reckoned that several times a generation a man might walk paths blazed by his father and grandfather, that he himself had trod in youth.

They wound their way toward a jagged volcanic peak. It rose a thousand meters above them, its jagged lip wreathed with mist.

Clark and Barbie stopped every few minutes to gawk and stare: The undergrowth was so raw, the rock so unweathered that it seemed that they had arrived less in another land than another time.

"A dinosaur just poked his head over that rock," Clark declared. "Riiight," his twin sister replied, but snuck a peek for herself.

Rude steps were carved in glassy rock, winding up a mountainside. The glazed black volcanic stone made the climb a nonstop torture, and they pushed and pulled and hauled each other up the grade. Then the path leveled out again, and they were in a little valley that one might only have seen from the air.

Running north-south, no more than two or three kilometers long and a single kilometer wide, the valley was perfectly sheltered in the sloping shadow of an extinct volcano at its northern edge. Its soil was as black and rich as ground coffee, dotted with clusters of fruit trees. A crystal-clear pool welled from the rock at the foot of the mountain.

Clarise wiped the dust and sweat from her grin. "Home, Chaz," she said. "This is sacred ground, very precious to my people." Wind and rain and volcanic action had weathered the raw, jagged ridges above them, but the valley floor was everything described by explorers in the eighteenth century: a virtual Eden.

The valley sheltered houses of rock and mud and wood, some of bamboo, and some decorated with shells carefully gathered on the beach a kilometer to the south. They were rude, strong, single story, clustered together with no visible gardens or fences. Sanitation ditches slitted the earth at the southern end.

Clarise made no sound, just stood and waited. As if some silent signal had been made, the Bdui left their homes and tasks and clustered below them, sun-cured faces upturned.

The inner Bdui seemed the same, genetically, as the outer. But they were a little smaller on the average, more wizened, eyes bright but teeth often pitted or twisted behind their welcoming smiles.

Lenore nudged Anson Teil. "We should call in the UN Dental Association Swat Team," she said. "They've been all through India."

Anson Teil laughed, and so did Chaz. "Protein and mineral deficiency," he said soberly. "The Blue Bdui take Xanadu's free protein. The White don't."

As Clarise descended, Chaz was again struck by how much taller she was than the other Bdui. She loomed over most of them. She was inundated with hugs, and laughter, and welcomed as if she were the most precious thing in the world. Little wonder that missionaries had spirited her away. It was not merely luck that she had received the finest nutrition and schooling and the opportunity to rise in the competitive modern environment.

She was, after all, a Walking Daughter.

\* \* \*

Without a grumble, workers diverted themselves from other tasks, assembled frameworks of bamboo and rattan, covered them with leafy sheets, and slathered on mud. In hours the sun had baked the mud dry, and the new housing was ready.

The Scouts and Lenore shared one rude but comfortable house, Teil and Minsky another. Chaz and Clarise were taken to a low-roofed house made of bamboo, straw, and some hardwood that he couldn't recognize. The interior floor was of dirt packed and polished until it was almost like marble. The light, powdery smell inside reminded him of unburned incense.

Their bedding was thin and hard enough to press the bones, but Chaz had no urge to complain: It was shelter and safety. He was unpacking their meager belongings when Clarise slipped her arms around his waist. "Be it ever so humble," he said.

She nibbled on his ear. "It gets better, Chaz."

A clamor drew them back outside, where a delegation of elders, men and women, waited, looking at Clarise expectantly. Every dark, wrinkled face beamed with curiosity.

"What is this?" he whispered.

Clarise seemed a combination of resignation and nervous expectancy. "It's time for this walking daughter to give back to her people."

The group formed a procession, and the outsiders fell into place, Minsky in the middle, the Sea Scouts and Anson Teil and Lenore Myles at the rear. Lenore had come to share responsibility for the Scouts. They traveled north to the end of the little valley and into a crack in the mountain wall Chaz had not seen.

*Lava tube*, Chaz thought. With torches held on high, they were led through a glassy tunnel with a roof three feet above his head. The footing was perilous, the slope a steadily rising grade, challenging to lungs and legs. He wondered if the tube would run on for kilometers, as they did in Hawaii. He would never make it.

The slick black rock beneath their feet suddenly became

terribly uneven, as if a stupendous hammer blow had split the ground, and the path ended in an ancient rock slide. Running water echoed in the distant dark.

Chaz inched his way around the fallen scree. His shoes were wet and slick, his toes gummy. The path turned narrow and scary. Clarise danced ahead of him; her feet seemed to remember the path.

A tight squeeze, a few passages that seemed more suited for the Sea Scouts (especially Crystal and Mohammed, who were scrambling about oohing and ahhing, having the time of their lives), and then they were through into another chamber.

It was gigantic, the largest lava-blister cave he had ever heard of. Its ceiling rose far beyond the glow of torchlight. He could only imagine that this place, disorienting and beautiful in a primal, primitive way, was created by a combination of molten rock pressure and water erosion.

"This is incredible." The inadequate words rang hollowly in his ears.

"The mother cave," Clarise said.

The others gawked speechlessly, words inadequate to describe the sight. Clucking happily, their guides took them to a smaller room off the side of that main chamber. Here the torches were able to fill the space with light. Once again Chaz was dumbstruck.

The chamber wall was a scrambled maze of paintings. Depictions of animals, men, huts, oceans, moons, fires and jungles. Modern ships and planes could be glimpsed here and there, but most could have been scrawled in antiquity. Some were smudged and indecipherable. Some were tiny stick figures scrawled with the end of a charred stick. Others were up to three times his own height. Bamboo scaffolds leaned against the cave walls like tired old men. He felt much as he had when first faced with the reality of Xanadu: that he was witness to the impossibly complex end product of uncounted thousands of hands, millions of man-hours.

"What is this place?" he asked weakly.

"This is the history of my people," Clarise said. "I was sent into the world to bring home a new piece of this."

"Those drawings in your apartment!"

She nodded.

Minsky smiled suddenly. "Two years ago. The art competition. You won in the n-neo-primitive category."

"I wanted to laugh."

"You're right, Clarise," Minsky said. "You really have come home." His eyes were the only thing alive in his face: He'd lost weight; his cheeks drooped from his skull.

Mending, hunting, fishing . . . for all of the semipermanence of their location, the White Bdui had no interest in cultivating their little valley, although they didn't seem to mind Chaz's fledgling horticultural efforts.

He rarely traveled outside the valley—that would have defeated the purpose of their perilous journey. As the Bdui began to realize his interests, they altered their daily routines to fetch him cuttings, samples of flowers and herbs from the surrounding forest. Some flourished in the rich, volcanic soil. Others died.

Weeks passed like clouds drifting across a frozen sky.

Chaz and Minsky's worlds had collapsed, but the twins and other Scouts browned and blossomed as if this were an extended field trip. Thanks to Anson Teil's inventive mind, that was the way it must have seemed to them: an endless round of cookouts, fishing expeditions, biology lessons, and orienteering competitions.

Somehow he managed to convince them that their parents were well, had survived, and that reunion day would come soon. Mohammed woke up crying once and was comforted by the others. The children played, learned, performed their chores. And often went south to the ocean at night, staring out across the water, perhaps crying. Arvad did that too.

Anson Teil was a master chef, and took the herbs, fruits, game animals, and fish and rendered them masterfully into palate-tempting dishes. Despite the fact that they seemed resigned to an almost Stone Age level of health and shelter, the White Bdui seemed content. They had found a niche in the food chain where they could concentrate their attention on those aspects of the world that brought them pleasure: song, prayer, and the daily rituals of hunting and gathering.

Their children were silent in the presence of their elders, unless addressed. Families seemed organized around the mother and her brothers more than the father. Men paid as much attention to their nieces and nephews as to their own children, but every child was a child of the village.

The Sea Scouts discovered *that* the first time Clark tried to steal a bit of dried sweet yam. A wizened, toothless Bdui grandmother had appeared from nowhere, and Clark writhed helplessly in her grasp as she administered a skilled spanking. Then, oddly, she enfolded him in her brown arms. Clark struggled for a moment, then collapsed against her, sobbing.

From then on, Clark and Barbie could scarcely be pried away from the old woman: They cleaned her hut, they washed her clothes, and she sang them to sleep at night.

As the days passed, the Scouts were gradually adopted into Bdui homes, and life in the valley began to normalize.

Sometimes Chaz went to the mother cave with Clarise. He helped her mix pigments of earth and rock and pig blood into a thick, pasty paint that she worked into the wall using bristle brushes, flat sticks, and a broad, sure hand.

As her paintings progressed a story emerged. In it, a girl-child left her people and entered a red rectangle crowded with happy-face circles: a schoolhouse.

A few drawings later, a boat ferried her to a hexagon-within-waves: Xanadu.

Her art was simple, its sense of proportions sometimes grotesque, but there was a calm center to it. She painted there for hours, and sometimes would wipe the sweat from her face and smile down at Chaz as he sat on the rocks beneath her, and he was warmed.


Day by day, the ache in his joints increased. At first, he didn't recognize the symptoms. He told himself it was just the effect of sleeping on a hard mattress, so close to the ground. He thought it a by-product of the cool, damp mornings or the cumulative stress and strain of recent days.

Of course, it wasn't that at all.

It took six weeks for the problem to swell from ant to elephant. On that fortieth morning he woke staring up at the roof with his heart hammering wildly in his chest. It took him a full minute to regroup himself, to remember where he was, that he was Chadwick Kato . . . wait . . . Chadwick Kato the Third.

He tried to eat more carefully and exercised daily, exerting himself in the disciplines that had once defined his life. Despite his best efforts, every day he felt a month older.

One day at their communal meal of plantain, rice, and fish he stole a careful look at Minsky, and saw the ashen tone of his friend's skin, his dry and cracked lips, the aimless tilt of his head. He made Arvad sit in sunlight and looked into his eyes.

The flickering white pinprick in his right eye, the digital camera: Arvad tilted his head left by a bit to see with that one. His living left eye, once clear, was now bloodshot and yellow cast, an old man's eye.

Time had caught up with Minsky.

"Arvad," he asked. "Are you all right?"

Arvad Minsky smiled vaguely. "As well as can be expected, Chaz."

"How old are you, Arvad?"

His friend looked at him wearily, and for a moment the smile deepened. "Right now," Minsky said, "older than God." And he shuffled away.

Chaz watched him go. He wanted to reach out and put his hand on his friend's shoulder, to touch him in some meaningful way. But there was nothing to say. With conscious effort, Chaz strode away, trying to put some bounce to his step.

Lenore had been spending more and more time with Anson Teil, and Chaz was glad of that. If her world had been torn apart by a war in heaven, something good might still come of it.

"We watch him," she said, meaning Minsky. "When the elders say it's all right, we go down to the cove."

Chaz nodded: He and the others went down there together as often as it was thought safe, generally at night. "It's peaceful there," Chaz said. "Moonlight makes it magic."

"Peaceful," Lenore repeated. "The last time we were there, Minsky thought that he saw Barrister."

Chaz sighed. It had been pure wishful thinking to hope for his friend's recovery. Within Arvad's soul burned an illness graver than a lack of dietary supplements. He wasn't even certain that it could be properly diagnosed.

# 46

It took Chaz a week to acclimate sufficiently to circumnavigate the valley. Every day he pushed his edge, experienced the bizarre sensation of his body trying to fall apart at the same time that his will drove him to greater and greater efforts.

By the end of their eighth week in the valley, he felt at least five years older, but reasonably fit, able to jog half the distance. In another three weeks, he could run the entire circumference.

His bones ached, and the tendons around his artificial knees, but his muscles were reasonably taut.

The Bdui washed their clothes and bodies downhill from the little pond that provided water to the valley. Chaz had already lost modesty. Washing with a soap paste made from plant extracts and sand, he examined himself: Did his knees look a little knobbier than they did just yesterday? God knew his wind wasn't good, but what could he do except push?

A pool away, Arvad Minsky washed himself in a circle of staring, giggling children. Arvad mugged for them, enjoying himself: Clarise Maibang's demon servant.

There had to be an answer. The trouble was that their answers lay in the outside world, a world he no longer had access to. If only he had been able to bring Nero!

Their contact with the civilized world was limited: Every week or so, the pale-skinned Xanadu refugees darkened their skin with berry juice and walked the trails to the outer village to listen to the short wave radio.

On one of these trips he listened to a roster of the Xanadu dead. The toll stretched into the hundreds. They were slaughtered in the initial attack, ripped to bits in riots; they were executed, or tried and then executed, or murdered in prison.

Yamato must have died while the Wetcat and its crew were still deep underwater. The Energy lord's armored limousine had been bombed into a twisted heap of smoking steel. Only tattered fragments of Yamato remained, identified by dental records and by whatever hadn't charred or melted of the hardware implanted in his head and torso. The news anchor seemed fascinated by how much of Yamato had been artificial, as if the Councilman had been no longer human.

Chaz wondered what the asshole would think of Minsky.

Arvad was too weak to trek to the radio. This trip, Clarise

and Lenore squatted with Chaz, listening to the news in the chieftain's hut. "This is beyond awful," he found himself saying.

Lenore looked to Clarise. "What do you think is going on?" she said.

"No, I'll ask you the same question."

"I think that the Council did something horrible and that the birds have come home to roost. Maybe you weren't involved, Chaz . . . ?"

"I was one of the patsies. Check me out, Clarise: Did a *lot* of people like me get selected sixteen years ago?"

"Over that year, more than sixty."

"Yes. We were candidates. We were brought to Xanadu, and then Saturn got very selective. A few got into the inner circle. Most of us were supposed to die in the riots."

"Saturn. Why not the whole Council?" He shook his head. She persisted. "They're powerful. They're elitist."

"Power isn't bad unless you hurt someone with it."

Lenore looked at him pityingly. "Grow up, Chaz, while there's still time."

That stung, and he might have barked back but for the sudden, joyous realization that her criticism was the work of a whole mind, a healthy ego. Her healing was nearly complete. So he smiled and said, "Too late."

Clarise and Chaz left the hut.

Lenore remained behind to enjoy the moments of contact with the outside world. Sometimes, when the weather was just right, they could pick up a BBC rebroadcast, radio dramas recorded during the 1950s and '60s. Those made her laugh, and sometimes cry. Now she carefully tuned the radio, searching, searching, until she found a show spotlighting old comedy songs.

*"All the world seems in tune on a spring afternoon—"*

She laughed delightedly and joined in: *"When we're poooisoning pigeons in the paaaark!"*

Anson Teil's voice joined hers. He sat with a graceless *huff*. "I didn't know you were a Tom Lehrer fan."

She studied him there in the shadows. His face, always pleasant but somehow bland, was transformed by the simple joy of singing along to one of the twentieth-century's most gifted satirists.

"Yeah," she said wistfully. "In college. We loved him."

"Me, too," Teil said. They hummed along to "Masochism Tango," and remembered enough words to "So Long, Mom (A song for World War III)" to actually try a little harmony.

There was a commercial break, during which Lenore and Anson looked at each other, and although the radio crackled, it seemed that the hut was silent. Finally Anson spoke. "I'm planning to have a fish fry with the Scouts tonight. I was wondering . . ." He cleared his throat.

"If I would accompany you?"

He nodded gratefully. "The weather should be clear tonight. The moon is full." He shrugged, as if hoping she would understand the rest.

"It sounds lovely," she said.

Teil sighed and turned back to the radio again. She kept watching him, realizing that she found his sunburned nose rather endearing, and giggled to herself.

Then, with all the enthusiasm they could muster, they launched into the soothing refrains of Lehrer's immortal "Pollution" and, after that, waited with great anticipation for a promised hour of the immortal "Weird Al" Yankovic.

One day Chaz returned from his grueling daily jog to find Clarise waiting for him. She followed him under their makeshift shower, holding her rich body close to his, and brought her mouth very close to his ear. "I'm pregnant."

Chaz looked at her, incredulous, then believing.

*Hey!* He and Ako had tried. Since then he had never seriously considered fatherhood, but *Hey!* The world outside might fall apart, and Chadwick Kato, like all men, would inevitably die, but a part of Chaz would go on. He amended that happily: a part of Chaz *and* Clarise!

He held her closely and felt her good solid strength. Their child would be healthy. Strong. Maybe it could grow here, away from the world, uncorrupted and free—and ignorant, starved of civilization's miracles . . .

God, the choices to be made.

One choice virtually made itself.

"Who do I have to bribe to get a wedding around here?" he asked.


The day before the wedding, the Sea Scouts and a few Bdui children ran down to the sea in search of mussels. There they found abandoned shoes and the bare footprints where Arvad Minsky had walked into the sea.

Chaz made the walk down, feeling a breathlessness that had nothing to do with his fatigue, though it was great. He held Minsky's worn sneaker, holes rubbed through at sole and toe, and gazed out at the ocean. They had tried to comfort Arvad, to be family to him in any way they could. But Chaz and Clarise had made a world with each other. Lenore and Teil had moved in together. The Scouts were children, and the Bdui, for all their hospitality, treated him like a visiting Martian.

Arvad Minsky, genius, multimillionaire, Council member, one of the most powerful men in the world, was a decrepit old half man, half machine, a slowly dying creature out of time and place, who ultimately had no one and nothing.

Chaz knew he should have watched him, should have anticipated that he was the one who would crack.

He was their first loss. Chaz knew he wouldn't be the last.


The wedding was simple, and profound. Pak Jute the Lurah asked Chaz if he loved this woman, this Walking Daughter come home. By the earth and the sky, would he swear to love her and hold her for the rest of his days, until the sun cooled and the moon fell from the sky.

He remembered Ako.

He had loved her! But Ako's husband had been a younger, shallower man, a man who made the terrible error of thinking that he understood himself, and in that understanding he had found something of value to give another. The simple words spoken by Pak Jute offered a different commitment, a different relationship. It was no betrayal of Ako. This was a different time in his life.

It was a different life altogether.

He said he would, and she said she would honor and love him and teach him the ancient ways. And to the cheers of Anson, Lenore, the Scouts, and the entire Bdui village they kissed until he thought the top of his head would explode.

For a few precious hours forgetting the fatigue that gnawed his bones, he danced until the campfires died down to coals and then held Clarise until dawn brought sleep and sweet dreams to them both.

Every third day at noon, Chaz left the valley and walked a kilometer west along a sheltered footpath and then across a beach, down to a little cove looking out on the blue vastness of the Indian Ocean.

To his great pleasure, Manny and Trish danced on the waves, awaiting his arrival. Few of the other scaliens and only one of the squarks had traveled as far east as Java. They'd lost interest or lost their way. Even Manny and Trish had vanished for one stretch of a week and a half.

Without asking, Chaz knew where they had been. He asked, "What is happening at Xanadu?"

"Xanadu people programming blow up," Manny said. "No one plays with us. Feeds us. Monitors us. No one goes to city."

He could easily read between the lines. Xanadu was controlled by joint Indian and Chinese forces preparing to bring charges before the World Court. Hundreds dead. How many captured? He was afraid to ask.

"What do we do, Chaz?" Trish asked.

He had no answer for them. Two dolphins and a squark were all that remained of their precious undersea experiment. Perhaps in time others would return to Squark City, if this hideous situation could be resolved. But how long might that take? And what remained of their augmented intelligence?

Their unmodified progeny might learn traces of a tradition, a habit of thinking. Evolution might shape dolphins or sea lions to use tools again over the next ten thousand centuries.

Or a dozen years from now, it might all be gone forever.

"Just meet me here when you can, Trish," he said.

Chaz slipped off his rock and into the water. Trish nosed up against him affectionately, a slick silken mass as affectionate as a house cat. He circled one arm around her as far as he could reach. He wondered if he and Minsky and the others, in giving the gift of greater intellect, had done a terrible wrong. Manny and Trish had no tribe but Xanadu, no family save their creators and the other scaliens.

"Love you, Chaz," Trish said, and for an instant Chaz felt the urge to stay with them, to swim out and out toward the horizon and never look back. Wished in that moment that he was one of these good and gentle creatures, not one of the gravity-bound mutations who had spawned the monster Saturn.

Every day health and youth slipped farther away. Age flooded back. Knees and spine and hands pulsed with arthritic agony. Sight blurred. Incontinence plagued him. Within two months after their wedding, Chaz's body failed to respond to Clarise.

If an answer couldn't be found, he might die of old age

before his infant son or daughter could walk.

In another life he had grown old like this . . . but he hadn't *fought* it like this.

Late mornings, after the customary run that had devolved to a hobble, Chaz worked the small straight cultivated rows where he strove to raise flowers.

He labored in the sun, aware that he looked like the old, old men back in Manzanar, working endlessly at gardens that bore little fruit.

One day, as he labored in his meager vineyards, Pak Jute approached him. Six or seven younger Bdui, including Mohammed, trailed along behind him.

Chaz wiped his forehead and greeted them.

"You look sick, my friend," Jute said to him haltingly, his ancient face creased with concern. "You have weakened much in the short time you have been with us."

"What do you call this?" Chaz asked, for a moment ignoring Jute's concern. He pointed to a fibrous bulb almost two feet tall, fleshy leaves at the base parting to allow its rather phallic blooms to seek light and air.

"*Bunga bankai,*" Jute said. "Corpse flower. When it blooms, it smells like a dead animal."

"Charming. Appropriate."

He stood creakily, glad that the *Amorphophallus titanum* wouldn't bloom fully until he was long dead. Chaz paused, trying to think of the right way to describe what was happening to him. "I took medicines," he said, "to keep me young. I am older than I look . . . looked. Older than you, I think, Pak Jute. Now my natural age is returning."

Jute's eyes widening with understanding. "Ah. That would be strong medicine indeed."

A flicker of hope. "Do you have herbs or potions for age?"

Jute looked at him and laughed uproariously. "My friend, if I had them, don't you think I would use them myself?"

Chaz's ears burned with embarrassment, increasing as

some of the others, and even little Mohammed, laughed at him. He said, "Duh."

Jute laid a withered hand on his shoulder. "We can help with many things, many pains, and illnesses. We can help a woman give healthy birth. We can even help a man who has lost his . . ." And here Jute made an anatomically specific gesture.

Chaz grinned ruefully. "I think we need to talk."

He glanced down at the flower whose Latin name meant "big, shapeless phallus."

The gods, he thought, had retained their sense of humor.


Lenore arrived as he was finishing his noon session with Manny and Trish. He usually conducted it on Minsky's Rock, the rock where Arvad Minsky had often perched, staring out at an empty ocean, waiting for Barrister.

There was nothing new to report on either side. Lenore plunged into the waves and swam with the dolphins. Presently the dolphins swam off to hunt. Lenore toweled herself off and sat beside him on the sand.

He watched her with an appreciation devoid of lust. Too vividly, he remembered the hormonal rush that had always accompanied the observation of such a perfect, sensuous form. Now . . . nothing.

He sighed. "Life," Chaz said, "is certainly strange."

"Compared to what?" She leaned her head against his shoulder. "I hope it's all right for me to do this. Anson doesn't mind."

"He's got no problem."

She paused, almost as if reading his mind. "God. You're married, and I'm living with Teil, and I still wonder if it's all right to talk about it. We humans are funny beasts, aren't we?"

"You're my sister now," Chaz said. "It's official. I'm sorry for everything that happened, but I'm not sorry I met you. I hope you don't regret it, either."

She didn't answer.

"Hey," he said, and thumped her thigh lightly. "I knew you had your mind back when you started winning arguments."

"I'm thinking ... oh, all right. It's strange, but no, I'm not sorry at all. But, Chaz, I would like to have Saturn's throat in my hands."

"Yes!" Bloodlust was an emotion he could still manage. Yes. Vengeance. "I can't even let myself daydream about it. It hurts too much. There's an urge, but no *image*. Do you really picture a throat?"

"Sure, what else?"

He saw his hands tearing a fiber optic cable out of ... flesh or hardware. Something.

Vengeance. Yes. To see Saturn die before darkness claimed him, as well. That would make it all fit together, would lighten the burden of inevitable death.

The breeze from the ocean blew against his cheek. "Do you smell anything?"

She sniffed. "No. What?"

Although the sun was still far overhead, the day was cool, and clouds promised rain. Something in the breeze was wrong. It smelled like oily smoke.

Or burning blood.

# 47

The fishing trawler arrived on the western island in the middle of the night. Its captain was paid lavishly, and advised to keep his bargain if he wished his children to remain well. Three men disembarked. One was Hiroshi Osato, whose grandfather's grandfather had served the Emperor of Japan.

They traveled inland, silent as the shadows of birds in flight, and came to the village of the Blue Bdui. There, safe in a shadowed hillside, they watched through digital spy-glasses of a power and compactness that would have aston-ished and delighted Osato's illustrious ancestors. One of his companions suggested that they use their stealth, their craft to enter unseen. Osato entertained the notion but spent an-other hour watching the little brown people, and some deeper instinct warned him against it.

Osato and his men built a hunting blind in the hills. From its shelter they watched the village carefully. For two days and nights without ceasing they examined the comings and goings of every human being, and a few minutes before midnight on that second day they identified one man as a Xanadu fugitive. Within minutes that information had been uplinked to the satellite: Chadwick Kato had been found. Arvad Minsky was nowhere to be seen.

Kato sat still in the sun while Osato studied him, the binoculars at high power. The man was a mummy. Xanadu wizardry had animated a corpse. If Osato had first seen him in such detail, he would not have identified him at all.

Minsky, he concluded, must be dying in some hut.

A beacon was set in place. Their work was done, Osato thought. Ninja hands could be hired by the highest bidder. They had served Yamato with love. Since Yamato's death, they had no goal save profit, and Osato felt the loss. Some-thing precious was gone from his life.

It would be prudent to leave, now that their contract had been fulfilled. But first he sprayed a camera. Later he and his father could watch what happened next.

## 48

Chaz was working in the northern garden. He bent to prune a series of small, delicate vines with flowers much like the orchids he so dearly loved . . . and in the next moment the ground beneath him slapped him into the air like someone shaking flapjacks in a pan.

He fell hard, the breath chuffing from his lungs. It was an old man's fall, painful to joints, jarring to spine and brain. At the southern sanitation trenches, dust and dirt and muck still mushroomed into the air. Only then did he manage to make sense of the sound first heard an instant before: a whistling sound that began at the highest end of the audible range and plummeted down until his bones rattled, ending in a roar perceived more in his bones than his ears.

For a bare, insane moment, he thought that the volcano had erupted, that vents beneath the valley had been building pressure for months while the children of Xanadu went native, while his body lost its slow battle with biological entropy. But the valley shook again, and yet again. There was no sound save that thunder: no screams, no cries, only the sudden blossom of death from afar.

Bombs.

On the ground next to him was Crystal, her little green eyes squeezed tight shut. Jaffie and several of the other Bdui children were scattered around them, eyes so wide that they might have been witnessing the arrival of the Almighty. They whimpered and tried to burrow into the earth.

Another blow came, and another, and again, smashing the earth every three or four seconds, rock and dirt and smoke and an incredible cacophony churning the air until he was certain he would go mad.

When it stopped, he felt as if the bombardment had been going on for hours, even if his heart knew that it couldn't have been more than a minute or two.

He couldn't hear anything.

He stood heavily, sobbing for breath, every day of his eighty-three years weighing on him like a stone. Knees and shoulders and ankles seemed clotted with rust and sand. He hurt *everywhere*.

All across the valley, he saw people he had grown to love sprawled on their faces . . . but they were moving. Confused and fearful, but not dead.

The bombardment had been laser-precise, intended to induce fear and confusion but not slaughter. It had been directed at the dead rock flats at the western end, not at the village, not at the gardens. That meant satellite surveillance. Was it Saturn seeking survivors from Xanadu? But using military hardware so compassionately?

But Chaz *knew* this pattern—

"Look!" Crystal stood shakily on dusty legs. She shaded her eyes and looked up toward the sun. A tiny black speck crawled across the clouds, seeding the sky with white blossoms.

"Paratroopers!" Chaz screamed. "We're being invaded!"

The Bdui were already fleeing toward the western edge of the valley, toward the jungle, herded by bombs at the southern end. Enemy troops would be waiting there. They'd have parachuted in last night, or come in overland. Next would come landing craft under cover of the fire, from ships hugging the horizon. In another few minutes they could count on a second burst of shells, clearing the way for the next stage of the invasion.

Air, sea, and land, a coordinated strike with pencil-point accuracy and timing, coordinated to take a minimum of life.

Chaz recognized these tactics. He had written them! He had developed war-games metaphors for India's naval forces. He had approved of their commitment to surgical precision: to no innocents harmed, ever. He had helped train them, and now they would be the death of him.

But he'd saved some lives!

Clarise emerged from the hut where she was resting, confused, fog-headed, swollen with child. He ran to her, arthritis temporarily forgotten. She shouted at him, but he couldn't hear.

To see her so disoriented frightened him. In many ways she was the most competent of them all, the only one who understood both worlds. Pregnancy put her out of the game . . . but the Indian invaders were forcing her to play.

More thunder from the skies.

Jaffie and one of the older villagers walked cautiously toward the southern end to inspect the smoking holes. Chaz screamed at them but couldn't hear his own voice. He bent to pick up some pebbles—

Both Bdui disappeared in a monstrous eruption of rock and smoke, instantly transformed from living, breathing human beings into ragged bits of meat.

So much for compassion. "It's the Indian Army," he bellowed in Clarise's ear.

"Saturn?"

"Indirectly. They want us alive. . . ."

The white blossoms over their heads were dropping fast. In a few more seconds they'd be on the ground.

"We'll take the Scouts to the mother cave," he said. His hearing was returning.

Lenore and Teil had joined him by this time, grayed with dust, faces strained with anxiety. Pak Jute squatted by him, the dark little man somehow calm in the midst of it all. He asked, "What can we do?"

Chaz said, "You said that the government leaves you alone."

"Yes. This is not the Java government. I do not believe they know of this."

"I agree," Chaz said. "This is some kind of very quick

in-and-out. Come like bandits, snatch us, run like bandits, deal with diplomatic consequences later. If we can hide for a few hours, a day at most, we'll get through this."

Pak Jute looked doubtful. "I think you are only partly right. They do not kill us now because they want you alive. You! After they have you, they will not want living eyes. They will hunt us down, if they can. Some of my people can disappear into the jungles. Perhaps the young ones. But the elders and your own children?" He looked very doubtful. "I don't believe you will escape."

Chaz forced himself to think. "Pak Jute, Clarise once explained to me why the Bdui were left alone. That your warriors would kill the enemy chieftain at any cost."

Old Pak Jute nodded.

"I can help you save your people. I think. There's one possibility," Chaz said. Here he looked directly at Clarise. "But you have to trust me."

The thunder of falling shells had ceased, and the first of the paratroops had hit the ground. The elder Bdui gathered up the children and headed toward the fissure in the valley's east end.

Once hidden in its folds, Jute looked out at the shattered village, his face savage. "Never in my life has anyone dared to invade one of our *kampong*."

"What is important?" Chaz asked. "The village, or the children?"

Jute's whole body trembled with rage. "Do not speak like a fool."

"I would rather sound like a fool than lose what is most valuable. That is the children, yes? Will you do as you promised?"

Pak Jute nodded. "I will do it." His eyes gleamed. "You will make them pay?"

Chaz watched as the paratroopers cut several of the women and children off from the jungle and guided them over to the side. They were not harmed. His sigh of relief caught in his throat as one of the men broke and ran. The soldiers shot him in the back.

He took Clarise in his arms and kissed her soundly. "Darling, get them out of here." He turned to Anson and Lenore. "You help her, and she'll help you. Keep those children safe. Keep Clarise safe."

Fully half the village was gathered in the fissure, the rows of brown faces looking to the elders as if hoping for a miracle.

He would give them that, even if he died delivering it.


The Indian incursion force commanded land, sea, air, and space.

A guerrilla army had been airlifted into the jungle the previous night, told to avoid all contact with the locals but to surround the valley. The air troops were hand-picked, two dozen of the Indian Navy's toughest special operations men, men who had, in better days, trained with the U.S. Navy SEALS and Russian *Spetznaz* forces. They were "Steriles," scrubbed of any marks that might identify them as Indian troops. All gear had been purchased on the international market. No man had an accessible military record. Any captured man, or recovered corpse, could and would be denied by the government.

The Steriles landed soft and hit hard, firing their weapons for maximum intimidation and minimum fatality.

The officers came in by sea, in inflatable rafts with silent, battery-powered engines, skimming through the surf from a battleship kilometers out to sea.

Lieutenant Chut was a tall, hard man whose own niece had been made infertile by a cause unknown. He was an educated man. In his life he had heard so many rumors and conspiracy theories that he was reluctant to believe what his government said of the Council.

But he had also seen enough to convince him that it was

possible. Whether he believed or not, it was Chut's task to investigate. His assignment was to find and capture any refugees from the artificial island, Xanadu, two such persons having been identified by reliable intelligence.

Through his command helmet, he accessed a virtual overlay of the entire operation. So far he was more than content. His flawless pincer tactics were more than the primitive local forces could resist. He assumed a three-hour window before the corrupt and troubled Indonesian government responded to the incursion. By then it would be over, his men extracted, captives firmly in hand.

Chut existed in two worlds: the world of choppy surf and approaching sandy beach, of grim-faced, well-armed men who would march into death and oblivion on his command; and a second world remarkably similar to an early video game. In that cartoon world tiny man-shapes marched along lines of a three-dimensional net, inexorably enveloping their target.

They hit the beach at 1100 hours precisely. Little three-wheeler bikes roared out of the rafts, tracking up the sand toward the valley, Lieutenant Chut bouncing along just behind the lead man. The bikes enabled them to cross the kilometer from the surf to the valley ridge in just under two minutes, and the climb to the top took only another hundred and twenty seconds. Then he was looking down into the declination, satisfied by what he saw.

The village was in rout. Most of the men and women were heading north to the cave mouth, as expected. The last of them disappeared inside as he watched.

A short, solid round man, a good man, Sergeant Tapas, joined Chut and saluted smartly.

"Any resistance?"

"None, sir, a rabble. They're abandoning their old and weak, and surrendering."

Chut snorted. These were the feared Bdui? Only savages feared savages. He would have this wrapped up in an hour.

The first captives had been herded to the midst of the

blasted area, its dirt still hot and smoking beneath his boots. Thermal rounds, smoke rounds, to induce terror and herd these primitives like the animals they were. If he chose Chut could have targeted, with pinpoint precision, a round for each hut in the valley. And used Xanadu's own technology to do it! At this he had to laugh.

The old Bdui were on their knees, hands behind their heads, moaning and bobbing in obeisance. Chut was disgusted.

Fleetingly he considered that these women might have been attractive in youth, but he found their sagging, ancient flesh oddly distasteful. Most of them wore heavy jewelry, knobby necklaces laced with bright stones. Nomads, they probably carried their entire family wealth around their necks. Gold perhaps? It might be worth a look, after all of this was over.

Several of his men approached, pushing a man in front of them. Chut was taken aback at first, momentarily uncertain of his perceptions. The man was Japanese, ashen and drawn, but not wrinkled. Simultaneously young and old. He was dressed in western-style clothes that might well have been clean before the bombardment began, but were now torn and covered with dust.

"You are Chadwick Kato, sir?"

The Japanese nodded, regarding Chut with eyes that were still very much alive. "Your command helmet is a Mark Seven, isn't it?"

Chut smiled. "You should be more careful where you sell your technology," he said.

Chaz folded his arms. One finger pointed at Sergeant Tapas.

When he did, a strange thing happened.

The Bdui women moved like a chorus line. They slipped off their necklaces and spun them once, making violent contact with the temples of nearby soldiers. It caught the Indians off balance for only a moment. Two soldiers fired shots.

One round struck an old woman squarely in the chest. She died without a sound.

Before Chut could bark an order, the old men attacked as well. They struck his Steriles with disorienting speed, changing from a cringing, worthless rabble into a churning storm of kicking feet and striking hands. After perhaps ten heartbeats of sudden, shocking violence, they broke and ran.

Because none of the old Bdui had previously offered the slightest resistance, Chut's Steriles had allowed themselves to slip into a sense of celebration, of mission accomplished. Now his soldiers were faced with the unnerving spectacle of old men and women fighting like demons, then scampering away with simian agility.

And two of the old men dragged a soldier toward the beach. Sergeant Tapas was trailing and bouncing like a dead thing. No more than fifteen seconds had passed. Chut's men brought their weapons up—

Into a rain of arrows. Pak Jute's men had crept around the valley's eastern edge. Light armor stopped most of the projectiles, but more than one Sterile caught an arrow in the calf or shoulder, and one through the back of the neck.

They returned fire. Another Bdui went down, mortally wounded. And another.

Sergeant Tapas was gone.

Chut cursed vilely. The Bdui had lost seven to this suicidal surprise attack and spirited one of his men over the southern edge of the valley.

He was about to order his men after Tapas when another barrage rained down on the soldiers. These arrows were tipped with fire and poison. His men retained their composure and returned fire, killing three more Bdui archers in a few seconds. The rest scampered away.

It all happened in about a minute, a complete reversal from sheep to warriors, from cowering old men and women to kamikazes using every tool and resource as weapons. Ten dead among the Bdui, and several disabled Indian soldiers: fractured arms, crushed ribs, concussions, a broken neck.

He would make them pay for that. His jungle troops would find them. What they wanted seemed clear. This desperate ploy was intended to split his forces and distract them from the caves. It wouldn't happen, now that he knew the enemy was capable of quick and vicious action. The Bdui must see that their desperate tactic had failed to distract him. They would break now. If they didn't they would all be killed.

But he would meet Chadwick Kato again. Now, for the first time, he began to believe that the man might just be the monster he was accused of being.

Chaz ran gasping, with black spots coming and going before his eyes. Sergeant Tapas was no longer with them. His throat had been slashed, his body left at the trail side. Chaz had been momentarily appalled at the casual murder, but these people were fighting for their lives, their homes. One invader was dead, and at least a dozen Bdui.

*Please, Clarise, stick to the plan.*

The Bdui children didn't whimper or complain as Anson Teil led them upward. Nor did their parents complain. It was as if they had prepared for these moments their entire lives. Fully half of the White Bdui clambered up the black floor of the lava tube toward the caves.

The crack in the tube wall opened up into the larger cave, illuminated by flickering torchlight. For a moment Lenore stopped to gape, as she always did, at countless thousands of painted images. Then she shook herself out of it and did what she could to help Clarise along.

Despite her pregnancy Clarise insisted on ensuring that every child and oldster went ahead of her. Her breath came harshly, and her complexion was unhealthily pale, but still she stopped to pick up fallen toddlers, to help oldsters deeper into the cave.

"Clarise," Lenore said. "Come on!"

Clarise looked at her with savage, desperate eyes. "I brought death to my people," she said. "I have to see them through."

Machine-gun fire echoed in the tube behind them.

At the far end of the cave the walls split again, opening to another lava tube. Kilometers above them were vents in the wall of the extinct volcano. The Bdui claimed they could find their way out again. Lenore prayed they were right. She had little taste for dying in the musty dark.

If Chaz could deliver what he promised. . . .

Clarise stiffened behind her, gasping, and Lenore stopped to check. The Bdui's Walking Daughter stared at Lenore, gritting her teeth. For a moment Lenore had allowed herself to forget that this was a pregnant woman climbing through volcanic glass and fleeing from armed men. They needed to stop, to rest.

Clarise would have none of it. "Go," she said, gripping Lenore's hand. "Go. Chaz is counting on us."

*Dear God*, Lenore thought. *How much more?*


Lieutenant Chut's troops fanned out warily, sweeping the caves with flashlights and sensors. All they had to do to close the trap was to move through the caves one chamber at a time, corner their quarry, and then go home. This time he would make no mistake.


The Bdui warriors virtually carried Chaz the last kilometer. Twice they hunched in the brush while soldiers passed within a few meters of them.

They reached a tiny cave in the outer valley wall. It was just a pocket, an overgrown and carefully camouflaged hunting blind. And there the men pulled branches over the entrance and huddled around Chaz expectantly.

He had promised them magic.

He pulled a plug of hair out of the back of his head. The men flinched a little: *Wizard!* He grinned at them and settled Sergeant Tapas's Mark Seven helmet on his head. He panicked for a moment when nothing happened, and then coughed at himself with disgust and flicked two switches at the back, thumb and forefinger, to turn the damned thing on. They'd added all these safeties because soldiers make mistakes.

The air before his eyes shimmered. His view bifurcated. It was not unlike looking through a mirrored window, seeing the world of the reflection and the world beyond. Here were the Bdui and the surrounding jungle; here was a world of lights and strange shapes, lines and curves. All thought ceased to wander, lost in a swirl of overlapping geometric patterns.

Finding a virtual keyboard was a simple thing in a domain he'd written himself. A few moments of searching, and he strolled through a three-dimensional cartoon of an office. He moved a cursor to change Bengali script to English.

Options flowed past. He was suddenly aboard a battleship, the HMS *Hyderabad*. Encryption was fairly primitive— mere recognition signals between Sergeant Tapas and the ship computer, defeated in seconds. The ship's walls became transparent, a momentarily disorienting effect. He found the main battery's ballistics computer. Nobody had bothered to reset the default codes installed by Chaz two years before. He laughed darkly, and in the other world his Bdui companions edged away.

He conjured up the targeting grid.

*Hurry, hurry.*

He had a satellite's view zooming down on Java, targeting a location, sending messages in, waiting for acknowledgment from the crew, and giving the authorizations. He signaled a minor change in targeting. Not much. Not enough to trigger alarms.

\* \* \*

Lieutenant Chut was content. The sweep of the outer cave was going very well, and they were prepared to enter the inner, larger cave.

He heard his men gasp.

The breath caught in his throat as he stepped across the threshold and swept his light around in a circle.

Floor to ceiling, on every side, the rocks and walls were covered with images of men and women, of animals, of plants. Images sufficient to fill a dozen museums. For a brief, shame-filled moment he felt he was trespassing in a shrine.

Then professionalism took over.

Where were his targets? Later there would be time to appreciate the artistry of savages—

Time ran out.


Lenore was scrabbling up a gravely rock fall, flickering torchlight the only illumination, when the first hammer-blows struck the mountainside.

No! Too soon! she thought, near to weeping. Chaz had done what he said, when he said, but estimates on how long it would take to get the children through the maze of tunnels had been off by minutes. Still, most of them were—

Ahead of her, Clarise lost her footing and slid, twisting and scrabbling for a handhold. Fingers found an edge of rock, she almost managed to right herself when another thunderous explosion tore it from her hand. She plowed into Lenore. Together the two women tumbled screaming down the floor of the tube. The slivered volcanic rock abraded her, jagged shards and outcroppings tested her bones and skin in the darkness. Her torch spun out of her hand, extinguished.

Lenore heard another harsh thump, like the bottom of the world stove out, and then nothing.

She was alive, and a sudden, raw outpouring of joy at that simple fact flooded through her even as the aches and pains of her slide began to burrow their way into her conscious awareness. She felt like a skinned snake. Dull pain in her armpit: Her fingertips found a sliver of rock embedded in the flesh.

Her subconscious cataloging of injuries stopped as she finally heard the labored breathing of another human being there in the darkness.

*Oh, God, Clarise!*

On hands and knees, Lenore crawled through the darkness toward the sobbing inhalations, her own fears forgotten for the moment. She skidded, tumbled again, caught herself, crawled until she felt a hand curl around her wrist.

"Clarise?" she whispered.

"Help me?" The voice was so small, so weak, after all of the strength she had witnessed Clarise exhibit, that she was suddenly and completely ashamed for all of the things she had thought, only now in this instant realizing that she had placed the Indonesian woman on some kind of a pedestal.

Wonder woman. Superwoman. Straddling cultures, conquering all, striding from the Stone Age to the Space Age in a single bound.

No, this was a frightened, pregnant woman, wounded in the dark, a million tons of rock above her, a homicidal army behind her. Those two syllables, *help me*, held all of the fear and lost hope that a human being could ever know.

"Clarise?"

"I'm here," Clarise said. "Help me."

"I'm here for you." She couldn't see. All light was gone now. "Where does it hurt?"

"Something inside me . . ." A sharp intake of breath, the sound of movement, and a yelp of stifled pain. Panting.

"I'm hurt. And . . . the baby."

Panic, barely controlled, seethed within Lenore. "Wait here," she said. "I'll get help."

"No!" The single syllable cut like a blade. All of the energy Clarise still had in her was in that single word. "Don't leave me here. Alone."

Lenore nodded, realized dumbly that Clarise couldn't see it, and said: "All right. I'll stay with you."

"No," Clarise said fiercely. "*You* have to help me get out of here. I don't want to die down here, in the dark." She paused. "I don't want my baby to be born in the dark. Please. Help me to the sky."

Lenore brushed one shaking hand across her forehead and swallowed, hard. She said: "We're a long way down, Clarise."

"I'll make it," she said, and once again there was steel, however slender and worn, in her voice.

Then it was gone.


The next half hour was the most horrible of Lenore's life. In the dark, she gripped an arm around the wounded Clarise, fought for purchase, struggled to brace her feet and her free hand where she could. Clarise's left arm was useless. Something warm and sticky leaked on her hands.

The darkness formed an intimacy that took Lenore by surprise.

They climbed for a hundred gasping paces and then rested. Then climbed for eighty paces and then rested again. Then fifty. Then forty. Sweat and rock dust drooled into her eyes, but she was ashamed to complain. On their sixth rest, Clarise finally more than merely answered her question: "Are you all right?"

She said: "Lenore?" And her voice was frighteningly weak.

"Yes?"

A beat. "When I first saw you, I thought you were a terrible woman. That Chaz had opened his heart to a terrible woman. And I hated you."

"I know," Lenore said.

"I just wanted to say that . . . I know why Chaz loved you. Loves you." Clarise sucked wind, every breath a torment. "And if things do not work with you and Anson, I would be honored to know that Chaz was with a woman like you."

Lenore didn't know what to say. *He's a walking corpse. How could I love him after seeing him like that? And there's Anson—*

She found her voice. "I don't want that kind of talk," she said. "We're getting out of here."

It was far too dark to tell, but she would have sworn that Clarise smiled at that. Then there was a rustle, and they were climbing again. Oddly, Clarise felt lighter, as if something had gone out of her.

"Yes," Clarise said, and her voice, weaker than Lenore had ever heard it, seemed almost transcendent. "Not far now. I want to see the sky."


The first explosion took Chut completely by surprise. The cave floor thundered as shells struck, *whump whump whump*. The walls of the mother cave, formed thousands of centuries earlier by molten rock and water erosion, began to collapse. The next sound was a grinding roar of shattering rock. A primal, awful fear of entombment overrode his training, and he screamed the retreat command into his throat mike. The tons of rock above his head blocked the signals.

The firing had stopped, but the walls and ceiling were splitting now and thundering to earth in a rain of dust and rock. He could hardly hear the men screaming around him. Discipline and order were forgotten in a mad dash for survival. The distant fire had triggered a collapse, and he wasn't going to die in it.

Screaming, pulling each other along, they scrambled down three hundred meters of lava tube with tons of rock raining down behind them, on them. Rock dust and the stench of ordnance filled their lungs as they tumbled out into the open.

One of his sergeants had a broken arm. An enlisted man had a shattered leg. A dozen men were still in there. Chut cursed and sputtered into his headset. "What happened?"

He listened to two minutes of confused, frightened explanations and then gave up in disgust. He had lost at least twenty men in the cave. Tons of rock stood between him and any who might remain alive. The operation was a disaster.

He had only the satisfaction of knowing that the bombardment had killed the rest of the Bdui. More would die in the jungle. As for Chadwick Kato . . . the whole world was hunting him. Today the hare had evaded the hounds.

Tomorrow would bring new fangs, new claws to the chase.

## 49

It was almost nightfall before the first Bdui returned to the ruins of their village. The invaders were long gone.

Chaz searched among them and could not find the Xanadu refugees. He was told that they were still on the side of the volcano. Pak Jute volunteered to take him to the exit vent, and together they began the slow, grueling trek around the sloping side of the great, extinct volcano. He had to stop every hundred feet or so, catch his breath, then steady himself to continue onward.

It was almost morning before he came to the first of the caves, and there, three miles from the opening, he found a clutch of Bdui huddled and afraid. Somehow, Clarise and Lenore, Teil, the twins, Mohammed, Jeffty, Crystal, and Nadine had seen each other through.

Lenore took his hand and pulled him along. The fear etched in her face banished his fatigue. "Come quickly, Chaz," she said. "It's Clarise."

\* \* \*

Her face was streaked with tears and powdered stone. Her ribs were fractured, and every contraction had to be torture. Clarise gripped Chaz's hand like a drowning woman clawing at a buoy. For almost five minutes she hadn't opened her eyes. When she did, there was nothing in them that recognized him.

Chaz's mind spun. Had everything he had done, everything he had fought for been a mistake?

Clarise gripped his hand, her dusty fingernails drawing blood. But she did not cry. As the contractions grew stronger, she grew weaker, but after every scream she mustered her energy and pushed, every time. It seemed that with the completion of every effort, she was a little farther away from him.

For minutes he watched her magnificent effort silently, completely lost for words. When guilt and grief and shame finally overwhelmed him, he opened his lips to say something, to apologize, to beg her forgiveness. But before he could say a word she somehow pulled herself out of whatever realm of pain and intensity she inhabited and focused on his face.

"Shhh," she said. "Love is never a mistake, Chaz." Then her eyes fluttered closed, and she began the next effort.

Chaz stayed with her until the old women bade him leave. He stepped out through the rocky vent into the open air. The sun was drowning slowly in the ocean, and he felt sadness beyond naming. He hardly knew it when a small, warm, lithe form fastened herself to his leg. He looked down and found one of the twins. Barbie? She was crying for him, for them, her hair plastered all over her forehead.

Together they watched the sun extinguish itself in a slow blaze of orange.

Pak Jute emerged from the tube an hour later, holding Chaz's son. Tears streaked his cheeks. "One life ends," he said. "Another begins. One age ends, another begins."

Chaz held his child in the moonlight and kissed the baby's brow for the first time.

*Boy.* He hadn't let himself remember. It would have been a betrayal. But Clarise had had the shot, and her girl-child would have been born sterile. *A boy can have children.*

After a time he gave the boy over to the women who had brought him into the world and went back into the slit in the rock.

Clarise seemed quite small now. She was bundled in a blanket, her face turned to the side as if she was sleeping.

Chaz sat in the darkness with his wife's corpse. Outside the cave, the Bdui sang their death songs.

"What do I do?" he said to her, although she could no longer answer. "If I stay more of your people will die. If I go they'll hunt me down. Tell me what to do."

Of course, there was no answer. She was dead now, with no fears, nothing to run from. She had shaped her life as she shaped her art. It was a thing to emulate.

So he had decided.

He kissed his wife's cool lips and promised her that he would join her soon. Then he went out to hold his son and tell the others their fate.

It took a week to dig corpses out of the mother cave. There were enough pieces of radios and other gear for them to spend another week cobbling together equipment for Lenore.

In a sergeant's smashed helmet Lenore found the man's personal tracking device. She showed it to Chaz with some pride. "This is how they'll find you."

Chaz chortled. "Smuggle that past Indian security? And Saturn?" He tapped the back of his head. "No need. Remember this?"

She watched him pull a plug of black hair from the black-and-gray around it. "Like Arvad?" Then she clapped her hands. "C-cyborg! Tooley called you a cyborg! It's a computer interface?"

"More than that."

# 50

They used the Blue chief's short wave to reach the Council and negotiate terms of surrender.

Chaz talked with his friends Manny and Trish. He told them what he planned and they tried to talk him out of it. As little as they understood human ways of thinking, how could they reason with him? Finally they agreed to do their part.

Chaz and Lenore used the jury-rigged military equipment to reach Lenore's friend Tooley. "You got a message to Lenore's ex," he told a recorded male voice. "To Levar. I know you can talk to his people. . . ."

Chaz sat with his son on Minsky's Rock, looking out at the ocean. The boy was quiet now, although he had cried as Chaz carried him down from the valley to the water.

"You'll never know your mother," he said quietly. "And I won't be back. But there are people here who love you and will care for you. After all this is over, they'll make their way back to the world and take you with them. Or maybe you'll stay here with the Bdui. You decide." He studied the boy, seeking to find, in miniature, the face of the woman he loved. There: perhaps in the curve of the mouth.

Certainly not in the tiny, pudgy hands or the wispy hair. Clarise was gone.

"I'm not going to give you a name," he said. "I don't think I have that right. But I will tell you that your father loves you. I hope that whoever raises you will never let you forget that."

Then he bent, touching his lips to the warm, soft skin of his son's forehead. His steps more uncertain than ever, every breath a laboring old man's, he carried the boy back to the Bdui village.


Her arms around Anson Teil's waist, Lenore watched Chaz climb slowly and painfully into a little fishing boat owned by the Blue Bdui and waved as it drifted out to sea. It would travel west and then north until they reached a larger village, from whence he would gain passage to Jakarta.

Her heart died for him. His sparse hair was still black at the tips, but it looked like a wig. His skin had an ashen, dry look to it, his posture was awful, and he could barely walk without wheezing. "I'll never see him again," she whispered.

Teil kissed the side of her neck. "We don't know that," he said. "We have to hope. Sometimes, hope is all we have."


Two days later she asked and received permission from the chief of the Blue Bdui to listen to his shortwave radio. Anson couldn't travel outside; she would have liked his company, but he was just too white. Skin could be darkened, hair combed with mud, but freckles and an aquiline nose still showed.

News broadcasts repeated sensational rumors of Chadwick Kato's surrender in Jakarta. Supposedly he would be turned over to United Nations authorities within a week. Lenore was about to switch it off when another broadcast broke in.

Someone was offering an audiotape purporting to be Chaz Kato's confession. *What?*

A rich and juicy voice boasted, rambled, laughed where nothing was funny, spoke hatred through clenched teeth; and when Lenore was about to switch it off, he broadcast the recording. She listened to the pirate broadcast and found it amazing.

She heard Chaz Kato bragging, not confessing. Chaz described how his circle had conspired to thin the human herd. He spoke of the One Race War. The voice was Chaz at his best, before he turned feeble. It was claimed to be the audiotrack of a holodisk retrieved from the wreckage of his apartment on Xanadu. This was his legacy to the future, made before the attack.

The speaker knew more than Chaz ever had about the conspiracy. He also knew Chaz Kato far too well, Lenore judged.

Afterward, commentators in Jakarta yammered complaints and threats . . . and Lenore turned the radio off, darkly depressed. The world would believe it. But no matter how many experts testified to its authenticity, Lenore never would.

# 51

Chaz was living his life in snatches of perception.

The Bdui had given him plant extracts and instructions. Take this before dawn, this yellowish powder after eating, mix this gray stuff with his food . . . but while he sailed toward Jakarta, he'd spilled the yellow stuff, a ground-up root. He'd kept to the rest of the routine for two days and then forgotten. It wasn't helping much anyway.

An Indonesian naval patrol picked him up dehydrated and hallucinating. It wasn't a rescue. He was battered, yelled at, mocked. The officers demanded details from a speech, a confession. They played it for him. It didn't sound like him, only nobody ever sounds like himself to himself, so maybe. But what was that about myelin sheaths and cytoplasm genetics? He laughed in the wrong spots and a junior officer hit him very hard, just above the right eye.

Then someone was pounding on his chest, and someone stabbed him in the elbow . . . tried to smother him with a rubber thing . . .

He shied away from that memory. He feared that he had died.

How many days?

The soft roar of motors, a whiff of fuel, vibration and varying gravity woke him softly. He must have boarded a helicopter. He'd slept through that, in a massive travel chair that was feeding him a broth of chemicals through four tubes.

He wriggled against straps. They had him anchored— even his head was immobilized in a rigid ring—but he rolled a bit within the restraint to look through the plastic.

He saw a tiny ocean liner trapped in a vast skeletal lily pad a thousand feet below.


They'd started Island Six, Huy Brasil, nearly two years ago.

*Princessa* was 700 feet long, 690 feet at the water line, with a 90-foot beam and 35-foot draft. She made a top speed of thirty knots and carried a 200,000 horsepower engine. Built in 1950, at its peak the enormous vessel was registered in Liberia and owned by a Dutch excursion line. She served up to 1,800 passengers and burned an average of eight hundred tons of fuel a day.

She plied the waters of the African continent, crossed to the Americas to run excursions from Mexico to Alaska, and made the crossing to Europe more than nine hundred times.

But in the last years of the twentieth century, *Princessa* was an albatross, not commercially viable. For ten years her twin funnels had been cold, her four 40,000 horsepower boilers gone dry. *Princessa*'s twin galleys, each capable of feeding two thousand people at a time, were empty. Her generators, each producing enough power for a town of eight thousand, were dark. Her propellers did not turn.

In 2017 she had been brought out of mothballs, extensively refitted, and returned to special service. Hauled to the middle of the South Pacific, she had been anchored, and there began the laborious task of growing an island.

The task was, by now, quite well understood. The *Princessa* carried a 100 megawatt Oceanic Thermal Energy Converter. After anchoring in the South China Sea, her crew lowered cold water pipes into the depths. *Princessa*'s engines began to pump up cold water, jump-starting the OTEC plant. The OTEC began to deliver its megawatts of power. The rest was accretion: the electrolysis grids, the precipitation of seacrete from the water, the slow and steady growth of an island already dubbed Huy Brasil.

Though the riots continued worldwide, according to what news reached Chaz, Huy Brasil had not yet been molested. For these two years *Princessa* had carried only blue-collar workers and technicians. None of the Council had been aboard. The government of Malaysia offered protection with that understanding. So long as money continued to flow, friendly docks and a landing pad were provided and no hostile staging areas or fly-bys tolerated.

Minor maintenance buildings had already gone in, and considerable underwater structure could be seen from this high. Two of the fish ponds were active; the water showed tints of green and bronze.

The liner grew tremendous. Chaz saw diminutive human shapes looking up from a lower deck.

He wondered who would own Huy Brasil when the dust settled. Some of the Council certainly survived. If Saturn was *not* a Council member, then he would not even be a suspect. Survivors could hide under new identities with Saturn to front for them.

But NERO had suggested another answer, hadn't he? And Chaz hadn't been able to follow up. Until now. . . .

It came to Chaz that he was growing lucid again. They had him hooked up and monitored. Was he getting tranquilizers too? He found he didn't care in the least.


The helicopter descended onto a tennis court on the *Princessa*'s main deck. Chaz imagined tennis players perfecting their serves on its surging surface while sea, air, and rolling waves complicated their game beyond anything ever experienced on land. Just one more thing he'd never live to try.

Three brawny men moved a ramp into place. Two wheeled Chaz out, having trouble with the chair's weight. The chair had a motor, but Chaz's controls didn't work. They'd left him a button to inject pain medication, though.

The tennis court was in the shadow of one of the gigantic funnels.

His attendants pushed him to the starboard side. Chaz had a moment's view of the ocean and the proto-island growing there, skeletal curves and swirls tinting the water. He wondered if this would be his last sight. A thousand tiny wrenches could have dropped into the machinery of his scheme. But if he'd done everything right . . . he might easily die without knowing it.

One pushed the chair, one paced him. They took a ramp down to the promenade, past a workman who looked at him with dull, incurious gaze, down past lifeboats that looked as if they hadn't been used or inspected in two decades.

Below was something unexpected: a large, English-style smoking room converted for dining. A dozen people waited. Chaz recognized faces: Phillipe Hernandez, Mary Kravitz, Diva. Three Council members. The rest might be Council too. Chaz didn't know them all. NERO had acquired pictures, but Chaz couldn't remember them.

They were all staring at him. They looked shell-shocked. As Kato's chair descended onto the hardwood floor, most of them stood. Were they about to applaud him?

No, their expressions were grim. Chaz wondered how much they knew. Which of them really thought he was guilty? Was it conceivable that the whole Council had been taken in?

But some—these—must stand with Saturn.

The nations wanted blood. All of the megatons of protein powder, the billion who didn't starve, diseases rendered extinct, construction projects in every nation, all of the Floating Islands' wealth and prestige and goodwill had bought the surviving Council only this much. *Give us a little time, we'll deliver the criminal.* He tried to see the guilt in their faces, or the savage relief that someone *else* would be fed to the dogs, and not them.

But Gregory Phillipe Hernandez lay in Mary Kravitz's arms on a roomy deck chair, his head just under her jaw. They hadn't moved. They could have posed for a travel poster, they looked that good, but they weren't smiling. Their faces weren't doing anything.

Out to save the planet from too many babies, these. They were both too bright to be lured or bullied into something so grandiose. They'd shaped the plan. But they hadn't guessed, none here *could* have guessed just *how much* hell they were raising.

Elders like Minsky and Mary Kravitz and even Chaz Kato: Those who reached Xanadu were the ones who could give up friends and family and all that they loved. There had to be a blind spot in their minds. Sajid Tata would have known.

Wayne and Shannon Halifax were dead already; the radio had said so. Chaz looked for them anyway, but they weren't here.

Their power had earned them places on the Council, but Saturn couldn't gamble that they would keep his secret. So they had been thrown to the wolves, and the publicity campaign Wayne Halifax would have controlled had never happened.

As Chaz was wheeled past, Phillipe Hernandez got to his feet. Chaz's attendants moved aside for him.

Hernandez pushed the injector button. "This work?"

The pain receded; things got blurry and sleepy. Chaz said, "Works fine. Might be a little strong."

"Might have a slow poison in it too. I'll replace it." He continued inspecting Chaz's chair, and Chaz. "This hurt?"

"Yes. Not much."

"Lymph nodes. Aspirin will take care of that."

Chaz started to ask . . .

But it might be best not to seem too lucid. After all, he didn't really care who Mary Kravitz had been humping in a corridor a year ago. What he really wanted to know was, why were they all staring?

Phillipe Hernandez finished his inspection and stepped back. "My God," he said softly, and Mary Kravitz shivered. "They did a good job, but . . . Kato, you look *dead*. You can't face the . . . Security Council, I guess . . . can't face them like this. We'll give you back your mind, at least."

"Mind." Chaz grinned, and liked the way Hernandez shied back. "My mind. How thoughtful."

His attendant cleared his throat. "Excuse me. Dr. Kato is required below."

"Of course," Hernandez said. "We'll take him from here."

Diva stood up, beautiful as a goddess, and raised an imperious hand. "Dr. Kato," she asked, "what's it like?"

Suddenly he understood the stares. They were looking at *their* future.

"It's like being drunk and hung over at the same time," he said. "You won't like it."

Diva said, "I won't run away without my medical system."

Chaz said, "Entropy wins. Sooner or later you'll wear out. It looks like this."

"Oh, go ahead." Diva waved him on. Mary Kravitz and

Phillipe Hernandez took the handles of his chair.

The elevator doors opened. Hernandez and Kravitz pushed him in. Despite the guards, despite his obvious infirmity, they were careful not to stand too close to him.

They were afraid of him. How wonderful.

He wanted to ask why. *WHY?* But he could guess how stupid it would sound. For power. For youth. For an arrogance crazy enough to believe that the values of a thousand generations of living, loving human beings could be disposed of in one massive con game, if a sucker could be found to pay the freight.

The elevator doors closed. They dropped through the decks, past the luxury quarters, down past tourist class, past the berths of the third-class passengers. Down farther, into the engine room.

They wheeled him along the tight corridors. He could see where the ship had been massively retrofitted with the technology and storage capacity necessary to fulfill its seed function. He had so many questions but hadn't the stomach to ask them.

So odd, going through the different levels of the ship, through areas meant for officers, crew, steerage class, and luxury class, across boundaries that *they* could never pass. Stranger still to walk between eras. Her designers had wished *Princessa* to hark back to a more genteel time, using relatively modern 1950s building techniques. What an odd, floating museum of social class structures and artistic styles, technological innovations and incongruencies.

Now she had been torn apart and refitted for the twenty-first century, and *that* social stratification was eerily similar.

His eyes took in every detail with an almost abnormal appetite. These might be the last impressions of his life, and he wished to savor every one.

The door slid open, and he allowed himself to sink deeper into his torpor. It wasn't difficult. Breath was labored, and his joints flamed at him, and that extra shot from Hernandez had him floating. He'd been sick and senile and dying. He was still sick, disoriented, and foggy in the head. But it was getting better! A pity there would be no time.

He could not guess when the hammer would fall. Word must leak across barriers of secrecy and paranoia . . .

They wheeled him along the corridor, along the hardwood paneling. Ahead, he smelled salt water. When he smelled that, he knew he had won.

They pushed him through the double doors, into the cabin-class swimming pool deck. A man sat in a chair at poolside. Glassy threads ran from his head down into the pool, where a white bullet of a predator thrashed with excitement.

"Minsky." Chaz gasped, contriving to sound surprised. "Barrister." *The kill*, Chaz thought. *He senses it. Be very very careful.*

"Hello, Chaz," said Saturn.

## 52

On Java, high in the mountains of the western section in another of the Bdui *kampong*, Lenore Myles slept beside the receiving equipment. When the signal came through, rerouted though the co-opted Indian military satellite before Chaz left, she almost screamed in relief. Then she swallowed her joy and went to work.

This was the signal from Chaz Kato's head.

She had seen the plastic socket in the bulge under Chaz's scalp. A medical computer could mate with the interface plug, to keep a patient alive. The tracer would bring help if an ambulatory patient had a relapse. After Chaz Kato healed, he'd asked that the tracer be taken out. The doctors of Xanadu could not be bothered, but they assured him that they had turned it off.

They'd lied, but Chaz had solved that. With NERO's help he had changed the identifying signal. The Council could not find him. Saturn could not. Lenore could.

Chaz was in the middle of the South Pacific—not an unreasonable place to find him—and he wasn't moving. Lenore was not reassured. This was just one more in a series of terrible decisions, as a master gamesman with no more room to negotiate made the only move he could make.

The impossible move, the move that a monstrous survivor would never anticipate or defend against.

No shark could conceive of martyrdom.

No chess player would ever plan a king sacrifice.

Lenore began the process of rerouting the signal in two different directions.

One went to Manny and Trish and the few squarks who still followed and obeyed them. There was far to go, challenges to overcome, and it was impossible to know how this would turn out. But for this to be over it had to end totally, and only Manny could guarantee that.

And the second message, the terrible one, the one that she dreaded, went to the Spinner Network. It would filter back through to the Indian government. She and Chaz were certain now that the Indians and Chinese had always sponsored the Spinners. She was giving them Chaz's finder frequency.

# 53

Mary Kravitz wheeled Chaz to the pool's edge, where he could peer down through the clear ocean water. The pool had been breached to allow Barrister access to the ocean. It wasn't as if *Princessa* still had to float.

Chaz doubted, now, that Barrister truly existed anymore. What had been a shark had been modified too often, had spent too much of its life linked to advanced computers and evolving programs and a disturbed, brilliant human mind. The minds of three previous sharks must live in those programs too. Maybe Barrister the Squark had never been more than an electronic puppet.

And Arvad Minsky might pretend to be a man, but what was *really* there was an aggregate personality, a many-lobed mind that sometimes called itself Saturn.

"Did you ever suspect?" Saturn asked through Minsky's mouth, something lazily predatory in his words.

"How could I?" *How can you really factor in the existence of a new form of intelligence? Even NERO barely glimpsed the possibilities; I couldn't program him for more. By God, we set out to create aliens, and we did it. It swam and hummed and walked among us and we never suspected.*

*Saturn had a shark's personality: the disregard for human life, the frenzy of the Ganesh ceremony, the tendency to circle even a helpless victim before striking. The programs let him think like a chess player, especially one who favors a rook sacrifice.*

*Rook, castle, stronghold. And you certainly sacrificed your castle, didn't you, Minsky? You let Xanadu be blown out of the water.*

*You just missed your timing, didn't you, Arvad? Didn't expect Levar Rusch to be in India. Couldn't expect Clarise to bring him right onto Xanadu! It was all most unlikely, and it screwed your timetable. You would have betrayed us to the mob, but where were you and Barrister planning to be? In Bali, watching from a beach? In a fishing trawler retrofitted for your perverse symbiosis? With a pouch of pearls for trade goods, in case everything went to hell.*

Arvad stared at him without blinking. Chaz realized that, in harness, there was nothing of the man that he had known and befriended. His fleshly eye was pink. He didn't blink because sharks don't know how.

He asked, "What were you hoping for when you turned yourself in?"

"Anything was better than just falling apart. I could feel my mind going, Arvad."

Minsky said, "Our doctors will take over your treatments. In a few days, when you're strong enough, you will be delivered to the United Nations."

"Just like that?"

"Not quite." Minsky stood, strolled over behind the wheelchair. "How is he?"

"He could stand up if he wanted," Mary Kravitz said.

"His *mind*, Mary!"

"I'd say this Indian patch job is putting him back together as fast as we could. Greg, love, would you—" But Hernandez was already replacing the painkiller drip that had come from India with Chaz. "He's lost some flexibility. He'll never run the heptathluge again, Arvad, but he'll be lucid long enough—"

"Phillipe. What is *this?*" Hands touched the back of Chaz's head.

Hernandez said, "I thought it must be a QQ25 or 26, adapted, but it might be older. Did I miss something? Shall we X ray him?"

"Indian doctors might have added a little something, I suppose, a mike or a camera . . . but what I meant was, this has been in Dr. Kato's head for *fifteen years?* Reprogrammed every few, just to keep up—"

Mary said, "I had one just like it until you upgraded me."

Hernandez nodded. "Yes, Mary, *exactly*. I upgraded you and Philippe and the rest so you could use the veeblefetzer array to mebble dup dub—" Chaz's tired mind wasn't picking up information any more, and they were using obscure technical terms and acronyms. He grasped that they were describing techniques used to make and monitor a microscopic life-form. They were all standing behind him now, probing his head, their voices a bit muffled. "—how can he be *me* for the United Nations court if he never had the *hard-ware* to mastermind the Marching Morons bacillus? We've already broadcast his confession, brilliant work, Mary, but it's exceedingly detailed regarding my *technique*—"

In some irritation Chaz said, "I'm still here, you know."

"Yes. Chaz, we're going to have to upgrade this. I've got a Word 555 plug somewhere. We would have had to do some work here anyway." Minsky's face poked around from behind Chaz's head. He smiled like a shark toying with a SCUBA diver.

"Chaz, a year ago you gave me an excellent idea. I am going to erase a few of your memories. That will cripple any defense you might attempt to muster. You won't deteriorate as fast as the Myles girl did, because I've improved the technique. You just won't remember some important things. In time you might come to wonder if the charges are correct, after all. Prep him, Mary."

"Wait!" Chaz barked, to no effect. Mary Kravitz set out a bottle and hypodermic. Filled the hypo. Stuck it into the tube that ran into Chaz Kato's arm.

No battle plan survives contact with the enemy.


At night Lenore listened to the news from India and China. The United Nations had agreed to wait thirty days for the prisoner to arrive. Five days were gone already. Chaz had thought that the governments would wait, and it seemed he was right. He was sure the Spinners would not.

She was coming outside too often. It wasn't safe.


Pain was eating through the torpor of anesthesia. Chaz waited it out, waited for his senses, his memory, his mind. He'd done this dance before, after Xanadu offered him his life again.

The pain was in his neck and the back of his skull. He

was sitting upright. Good God, he was still in the wheel-chair!

"You're awake," Saturn stated.

"People used to be less casual about brain surgery," Chaz said. His tongue felt as big as a Pekingese.

"We got better at it," Mary Kravitz said. "How are you?"

He was under a plastic tent. He couldn't move his head. It was locked in the brace.

He said, "Hasn't started hurting yet. What have I forgotten?"

"Oh, we'll do the editing later. Arvad wants to talk."

Chaz started testing his add-on capabilities. See ultraviolet, take a random tenth root, listen for the most distant voice . . . but his senses were screwy. At least his eyes worked. Saturn was in the pool, swimming a side stroke alongside Barrister. In infrared the pool was black with a hint of motion. Zoom: Barrister had been modified again.

What had they done with what they took out of his head? It wasn't in sight.

He said, "Tell me what you did."

She lifted the oxygen tent and moved it aside. "Say 'Saturn, Tutorial.' "

Chaz did. Instructions appeared before his eyes.

He began to play.

His new software would do most of the work his old programs had. Some of the instructions were different.

He ran the recording of his operation. Quick and simple: Split the scalp, yank the QQ26, plug in a plastic thing that flexed like jelly, three times as big. He felt the back of his head and found the bigger bulge. His capabilities had been vastly upgraded.

He still had infrared vision. He could ignore extraneous sounds, focus his hearing on human voices, emphasis on consonants. Kravitz and Hernandez were whispering, echoes distorting the sounds. He heard:

"Waste of time."

"Never know with Minsky. Think you figured him out, he's gone somewhere else."

"Used up old man—"

"He's my age! All right, Philippe, I see your point, *I* never spent months cut off and living like a savage, but you couldn't *buy* a way to get this kind of practice! What does it take to bring him back up? Phillipe, one day this will be you!"

The computer link was amazingly fast. Mistakes could be fixed, and it learned. He was hearing every word now. If he was wasting the last minutes of his life as a guinea pig for these monsters, what the hell. This was fun.

Chaz found a role-playing game named "Civil Rights" under his own company's brand. He called, "Phillipe! Is there a monitor around here?"

"Sure." Hernandez wheeled his chair around to face a wall. Chaz just glimpsed something fist-sized, a small steel and wire spider sitting in pooled blood in a steel tray. Stiff black hair stuck up from the patch at one end. It was the obsolete interface plug that Saturn had taken out of his head. They hadn't destroyed it!

"We wondered if they might have put a camera in there, in India," Hernandez said, "but there's nothing."

Chaz said, "They X-rayed me, but they didn't change anything. If they hadn't found that . . . QQ25? . . . they'd have been upset." Chaz smiled and brought up "Civil Rights" on the wall.

Cartoons for actors, imitation Disney Cinderella, but the game was very realistic. It was a game of politics. From 1776 in Philadelphia to present time, guard your civil rights, block parasitic growth of the national government. Subverting the Continental Congress . . . didn't work. Just moving Congress out of that patch of swampland near Baltimore was a waste of time . . . allowing Washington's defeat of Vermont's Green Mountain Boys was a major blunder . . . touch of Libertarian philosophy here?

Dinner appeared: tuna and fresh vegetables. "We're

having trouble getting lettuce. We don't want to import anything we eat, Dr. Kato. Dangerous," said Mary Kravitz.

"Mmm." With a thought Chaz saved "Civil Rights" where
Bobby Kennedy was erasing the constitutional protection
against double jeopardy. He couldn't see a way out of that
one. Hey, you didn't win a game on the first pass. Chaz
scanned the limited set of files in memory, pulled up
"Marching Morons" just because he liked the title, and was
being asked for a password.

Chaz looked around. He could turn his head about forty
degrees.

Saturn was ignoring him. Man and shark were writhing
together in an obscenely playful game of tag. Barrister's
right-side arm had been altered. Now it was jointed mechanical tentacles; the left was still flashy flattened fingers.
In the water Minsky wore a wireless plug. It bulged out into
a hemisphere, distorting his head, with no such vanity as
faked hair.

Chaz shouted, "Arvad! 'Marching Morons'! Password?"
The effort hurt his head.

"Recess!" Saturn returned.

"Recess," Chaz printed, the work of an instant, and he
was looking at plans that had become the One Race War.
It was a rainbow maze of planes and angles in four-space.
Paths splayed away, dividing again and again, each line
showing pop-up color-matched labels all along its length.
Take one fork and other options were gone. Sometimes they
rejoined.

*Here* was the choice that allowed Saturn an advertising
blitz. Halifax wasn't to be in charge. The campaign would
have started a year ago, about the time Lenore discovered
what the inoculations were all about. Show the world its
own face: humankind packed shoulder to shoulder, no food
but dole yeast and everyone starving anyway. The population explosion, every baby a grenade. Wars fought for
patches of land that any modern war would destroy. The
stars our destination, but all resources gone, no way to build

so much as a hang-glider. A thousand ways to die in childbirth, in living color on every news channel, nothing edited out. Every public voice shouting the same message for a year: DON'T MAKE BABIES! and then . . . girls aren't getting pregnant.

And the riots begin anyway, but when civilized voices speak, now nobody listens at all.

"How old is this file?" Chaz called.

"Two months. Updated right up to when the shit hit the fan. We'll wipe it, of course. You too. You won't remember anything that happens here. You stayed in Jakarta until you came out of your coma, then went directly to the Security Council."

Chaz didn't expect to live long enough for them to put holes in his mind. Now he was looking at what Chaz Kato had confessed to, in several drafts. Saturn must have written this himself; early phrasing was weird, inhuman.

Philippe Hernandez said, "I thought you'd ask why."

"A billion less humans on Earth. You thought you could handle the payback."

"We are."

"Philippe, you haven't seen it all."

"What should we have done, Dr. Kato?" Hernandez demanded. "Ended the population expansion with persuasion? Free condoms. Free vasectomies. Propaganda. What are you breeding for when you persuade people not to have too many children?"

Chaz wasn't really interested in Philippe's justifications. In the main line of the "Marching Morons" file, Xanadu's destruction was scheduled ten days later than it had happened. Thank you, Levar—

"Unpersuadability!" Philippe Hernandez shouted. "You breed for people who don't read or don't listen or don't understand the arguments. People who can't figure out how to use a condom. People who understand the population problem, but they don't give a shit."

"What if I could persuade you you're wrong?"

"How?" Hernandez asked.

"Who cares? You've already done it. There's nothing left to argue about."

Silence. Angry footsteps stamping across hardwood-on-metal.

Chaz Kato read on. Asimov's *Second Foundation* must have been planned like this. Control freaks . . . but the "Marching Morons" scenario was ingenious and flexible. Its worst problem was that the "acceptable" death rate was insanely high . . . as with the *Foundation* stories.

A voice asked, "Chaz, who am I?"

Chaz looked around. Kravitz and Hernandez were gone. Arvad walked around from behind him, dripping salt water.

"What?"

"I would not ask my associates . . . my *school*. They might get the wrong idea. I do not doubt my abilities, Chaz. I only wonder who I am." Arvad Minsky pulled the plug from the back of his head. The hole it left was pink.

Chaz saw his face change. Minsky wasn't Saturn anymore. He moved with more caution, concentrating on a simple task: set the plug under a UV lamp, then pick up what was sitting there, a smaller plug two inches across, with a spray of little fiber optic cords running into it. It ran to a spool to keep it taut. Barrister was still plugged into the other end.

Arvad inserted it into his head and was Saturn again.

Chaz asked, "Did Barrister get you off the island?"

"Yes. I was afraid I might eat me, but some of Barrister's intelligence is an implant. He figured it out. He towed me to a little village where I stole a boat with a radio. I was able to contact Diva. Anything else, Dr. Kato?" His eye wasn't blinking. Chaz wondered what primitively vicious memories and sensations Barrister's brain might be uploading to Minsky. "I'll answer any question. You won't remember."

"How long has this been going on? How long has there been a Saturn?"

"Since Geryon. Everyone around me was doing their experiments with dolphins, but I . . ." That unblinking stare. "I didn't want to share what was in my mind with a dolphin. Too bright. Geryon and I—"

"The second shark."

"Right. Nothing stopped him, you understand? I was never afraid when we were together." He paused, then added thoughtfully, "Sometimes I think Minsky never existed at all. How long has there been a NERO?"

The question was unexpected. Chaz gaped. Then, "Since you attacked Lenore Myles. I *had* to look. We had your programming style, but we just couldn't find you."

"Hah." Jaws went wide, a shark's smile, but Saturn had forgotten how to lose control of his breathing: how to laugh. "You couldn't describe me, Chaz. You couldn't tell a computer program what to look for. Worse! I've been upgrading as fast as new stuff came on-line. I was never the same! Every time you looked, you and your toy detective, I was further evolved."

"Life-forms seek homeostasis. Whatever state they're in, they try to keep things that way."

"I can upload biology texts too, Chaz, but everyone on Xanadu is an *exception* to that rule. It's human to want upgrades. You did."

"Yes."

"How do you feel now?"

"My head hurts where you did the carving." But all the aches had gone away. His chemistry was back in balance. He flexed his arms, his legs. Would the straps hold him? He said, lying, "I think all my limbs have gone dead."

"And you've been playing with the upgrades. A year ago you were playing with a stud's body. Twelve years ago you spent a month hang-gliding. Change, always change," said Saturn, "but couldn't you see what the end would be?

"Each of us, everyone on this ship, uses his wealth to buy more intelligence, data, sensory versatility, medical treatment. With his intelligence and his data sources he runs the stock market. More wealth buys more brainpower and better senses and better data sources, and better medical techniques to keep him functioning even longer. *One* of us was going to be the brightest mind on Earth. That one would cut off resources for the rest. Would *rule*. Didn't you see that coming? And that one will be me."

"Well," Chaz said, "briefly. You're still changing."

Minsky smiled wide enough to hurt his face. Barrister thrashed in the pool. "But am I human?"

Chaz said, "There are a lot of ways to be human." He did not believe Saturn's was one of them.

"Let's exercise you a little," Minsky said. He pulled the Velcro straps apart and freed Chaz's arms, wrists, torso, legs, ankles. He slid his hands into Chaz's armpits and lifted. Chaz gasped: Minsky was *strong* now. Chaz fumbled for his footing as Saturn turned and walked him toward the pool.

His legs were a bit unsteady. He was nothing like crippled; he'd lied about that. He tried to match Minsky's pace, but that wasn't easy, because Minsky's iron grip was lifting up under Chaz's right shoulder.

Barrister was swimming round and round a few feet from the rim of the too-small pool. He came toward Chaz, and Chaz realized how close he was to the water and the monstrously altered shark. How easy it would be to topple him in.

Saturn enjoyed intimidation.

"Are you human?" he asked suddenly, letting go and turning to face Chaz. Chaz wobbled, then found his stance. "You're constantly changing too. I studied you. Chaz Kato, concentration camp inmate, unwanted child. Workaholic. Husband. Tycoon. Widower ready to die. Then we rebuilt you and you dove into your second life like you'd never wanted anything but to be a Greek slave. I didn't know about NERO; at least you took *some* control of your destiny. Then Clarise Maibang! That startled me, Chaz. I didn't get it."

"Now you do?"

Saturn smiled a Minsky smile, an echo of the past. "Not really. I don't date."

"Yeah."

"When the attack on Xanadu came, you were out of there at a dead run with no medical support. Old and dying again. You must be getting used to that."

"I have to admit it," Chaz said. He was still at the edge of the pool. He refused to step back; he wouldn't give Saturn the satisfaction. But Saturn had detached him from the medical chair, and *that* bothered him.

"I didn't choose very much of that," Chaz admitted. "When I came to Xanadu, that was a damaged brain at work. The rest of it just happened, or other people made it happen. But you, Arvad, you change on whim."

"You've still never hooked your mind into another lifeform. There's other stuff, now that you've got Word 555. Chaz, everybody's changing. When was the last time you saw anyone wearing glasses? I mean with just lenses, and even those were a prosthetic, like crutches, or a torch in the dark. The human race changes because it wants to. Shall I download your mind before we send you to the Security Council?"

"Good God." Looking into Minsky's unblinking eyes, Chaz simply could not decide if he was serious. "And where would you run the download?"

"Maybe a dolphin. Maybe a sperm whale? Have you ever wanted to be Moby Dick? Then later we'll find a marine biologist who wants to link with you. Best of both worlds."

Arvad waited, but Chaz had no answer. And in the silence he heard a kind of scraping sound above the *sh, ss* of waves. The whole hull had been just barely rustling, for minutes.

# 54

Beneath the water line *Princessa*'s defensive perimeter was exquisite, but no defense is perfect. Not if your enemy knows where to find you. Not if his technology is equal to yours. Not if he is willing to die in order to kill.

The submarine was designed for both active and passive resistance to sonar: It scanned like a dense school of tuna. Of Russian design, it was owned by the Republic of China, and had been reported stolen by a terrorist group a year ago. It maneuvered its way through the electronic surveillance apparatus. Frogmen swarmed out, a revenge squad formed at the highest levels: Russian *Spetznaz*, American SEALS, British Royal Marines. Operating with lethal precision, they set mines on *Princessa*'s hull, then withdrew.

"Moby Dick. Tempting," said Chaz. His voice must serve as distraction. He held it low so that Saturn would have to listen. "I'd have liked to hang around and see what you become. Maybe you'll turn merciful, or turn into a pool of one-celled goo. That always happens in the old comic books."

"Before my time. I'm only eighty-four, Chaz."

"You call yourself by the name of the oldest Roman titan. Why?"

"Sharks are older than dinosaurs."

"Arvad, sharks don't change! You're mercurial, not saturnine. Keep changing yourself and sooner or later you're bound to reach a stable state."

"Formless protoplasm? A wise and just and merciful god?"

"Dead is very stable," Chaz said, and he saw that smile again, so wide that it must have hurt Arvad's face.

Came a bang like worlds colliding. The hull slammed inward, a titanic dome-shaped bulge. Shelving, floors, walls buckled: Thousands of square meters of steel deformed, and polished hardwood floors splintered and cracked as if caught in a massive earthquake.

Chaz was instantly deaf. The shock wave set him reeling.

Saturn lunged, both of him. Minsky still wore the shark's grin.

Chaz hurled himself away from the pool. Barrister rammed the pool's edge and slid over, half out of the water, teeth snapping four inches shy of Chaz. But Minsky lunged and had him, iron fingers gripping his arm, flat human teeth snapping at his neck. Chaz screamed in horror before the deck tilted. In the slosh and sudden inclination Minsky slipped and fell at the pool's edge. Chaz kicked him in the head and lost his own footing in the process, slamming down not three feet from Minsky.

Barrister's hardware arm pulled him back into the pool. He turned and watched. And Chaz was on his hands and knees, dazed, terrified—but also, paradoxically, hopeful.

Missiles, soldiers, bombs, whatever the Spinners sent would have zeroed in on the back of Chaz Kato's head. Chaz had not even considered trying to save his own life. Phillipe and Mary had changed everything when they removed the interface plug and left it bleeding in a tray.

Suddenly there was a bare chance of survival, if Chaz Kato could separate himself from the old QQ25 interface unit.

But Saturn had guessed what the explosion meant, and Saturn meant to kill him.

Chaz rolled away from his adversary and was on his feet, his elbow screaming, breath laboring. He stumbled toward the stairs. Minsky moved in a shark-blur, blocking the stairwell and edging toward Chaz, fingers spread, eyes fixed, legs bent and ready to spring.

Chaz lurched among the deck chairs. Kicked one across the tilted, sloppy-slick, broken deck. Minsky sprang like a spider, leaped over the chair and came on.

Panic and adrenaline and what Saturn had done to his head gave Chaz an uncanny clarity. He picked out the smallest chair, moved as only a man facing mortal peril can move, *through* the pain in his back and shoulders, wrenched the canvas-backed wood frame in an arc as tight as a baseball swing, meeting Minsky's jaw in midair.

Minsky dropped and rolled and bounded up. Chaz, exhausted, ran, tumbling deck chairs behind him. Minsky wove through the deck chairs like a shark . . . and the racket had become near intolerable. Footsteps were pounding down metal stairs.

A guard ran out of the stairwell. Saturn had summoned help.

It was over. Chaz accepted death, snatched up a chair and faced Minsky.

The man stopped, bug-eyed. Minsky whirled around at the horrible strangling sound he made. Then blood gushed from the guard's mouth in a tide, and he rolled thrashing down the stairs.

What the hell? Chaz zoomed, and saw a tiny trickle of blood in the man's throat where something that looked like a tiny arrowhead now projected.

Minsky dithered. Chaz zoomed on Barrister: The shark watched fascinated, but at least he wasn't coming out of the pool for him. Chaz looked beyond the guard and saw something that he couldn't quite credit.

The wall was *alive*. A section of metal tubing was flexing, dropping, resolving into a human form. Impossible. Twenty feet away, another section of wall—no, of stairs—shifted. More of Minsky's guards pounded past without seeing it.

Minsky lunged. Chaz threw a chair and danced away, huffing, and almost missed what happened next. The humanoid wall segments flickered, and two more guards were dead, projectiles in their necks. The pounding footsteps stopped.

Chaz barely registered the other sounds: screaming and explosions from elsewhere on the ship. Chaz turned to face Arvad Minsky. His employer. His friend. One-half of the most evil, destructive creature that had ever lived.

"Check," Chaz announced.

Saturn lunged toward Chaz; spun, swatted an unseen fly twice, and Chaz's zoom showed him two darts knocked away. Saturn made a vicious hissing sound, jumped a chair, and dove into the water.

Chaz was weirdly calm. He watched, still holding his chair-weapon, as some kind of sophisticated camouflage suits, liquid crystal sandwich cloth programmed to blend into the surrounding area, lost power, and human beings appeared.

"Dr. Kato," the tallest of the man-shapes said in a muffled voice. "You are to come with us."


Saturn was whole again, even if in flight. He scrambled Minsky into skeletal Xanadu rebreather gear; he held Barrister until Minsky was in position before they fled through the tunnel in the side of the pool.

Above Saturn, pawns were dying, killed by men who blended into walls. This would be dealt with, once Saturn reached safety. He had used the Ninja. Now someone had turned them against him, and that would not be tolerated.

A pair of pressure doors opened, Saturn swam forward, and the doors closed behind him. The outer hull doors opened at his urging.

It would be a simple matter to relocate to one of his other bases. No machine could track him, or catch him. Even if every human being died, it was inconsequential: There was no computer system he could not penetrate, and that was the key to power.

As he swam out into the open water, the human half of him was struck a thunderous blow, hundreds of kilograms of dolphin driving at top speed, aiming not at the shark but the man-thing riding it.

Chaz had begged them to follow his signal. They were afraid of Barrister. They had almost changed their minds, but Lenore had begged them, as well, and finally they had agreed. It had taken long, exhausting days to reach Huy Brazil. They had waited for almost twenty hours knowing that if their teacher and greatest friend was right, the misshapen shark and his human symbiot might seek to escape by water.

*I can't tell you what the circumstance might be*, Chaz had said. *I have to trust you both. You are intelligent beings. Improvise.*

Chaz was dead now. There was vengeance to be had.

Improvise meant *think*.

Barrister thrashed, driving at his tormentors, but Manny and Trish wove in and out, and every motion of Barrister's merely exposed Minsky to another jolt.

The two bodies were linked intimately: Pain and shock confused the shark's linked mind, slowed his responses, filled the merciless predator's mind with unaccustomed fear and confusion.

Barrister's gnashing teeth finally caught Manny's rear fin. Trish butted Minsky's head from the other side. Minsky's body hung limp, blood gushing from the open mouth, eyes staring blankly into salt water.

Still following the last blast of panic and pain, Barrister fled.

Trish inspected Manny's rear fin, making little nuzzling motions against it and then sliding along his side with hers, scooting ahead, delighted when he joined her. It was time to leave. They had barely begun their trip west when the ship detonated above them. A million liters of flaming oil vomited out into the Pacific, lighting up the horizon for a hundred miles.

Manny and Trish swam hard. Shock ripples drove them farther out, the water above them licking with flame.

They were famished for oxygen before they let themselves break the surface again. Looking back to the east, they saw the blazing ship filling the sky above with smoke.

They chittered to each other. They had done what their friend and father, Chaz, had asked of them. There was nothing more to do. They would return to Java. Every full moon they would return to the little cove where they had seen him last.

Chaz was very smart. Perhaps he was wrong. Perhaps he had survived. If they were very, very lucky, perhaps one day they would see him again.

# 55

Chaz drifted in and out of sleep, his body belted into the same cot in the same helicopter that had originally brought him to the *Princessa*.

His companions were three quiet men who still wore delightfully strange camouflage clothing. They had taken off their headpieces, revealing square-faced, somewhat hollow-cheeked Japanese. The camouflage cloth seemed to bend light with about 90 percent accuracy. From any direction Chaz seemed to be staring right through his rescuers' muscular bodies, to the controls, windows, or walls beyond. The effect, to his woozy mind, was much like watching disembodied heads floating around the cabin.

His rescuers didn't seem to mean him immediate harm. In fact, they treated him with a certain awe. He could understand that. He was, after all, the greatest criminal in the world.

They had spoken little.

Three men. With stealth uniforms, exceptional fitness, and absolute ruthlessness. They had dealt with guards and Council members like terriers killing rats. He had seen Hernandez's corpse, a miniature crossbow quarrel projecting from his throat. Kravitz hunched over him, sobbing.

With savage satisfaction, Chaz imagined those tears, crocodile or real, evaporating three minutes after their flight, when the *Princessa* dissolved into a blinding fireball.

He drifted in and out of sleep, and so was uncertain how many hours passed before the helicopter landed. A tiny window next to his seat displayed ocean, islands, occasional patches of misty green. Mostly he slept.

He dreamed of Clarise.

He awakened as the helicopter landed. When the door opened he smelled salt air, and had a desperate urge to stand up, to see the ocean again. His joints were sore again. His back seemed fused into an unyielding mass. There must be a limit to how often will and adrenaline could force him erect and coherent. If these frightening creatures intended to torture him for their amusement, he might not even have strength to object. But this time—one last time, perhaps—Chaz Kato would meet the world on his feet.

He waved aside the wheelchair and stepped out of the helicopter on his own. The air was bitingly cold. He could hear, but not see, the ocean.

He slowly turned.

At first Chaz was convinced that his eyes deceived him. They stood in a cobblestone courtyard broad enough for a dozen such helicopters to have landed side by side. A hundred meters away rose such a structure as he had never seen in life. Fifty meters and six stories high, roof composed of countless overlapping tiles as perfectly arrayed as scales on a Samurai's armor, so perfectly preserved he thought he might have stepped into a story book, a Japanese castle dominated the end of the courtyard like some vast primeval god of war.

How . . . ? Where . . . ?

At least thirty Japanese men in dark, quasi-military pants and tunics waited for him, lined up in two rows leading from the helicopter into the shadow of the castle, as if anticipating the arrival of a head of state.

"Where . . . am I?" he finally managed to ask, not really expecting an answer. Expecting instead, perhaps, to be driven to his knees with a rifle butt or the side stroke of a trained hand.

Instead, one of the men approached him. The man was solidly built and moved like a tiger. He seemed to be in his mid-forties but could have been of any age.

To Chaz's shock, the man bowed deeply. "Allow me to present myself," he said in flawless English. "My name is Hiroshi Osato."

When Chaz was too fatigued or tongue-tied to reply, Osato continued. "When Yamato died, my father and I assumed that the architect of the glorious plan was gone. We know now we were wrong."

Wrong? They were . . . ? Chaz's mind boiled with possibilities.

"—we waited to see what you would do, and when it was clear that you intended to meet your fate as a Samurai, we decided to intercede. We would be part of your army."

Chaz stared at them in shocked surprise. His old bones could barely keep him upright, but the implications of the last few sentences had electrified him. If he could play the role demanded, if he could stay alive another few days, the treatments could be resumed. He knew they had access to the technology. These men had served Yamato. They might well have access to his life extension technology. . . .

It all depended on what he did and said next. He chose his next words with some care.

"No man should refuse an army when offered," he said gravely. "I accept with gratitude. Mr. Osato, you have surely guessed that I have no plans beyond . . . two hours ago."

"Oh, yes," the Ninja said. "But you have left the world a safer place already. You shall have time to heal. We are putting together a medical system for you. Huy Brasil is destroyed, of course, but did you leave a backup system elsewhere in the world?"

"No. Mistake!" He had, but the Security Council must have it by now . . . and it wouldn't matter. Thinking paranoid was not a new skill, and Chaz Kato had been trained by the NERO program. "Test me. Use your own doctors. Start at the beginning and learn what my body will do." He surveyed the castle, self-consciously stiffening his posture. *They expect arrogance. Imperiousness. These men crave a leader. Give them one.* "We can take our time. We never want anyone to wonder why a private army busted their arses to find a medical system for . . . for the late Chaz Kato the Third."

"You are wise. Chaz Kato must be presumed dead. How shall we name you?"

And that, finally, was an easy choice. *Clarise. This is going to work. There is still work to do, darling, and I swear on our son's life that I will do it, no matter what.*

"Call me Saturn," he said.

# 56

In the Pacific Ocean, the dead hulk of a ship rested like a spider in a web of seacrete. Wreckage covered a five-square-kilometer area, along with slicks of burned oil and more esoteric chemicals.

And on the far side of the slick, Barrister hid, concealed behind a splintered glass wall.

The dolphins had caused him pain. The explosions more

so. His skin burned from the very feel of the water that flowed out of the twisted hulk.

Glassy lines ran from the shark/squark to the floating human corpse trailing it. Barrister thrashed from time to time, trying to free himself. Once he actually got the glassy lines in his mouth and savaged them with his teeth, and still couldn't sever them.

At first Barrister didn't think of the corpse itself as food. He saw it, and even knew that it was bleeding, but it took time before it really registered. Some factor inhibited the feeding response that had been hard-wired into his kind for over a hundred million years.

When hunger finally overwhelmed Barrister the resistance vanished, and he ate, still watching for the dolphins to come back. Tasteless crunchy stuff was part of its flesh, but Barrister swallowed it all.

The dolphins had been gone a long time.

Now the torpedo shape of a shark with hands pulled itself out of the water onto a hardwood deck. Barrister's right arm was rigid, almost dead. Partly it was hard stuff; it had no smell, no taste. Both shoulders still worked. Drowning in air, Barrister pulled himself across the deck, around a crumpled elevator shaft, toward a cratered wall. His arms lifted most of him over the jagged edge, but his flank and tail trailed, and fresh blood followed him into the sea.

The dead arm pulled him in circles. He had to concentrate to swim straight . . . and concentrating was hard. Much more of him had died than just an arm.

He had lost a universe. The space inside his mind had been vast and roomy and intricate. His enemies and his prey were as complex as himself, and the hunting was a marvel of intricacy. Now nothing was left but . . .

Hunger? Even when he was Saturn, he could not remember not being hungry. He could remember choosing not to eat. That puzzled him . . . but he was losing the capacity to be puzzled.

The capacity for sorrow, that was fading too. But for a

small time Barrister's world had expanded, and in that time, he knew, just *knew* that he would eat all of it.

Barrister swam away from the ship. Blood was in the water, human blood, and his blood too, from wounds that he could not staunch. The smell caused an unfamiliar mix of emotions, alien thoughts, disturbingly frenzied images.

If he swam fast enough and far enough, perhaps he could escape those images. If he dove deep enough, he might cleanse himself of the strange, raw sensation of fear coursing through his mind: fear that his wounds were mortal. Fear that other predators even now approaching, following the trail of blood, circling at a safe distance, would decide that he was too weak to resist.

Fear that he had lost what he could never regain.

*No!* Barrister thought. *I am a thinking being, I am powerful and fierce.*

Then:

*I am going to survive. . . .*

Then simply, and terribly:

*I am.*

# ABOUT THE AUTHORS

Larry Niven is the multiple Hugo and Nebula Award-winning writer of *Ringworld*, along with many other science fiction masterpieces, including his most recent, *Rainbow Mars*. Larry Niven lives in California.

Steven Barnes is the author of several science fiction classics. His last novel was the highly praised supernatural thriller *Iron Shadows*. Steven Barnes lives in Longview, Washington.

Both Barnes and Niven have collaborated on many *New York Times* bestsellers, including The Legacy of Heorot and Beowulf's Children together with Jerry Pournelle. Now Niven and Barnes collaborate again with a wondrous tale of biotechnology and artificial intelligence.